SCARLE[illegible]ING AND NADINE O'KEEFFE

Fractured Faith

For Sas,
Happy Reading!

Nadine O'Keeffe
Scarlet King

First edition

ISBN: 978-1-7399387-7-2

Cover art by Samantha Wildeboer of Sunset.Bibliophile Graphics

This book was professionally typeset on Reedsy. Find out more at reedsy.com

To the universe, who fucked us in the ass the entire time it took to write this book...

at least when we do it to our characters we give them lube.

Contents

Authors' Note

Fractured Faith is an ADULT, DARK MMF polyamorous mafia romance. This book is written in British English. It is the second in the Blessed Hearts series, and while we recommend reading the first book (*Broken Vows*) first, this book can be read as a standalone. All the books in the Blessed Hearts series follow different main characters.

This book contains explicit sexual content, including kink, and is NOT, in any way, representative of safe sex or kink practices. This is a work of fiction and not in any way meant to represent realistic BDSM or sexual activities, nor should it be taken as such.

Fractured Faith contains content that may trigger some readers, and we heavily advise you read the following list before continuing.

Trigger Warnings:

Anxiety

Blood

Cheating (Some may not consider what happens in this story as cheating, while others may. None of the three main characters have relationships with anybody other than the two others, and everybody ends up happy and together. If you need more details please contact either Nadine or Scarlet)

Death

Depression

Discussions regarding parental death

Gang violence

Graphic sex

Graphic torture

Kidnapping

Mentions of rape and assault (no graphic scenes)

Mentions of sex trafficking and detailed accounts of where the victims are held hostage

Sacrilege and sexualisation of religion

Suicide

Self harm

Symptoms of PTSD

Violence - including gang, knife, and gun violence

The following is a list of kinks included in this book, some of which may be triggering for some readers: bondage, D/s dynamics, edging, humiliation, praise, sexualisation of religion, voyeurism/exhibitionism

Pronunciations and Translations

Irish Names:

Oisín: Ush-een

Siobhán: Shiv- awn

Seamus: Shea-mus

Aoife: Ee-fa

Gráinne: Graw-nyuh

Irish Translations:

Máistir - sir/master

Craic - fun/enjoyment (used colloquially in Irish and Scots slang). Can also be used in phrases like "what's the craic?" meaning "what's up?" and "how are you?"

Dearth※áir - brother

Eejit - idiot (used colloquially in Irish and Scots)

Deirfiúr - sister

A rún mo chroí - secret of my heart

Tá - yes

Tá mé i ngrá leat - I am in love with you

Bhí mé i ngrá leat i gcónaí - I have always been in love with you

Sea - another word for yes

Italian Translations:

Stai zitta - shut up

Cazzo - fuck
Puttana - whore
Vaffanculo - fuck you
Testa di minchia - shit head
Pezzo di merda - piece of shit
Figlia cara - dear daughter
Bentornati - welcome back
Testa di cazzo - dickhead
Io ti sfido - I dare you
Mi dispiace - I am sorry
Ti chiedo tanto perdono - I ask for your forgiveness
Grazie - thank you
Certo - certainly/of course
Ho già detto prima che non so niente - I've already said I don't know anything
Bugardio - liar
Ti ho detto tutto quello che so - I've told you everything I know
Apri la porta - open the door
Uccidimi - kill me
Per favore - please
Non importa come lo fai, ma ti prego, uccidimi adesso - It doesn't matter how you do it, but please kill me now
Dio non è qui - God is not here
Ti amo - I love you
Siete pronti? - Are you ready?
Sono qui! Va tutto bene - I'm here! Everything's okay
Una volta che saprò chi c'è dietro, ti prometto che non ci sarà un solo pezzo del bastardo lasciato intatto dal mio coltello - once I know who's behind it, I promise you there won't be a single inch of the bastard untouched by

my knife

Li distruggerò. Te lo giuro sorella - I will destroy them. I swear to you sister

Lo so - I know

Hai ragione - you are right

Vuoi un caffè? - do you want a coffee?

Sono fiero di te - I'm proud of you

French Translation (because Sebastian is a flirt in every language):

Vous le vous cochez avec moi? - will you sleep with me?

Prologue

Serafina
Three Weeks Ago

"My darling daughter," my father says with a sigh.

His deep voice startles me from the fictional world I'd escaped to, and I peer over the rim of my sunglasses to find him standing beside me. I place the book I'm reading on my lap and search my father's face, hoping to find a clue as to why he's interrupting the few minutes a day I have to read and relax.

Dark, puffy circles mar his under eyes and his hand shakes as he reaches for the half empty bottle of wine on the table beside me.

Something's not right.

Checking my glass still holds some of my wine, I reach for the stem. Nothing good is going to come of this conversation - I can tell from the tight set of his lips as he sniffs the edge of the bottle.

Settling the bowl of the glass into the palm of my hand, I swirl it slightly and watch as the deep red *vino* slides up the wall of the glass. The colour catches the evening sun rays, and I allow myself to focus on it as I wait for my father to speak.

My father doesn't call me *daughter* with that regretful tone unless he's about to ask something of me. Something he knows I won't want to do.

It's a fine game we play - he asks me and I say yes, as if I ever truly had a choice to begin with. He wouldn't punish me if I said no, but there's more at stake than our familial relationship, and I'm all too aware of it.

I am Renato DeSantis' daughter, an heir, a princess of blood, and the choices I make are rarely choices at all.

My father takes a seat at the end of my deck chair, and I sip on my wine to distract myself from the tension seeping out of him.

"Papà?"

"I just spoke to Thomas Cavanaugh."

"Ah, *cazzo,*" I mumble, taking a gulp to muffle my curse. I like the Irish bastard just fine, for all that I've heard about him from my father, but there is no way in hell that he called just for a fucking chat.

Not with the state of Killrover and certainly not with the mess we've spent weeks trying to clean up here in San Jarno.

I cross my ankles to keep myself still, my body already preparing for a fight. Papà looks up at me, pinching the bridge of his nose the way he does when he's been thinking too hard, and exhales sharply.

"It appears they've run into a bit of trouble," he says slowly, voice strained.

I wonder how much of the day he's spent hiding his own stress, stowing it away behind a careful mask of boredom so the others don't see the toll this shit is taking on him.

I can count on one hand the amount of times anyone other than my sister or I have seen that mask slip.

Lately, it feels like that mask has been at risk of slipping more and more.

The garden is quiet now, the birds settling as the sun dips into the horizon, hidden behind the trees lining our property. I lift my sunglasses from my face and rest them on my head as I take a deep breath. The smell of freshly mowed grass and wine floods my senses, though that could be because I'm still holding the glass to my face.

Papà shifts slightly to the side, and I watch curiously as he pulls a small notebook from his pocket. He flips through the pages until he finds the one he wants, and leaves it to rest on his lap. Illegible scribbles cover the open page and I squint as I try to make out what he's written. Before I can, he tears it out and holds it over the stone path beneath our feet, grabs the lighter from his jacket pocket and flicks the flame open. The bottom corner catches first, but the fire spreads fast, engulfing whatever he'd written until the smell of burnt paper surrounds us. When nothing but the last corner remains, he blows the flame out and lets the charred edge fall to the ground.

I take another silent sip, not daring to question his actions.

I know when my father wants my opinion, and this is not one of those times.

"His son," my father starts again, relaxing as he looks at the specks of ash beneath his feet. "The heir. He's in need of safety."

I frown, putting my glass back on the table beside me as I lean forward, drumming my fingertips on the cover of the book resting against my thigh.

"Safety?" I echo, rolling the word over my tongue. My brow arches as I make note of my father hiding his smile behind tightened lips. His jaw twitches, and I can't help the bubble of amusement that builds in my chest.

"His bride apparently did not agree to be married. She brought a gun to the church and decided to test out her aim on her own father. A parting gift if you will for his desire to see her wed to their enemy," my father explains with a smirk.

A laugh bursts out of my mouth.

As ridiculous as it all sounds, some small kernel of me can't help but respect this woman.

"Whatever alliance Cavanaugh was trying to form went up in flames," he jokes, as he nods at the burnt paper on the ground. "Regardless, he wants his heir protected."

He shoots me a weighted look and I blink as realisation washes over me.

Fuck.

"Here?" The word slips from my mouth, astonishment clouding my mind.

My father dips his chin in acknowledgement and my eyes widen. When he inhales deeply, I hold my own breath.

The look on his face tells me there's more. I shouldn't be surprised really - there's always fucking more.

"On what conditions?" I ask, trying to keep my voice calm and cold. Nothing good can come of housing a runaway mob heir. We've had dealings with the Cavanaughs in the past - business, not pleasure, and I've never even met the heir Papà's speaking of. But something tells me that this isn't going to be easy. That *he* is not going to be easy.

"They help us with our cockroach infestation, we give the kid a safe haven." My father's dark eyes track my reaction, and I wait, doing my best to keep my face neutral.

I know better than to say anything just yet, to allow myself to think that I can voice my opinion on the matter.

"Of course, we need to ensure that both parties are… trustworthy. I will not bring a threat into our territory, or into our home. Nor does Cavanaugh want to entrust his only son with a tentative ally. Especially one whose territory is being swarmed with *vermin*."

Cockroaches would be preferable. Our infestation is far more worrying.

"The kid's wedding never went ahead," Papà says slowly, and I go cold at the not so subtle implication of his words.

"Why is Frankie not here for this conversation?" I interrupt, dread pooling in my gut. I know fine well why, but I want him to admit it.

"You're my heir, Serafina." He enunciates every word like it holds weight. I feel the pressure of it resting on my chest, a lead brick keeping me grounded. Reminding me of my responsibilities, and the duty I have to my family.

"My brutal, deadly, dangerous, daughter. I adore Francesca, but she is younger and untried. She isn't made for this sort of thing."

Any other time, I'd take being called deadly by my father as a complement. Hell, I'd preen at his words. I take pride in how well I took to this life, not that I've known any different. But I've never shied away from the darkness I was born into. I embraced it, thrived in it, relished it.

I'm not ashamed of who I am or the things I have done to strengthen the DeSantis name.

And yet, the pause in the air between us makes my palms sweat.

"An heir for an heir," Papà says finally.

I say nothing. I wipe my hands on my white linen trousers and straighten my shoulders. I exhale slowly through my nose.

I understand now why he held the bottle of wine I'd been drinking captive.

I expect the idea to fill me with disgust or disdain. Instead, I'm surprised to find I don't feel anything at all.

"A husband."

The words fall thick and heavy from my mouth.

I suppose it had to happen eventually.

"I would not marry you to a cruel man, Serafina," my father continues. "I've dug as deep as I can, short of cutting off the boy's skull to dig around inside his brain. I can tell you everything there is to know about him. He's quiet. Dangerous, of course, but not to you. I swear it."

I raise a brow at that. "When has a man ever laid a hand on me without it being broken in return?" I ask with a small smirk. My father chuckles darkly at the remark.

"I'm not worried about him," I say, my tone dry as I struggle to picture myself married to someone I've never met. "I would have liked to have been consulted regarding this grand scheme you two have thrown together, *before* my hand was offered to a stranger."

Papà winces at that, nodding knowingly. "You and your sister are my pride and joy," he said, voice low. "You know I'd never ask you to do anything that wasn't absolutely necessary, *cara mia*."

"I understand," I assure him, shrugging. "Marry the Cavanaugh boy so he can stay under our roof and away from the gunfire, and they help us with the *pests*."

My father nods once, threading his fingers together as he rests his elbows on his knees. He seems even more tired now, as though this conversation is draining every ounce of energy he has left.

"I'm aware this probably isn't what you dreamt of when you thought of marriage-"

I break him off with a scoff, leaning back on the lounge chair and scooping my glass again. The move is meant to settle Papà more than me, and it seems to do the trick.

"I didn't dream of marriage," I tell him honestly. I'm not against it, but I've never found a person I could picture myself marrying. I've had sex, a lot of it, but love? Love is messy and cruel. I've seen the pain it can cause. My father isn't the same man he once was. Losing my mother and the love she gifted him did that. It changed him.

Take the issue of love out of the equation, and this marriage would be far from the worst thing I'd done for my family.

And, truthfully, I'd do far worse now if it would help dig us out of the fucking hellscape we've been dragged into.

"Does Thomas really think he can help? What can he do that we haven't already done?" I ask, tapping my nails against my book once more, the steady rhythm keeping me calm. My eyes narrow as I try to steer the conversation away from such emotional topics.

"We can't afford to seem weak right now," my father sighs, content to discuss strategy instead. "The wedding will be a show. A sign that we're not alone, and that our territory will not be taken so easily. We need to show *them* that they have something to worry about."

I nod sharply, careful to keep my expression guarded as I lift my glass a final time. I swallow the wine, the taste no longer as soothing as it was when my father first joined me, and lock my eyes with his.

"Okay," I say simply, raising my brows in expectation.

"When's the big day?"

1

Oisín

Serafina DeSantis is beautiful. Gorgeous. Glorious, really, clad in her skin tight white wedding dress. It's simple but cut perfectly to fit her body. The neckline is so low I swear the priest performing the ceremony blushed as she entered the church. The silky material shines in the light, and the bright red lipstick she has on is smudged slightly from the kiss that sealed our fates.

This is not the first wedding I've had, but it is the first that's gone to plan. It's barely been a week since my last botched wedding, a poor attempt to secure an alliance with the Branigans back in Killrover.

That wedding ended before it could even begin with my wife-to-be shooting her father in the shoulder. Annoyingly, she missed the fucker's heart - having Seamus Branigan dead would've been the best outcome.

Instead, Siobhán Branigan started a fuckin' war.

Tensions between our family and the Branigans have been high for years. We're enemies down to the bone. Seamus encroaches on our territory, disrupts our supply lines, and has the fucking nerve to act like he knows shit all about it. Being the Cavanaugh heir, and marrying his daughter, the Branigan heir, was supposed to result in a truce. To return some semblance of peace to Killrover.

Instead, after starting a needless fucking war, my ex fiancée *ran.* Da couldn't risk having me killed in the fight, not as his only heir, so here I am - wedding round two. This time, to our Italian allies, the DeSantis family.

I spent the whole ceremony with my breath held, half expecting hear bullets ricocheting off the stone walls again. Fortunately, Renato wants this alliance as much as Da does.

The gold ring on my hand feels heavy, but I don't mind it. I've known my entire life that my marriage would be born of necessity. That love would play no part in it. Da kept me informed of my future, and given that his only marriage resulted in my fuckin' Ma running off and abandoning me, I was far from giving a shit about love. I wince as my mind conjures images of the only person I've ever attached that word to. I left him behind in Ireland, in the midst of the chaos Siobhán created.

I try not to think about him. I can't afford to.

A warm hand slips into mine, our palms pressing together. My wife tugs gently, leading me onto the dance floor and I blink rapidly to force myself back into focus. Fuck, this whole day has passed in a blur.

"Last dance," Serafina whispers as I go through the motions of cupping her waist and twirling her to the classical music played by the string quartet Renato hired.

I like her, despite the fact I just met her days ago. She's confident, stunning and powerful. She has dark brown hair, currently curled at the ends in an effortless wave, deep chocolate eyes, and sharp cheekbones. Her tanned golden skin shimmers with some sort of glittery makeup. She looks fucking *radiant* as we move around the dance floor.

"And then what?" I murmur as I dip her, hearing the click of the photographer's camera as he captures the moment. We smile, all too aware that we're being watched, and continue to play the roles we've been given: a happy blushing bride and a prideful groom. Our guests are circling the dance floor, muttering and laughing as they watch us.

As I twirl my wife around the room, I wonder how the hell it's time for the last dance already. I've spent the reception in a haze of relief and concern, too focused on the war at home and ensuring I played my part perfectly.

I lead Serafina in measured, rhythmic steps around the dance floor, forcing myself to remember that there's nothing I can do for my family but this.

Securing this alliance with the DeSantis, in case we need the support back home, is all I can do while keeping our lineage safe.

God knows the Branigans aren't to be fucked with, but that's exactly what we've done. My da, however, has informed me that Nessa - one of our best enforcers and my only other close friend - has captured my runaway bride.

Seamus hasn't struck back yet.

Knowing that he's out there, waiting and planning his attack sets my teeth on edge. It doesn't matter that we were just as surprised by Siobhán's attack at the wedding as Seamus was. The tentative alliance is broken, and he's out for blood. There's nothing I want more than that fucker dead and buried.

Hell, at least Serafina seems happy with our marriage, or maybe she's just as unbothered as I am. Even while walking down the aisle, Siobhán had been shifty, clearly uncomfortable at the thought of marrying me. Siobhán's father is an asshole, and though I'd have gone through with the marriage if she'd said the vows, I'd have felt like shit for forcing her hand for the rest of my life.

No, this is the better option. A wife who's used to the political games that control our lives, and doesn't resent her position.

"Well..." Serafina smiles as her hands slip up to cup around the back of my neck, swaying against me.

"They say a marriage isn't sealed until it's consummated," Serafina says casually, and my jaw tightens. The tiny strap of her dress slips over her shoulder, and her finger traces under the collar of my shirt.

My skin lights up under her touch and I swallow hard. Since I met her, the attraction between us has been undeniable. And, *fuck*, the kiss at the altar...

Our first kiss, in front of an audience and God, to seal our marriage. But soon, we won't have an audience and God has no place in my bedroom.

"Is that so?" I reply, my voice low. My hands flex on her waist. Her dark eyes glitter, the music fading into the background as she smiles up at me.

"I'm going to cut to the chase, Oisín," she says simply, pressing closer as we sway. "I don't intend to spend my marriage acting like I'm not attracted to my spouse. We can fulfil our responsibilities as heirs while enjoying ourselves, can't we? Of course, if you'd rather, we can let that kiss be our last, and go fuck other people in private. But I won't pretend that I want to spend my wedding night alone."

My cock jumps in my suit trousers, and I tug her closer

to hide the bulge. She grins, swaying her hips against mine, lashes lowering as she feels the evidence of just how much I agree with her.

Serafina is hot as hell, and fuck if I'm not picturing taking her up to our honeymoon suite right the fuck now. Tonight may be the only night we can just be newly weds and not political props for our respective family names.

Still...the knowledge of what I left behind, of *who* I left behind in Killrover feels like a rock in my stomach. I ignore it.

There's no point letting myself linger on what I can't have. What I could never have. I have a beautiful, strong woman in my arms whose touch is making my blood ignite. Who I am *married* to.

I hate myself for the way that this doesn't feel like enough.

"How fast can we run away from the *thank yous* and niceties?" I ask her, dropping my head so I can whisper the words into her ear. The slightly spiced scent of her perfume hits me, and I inhale deeply.

Serafina laughs and the sound drowns out the music. I'm so fucked.

"I'll race you through the crowd," my new wife dares, and I nod once as the quartet finally finishes their song.

"Run then, little wife."

2

Sebastian

T*wo Weeks Later*

Standing outside an abandoned church listening to my best friends fuck is not my idea of a perfect afternoon.

At least earlier I'd been happy while taking my anger out on the Branigan fuckers. After the hell they've put us through this past month, I'd relished the spray of blood hitting me with each bastard I'd killed.

Not one of the fuckers involved with Seamus Branigan deserved to keep breathing. Or at least I'd thought as much until I'd gotten to know Seamus' only heir, Siobhán Branigan – the woman currently shagging my best friend six ways to Sunday, and in a church no less. It hadn't taken long for me to realise that the woman who'd run from her own wedding with guns blazing was broken and desperate for freedom. Siobhán was just as much a victim of her father's actions as we were. Once we learned how badly her father treated her, I couldn't blame her for running, or for shooting him in the shoulder on her wedding day. I only wish that her aim had been better.

The rest of the Branigan rats however? Each and every one of them played their part in trying to disrupt our supply lines, and wreak havoc on our businesses. All of them were complicit in forcing Siobhán's hand in marriage, and they'd all picked the hill they chose to die on.

I won't lose sleep over any of my kills today.

The streets of Killrover ran red for weeks because of Siobhán's refusal to marry Oisín. But all of that ends today. The stress of keeping Siobhán under lock and key, the games between her and Nessa, and the war between us and the Branigans is all done and dusted, buried six feet under with Seamus' body.

I can only hope whoever takes his place as head of the Branigans doesn't want more bloodshed between the lot of us.

Minutes pass as more moans seep through the church doors, and I shiver at the cold air. I've been out here for fuckin' ages, and the longer I'm exposed to the cold air, the more the blood drying on my skin begins to itch. I grimace at the feel of it pulling at my flesh. I hate the way the rust coloured flakes cling to my scars, dragging up memories better left forgotten.

Siobhán cries out from behind the old wooden doors and I groan, frustration building as I lean back on the cold brick of the church's exterior. The old stone presses against my skull, and a low ache builds behind my eyes.

I press my fingers against my temples as I try to remind myself that this is good.

That I'm happy for them.

And I *am* happy for them. Truly. Wonderfully, ecstatically happy. Nessa, the bitch that she is, deserves love more than perhaps anyone else I've ever met. Yet, as much as I love my best friend, there's never been an ounce of attraction between us, and I sure as fuck have no intention of making her scream like Siobhán currently is.

I'm happy for them.

But I'm also pretty sure my heart has shriveled up to the size of a fucking raisin. I can feel it shrinking inside of my chest as I think about how lucky she is, how she finally has the person she loves in her arms.

Jealousy burns in my veins and I do my best to pretend it's not there, eating me alive.

Folding my arms across my chest, I repress every fleeting thought of *him*.

I refuse to let my heart break over someone who never let me into theirs.

I won't let what I can't have hold power over me.

Ignoring the noises coming from the church, I try my hardest to focus on literally anything else. I count the bricks on the building across from me, the cracks in the pavement, and the rate at which my heart pounds inside of my chest. I check in on every inch of my body, twisting and turning to see which bruises ache the most after the fight with the Branigans.

If I try really hard, I can almost pretend that the pain's not there.

My dick on the other hand…

Painfully neglected.

It's working overtime to remind me just how alone I've been this past month.

It's not like I've ignored it. I've tried, multiple damn times, to sort that issue out. But no matter how many pretty people I've kissed in bars, or how many offers of a good time I've gotten in the dim light of *Sinners*, neither me nor my cock have had any fucking interest.

In anyone.

Anyone but him.

It's is incredibly fucking inconvenient for me and my dick. There's no fixing this. Not when his father smuggled him out of the country the second Siobhán fled their wedding. A wedding day I'd really fucking love to pretend had never been planned at all.

I grit my teeth at the memory of Oisín dressed in an immaculately pressed black suit with a little white flower in the buttonhole. Handsome, hot as fuck, and one hundred percent *not mine*.

Never fucking mine.

Absently, I rub at the heavy ache spreading through my chest, so lost in my own Goddamn misery that I'm startled by the church doors being yanked open.

I spin on my heel, hand dropping back to my side as I make eye contact with Ness.

Her cheeks are flushed, and her pupils are wide. Her hand is still wrapped around Siobhán's waist and they both looked *satisfied* as fuck. It's almost as if she can't bear to stop touching her.

I swallow the bitter taste in my mouth as the thought creeps across my mind and look at both of them closely.

Nessa's covered in blood, more than Shivy and I combined. Apparently sex was more important than stitches, but as fat scarlet drops hit the pavement, I'm questioning her priorities.

I narrow my eyes at Nessa as she looks at the blood staining the concrete, but she simply smiles at me like the sadistic fuck she is.

Siobhán looks remarkably calm for someone who's just killed their da, in fact it may be the calmest I've seen her yet. Her shoulders aren't curved inward, she's standing tall beside Nessa, and her eyes seem… *lighter,* almost. As if the weight of the world has been lifted from her back. Who would've thought that the daughter of our sworn enemy would become one of my closest friends when we kidnapped her?

I push aside the desperate part of me that wonders if Oisín will come home now that Seamus is gone.

Flinging my gaze back to Nessa, I smother my laugh as she hits me with one of her looks. If I didn't know better, I'd question if she wanted me six feet under for daring to look at Siobhán as closely as I have.

"Do you think you could scream any louder?" I ask dryly as Nessa glares at me. It feels good to take my mind off of Oisín, and to focus instead on the two people I care about standing right in front of me.

Siobhán grins at me without missing a beat. "Nessa had a lot of confessions to work through."

I snort, shaking my head at the pair of them. Nessa is the closest thing to family that I have. Hell, we were practically raised together. We were two cocky ass teenagers, tied at the hip, doing everything we could to piss Thomas off, and even after all these years, nothing has changed. Seeing her stare at Siobhán with something akin to awe has a spark of warmth chasing away the gross, cold feeling sticking beneath my ribs.

Thank God indeed.

"I'm sure she did," I say with a wink. "C'mon, I'll drive."

I walk ahead of them to the car, and open the back door like the gentleman I am. I sigh in relief when I slip into the driver's seat and slam the door behind me, gripping the wheel like it'll save me from the well of emotions I have no desire to feel right now.

Fast cars fix everything. I refuse to hear otherwise.

The hum of the engine sparks through me as I slam my foot on the accelerator and speed us away from the church.

"Don't bleed out on my expensive leather," I call back to Nessa as we pass the city limits and the grim grey of Killrover yields to the open countryside. Even with the trees stripping themselves of leaves and the ever present clouds turning the sky a grey darker than the concrete, I swear my breath comes a little easier.

"Oops," Nessa teases from the back, voice flat in the way that tells me she isn't sorry in the slightest.

"What's going to happen when we get back?" Siobhán asks, looking at me in the rearview mirror. The words are steady, far calmer than I expected her to be after the massacre we just took part in.

"We'll be put under investigation," Ness answers with a long sigh that makes the corner of my mouth twitch.

"You've got a good pain tolerance, right, sunshine?" I check with Shivy, taking my eyes off the road to grin at her over my shoulder.

The redhead just glares at me and sighs. Damn, Nessa's attitude is catching.

"Drive faster," she demands. "Let's get this shit over with."

Given that Nessa is technically now a traitor to the Cavanaugh's, I should vow to end my friendship with her and kiss the fucking ground that Thomas walks on as I beg him not to torture me. I should be doing everything I can to escape the interrogation rooms, to keep myself from their clutches entirely. No part of me wants to step into one of those rooms and feel like a victim ever again. But I've never been one for taking the easy way out and, more than that, Nessa has spent years proving how much she deserves my loyalty.

Sure, she fucked up. Bad. Like, *we might have our eyes gouged out by the man who raised us* kind of bad.

But who amongst us hasn't made mistakes?

I sure as fuck have made plenty of them, and Nessa's always been there to cover my arse when I needed her the most.

I won't abandon her now.

Even if it means triggering those memories. Even if it means destroying what little sanity I have left.

The front door of the manor swings open before we even reach it. Thomas Cavanaugh stands at the threshold, glowering at us. His pale blue stare is eerie, but I've had years to get used to it. Combined with the scar splitting his top lip, he looks every bit the executioner I'm sure he imagines himself to be.

My pulse quickens as I watch him narrow his eyes. We're fucked. Completely and utterly fucked.

I've talked my way out of a lot of shit, but I don't know if I can talk my way out of this.

"Inside. All three of you. You know where to go," Thomas snaps. The ice in his voice makes Nessa's spine straighten but it only makes me raise a brow.

I'm not great with following instructions, unless they're

given to me in the bedroom.

But I do owe this man my life, and we did just murder the head of our rival gang. Hell, we only ended up in this position because my idiot best friend refused to acknowledge her feelings for said rival's daughter.

Fucking eejit.

I walk by her side down the familiar corridors, knowing the route to the interrogation rooms like the back of my hand. Normally, I'd be dragging some poor sap with me. *Oh how the tables have turned.*

Knowing that I'm the poor sap in this scenario does something to me though. My body vibrates with a sense of impending doom as memories that haunt my dreams come back to the surface.

The flash of knuckle braces catching in dim light.

The taste of blood in my mouth.

The searing heat of a blowtorch pressed to my back.

Fuck.

Shaking the violent images away, I collect myself as we keep walking the length of the hall.

I don't know why Nessa ever thought she could go behind Thomas' back and get away with it. She had to have known he'd find out eventually. The fact that she aligned herself with Seamus in any way is enough for Thomas to execute her. Hell, I've seen what he does to traitors. I've helped. My own damn mother was shot in front of me for foolishly doing the same shit Nessa has done.

I don't fucking care that Nessa never planned on supporting Seamus, or actually giving Siobhán back to him. Her half baked plan of swapping Siobhán for information on Thomas was as dumb then as it sounds now.

I'd warned her of this. Of the mess she'd cause if she followed through on it. And now here we are, reaping the rewards of the seeds she sowed.

Fuck. If she'd just been less emotionally fucking stunted, if she'd just talked to Thomas, none of this would have happened.

Half of me wants to strangle her for subjecting me to the shit show ahead of us, for making me care about her enough to stick myself in this situation willingly. But the other half of me knows that it's worth it - that it's only because of her betrayal to Thomas we managed to kill Seamus.

Before long we're in the basement, the short row of doors staring at us and I know that there's no point postponing the inevitable. I reach for the handle of the first door, and it swings open easily.

The smell of bleach assaults my senses and my nose wrinkles. Thomas turns to us when we enter, utter disappointment clear as day on his face. His eyes catch on Nessa, holding her stare and I watch, shocked, as her shoulders slump under the weight of it.

Of the two of us, I didn't expect her to be the first to break.

Anji and Aoife wait inside with Thomas, the former with a med kit splayed out on the small wooden table in front of him. Aoife, our resident weapon's coordinator, just watches us with her arms crossed, deep brown eyes betraying nothing of how she feels. Anji is cold and logical, but Aoife is softer. It doesn't bode well that she's not giving us any sort of reassurance.

"Stitch her up, Anji," Thomas instructs, but I don't get to stick around to watch him do just that.

As Anji picks up his needle, Aoife slips away from Thomas'

side. She grabs Siobhán's arm, then nods for me to follow her. I'm grateful she doesn't try to touch me too, because right now my skin feels like there are spiders crawling over it. The horrible, sinking feeling that something is very fucking wrong creeps over me, and I tighten my jaw.

I'm not scared, but the air is thick with tension and I swear I feel eyes on me as I let Aoife instruct me into the neighbouring room. She leaves me there alone while she drags Siobhán away. The door locks with a *snick* that echoes through the bare space.

This room smells slightly less like chemicals. Damp stone and earth flood my senses and I'm grateful for it as I suck in lungfuls of air. It's empty aside from the table and two chairs and the hook embedded in the ceiling. I don't let myself look at the hook for too long, instead plopping down on one of the chairs. The shitty rusted metal groans a little as it adjusts to my weight. It's uncomfortable as shit but I have nothing else to do but sit here and wait.

Vaguely, I can hear Nessa and Thomas' voices through the wall, though I can't make out what they're saying. There are no screams of pain so that has to be a good sign. Thomas is a brutal bastard, but even after complete betrayal, it's hard to imagine him hurting Nessa. Or me, for that matter. He's never been soft though, never been one to let shit like this slide. He's put a lot of time into us, years of training and feeding and protecting the kids he accidentally took responsibility for. He's never treated us all that differently from his actual child. But I doubt that will stop him from dishing out the punishments we both deserve.

Shit, I don't fucking know what's about to happen.

I rock back on the chair, letting the motion distract me

from any thoughts of us as kids, or of Oisín, of when we met, of the way we stared at each other, and every fucking stolen look since.

He can never be mine. I've always known that.

I was content with the hidden moments we had - finding shadows to hide in, using each other to drown out reality, of sneaking into his room at night, of remembering the way his teeth nipped my neck, the way his hands searched my skin, the way his eyes flutter closed when I-

No.

Bad Sebastian.

Not happening.

Oisín isn't in the fucking country.

Hell, he isn't evening answering his phone, or acknowledging the millions of texts I've sent since he left three weeks ago.

He's as good as gone.

It shouldn't hurt because there's nothing to grieve. We were never *anything*.

Christ above, I'm a shit liar.

The door finally opens and Anji enters. I'm grateful as fuck when his glowering face drags me from my self pity.

"Afternoon, Anj," I greet, waving enthusiastically at him.

If I'm going to be stuck in this fucking room having the shit kicked out of me, I'm at least going to have a little fun first.

The man furrows his brows at me, locking the door behind him before settling into the chair across from me. I lean forward, elbows on the cold metal table, meeting his glare.

"What a shit show you've gotten yourself into," Anji comments. The shitty lightbulb above us flickers, making his expression seem much more ominous.

Anji is handsome, with high cheekbones, a strong nose and medium brown skin. He's also fucking terrifying when he wants to be. I should be used to his intimidation tactics. He spends most of his time hacking shit for Thomas but occasionally he drops in on my *information collecting* sessions to lend a hand. I've seen the damage he can cause.

I know better than to doubt the power he holds in those giant hands of his.

I grimace. "I prefer *one man improv show*," I say.

"Considering Nessa's the one who betrayed everyone in this fucking building with the shit she pulled, I wouldn't be calling you the head of the operation."

I bark out a laugh at that. I like Anji, but right now, I'm too highly strung to shrug off his words like I usually would.

"You insult me," I say, trying to keep my tone light.

"Not nearly enough," he shoots back.

I grind my teeth. "Look, I get it, you're pissed. But hey, it all worked out. Seamus is dead and we've got our supply lines back, and Killrover isn't running red with blood anymore. What more could ya want?"

"How many of our men were lost in the process?"

I go still. Ah. I see.

"Your brother was a bit of a dick anyway, Anj," I say and immediately his hands ball into fists.

I don't bother trying to dodge the punch. I let him hit me, square in the left eye, and savour the bright burst of pain. I deserved that.

I deserve this, and much more.

3

Sebastian

Anji hit me once more before our investigation came to a close. He established pretty quickly that I'd done nothing wrong outside of failing to report Nessa's betrayal to Thomas. In truth, I'd helped to protect our guys regardless, so he let me go.

I'm dabbing blood off my cheek with my sleeve as we step out of the room. The dull throb of pain from Anji's hits barely registers, even as I prod at my skin.

The hallway is empty, and my stomach churns as I wonder what the fuck they've done with Siobhán. Sure, she wanted her father dead just as much as we did but at the end of the day, she still carries the Branigan name.

I feel sick as I wonder if she's secretly suffering. If the guilt is eating her alive. She didn't seem to care too much earlier, but I worry that if she's been left to herself she'll have nothing but time to think about what's been done.

I swear under my breath, storming to the door Aoife had taken her through, determined to check on her. I stop in my tracks once I reach it. It's hanging open, the small, nondescript interrogation room empty. *Where the fuck-*

Nessa's voice cuts off my train of thought, snappy and clearly frustrated as hell. I pause in the hallway, listening to her list off the short version of today's events.

I wince as she goes through it all, desperate to know just how badly Thomas has hurt her. The fact that she's still breathing gives me hope, but my best friend lives to give me fucking heart attacks, I swear it. In fact, my entire sternum is aching right now, only half the pain from the fight.

My body freezes as I hear the next words filter out of the door.

"Jesus, Mary and Joseph you've gone and fucked it right up for yourself haven't ya?"

That voice.

That fucking *voice.*

It's tinged with anger and tiredness, gravelly and low. It washes over me, drowning me as I shudder. I brace myself on the cool stone, blinking rapidly like I'm trying to come out of a dream.

I'm moving before I even make the conscious choice to, throwing myself down the short hall and into the doorway of the first interrogation room.

My brain repeats his name over and over and over until I swear my very heart beat is chanting it, too. Nessa begins talking again, Thomas, too, but I can't hear them properly over the sound of his name.

"Oisín."

Even to my own ears, my voice is strained and tight. My eyes are wide, desperate to take in every inch of him I can.

He's here.

He turns to me, his eyes wide - the same merge of blue and

green I always told him reminded me of tropical seas I've never seen. I don't know when the fuck he got here, only the creases in his black shirt telling me he's been wearing it for at least a couple of hours. His curly brown hair grazes his shoulders, mussed like he's run his hands through it the way he does when he's stressed. Or when *my* hands have been tangled in it-

His mouth opens, but he turns away from me without a word.

A bomb detonates in my chest. I'm at once burning and so cold my heart skitters to an icy stop. I think I'm shaking but I can't be sure because I can't feel my fucking hands. My ears are ringing like someone's fired a gun too close.

I thought I could do this. That I was okay with knowing he wasn't mine. I was so fucking wrong.

Siobhán looks at me, her lips parted in a silent *oh*. I force my spine straight again, blinking as I shut myself the fuck down.

Shut it down.

Shut. It. Down.

I smirk at her, but I see the way concern creases her forehead. She doesn't believe me.

I'm about to think of some witty thing to say to distract from the fact my heart has just been pulled out of my chest and stomped on right in front of my friends. Anything to interrupt the freezing silence engulfing the room, and the way I want to scream *why won't you even look at me?*

Arms wrap around my waist and my heart jerks itself to life again with a series of thundering beats. But it's just Shivy, her body smaller than mine, holding me tight, holding me together.

"You're okay," she whispers, relief evident in her words. I can't tell if she means *you didn't get beaten half to death for not ratting Nessa out when you should've* or if she's trying to reassure me that having Oisín ignore me entirely doesn't mean I've actually ceased to exist.

The latter hurts too much, so I go with the former.

"I'm alright, sunshine," I reassure her. My voice comes out a little rough, but I press on. "I just pissed Anji off a little more than I probably should have before he set me free."

Her eyes trail over my face, clocking the bruise and the cut on my cheek, before she evidently decides I'm telling the truth. She nods but doesn't pull away, tucking herself into my side.

I'm so grateful for her at that moment that I can't speak. The weight of her against me holds me down, tethers me.

"So, Italy, huh?" Nessa says to Oisín, moving on from the awkwardness with ease. She looks alright, tired as fuck but not injured. Well, no more injured than she was earlier. Her wounds have been stitched, and she's standing on her own two feet, which I take as a good enough sign.

"Yeah, Italy. Da sent me over there to deal with the DeSantis family. Ended up married to their mafia princess too," Oisín laughs.

He laughs.

I go rigid. My fingers tighten on Siobhán's shoulder but I can't help it. I can't *breathe*.

Married.

Married to some Italian mob princess.

Married.

Not to me.

The world swims and I realise with a sinking, awful horror

that the stinging in my eyes is tears. I try to swallow my heart as it rises in my throat, desperate to crawl its way to Oisín, but it gets stuck. My body goes fuzzy, my brain static.

Siobhán grabs my hand and squeezes.

I force my eyes away from him before the tears begin to betray me, staring down at my friend instead. Siobhán's gaze is glued to Ness, worry clear in Shivy's brown eyes. I can't stand it.

I feel sick.

Somehow, the conversation passes. Somehow, it ends and Siobhán is with Nessa and I'm standing there, numb and shell shocked. Somehow, this is fucking real.

I throw myself into the hug Nessa and Siobhán are sharing, needing them to ground me. I wrap my arms around them, feeling Shivy laugh and Nessa groan at the move.

"How cute."

Oisín's teasing has us breaking apart, and Nessa rolling her eyes. He's not looking at me. No, his eyes are curious and bright with intrigue as he aims his comment Nessa's way.

I don't exist.

Years, we've spent together. Years of friendship, of kisses, of warm bodies and whispered confessions, and more than once cleaning each other's blood. Years of intimacy and hope and -

Nothing, I realise with a start.

Nothing.

He feels nothing.

After everything, I don't even warrant a *hello?*

This time, it's not the betrayal or the sadness, it's the anger that spurs me. A burst of bright, burning hot rage has me stepping forward towards him, baring my teeth as I spit accusations his way.

"You have so much fucking explaining to do, asshole," I hiss.

He doesn't even bother answering. He only tips his head up to look at me, and we're so close I meet his gaze through his fucking eyelashes. Long and dark. I've seen the way they flutter when he's panting, I've seen them skim his cheek when his eyes close, I've seen them stuck together with tears.

I hate his fucking eyelashes. I hate him.

My hands flex at my sides, desperate to grab him, to pin him against the nearest wall and...

And what? Kiss him until he remembers he's supposed to be with me? Demand answers? Tell him how much I despise him?

I can't do anything because Thomas' hand lands heavy on my shoulder, pulling me back from his son and pinning me with a dark glare.

"Bloody children, the lot of yis," he huffs, and I hate him too.

Days after the first failed marriage, he found another wife for his fucking kid. Is he that desperate? Does he have no other plays to make?

"Go get yourselves cleaned up," Thomas orders us, oblivious to the war raging inside me, waving his hand through the air like it's all nothing, like we're all nothing.

I'm just *nothing*.

Not even a fucking thought in these men's heads.

Aoife appears at Thomas' side from fucking thin air, leaning up to whisper something in his ear. I turn away before I do something incredibly stupid like hit him.

I want to grab Ness or Siobhán or, fuck, even Anji - anyone to ground me. But the girls are kissing, whispering things against each other's mouths and soothing each other and guilt slaps me across the face.

Siobhán's just killed the only parent she had left, Nessa's just had herself stitched back together and I'm standing here wanting them to comfort *me*?

I stumble like I'm drunk, shoulder hitting the doorframe. Oisín's ahead of me, climbing the stairs out of the basement without a single glance back.

I rush after him, taking the steps two at a time. I slip at the top, hand connecting with Oisín's arm to stop myself falling. He stills as I right myself, panting, staring at him wide eyed.

"What the *fuck,* Oisín?" I hiss, aware of how reedy my voice sounds. My skin is buzzing, my body all too aware of how close we are. I'm still leaning on him, hand gripping his arm like it's the only thing keeping me upright.

Oisín flicks his gaze down to where I hold him. "What do you want, Sebastian?"

His words echo around my head. "What…what do I *want?"* I snap, fingers tightening on him. "An explanation! You had no right to marry her without speaking to me first!"

Silence hangs thick and heavy between us. Oisín shakes his head sharply and yanks his arm back to his side, dislodging my grip on him.

I sway on my feet, unmoored, as he turns without a word and stalks off.

The world's all blurry and that ringing noise is back again. The air's gotten colder, thicker, harder to take in. What the fuck is happening? I glance around frantically, but nobody else has climbed the stairs yet.

I end up in my room. I don't know how I got here. But the door's locked, the light's off, and I'm on the floor.

I'm on the floor hearing *fuck, Sebby, yes,* and *God you're beautiful.*

I'm on the floor hearing his voice, hearing *married,* hearing *mafia princess.*

I'm on the floor hearing my own heart break, and it sounds a lot like absolute fucking silence.

4

Sebastian

Warm air and the rich scent of freshly brewed coffee greets me as we step through the door to Libby's Diner.

The place is spacious with rows of booths nestled against the windows, facing out onto the street. A handful of tables are set up between the booths and the counter and risque art pieces hang unashamedly on the pink walls. I smirk at the pop art style print of a woman with her eyes closed and her tongue sticking out. Libby's taste in art is much like her personality - bold and in your face. Everything about her and this place screams *I don't give a shit about your opinion.*

The diner sits on the corner of two streets, nestled between both territories claimed by the Cavanaughs and the Branigans, making it the perfect neutral ground for meetings like this. There's no other place like Libby's and no other woman that could handle keeping both sides of the area in check.

I automatically sweep the room with my eyes, checking the exits are secured. I spot Patrick Branigan immediately with his long copper hair tied in a braid and tattoos adorning every inch of visible skin he has on display. My eyes snag on the lip ring nestled in the centre of his mouth. I sink my teeth into my own lip, wondering if I should finally bite the bullet and get the same piercing. Avery would jump at the chance to pierce me in a visible place for once.

Patrick sits in the farthest booth from the main door, but I wait for Shivy to make her move, standing patiently at her back.

It's been less than twenty four hours since the shoot out with the Branigans that resulted in Seamus' death and I can practically feel the tension radiating from Shivy. From all of us really. Siobhán's been far too calm for my liking, especially after murdering her Da. I suspect that the weight of it all will eventually hit her, and I swear I'll be there to help her through it - as much as Nessa will allow me to be anyway.

That girl is damn possessive.

Oisín, Nessa and Thomas stand behind Siobhán, waiting for her to spot Patrick. We're here to present a unified front, but I'm trying my hardest to ignore them. I don't want to think about the mess they're in. Or the fact that Oisín still won't look at me.

I catch the exact moment Siobhán spots her cousin. It hadn't taken long for her to rescind her claim as heir to the Branigan gang, choosing instead to let him take over. I couldn't help but admire her when she told us that all she'd ever wanted was to be free of Seamus and the entire syndicate, and to be fair, she got exactly what she wanted through Seamus' death.

Patrick stands, and Siobhán hesitates for just a second before throwing herself at her cousin. Patrick catches her easily, their red hair blending together as they smile and joke with each other.

Introductions are made quickly. Patrick, Nessa, Thomas and Siobhán sit at the table as Oisín and I stand guard behind them. We're as far apart as we can get while still doing our job, and I swear every inch of space between us feels like a wound. There are a couple of men standing behind Patrick, though none of them look as though they're bothered by our presence. I catch Siobhán's brow furrowing as she takes them in.

Her confusion is made perfectly clear when she says, "What happened to Da's men?"

"Told 'em they could pledge allegiance to me and be punished for their involvement in your father's shit, or they could get in the grave." The grin on Patrick's face is feral. I like him already. "Most of 'em told me to get fucked so we dealt with 'em like the traitors they were."

My brow arches in surprise, and Siobhán fails to hide her smile. Still, I keep my eye on the men Patrick brought with him just in case. I won't let myself rest until I'm sure that Shivy is free, and that she'll never have to face that nightmare again. The sooner we get this deal sorted the better. I've had fuck all sleep, what with Oisín plaguing my every Goddamn thought, and I don't think even a gallon of Libby's coffee is gonna cut it.

"Right then, let's get this treaty sorted shall we? I have a whole gang to renovate ya know," Patrick starts, leaning his elbows on the table. The grin never leaves his mouth. My surprise is echoed on Thomas' face - Patrick is nothing like the Branigans we're used to dealing with.

Thank God.

Siobhán snorts and I try to smother my smile, but I can tell that even Nessa and Thomas are struggling to contain their smirks.

"Fine," Thomas agrees, and I nod my head too as we wait to hear what Patrick proposes.

"Alright, wedding round two. Same rules as the botched one, I assume. Shivy marries Nessa and the feud ends. One of mine and one of yours, joined forever in *holy matrimony*. A lovely, giant metaphor for two families becoming one."

I can't hold in my laughter anymore, not when I see Patrick dramatically holding his hand over his heart as he leans forward, and Nessa buries her face in her hands, groaning.

Before Thomas has any chance of answering Patrick, Libby, the older lady who's owned this diner longer than I've been alive, comes over to greet us with the usual warning.

"Order up or take your little lackeys and meet on another street corner."

We quickly rattle off our orders, none of us daring to disobey her, before settling in to discuss the terms of the treaty.

The hours pass quickly, helped by two more rounds of coffee, as Patrick and Thomas finally agree on the terms of our alliance. Siobhán and Patrick bicker over the importance of flowers, colour choices and seating arrangements, while Nessa rolls her eyes. By the time Siobhán snaps and reminds her cousin that she's already had a wedding, my light-hearted mood has disappeared.

Nessa glares at Oisín, and I swallow the lump in my throat.

Suddenly, the shiny linoleum floor is *very interesting*. Who'd have thought I'd find black and white tiles so fascinating? They're a hell of a step up from searching the face of a man who's stoically pretending I'm not even here. A man who was set to marry Siobhán not more than a month ago. By the time I get my shit together enough to look up from the floor, the terms are finalised.

"One week," Thomas states, and we all nod in agreement.

One week, and this nightmare of a war will finally be over. One week and I can go back to wandering *Sinners,* trying to convince my dick to want anybody other than Oisín without the threat of a Branigan weapon between my eyes.

The week passes in a blur of dress appointments, suit shopping and alcohol.

I stand near the altar in The Church of Blessed Hearts, my feet aching in my new fancy shoes, as I watch Siobhán float down the aisle. She and Ness look perfect together. Nessa's hair is tied back, a few loose strands framing her face, wearing a hot as fuck black dress with a slit so high it exposes the dagger strapped to her thigh. Siobhán looks every bit the ray of sunshine she is in her crimson gown with her hair flowing down her back. She'd made it very bloody clear that she'd never wear a white dress again, and I don't blame her considering her last one ended up red anyway.

The church is empty aside from the brides and a select few family members. Father Donnelly, the crooked excuse for a priest, is visibly worried, sweat beading at his brow. I shoot him a smirk as he clears his throat and begins the ceremony.

"Let's try this again shall we?" he asks, lips pursed. "Siobhán Branigan and Nessa Tobin, have you come here to enter into marriage without coercion, freely and wholeheartedly?"

"Say yes this time," I call out in a helpful reminder, grinning. My heart may be half dead, but even it swells as my best friends bind themselves together with their vows.

Bind our families together.

I twist my hands together, my right index finger tracing over the empty knuckles of my ring finger. Fuck me, I've turned into a sap. I check my grin hasn't faded, though everything feels blurry now. I'm beyond happy for them, beyond proud of them, and yet the empty, hollow feeling inside my torso threatens to swallow me whole.

I think I might hate weddings.

I manage to blink myself back into reality long enough to fumble for the girls' wedding rings, and then it's over. Or, it's just begun, I guess. A long, happy, married life stretches out in front of Siobhán and Nessa and they're speeding away headlong into it as the rest of us stand on the steps of the church waving them off.

I half consider crashing their honeymoon. I've never been to France, but anywhere is better than the fucking manor at this point.

I cringe as I think of what waits for me back home. A whiskey stained wall, shattered glass bottle in a pile on the carpet because I had no time to clean it up before the wedding, and pictures littering my desk.

Pictures of Serafina DeSantis. Of course I fuckin' looked her up. I regretted it immediately, but shit I'm only so strong. Her long black hair is always perfectly styled, the business-casual suits she wears perfectly pressed and fitted, and her no fucks given attitude present in the arch of her brow or the curve of her lips.

She's fucking stunning.

And she's his fucking wife.

5

Oisín

"She's your *sister?*"

I nod my head, staring at my wife through the phone screen. Serafina's eyebrows are nearly touching her hairline, and her jaw is wide open.

"Apparently Da didn't think to tell me. Or Nessa for that matter," I grunt, pissed that for eleven years I've been living with my sister and didn't even fucking know it. Hell, I've gone twenty-nine years on this earth not even knowing I *have* a sibling, never mind the fact that I'm related to my best fucking friend.

Fuck, at least I like her. And, now that I think about it, we treat each other the way I imagine siblings do anyway; fighting as teenagers, pissing each other off, but always being there for each other. More than that, Nessa may have used our mother's last name - Tobin - but she's always fit in like a Cavanaugh.

"What are you going to do?" Sef asks, and I laugh.

"What's there to do? It doesn't change anything. Not really."

She shakes her head at me and I can practically feel her

frustration through the screen. "This changes *everything,* Oisín. She is your blood. Your family. You cannot pretend that this does not affect you, or your life." The disapproval in her voice makes me grit my teeth.

Sure, family is important. I care very fucking deeply for my family, and the fact that I'm married to Serafina attests to that. Christ, the fact that I'd been willing to marry a fucking Branigan proves it. But the reality is that I've always viewed Nessa like a sister. It won't actually change things, at least, I don't imagine it will.

"I don't exactly see Nessa going from the ruthless menace she is to suddenly wanting to have Sunday dinners and spend every waking moment comparing our childhoods, do you?"

"No. From what you've told me of her she definitely doesn't seem like the type of woman to care about those things. But still...you need to make an effort Oisín. To show her that you value her, not just as the person she was to you as a friend, but as your sibling. She needs this. And so do you. Do not try to tell me otherwise, husband."

I consider her words, breathing deeply. Truth is, as much as I sneer about it, I do want to know what her childhood was like. When our mother left, she took Nessa - still a newborn - and left me with my father. I don't remember my mother, I was only two for fuck's sake. Do I want to know about the woman who abandoned me without a care? Do I want to know how much my sister suffered because our father failed to bring her back home? Do I want to imagine what my life could have been like if Ma had taken me, too? Or if she'd just stayed, or been fucking *normal* - filed for divorce, shared the kids at Christmas.

My life's even more of a shit show than I thought.

"Fine. I'll try to be, I don't know, *nicer*? Fuck knows how I'll make that work, or if I'll survive her stabbing me for daring to be kind to her. If I die, just know it's because I listened to you."

Serafina laughs, and a smile stretches across my face. I love it when she's like this. Relaxed, happy, comfortable to be herself.

Footsteps approach from down the hall. When I lift my head, I spot my da entering his office. I've been standing here waiting for him for over twenty minutes. I need to jump now if I've any chance of speaking to him freely.

"I need to go, angel. I'll call you later?"

Serafina agrees and I pocket the phone quickly before rushing to follow my father.

I sip at the whiskey on the rocks in my hand as I sit across from my father. It's been weeks since we've sat and talked properly, but given the mess the girls created while I was gone, I can't blame him for not taking the time to see me any sooner.

I look at him as he bounces back in his chair, a matching glass in his hand and a cigarette burning away in his mouth.

He looks completely worn out, as though the last month has taken a piece of him. Cut something vital from his soul.

"Christ above, say what it is you want to say, Ois," he grumbles and I can't stop the smile that etches across my face.

"Nothin' at all Da, just taking a look at ya is all. You seem tired," I comment and he peeks an eye open to glare at me.

The side of his lip with the scar twitches as he struggles to hide his grin. We look alike, the same slightly crooked nose - though his is worse than mine given how many times it's been broken - and my eyes have more green than his. A trace of my mother, I suppose, considering the colour of Nessa's, too. My sister.

I'm not sure I'll ever get used to that.

"There it is, you prick," he laughs, and I join him.

But our laughter dies fast.

When I came home, married to Serafina DeSantis, I knew I'd be walking into a new line of fire with Sebastian. But shit, it hurts more than I'm willing to let myself think about. I take another long drink of liquor, letting it burn away the ache.

Despite the shit show I've just come out of, I'm grateful to be able to spend time with my father. Grateful we all survived. Given the state of things, it's a Goddamn blessing.

Anger twists my gut as I think about Nessa's betrayal. Because of her, we could have lost him. I love that girl but, fuck me, sometimes I just want to smack her upside the head and knock some sense into her.

"Hey, none of that, son. I know that look, and I think we can both agree that Nessa's been put through the ringer enough," my father commands, and I grunt before nodding my head.

"I know. I just can't help thinking about how wrong it could have all gone. For all I know, I could have been coming home for your fucking funeral and not to word of Seamus' death," I growl. I've hated Seamus Branigan my entire life, but after hearing about his treatment of Siobhán I wish I could have strangled him myself.

I don't particularly care for the girl, but no parent should ever treat their own flesh and blood so horrifically. An unpleasant, heavy feeling sinks in my stomach as I realise my own father *has* treated his flesh and blood so terribly. Thinking of Nessa alone in the system, then on the streets, with nobody to fight for her, makes me sick.

I push those feelings down, too.

"Well, I'm still alive and kickin' and you won't be getting rid of me anytime soon. Now, tell me where we're at with the DeSantis."

I swirl the remainder of my whiskey in the glass before knocking it back and draining it.

"The Russos are pressing them hard. They've got good trade going with the guns and the drugs, but Renato thinks the Russos are pushing to set up skin markets across the country. It's bad Da, they're gonna need us," I tell him as I reach for the decanter on the desk. I fill my glass to the brim. If I've to discuss the horrors I've witnessed these past few weeks then I'm going to need to be a lot less sober than I am now.

"Talk to Nessa when she gets back from her honeymoon. You're going to need her. Sebastian too," Da sighs, pinning me with a look as he leans back in the chair again.

My heart twists at the thought of Sebastian. Turns out, no amount of whiskey will drown that out.

You had no right to marry her without speaking to me first!

He'd been fuming after finding out that day. And in truth, I can't blame him.

He's right.

But I had no choice. Not when it came to building alliances we desperately needed during the war. And especially not when it meant saving Nessa's arse from their revenge plan.

Realising that I haven't responded to my da's order, I nod my head.

Rapping my knuckles on the desk once, I stand up and say goodnight to my father before heading towards the door.

If I've any chance of getting ahead of this mess, then I need to find Sebastian.

I just hope he can forgive me before it's too late.

6

Serafina

I stare out the window at the pool and deck, glaring at the dark clouds collecting in the sky above. It's colder than usual today, and as much as I want to say fuck it and swim anyway, I don't want to subject myself to being cold and wet without Oisín here to warm me up after.

Anger flashes through me quickly at the thought. I don't need a fucking man to keep me warm. I've spent twenty six years without one and it pisses me off to no end that within *weeks*, my husband has me craving him. It's only been two weeks since he flew back to Killrover. I refuse to mope about it.

I'm about to jump in the damn pool out of spite when my phone rings. For a second, I consider ignoring the ringtone in favour of doing whatever the fuck I want, but duty wins out.

I snatch the buzzing device off my bedside table and catch the name of the caller on the bright screen. My chest tightens.

"Husband," I answer mildly, glad he can't see the way my lips tip up in a smirk. He doesn't need to know just how much

I've come to like him. I don't want to stroke his ego.

"Wife," he says back, his voice low and velvety. Butterflies flutter in my stomach and I frown down at my body for its betrayal. "How are ya, dear Seffy?"

The Irish lilt in his voice makes my heart race. I want his lips on my skin and his filthy words whispered in my ear as his accent draws shivers from my body.

For fuck's sake. When did I become so desperate for him?

I press the phone between my ear and my shoulder, twisting my wedding ring on my finger.

"Missing the Italian sunshine?" I hum back, neglecting to inform him that there's barely been any since he flew back home.

"More than you know," Oisín replies smoothly. If he was here, I'd elbow him for that. Flirt.

"How's the homeland?" I tease, watching as a spatter of rain begins to fall out in the garden.

My bedroom has the best view in the house. The outward facing wall is almost entirely glass, with large patio doors leading out to the back garden. The pool stretches wide, the water blue and warm usually, though now the cover's been rolled over so all I can see is the grey tarp. My father puts a lot of work into the garden, not that he'd be caught dead actually gardening though. I bought him a little potted cactus for his birthday when I was younger, and he killed it in two months. To this day, he swears he did everything right, but the poor thing shrivelled up and fell sideways.

Good thing he's a better father than he is a plant parent.

"It's fine."

Oisín's reply is snappy, his voice losing any warmth. I stiffen, releasing my grip on my ring to straighten and hold the phone in front of my face.

I hit *video call,* waiting for it to show me my husband's face.

Instead, Oisín rejects my request.

"What's going on?" I snap at him.

"Nothing."

"I've been married to you for a month and already I can tell that's a fucking lie," I seethe. Sure, he doesn't owe me a detailed explanation of his entire day, but part of our union was supposed to be *honesty*. In a business sense, sure, but it's hard as fuck to separate the two when you're sharing a bed.

"Sef.." Oisín sighs heavily. "I just can't video call right now, understand?"

"What, don't want to show off your wife?" I snark back, anger bubbling inside me.

"You have no idea just how much I'd *show you off,*" he says darkly, and I suck in a sharp breath at his meaning.

"Don't try to distract me with sex."

"Why not? It works."

"You bastard-" I start, but his low laugh cuts me off. Even still, the sound is strained, forced.

"How's the vermin problem?" He changes the subject but I don't call him on it.

"They haven't miraculously disappeared if that's what you mean." Sarcasm drips from my words as my irritation grows. "How's the war in Killrover?"

I'm determined to find out answers, no matter how much he tries to distract me from them.

"Over," Oisín grunts. "Truce. New head of the Branigans and all. Ah, fuck, Seffy, I've got to go."

"Wait, Oisín-"

The dial tone answers me. I swear, glaring at my phone,

gripping it tight.

"What the *fuck?"* I hiss, throwing the damn thing back onto my bed. It bounces on the mattress, narrowly avoiding falling right off the other end.

"What the fuck indeed."

I look up at her voice, finding my sister standing in my doorway, her dark brow raised.

"Trouble in paradise, sister?"

I shake my head, feeling a little of the tension flee from my shoulders at her presence. Francesca's always had a way of doing that - making everything seem a little brighter than it had been.

"Just the *love of my life*," I groan, the words bitter on my tongue, the joke falling flat.

"It's been what…five weeks?" Frankie laughs, flopping down on the edge of my bed. "Honeymoon phase over that quick?"

"*Stai zitta.*" I wave my hand through the air like it'll silence her faster. She just grins at me. Our smiles are similar, inherited from our mother. It hurts a little to look at Frankie when she's grinning like this.

"Never. I don't know how to shut up," she teases, winking. "Seriously, Sef, what's wrong?"

"Fuck if I know," I say honestly, sighing as I sink down next to her. "Where's Papà? I thought you were with him."

"I was," she says, leaning against me and letting me sap some of her strength. "Beat his ass at *spit*."

I snort at that. My father hates that fucking card game, but he plays it every time Frankie asks. I think she only does it so she'll win.

"He got a call from Lorenzo."

"*Zio?*" I ask, wondering why the hell our uncle's calling. Dread pools in my gut.

"Shop got broken into," Frankie summarises. "Or, at least, the windows were smashed. Someone's trying to piss us off."

"Cockroaches," I mutter under my breath, but Francesca hears anyway. I feel her nod against my shoulder. "*Cazzo.*"

"Guess I should freshen up my aim, huh?" she jokes, but I'm already agreeing with her.

"At the very least, you should keep on top of your training."

Francesca groans at the prospect, falling backward onto my mattress. "But being in bed sounds so much better than being in the gym."

"Tough," I decide, standing and dragging her with me. This is just what I need to distract me from whatever fucking secret my husband is refusing to tell me. And Francesca has been slacking lately. It'll be good for her to face a challenge.

Like me.

"Just don't give me a black eye like last time," she makes me swear as we trudge out of my room.

"No promises."

7

Oisín

"Missing the Italian sunshine?" my wife hums down the phone, a teasing lilt to her voice. The sound of it makes my nerves settle a little.

"More than you know," I answer truthfully, pacing from wall to wall in my bedroom. I swear, if I look down, I'll see the tracks I've made on the soft carpet.

I've only been away for a few weeks but it's odd to be back here. Alone. Serafina has never seen this house, this room with its dark wood bed, high ceilings, bookshelves stacked full of every book I've ever read. I've peeled back the black curtains from the large window, though there's fuck all sunlight to stream in given that it's November in Ireland.

It's a fucking miracle if we get so much as a break from the constant rain and wind that batters our shores.

I stare out the glass at the pissing rain just so I stop staring at the bed. So I stop imagining the sheets rumpled, and dark hair on the pillow, and boxers on the floor beside it.

So I stop fucking imagining it the way it was the last time I was here.

"How's the homeland?" Serafina asks, and I try to focus on her words and not the nightmare I've come back to.

Until said nightmare walks through my bedroom door.

I spin on my heel, chest tight as I meet Sebastian's eyes. His hand is still on the door handle, long fingers curled tight around the metal. Nearly a week since I told Da I'd speak to him, and I've done fucking everything to avoid it. Avoid *him.* Hell, my damn sister got married and had a honeymoon in as much time as I've spent hiding from the man. I'm a fucking coward.

I rip my gaze away.

"It's fine," I say to my wife, every muscle in my body tense with awareness as I give Sebastian my back. Da might insist I need him to deal with the shitshow in Italy, but I can't fucking bear to look at him right now.

My phone buzzes, an incoming video call. Fuck. I swipe *no,* a headache building thick as a storm behind my eyes.

"What's going on?" Seffy asks through the phone, her voice sharp, and I grit my teeth as the *click* of my door closing makes me tense.

I know better than to hope it's him leaving. Sebastian doesn't back down. Even when he should.

"Nothing," I mutter back, pulling the phone away from my ear as Sebastian crosses the room to stand in front of me, forcing me to acknowledge him.

Vaguely, I hear Serafina call me a liar, and Sebastian raises one dark brow at me. The way he's holding himself is stiffer than normal. I fist my free hand to stop myself reaching for him.

I can't make this wound better.

"Sef..." I sigh heavily. Sebastian cocks his head at me,

curiosity and anger forming in the crease between his brows. He doesn't say anything, and I'm not sure if I want him to. What the fuck can either of us say? "I just can't video call right now, understand?"

Sebastian can hear her clearly now, but he doesn't try to end our phone call, or interrupt. No, he leans against my wall, one foot up, arms crossed over his chest.

"What, don't want to show off your wife?" Serafina says.

Sebastian snaps his head up at that, lips pressing into a harsh line like he's physically withholding himself from speaking. The word *wife* echoes in the suddenly stuffy air of my room.

"You have no idea just how much I'd *show you off,*" I say in a low voice. I meet Sebastian's eyes as I speak. I should know better. I see the fire there, the interest flaring. I swallow roughly.

"Don't try to distract me with sex."

"Why not? It works."

Sebastian stares at me, and I can't look away. His hands flex. His eyes dart between me and the phone. I make the grave mistake of looking him over, only to find him straining in his pyjamas, the thick outline of his cock visible.

Serafina calls me a bastard, and I turn away from Sebastian entirely. Wife. I have a goddamn *wife*.

I move the subject from fucking before my own body gets the wrong idea. I can't think about sex while I'm in the room with him, while I'm looking at the bed we lay in together before my first fucking wedding, my cock in his mouth, and his cum on my chest.

My answers are robotic now, my mind barely processing what Serafina's saying. I can *feel* Sebastian getting closer to me, his presence like a hand on my neck.

I want to put mine around his for the shit he's pulling right now.

A punishment. That's what he fucking needs.

No.

No.

"How's the war in Killrover?"

Serafina.

"Over," I grunt. "Truce. New head of the Branigans and all."

Hell, I was there for the peace treaty negotiations. Patrick Branigan seems far more tolerable than his late uncle and it's obvious he cares about Siobhán. Given that she's now a Cavanaugh by marriage, it bodes well for peace.

Sebastian's hand wraps around my waist from behind me and I jolt like his touch is lightning. "Ah, fuck, Seffy, I've got to go."

I shove my phone into my pocket and grab Sebastian's hand in a harsh grip, throwing his touch off me like he's a spider I found crawling on my clothes.

"What the *fuck* Sebastian?" I hiss, glaring at him over my shoulder.

"Me?" he snaps back, indignation bright in his voice. "What the fuck have you done, Oisín?"

"My duty."

"Fuck your duty!"

I turn fully, facing him and giving him the fight he so clearly wants. It hurts to look at him. I can't stop.

"Does your wife know whose bed you were in days before ye were married?" Sebastian says slowly. "Does she suck your cock as well as I do? Does she submit like a *good girl?* Or does she fight you like we both know you want? Huh?"

"Don't fucking speak about my wife."

"Does she even know?" he presses, stepping closer. I have to tip my head back to look up at him. Every instinct in me screams for me to force him to his knees, to force him to look up at me instead. "Do you make love to her, is that it? Soft and sweet and *boring*."

I'm near shaking with anger and something darker, something I refuse to analyse. Because fuck him, and fuck the fact that I can't fuck the attitude out of him.

I don't have an answer.

He's right. I haven't told her what I like in bed. But hearing him imply that fucking my wife could ever be *boring* makes me want to shut him the fuck up.

Preferably with my cock.

He's so close now our chests are touching and I can feel his breaths are as heavy as mine. I fist my hands. *Do not touch, Oisín. Not yours to touch.*

"You knew this was coming, Sebastian," I tell him darkly, spitting anger at him. The rage is a shield, but I won't lower it. "Don't act like we had a future."

He winces, blinking rapidly like he can hide the flash of hurt in his eyes. Like he can hide anything from me.

"I thought you'd at least be in the fucking country!" Sebastian shouts. "That you'd be here, and we could sneak off at dinner parties and fuck in your marriage bed while your wife, who was supposed to be a Branigan let me remind you, charmed your guests."

"Sebastian." His name melts like chocolate on my tongue.

"Don't lie to me now, *Máistir*." Sebastian presses closer still, and I curse myself for getting trapped between him and the bed. I want to push him away, but that means touching him again. "No matter which spouse you take, you'll always be mine."

I find my strength, bracing my hands on his chest and shoving him back. He goes easily, and I pretend like the touch didn't burn my very fucking soul.

"I was never yours," I tell him. "I never will be."

"Fuck off," he says, but there's less venom in his words than before. "Don't act like all those years meant nothing."

"Get out."

"Don't do that, Oisín. You've avoided me all week, I deserve-"

"I owe you *nothing*." I need him to leave. I need him to leave now or I'm going to pin him down by the throat and ruin everything.

Sebastian stands between me and the door, mouth open but no words leave him. He blinks at me, eyes wide. The shock dissipates and his eyes narrow as he points to my bed. The black sheets are perfectly made, tucked in at the corners.

"I hope you go to sleep at night thinking about everything I did to you on that mattress," he says, eyes dragging over my body. I feel myself ready for him, but tell myself it's nothing more than muscle memory. I know he notices, by the way the smirk returns to his face. "I hope you dream of me, on my knees for you, and I hope you wake up covered in your own cum."

"Sebastian."

"I hope you stop fucking lying to yourself," he continues, voice growing quieter. "You can try and forget those *years* we had, but your body remembers. It knows what's good for it."

"I can't do this."

His eyes are trained on mine.

"Let me," he whispers. I watch, unable to look away, as he falls to the floor, knees hitting the carpet. "Let me."

I bite my own tongue to stop myself saying *yes, fuck yes* because he's fucking gorgeous, face tilted back to look up at me.

"No," I say instead. "I'm married, Sebastian."

"For barely more than a month," he murmurs. "We had *years*. You don't get to leave me behind with no explanation, Oisín."

"You need to leave."

He nods, standing and readjusting himself in his jeans with no subtlety. He backs towards the door, silent until he's halfway out my room, lips tipped up on the right in a smirk.

"Sweet dreams, *Máistir*."

8

Sebastian

The shower's fucking freezing but it doesn't help. My body is still on fire, anger and lust burning me up. I slam my open palm against the tile, wincing as the impact reverberates through my wrist.

My forehead hits the wall, the spray of the water hitting my head as I squeeze my eyes shut and pray for my dick to stop reminding me how badly I need him. How much I miss him. How desperately I want to swallow his cock down my throat and remind him who he truly belongs to.

Fuck!

I knock my head against the tile a couple of times as my dick bobs against my stomach, ignoring the icy water slipping down my body.

My hand wraps around my length and I hiss as pleasure sneaks up my spine. I give myself a harsh tug, before letting go and shaking my head.

I can't. I won't.

I refuse to get off while thinking about him.

I won't do it anymore.

I won't let him control me like this. My needs, my desires, they aren't his to own. Not anymore.

According to him, they never were to begin with anyway.

Pain lances through my chest, but I ignore it.

I focus instead on taking deep breaths, desperate to settle my body and mind. I curse beneath my breath as my dick only grows harder.

I run my hands through my hair, lifting it from my face before reaching for the shampoo from the floating shelf beside me.

Grabbing the body wash next, I clean every inch of myself, expertly avoiding my dick in the hopes that I can just pretend my erection isn't there.That my body isn't shaking, begging for release. For the pain in my chest at his rejection to be softened with the pleasure I know I can give myself.

By the time I've rinsed myself off, my dick is practically weeping with the need to come.

Frustration burns in my veins as I wrap my hand around my cock. I swipe my thumb across the tip, precum coating it as I squeeze myself harder.

Bliss sneaks up my spine and I shiver. My nipples are pebbled, straining between the icy water and the desire riding me hard as I drag my fist down my length.

My hips buck, pushing my dick into my hand and I let go of any reservations I had.

Fuck this, and fuck him.

I'm not going to let him wreck me like this.

I twist my body so that I can rest my back against the tile, the harsh bite of the cold water hitting my abdomen and I hiss at the contrast between the heat of my cock in my hand and the water trailing over my thighs.

My eyes slip closed as I move my hand once more, twisting it at the head to gather more precum. I scrunch my face as my mind automatically drifts back to thoughts of Oisín. The way his muscled back flexed as he held the phone to his ear. The sound of his voice as he taunted me. Flirted with *her* while glaring at me.The sharpness in his gaze as he'd looked at my tented sleep pants, want burning in his eyes.

He couldn't have hidden that from me if he'd tried to.

Heartbreak dampens the bliss I'm feeling as his rejection hits me all over again.

He told me to leave.

Denied my touch, and threw me aside.

Tears burn the back of my eyes but they don't fall.

My hand never stops moving despite the fact that my heart shatters inside of my chest. If anything, I pick up the speed.

Wet tracks flow down my face now but I pretend that I can't feel it.

It doesn't matter. He doesn't matter.

My breath quickens as my balls draw tighter, and with a few aggressive tugs of my length, I'm coming.

My knees lock and my eyes fly open, tears freely streaming down my face now as I watch my release swirl down the drain.

Lifting my free hand to my mouth I muffle the sob trying to escape me. I can't do this.

I can't pretend.

I've loved him for so fucking long, and to know that he never loved me the same way breaks me more than I ever thought possible.

I feel fractured. Torn apart. Like pieces of me are missing, and I'll never be whole without them.

My vision swims as the pain crushes me from the inside out. My legs buckle under the weight of my heartbreak and I slide down the wall to collapse on the floor. I can't stop the onslaught of memories. The times we spent training together, messing about with Nessa, driving her insane. Secret stolen moments together in hallways and empty rooms.

Fuck him for doing this to me. To us.

Fuck him for never caring at all.

How could he let this happen?

My hand flies from my face, my knuckles colliding with the tile. My skin splits and I hiss, relief filling me as I welcome the pain. I'll take anything over the devastation that wreaked havoc on my mind.

Anger takes a front seat as I watch blood drip down my hand, mixing with the rush of water swirling down the drain.

I shake my head, scrambling to collect my thoughts.

I don't know where to go from here.

All I know for sure is that Oisín has hell to pay. He doesn't get to hurt me like this. Not after all we've been through.

I stand abruptly, careful not to slip, before shutting the shower off.

Wrenching the door open, I reach for the towel and wrap it tightly around my hand as I step out. I don't care that there's water dripping from my body to the floor below. I don't care that I'm freezing, naked and wet.

I storm out of the bathroom determined to never let this happen again.

9

Sebastian

"Oh for Christ's sake, Sebastian put some fuckin' clothes on!" Nessa shrieks, covering her eyes dramatically as I freeze in the doorway.

"What the fuck, Ness?" I spit back, lowering the bloodied towel fisted in my hand to cover my dick. I'm still dripping wet and shivering and now I'm confused as well as pissed off. It's a bloody *marvellous* combination. "When did you two get back?"

I close the door behind me, not giving a single fuck that either of them can see my naked arse. As I turn back to face them, I take a good look at my friends. Nessa's standing by the large armchair Siobhán's sitting on, her hand still held over her eyes.

"Three hours ago," Shivy answers cheerily, unconcerned with the state of me. "Wanted to come see my favourite Cavanaugh member. Missed you."

Nessa glares at her for her comment, hand dropping from her face. Siobhán just smiles, and a rough chuckle works its way out of me.

"Missed you too," I offer. "How was France?"

Maybe if they distract me enough with talk of their honeymoon it'll fill the hole in my chest. Worth a damn try.

I drop my towel from my dick, much to Nessa's complaints, and wipe myself dry. I snatch whatever clothes are nearest to me from the floor, and chuck them on, sniffing at them to make sure they're not old gym clothes. I'm behind on laundry as per fucking usual.

"It was lovely," Shivy grins. "No freezing fuckin' rain."

I rub the towel through my hair before letting it drop to the floor.

"Does this mean yous got the lovey dovey nonsense out yer systems? Or can I expect to feel violently nauseous around you still?" I joke, my chest squeezing tightly.

In answer, Nessa leans down to kiss Siobhán. It's brief but I look away regardless. I suppose it's revenge for finding me naked and fresh out the shower but in my defence, how was I to know they were in my room?

I roll my eyes as they pull apart, only to find Siobhán squinting at me.

"Your eyes are red," she comments, standing and cocking her head.

I look away. "Too much drink last night is all."

"Must be some fucking hangover to have you looking like that at eight o'clock the next night," Nessa says suspiciously, eyeing me.

"Yup," is all I say. Even to my own ears my voice is tired.

"What did we miss, Seb?" Siobhán asks, and I hear their footsteps approach.

I sigh, giving up as I sit on the edge of my mattress, leaning my elbows on my knees.

"Fuck all."

"Sebastian-"

"No," I continue. "No, literally, *fuck all*. That's the problem."

"Maybe you are still drunk," Nessa mutters under her breath. Siobhán elbows me over and sits beside me, but Ness stands, looking down at me.

"He's ignoring me."

There's a beat of silence in the wake of my confession, and I almost try to take it back.

"Oisín?" Nessa asks, like she has to confirm we're talking about the same person.

"Obviously."

"*Oisín?* Like, my brother? The guy you've been stuck to since you were fourteen fucking years old? Son of-"

"Yes, that Oisín," I snap at her, irritation making my skin crawl. It takes more effort than I want to admit to keep my anger under control. I hate this rage.

"It's just…why?" Nessa murmurs, frowning at me. "What did you do?"

The laugh that burst from me is cold. "Me? I'm not the one who fucked off to a different country, ignored every call and text, and got shacked up to an Italian mafia princess. *I* haven't done anything."

God, even recounting what he's done makes me feel sick.

"Ah," Nessa hums.

"What was…is…going on between the two of you?" Siobhán asks softly, her hand landing on my arm. I shake her off, hating the feeling of her skin on mine. I don't want anybody's touch but his and I hate myself for it.

"Nothing that matters," I hiss.

"That's not true, it clearly matters if you're this upset," she argues.

"I'm not upset!" I snap, immediately shaking my head at myself. "I'm just...fine. Fine. Okay, I'm pissed. He fucking *abandoned* me."

"You love him," Siobhán murmurs, brows drawing together as she looks at me. The sympathy in her dark eyes forces me to look away. I don't want pity.

"He doesn't want me," I answer instead. "He's made that very fucking clear. But he doesn't get to just ice me out without so much as an apology."

"He was supposed to marry me," Siobhán reminds me. "Were you pissed at that, too?"

"Less. At least he'd have been close. We could've..." I trail off, catching myself before I tell her I'd planned on making her husband cheat on her with me.

I'm not even embarrassed by the state of my morals. I've never claimed to be a saint and working for the Cavanaughs has only further darkened my world view.

"Glad I shot down that marriage before I was tied to a cheat then," Siobhán says with a roll of her eyes.

"He's far too up his own hole to have taken me up on the offer anyway," I mutter. "Least of all now. He's already in love with this one."

There's an uncomfortable silence. We all know that there's nothing Ness or Shivy can say that will make this better.

"He's married, Seb," Nessa says finally, and I clench my jaw. "That's the fact of it. "

She says it with such finality that I deflate. It's the truth and I know that. I can't do anything. I can't force him to want me. I can't beg him to choose me. The choice has been made, and I wasn't even there for it.

The world goes all blurry again.

"Let's go out," Siobhán suggests, trying to inject some life back into me as she elbows me encouragingly. "Get drunk. Find a pretty person to take your mind - and your dick - off him."

I can't even muster enough effort to pretend to consider it.

"Won't work. Tried it," I admit. God, he's condemned me to a life without love and a life without sex. Prick.

"Well, you need to get over it somehow. I'm not listening to you moping 'bout him until the end of time, and I'm sure as shit not dealing with the two of you being weird as fuck around each other," Nessa tells me, voice as brutal as her words. I glare at her.

"If Shivy married someone else and I told you to *get over it*, how badly would you want to punch me?" I ask her in a low voice. Her hands fist at her sides, and her gaze turns to Siobhán like she can't bear the thought. "Exactly."

"It'll be okay, Seb," Siobhán says, leaning her head on my shoulder in a sideward cuddle. I don't flinch away this time, but I don't return it either.

"Thanks, sunshine," I murmur.

I don't tell her that I don't want to be okay without him. That I can't fucking settle for okay after I've spent years feeling like a god in his arms. That I've spent so long imagining a future with him, one where we didn't hide, and I can't accept losing that.

I can't accept losing him.

10

Oisín

The air smells like blood and piss. It's cloying, and I pant as I try to get any oxygen into my lungs. It's so dark that I can't see my hand in front of my face.

I don't have a fucking clue where I am.

There's a brief sound like nails scratching at concrete, then a sharp cry before it's silent again. My skin goes cold.

"Who's there?" I call out, trying to step forward, further into the darkness. But my feet won't move, and my body doesn't feel real. I'm stuck, trapped in an abyss.

"Oisín?"

"Serafina?"

It's her. I know it's her, I'd recognise her voice anywhere. Except now, it's strained with pain and thick like she's been crying. She doesn't call out again, and I still can't move. Panic rises as hard and fast as a tidal wave, and if I could feel my body, I'm sure I'd be shaking.

"Serafina!"

Silence, then footsteps.

"Where's the bitch?" The voice is gruff and male. I don't

recognise it at all. It sounds like I'm listening from underwater; everything's distorted.

"Which one?" Another voice, like static.

"The newest."

I want to move. I want to find my wife. I want a weapon and I want the blood of those bastards on my hands.

"Ah there she is," the first one says, and something rattles. Metal on concrete. Serafina's sob.

"Please don't," she says. Her voice is much smaller than usual. Serafina doesn't cower, and yet by the sound of her plea, I can practically see her curled up, arms over her head.

"Don't fucking touch her!" I shout out, but either they can't hear me, or they choose to ignore me completely.

"Such a pretty face is wasted being kept up in that house," the second voice sneers. "You'll be put to good use here, puttana."

"Tell me, has a man ever made you scream?" the first laughs.

Serafina shouts out, and the rattling starts again, like they're shaking a cage. Like they're shaking ***her*** *cage.*

"Leave her alone!" I scream. The darkness seems thicker than ever, and I want to slash through it, to fight, to kill.

I'm powerless.

"Let her go, you fucking bastards!"

Serafina screams.

"SERAFINA!"

I jolt upright in bed, sweating and shaking, the sheets sticking to my skin. I thrash, trying to shove them off me but only succeeding in twisting them tighter around my limbs. Panic grips me so hard I can hear my own pulse, and my throat is raw from shouting my wife's name.

But this darkness isn't all consuming. No. The darkness

now is split apart by shafts of moonlight streaking in through the window. I didn't close the blinds before I collapsed into bed. I didn't even intend on sleeping. I'd just wanted to lay down to recover from the shit show with Sebastian before I called Seffy back.

Fuck, Seffy.

It's only when my pulse calms and my ears stop ringing that I realise my phone is vibrating. I curse, trying to find it, finally managing to get the sheets off me.

I snatch the phone up from where it was hidden under the duvet, and swipe to answer the call.

"Seffy?"

"Oisín."

The panic comes rushing back stronger than ever at the rasp in her voice. Something's wrong. Something's very fucking wrong.

"What happened?" I ask immediately, moving to stand, needing to do anything other than sit in that fucking bed. "Serafina, are you okay?"

"No," she rushes to say, voice shaking. "It's all gone to shit, Oisín. It's all gone to shit. *Cazzo,* they…the bastards. The bastards took her."

I freeze in my pacing. "Took who, love?"

"Frankie."

"Your sister?"

"She's gone."

I swear, resuming my back and forth, shaking my head. "What the fuck happened? The Russos made a move?"

The Russos and the DeSantis have a long history. Mostly a peaceful one. But ever since the Russos began talking about making coin in the skin market, tensions have been high.

They're immoral fucking cunts that don't deserve the ground they walk on.

They're also richer than God and good at covering their tracks. In the months Renato DeSantis has been digging, he's found no evidence of their involvement with the underground market that's festering in San Jarno.

"They're denying everything, the cunts." Her words are sharp and rushed. "We need backup, Oisín. We need..."

"My father."

There's a brief beat of silence in which I can hear her panting, like she's been running for miles. Worry makes my skin crawl. Francesca's as well trained as any of them, though less vicious by nature than my wife.

How fast will word spread that Renato DeSantis' daughter is missing? How fast will word spread of their weakness? How fast will someone take advantage of the fact their focus is on finding her, and not their business?

Fucking *hell.*

"Fly over, Seffy," I tell her, needing her close to me.

"I can't leave-"

"You have to." My voice is harsher now, demanding. "You can't be a sitting duck, Serafina. They've already got Francesca, what's to say they won't take you, too? Strip Renato of all his heirs?"

Her sharp intake of breath makes me tense. "I am not a *sitting duck,* husband." She uses my title like an insult, and it makes my lips curve up. I want to punish her for it as much as I want to protect her. "Let's see them try to take me. I'll relish watching them fall at my feet."

"I know you're angry," I try to reason. "But be smart. For your sister. Come over. Speak to my father while yours does everything he can to get your sister back. We have to be careful here, Serafina."

"I can't leave my father right now."

"Ask him," I insist. If I know anything about the man, it's that he protects his children with his life. He will encourage her to leave if only to come back with backup, and we both know it.

"We need to push the Russos for information, we need-"

"You need to do nothing but get on a plane and come to me."

"Oisín, do not think you can control me because I wear your ring."

"I wouldn't dream of it," I tell her honestly. I love the bloodthirsty, feral look she gets when someone's pissed her off. I love it even more when it's trained on me. "But think through your anger. There are tens of people under your father's command that can push the Russos. You're better served to make use of the alliance. Come over, Serafina, and demand help."

"*Cazzo,*" she curses, rage bleeding into her voice in earnest. "I'll be there tomorrow."

I grin, despite the fact she can't see me. Worry is still simmering in my blood, residual panic from my nightmare still lingering. Panic seizes me for a brief moment as I realise just how close that dream was to reality.

But if she's here, she's safe. I can't convince her not to fight back, not to search for her sister, but I can make sure she's protected while she does.

"I'll have someone meet you at the airport."

"See you soon, husband."

11

Sebastian

"Serafina?"

Oisín's sleep coated voice bleeds through the wall, and I grip the bedsheets in my fists.

Fate cannot be this cruel to me. It was bad enough having him come home *married,* bad enough being brutally fucking rejected, without having to listen to him shout out his wife's name in his sleep.

Who the fuck did I piss off in a past life to deserve this shite?

"Serafina!"

His voice is hoarse and thready, and the sound of his fear makes my stomach clench. I release the bedsheets to press my hands over my ears, leaning forward until my head is between my legs at the edge of the bed. I stay like that, curled into myself, nausea rioting in my stomach.

I can't fucking do this.

It's inhumane.

"SERAFINA!"

I curse as I shoot to my feet. I'm at my door before I know it, unable to fucking stand the raw pain in his voice. He sounds like he's terrified - the name being ripped from his chest in a scream.

My muscles strain with the need to go to him. To comfort him. To hold him until he's okay.

But it's not my name he's shouting for.

It's not me he's scared of losing.

I hesitate, my hand shaking over the door handle. I can't open it. I can't go to him.

He doesn't fucking want me.

The sound that rips out of my throat is something akin to a growl, and I'm shaking so badly I stumble on my way back to the bed. The sheets feel too warm against my burning skin, and I kick at them, burrowing my face in the mattress and shoving the pillow over my head.

I can still hear him begging for her.

I fall asleep wishing he'd beg for me like that.

12

Serafina

My ears pop as the plane finally levels out and my body adjusts to the new height. The jet is silent but for the hum of the engine that radiates through the seats, and my sigh sounds loud in the stale air.

It's so early the sun has only just risen, radiating bright orange across the clouds below us. I stare at the glow until my eyes blur, and when I look away, the sun is imprinted on the back of my eyelids.

"Good morning," the air hostess greets with a tight, professional smile. "Can I offer you a drink, or some breakfast?"

I almost feel bad for the last minute flight plan, but we pay her and the pilot double what they'd get on a commercial plane so my guilt fades quickly. She's around my age, with neatly curled blonde hair and red lips. I can't remember her name, but I nod at her.

"Espresso. And whatever pastries you've got," I answer, forcing my own tight smile in return. It hurts my face, but I don't want to scare the woman charged with helping get me to Ireland safely.

"Of course."

She leaves in a hurry to fill my order, and I sink further into my seat. I'm fucking exhausted. Exhausted beyond just needing sleep. Worry weighs my body down with every moment that I'm away from Frankie. I feel like I've been filled with concrete, stress and the bone deep tiredness is pulling me down as I struggle to figure it all out.

It's been years since I've flown alone, and I struggle to sit still. The sooner this flight is over and I can get to the Cavanaughs, the sooner I can come home to find my sister.

The air hostess returns with a little cart and begins to set out a selection of food and my cup of espresso in front of me. She's silent as she does so, my bad mood bleeding into my facial expression. I fight to keep myself from sneering at her sheer closeness. Thankfully, she leaves quickly with a small nod in my direction.

I sip my coffee and scald my tongue, hissing at the sting. The nerves coursing through me have my stomach tangled in knots, but I reach for a croissant anyway, flaky pastry falling as I pick it up. I barely taste it as I eat.

I choke it down regardless, and finish the last sip of espresso, tipping my head back to get the dregs of coffee that stain the bottom of the cup. My fingers find the ring on my left hand subconsciously, twisting the sparkly wedding band. The thing's ridiculous - the entire band set with alternating rubies and diamonds, curved around the huge ruby stone of my engagement ring. Our *engagement* was non-existent, but I appreciate the pretty jewellery nonetheless.

Our wedding is a blur in my memory. A blur of champagne and satin and smiles from people I barely knew. Fuck, Oisín's own family wasn't even there. Too busy trying to survive as war raged in Killrover. My gut clenches again. The wedding doesn't matter.

At least the consummation was good.

Really fucking good.

Fuck, I miss him.

Not just because of the sex. Although, truth be told, I miss that too. But because, despite the fact I've only known the bastard for barely more than a month, he's wormed his way under my skin.

I didn't want to be apart from him. Not when we were only just getting to know each other, getting comfortable with each other. I like him, and I don't want whatever spark of connection there was between us to be snuffed out by distance.

Our marriage is not one of love, but necessity. But that doesn't mean we have to suffer with the choice for the rest of our lives.

I don't want to resent him, or myself, for the way we've been brought together. Francesca had thought I was ridiculous for *swooning* over the man, and I'd scoffed in her face for the assumption.

God, she'd tease the hell out of me now for being so nervous to see him again if she was here.

But she's not here.

And the fact that we don't know where the fuck she is has my breakfast threatening to come back up.

I shake my head like I can clear all the worst case scenarios from my brain but the reality is that my baby sister is *gone*.

She's gone and I'm on a fucking private jet to Killrover. Gone, and I've left my father to find her himself. Gone, and I'm worried about my fucking husband who's practically still a stranger.

Guilt makes my blood turn cold. I have to dig into my bag and find an extra jumper, tugging it on over the comfy sports bra style top I'd worn for travel.

I'm doing the right thing.

I'm doing the right thing.

Am I doing the right thing?

I need to meet Thomas Cavanaugh and I need to ensure he's going to keep his word with this alliance. We kept Oisín safe - as safe as fucking possible given that we made him a member of our family.

And now my sister is God knows where being put through God knows what. We need him, and I won't take no for an answer.

The Russos are denying all involvement. Which is a massive fucking problem because we've been *sure* they were behind the trafficking ring that had popped up beneath the streets of San Jarno. The Russos have a long, complicated history with us and none of us would put it past them to stoop as low as shit to make money.

We may be fucking criminals but we have morals.

Apparently, they're insisting they do too.

I don't trust it, but Papà spent all night demanding I let it go. He was ruthless in reminding me that it wasn't my problem to solve, especially as his heir and not the head of the family. No, my problem is now convincing an Irish gang leader to leave his own territory to help us defend ours. Like we're fucking packs of wolves.

It has to work.

I won't return without them.

I imagine meeting my husband's father for the first time

under normal circumstances would be nerve-wracking, but with the added pressure of demanding his help in saving my sister, my mind is spinning. He's important to Oisín, and I know the rest of the close members are too. He's spoken about Nessa, Anji, Aoife and his father the most.

I want them to like me. More than that, though, I need them to respect me. I won't be viewed as just *Oisín's wife*. I'm Serafina DeSantis and I will not let a man define me.

Even to his own family.

I spend the entire two and a half hour flight in a state of restlessness, almost sick with nerves. By the time we're landing, my ears once again popping painfully with the change of pressure, I'm antsy and snappy as fuck.

My husband has promised someone will be at the airport to collect me. I wonder how much they'll expect me to talk, or if they'll let me sit in the back of the car and try to remember how to breathe like a normal person until I'm delivered to my father in law to beg him for help.

With my fucking luck, I'll get the chattiest member of the entire Cavanaugh gang driving me to Killrover.

Just the thought makes me want to board the plane and go home again.

I exhale slowly, trying to tame my body language into something remotely welcoming, and check my phone. There's a text from Oisín, telling me there's a car waiting for me, and that he'll see me soon.

This will go well, I tell myself as I collect my bags and make for the pick up point.

It has to.

13

Sebastian

"No."

"Sebast-"

"Absolutely fucking not. I'd literally rather chop my own dick off. And that's fucking saying something, Thomas, cause I'm rather fond of it."

"I wasn't giving you an option," Thomas says pointedly, scowling down at me.

"Fuck it, I'll chop off my balls too. Hell, I'll even let you do it for the craic. But I'm not playing taxi to your son's new wife," I spit out, shaking my head furiously. "That's my hard limit."

"Need I remind you that you're not in my fuckin' good books right now, son?" Thomas' tone is ice cold now, far worse than the annoyed snap from before. I go still, seething silently. "This is a job you can't fuck up. If you want to earn my trust back, Sebastian, you'll do as your fuckin' told."

My hands ball into fists but they stay at my sides. I'd have to have more than a few missing brain cells to try and fight Thomas Cavanaugh. The man's fucking deadly.

But right now, I'm almost up for the task.

"Thomas," I try, nearly pleading. "Surely there's someone else. Like literally anyone else."

"You and Nessa are going. That's fuckin' final."

I know he's making us do it as some form of punishment. It's a boring as fuck job, normally, playing taxi from the airport to the manor. If it was anyone else, I'd grumble but do it without much resistance because even I know I've pissed off Thomas enough for one week.

Except it's not just anyone he wants us to go and collect.

It's Serafina fucking DeSantis.

Otherwise known as Oisín's wife.

Otherwise known as the last bloody person I ever want to see.

"Nessa's waiting in the car. Don't be late."

It's a dismissal and we both know it. Still, I stare Thomas down for a few seconds, hoping he'll take pity on me. I can't very well stand up here and tell him *why* I don't want to do this. Not when that would mean explaining that I've been fucking his son in secret for years.

Without the Cavanaughs, I have nothing.

So I have no other choice but to nod my head reluctantly and back out of the library, dragging my feet behind me like a kicked dog.

When I make it out, I find Nessa is indeed waiting in the car. In the driver's seat, no less. That only makes my mood sour more, and I glare at her as I slide into the passenger seat.

"Bitch," I accuse, glowering her way as she pulls away from the manor.

"You snooze, you lose, dickhead," she taunts back, grinning far too wide for the circumstances.

"Take pity on me," I whine, the back of my head thumping against the headrest. "At least run me over so I don't have to do this."

Nessa snorts. "As dramatic as ever I see. Good to know the heartbreak hasn't changed you."

I debate whether or not I can punch her without her crashing the car, eventually settling on giving her a death glare instead.

"God, how did I not figure out you're Thomas' kid before now?" I grumble back to her. "You're both complete pricks."

Nessa just shoots me a grin and a wink. In retaliation for her stealing the driver's seat, I turn my music up as loud as it'll go and sing along, purposefully butchering every note, as she threatens to let go of the wheel just to cover her ears.

It's as much revenge as I'm going to get, so I take it with a grin.

The private airport is tiny and apparently empty. We pull up to the pick up point right on time, but there's nobody there. Nessa parks anyway, and gets out, opening my door to drag me out with her. I groan but let her, leaning against the side of the car while she takes a few steps ahead.

"If she's not here, we can leave, right?" I say hopefully, tapping my foot on the pavement.

"Stop your fucking whining," Nessa snaps back without even looking over her shoulder. I glare at her back.

I'm about to get in the car and tell her to find her own way home when the sound of heels clicking on concrete and suitcase wheels approaches. I stiffen.

"Serafina DeSantis?" Nessa calls out as the woman herself

steps around the corner and into view.

I want to gauge my own eyes out.

She's as gorgeous in real life as she is in the photos. The kind of gorgeous that seems unfair, because she's been on a fucking plane for nearly three hours at the crack of dawn and should at the very least have puffy eyes or messy hair.

Of course not.

She's tall, though that's helped by the red bottom heels, and her thick, dark hair is pulled back into a ponytail. Her brown eyes are so dark they look black. They're trained on Nessa as she steps forward with her hand outstretched to help Serafina with her bags, not missing a single move that Nessa makes. Oisín's wife is the picture of poise and politeness as she smiles widely at Nessa, pink lips full and glossy.

Serafina DeSantis is hot as fuck and I hate her for it.

Or, rather, I hate Oisín for it. Or maybe myself. Regardless, I'm pissed.

"You must be Nessa?" Serafina asks as she and Nessa round the car to try and fit her three suitcases in the boot.

"That's me. I'm not sure it bodes well that you've heard of me enough to recognise me," Nessa quips back with a kindness she never directs at me. Traitor.

"Well, your wife was supposed to marry my husband," Serafina laughs and my stomach turns.

The boot is slammed shut and the sound shakes me. I push off the side of the car and give Serafina a sharp nod. I can't bring myself to actually speak to her.

"I'm Serafina DeSantis, heir to the DeSantis family," she introduces anyway, that pretty, polite smile directed my way now. Bile stings my throat at the sickly sweetness of it all. For fuck's sake, the woman's gorgeous and nice and that's just *fucking perfect isn't it.*

I don't answer, and her smile falters just slightly.

"I'm sorry, I don't think I caught your name?"

I stop in my tracks.

She doesn't know who I am.

"Sebastian," is all I can manage to choke out.

"Oh, sorry, Oisín's just never mentioned you!" she chirps apologetically.

Nessa holds the back door open for her and she slides inside while I stand there like a fucking idiot, frozen to the spot.

Oisín's never mentioned so much as my Goddamn name.

The knife in my back twists deeper.

I snatch the keys out of Nessa's hand.

"I'm fucking driving," I growl at her, and to my shock she doesn't argue back. She just slides into the passenger side without a word.

The second my ass hits the chair, I'm slamming the accelerator to the floor. Our cargo lets out a surprised squeak from the back seat, then shuts up, and I avoid glancing in the rear view mirror so I don't have to look at her.

"So, how do you know my husband?" Serafina asks, trying to ease the thick, cloying tension in the car. The engine growls as I push the car faster.

Because he was fucking me long before you came along, I want to tell her. *Because I'm the one he learned what he needs with. Because it was me who he called his first.*

But only behind closed doors. Oisín calls Serafina his loudly and proudly and with his whole damn chest.

I ignore the question, and Nessa fills in, changing the subject quickly. Their voices are nothing but a low drone that melds in with the engine. The entire drive passes in a blur and I'm pulling up outside the manor having driven the whole way on auto-pilot.

I'm slamming the door shut and racing inside before either Nessa or Serafina can stop me.

14

Oisín

Fucked up doesn't even begin to describe the state of my life.

"You're going to wear a path into the floor," Anji grumbles as I pass through the kitchen for what feels like the hundredth time today.

I can't fucking sit still. Not since Seffy texted me to let me know that Nessa and Sebastian had picked her up and that she was on her way.

The second I read his name on the screen my heart dropped. Nothing good was going to come of them meeting for the first time without me there. Sebastian is fucking terrible at keeping his mouth shut and I couldn't risk him telling my wife what we were…had been…together.

What the fuck had we even been together?

Nothing. *Nothing.*

The pain in my chest calls me a liar. *Fuck.*

Could I even blame him if he told her everything? The kind of asshole I was? But he knew, we both knew, that there was no future in what we were doing. We could fantasise about it all we wanted but the second my father mentioned an alliance with the Branigans, it was time to wake up from the dream.

Sebastian was never mine.

No matter how much I wanted him to be.

There's nothing I can do, least of all now that I have a wife. I have a fucking wife and here I am pacing the manor and thinking of the fucking man I can't have.

I want Serafina.

I want Sebastian.

And they don't even know about each other.

I scratch at my chest absently, as though I can dig out the burning sensation simmering beneath my ribs.

I can't lose Serafina and we can't lose the alliance, not now that Francesca is in danger. This is far from the time to have this shit blow up in my face.

I should've told her. She deserves to know but I can't bear to speak his name out loud to her.

I've done nothing wrong, I try to tell myself. It doesn't matter that days before I was shipped off to Italy for my wedding, I had Sebastian panting and begging for release in my bed. It doesn't matter because the second this ring was placed on my finger, my future was sealed.

My future, without him.

Anji catches my arm, jolting me. I stop on instinct, whirling on him, wide eyed and antsy.

"Whoa," he murmurs, frowning up at me. "What the fuck is up with you, Oisín?"

He shoves a mug into my hand, and I take it wordlessly. I'm worried that if I open my mouth, their names will spill out.

"Drink that, you clearly need it more than me," he continues when I don't answer. I sniff at the concoction, smelling coffee and the sharp tang of alcohol.

I sip it and cough. The bite of liquor finally frees my tongue up. "What the fuck, Anji? It's barely noon."

"Maybe for you," he scoffs, taking the cup back. "I haven't slept in twenty six hours. Time means nothing."

My eyebrows shoot up at that, but I just nod, not wanting to be the one that pushes him over the edge. "I think sleep is the answer, not spiked coffee."

"Well, you know fuck all," he snarks at me. "I'm not taking advice from the guy who's walked this entire house twenty times in the last hour."

Fair point. Anji pins me with a look, and I see the way exhaustion has painted purple marks under his eyes and how his movements are slower than usual as he stalks off, leaving me to my pacing.

I'm never usually restless. This is all Sebastian's doing. That man can never be still, not unless I tie him down and make him.

Even then, he tries to break free.

I hate that I've picked up his habit. Hate that he's so much a part of me that I can't fucking get him out of my system. Hate that it feels like the bastard's reached into my chest and stolen half of my heart.

Hate that it's taken me *years* to realise he couldn't have taken anything from me that I didn't willingly give.

He's not a fucking thief.

I'm just a complete and utter prick.

It's too late. I can't take any of my actions back and if I'm honest, I don't want to lose Serafina. Fuck, I didn't want to lose Sebastian either. But it was inevitable. I can't ask the man to wait around for me knowing I can never give him what he wants. I won't cheat on my wife, I won't ruin the relationship between our families or the relationship we're building.

I don't want to have to choose.

But it's too fucking late. The choice is made. I could blame my father, I could tell Sebastian I had no option, I could pretend I had no hand in this. But I went to Italy willingly. I said those vows with my whole chest and I never once argued with the arrangement.

I could love Serafina. Easily.

I can't think of love and of Sebastian. I can't think of any of this. I can't fucking think.

Downstairs, a door slams. Even from the kitchen, I can hear heavy, rushed footsteps and I've memorised the rhythm of them. Sebastian's back.

Ah fuck.

15

Serafina

Sebastian runs from the car the second it stops. Wide eyed, I watch him leave like the thing's on fire. In the minute it takes Nessa and I to exit the vehicle and grab my things from the back, the man's disappeared.

I narrow my eyes at the door of the manor, wondering what the hell I did to piss off a guy I said maybe two sentences to. Nessa doesn't comment on it, just nudges my shoulder with hers slightly as she drags two suitcases over the gravel.

The Cavanaugh manor is huge and clearly old, though well taken care of. It sits in the middle of nowhere, surrounded by wide open fields. The air is freezing, my lungs stinging a little as I inhale, and the skies are grey. The house itself is made of weathered, pale stone and the entire front wall, which stretches three stories high, is covered in ivy.

It's stunning.

Nessa and I lug the bags up the stairs and she shoulders the door open. It swings inward with a soft creak, revealing the grand entrance. The interior opens into a long hall, lined with large windows that I imagine would let in a glorious amount of sunlight if there was any.

The foyer is relatively small in comparison, a cupboard and coat rack to the left and a small, dark wooden side table.

The second my husband appears, my curiosity is abandoned.

I drop my suitcase and run to him as he comes to a stop in the hallway, arms outstretched for me. I practically jump onto him, wrapping my arms around his neck.

Weeks is far too long to spend away from the man I've only just begun to know. I'm not ashamed to say I've missed him, and the comfort of having him hold me eases the tension from my shoulders. I relax against him, his arms wrapped around my waist as I stretch up on my toes to be able to kiss him.

His mouth meets mine hungrily, our tongues sweeping against each other the second my lips part for him. I press closer, eager for the way he's devouring me, heat rushing through me.

The man kisses like he's starving.

Fucks like it, too.

I cut off the moan in my throat by pulling away from him, feeling how hot my face is. How hot my entire body is. I fight to keep my breathing even, smiling up at my husband.

His eyes are half lidded as he looks down at me, the ring of green around his pupil bright before it fades to blue. His brown curls are pushed back from his face, longer than they were at our wedding. I wonder if he'll cut his hair, and whether I'll get to see if it's as good for gripping onto as I suspect it is before he does. The black jeans and tight black t-shirt are doing nothing to ease my desire for him. Oisín is slim but strong, and I trace him with my eyes, snapping my mouth shut before I do something stupid like ask him to show me his room.

I'm so lost in my own needy thoughts that I almost miss Sebastian. I catch a glimpse of him over Oisín's shoulder, standing on the huge staircase, eyes fixed on the pair of us. I swear I see hurt flash through his dark blue eyes, his mouth parted and hands open and shaking at his sides.

"You know I really could live without watching my brother make out with his wife like we're not all standing right fucking here," Nessa says and I start as I realise two more people have appeared while I've been busy.

"It's…sweet," the other woman says hesitantly, a kind smile on her face. She's short and curvy, with long red hair and pale skin covered in freckles. Nessa loops her arm around her shoulder and tugs her closer to her side and I realise who she is.

"Siobhán, right?" I ask, clearing my throat as I put some distance between me and Oisín. He's having none of it, and his hand grasps mine, fingers twining with my own. I can't stop the grin it puts on my face.

How the fuck this man's mere presence can comfort me after such little time together is beyond me. Oisín is steady, and I like knowing I can lean on him, even now.

Fucking asshole making me fall for him like our marriage is more than convenience.

"You must be Oisín's wife!" Siobhán greets, ducking out of Nessa's embrace to offer me her hand. I shake it with a smile, nodding.

"Call me Serafina," I say, letting her off the hook. I'm my own damn person, not just *his wife,* but this is the girl who was supposed to be his wife before me.

"You have a beautiful name," Siobhán compliments, squeezing my hand a little before tucking herself back at Nessa's side, lifting her wife's arm over her shoulder like it had been before. Nessa huffs at her, but I note the way she holds her a little tighter.

They're so obviously in love it makes my chest tighten.

I'm glad my husband's first marriage was a complete fucking failure and I'm not sure I care if that makes me a bad person. It's hard to imagine the redhead with a gun in her hand, but then again, I know better than to underestimate a woman. The band on her left hand matches Nessa's, and side by side they compliment each other.

"Da," Oisín calls out, and I turn my attention away from the women.

Thomas Cavanaugh meets my eyes.

"You must be my newest daughter in law," he says, voice low and gravelly. "Welcome to the fucking shit show." He spreads his arms wide and I notice more people have gathered at the top of the stairs.

And that Sebastian's disappeared.

16

Sebastian

My knuckles sting where the skin has split apart but I don't slow down. I can't. If I stop moving, my anger will tear me apart from the inside. Even now, fists flying, the punching bag rattling on its chain, the anger feels like a living thing - writhing, fighting, desperate.

I'm too fucking angry to even register the pain properly as I throw my fists again and again, sweat making my hair stick to my forehead. I should've changed before I came here, my jeans and shirt are only making this harder. But I couldn't face going back to my room. I can't stand there, alone, while Oisín is kissing his bride like she's the only thing he'll ever need. Like she's the fucking oxygen he breaths.

He doesn't give a fuck that I can't breathe.

Doesn't give a fuck about me.

He.

Smack.

Doesn't.

Smack.

Care.

Smack.

The punching bag is wet with blood now and my hand slips as I hit it, throat burning as a low, guttural shout rips its way through my teeth. My sleeves are shoved up to my elbows, but they restrict my movement and suddenly I feel that suffocating feeling so much more acutely.

I can't stop fucking seeing them.

Serafina, beautiful, sweet Serafina, running into his arms. Him, catching her, their mouths meeting, their tongues twining, their chests pressed together.

My eyes sting. I'm panting, breathing so heavily my chest strains against my sweat soaked clothes.

I can practically hear Nessa in my ear telling me to get a fucking grip. To get over it. Get over *him*. But I don't know how to.

More than that, I don't *want* to. Oisín might be insisting that nothing between us ever mattered, but I can't separate myself from our history so easily. He was the first person that I ever wanted for more than a night. As a teenager, I'd slept with a few others before him. At parties, at *Sinners*, when the other recruits and I managed to convince the bouncer to let us in. I'd been young and cocky and horny and yet nobody had ever made me crave them the way Oisín did.

At first, I thought it was because he was the heir. He was unattainable. I'd known him since Thomas took me in at fourteen, and we were close in age, but there was always an unavoidable gap between us. I was a nobody - an orphan his da had taken pity on. Quickly though, my obsession became much more than that.

Oisín was withdrawn - cold and curious. He spent most of

his time in his room or the library, nose in a book, only really interacting with the rest of us when he was forced to train. He was smart, scarily smart, and always had the answer to fucking everything.

I think I annoyed him. I never shut the fuck up, always said the wrong thing, teased the crap out of him and Nessa and whoever else was around.

I was nineteen when he kissed me for the first time. I'd been distracting him from whatever book he was reading. I was bored, it was late and everyone else was asleep.

I remember the entire damn thing like it was yesterday. The way he'd sighed heavily, closed his book so loudly I'd jumped then burst out laughing because of the look on his face. *Christ* the look on his face...

His eyes had darkened, and he'd taken his glasses off, folding them up on top of the book. He stood slowly, pinning me with his eyes, and stalked toward me in long strides.

My back was against the bookshelves, my heart beating so loud I barely heard him when he said *do you ever shut the fuck up?*

Only when my mouth's full, I'd snarked back to him, grinning with false confidence. I'd had to fist my hands at my sides so he didn't see them shake.

He'd scoffed, and then his lips were on mine and his tongue was in my mouth and I couldn't have said a damn thing because my brain had exploded.

And now here I fucking was. Bloody knuckles and stinging eyes and a shattered fucking heart.

It'd been another year after that kiss when we finally pushed our friendship further. But even then, he'd told me we couldn't be together. Not really. He had duties to fulfil and I couldn't distract him. There had always been a feud with the Branigans, and Oisín didn't want any weaknesses.

But I was devout. I had blind, blissful faith. I'd convinced myself, on my knees, hands open in prayer, that there was something more.

I should've fucking listened.

But I'd *seen* the way he looked at me. Felt the way he touched me. Heard him whisper his devotion to me when he thought I was asleep.

Stupid fucking boy.

I stare down at my hands. They don't hurt nearly as much as my chest does. I want him. I want him so badly I don't know how to function any more.

Fuck, I'm still that same kid that doesn't know when to give up.

I won't be discarded. I won't.

I won't lose another precious thing.

I'm still staring at my palms when the door to the gym opens. I haven't even bothered turning the lights on, and when they flicker overhead I wince. My head is pounding.

"Jesus, son."

Thomas.

I don't look up. I have nothing to say to him.

I can't even fucking blame him for marrying Oisín and Serafina. I understand why. I'm loyal to him, and as his enforcer I know why the alliance with the Italians is a good thing. Hell, between Oisín's marriage and Siobhán's cousin taking over the Branigans, we've never been in a better place.

Still.

"Look, kid," Thomas sighs heavily, and I feel him walk closer to me. His hand hits my shoulder, warm and calloused. I respect him, and because I do, I can't look at him right now. Fuck knows what will happen if I say something I know I'll regret.

I don't think he'd kick me out, but can I trust that?

He can call me son all he wants but it's not like I'm actually one of his kids.

"I know you love him."

That makes me startle. So much so that I stumble sideways, only just finding my balance before I fall onto the mats.

"What?" I manage to get out, my throat tight.

"You think I don't know every feckin' thing that goes on under my roof?" He laughs, dark and short. "Ya think in all the years you've been here, I didn't know where you were when you weren't in your own damn bed?"

I feel like he's doused me in ice water.

"Thomas-"

"I don't care that you were sleeping with my son," he says, and I choke on my own spit.

"Jesus Christ," I wheeze, finally raising my eyes to his. True to his words, he doesn't look the least bit bothered. Apparently, he hasn't been this entire fucking time.

"But he's married now," Thomas continues, like I'm not one revelation away from an aneurysm. "I need you to respect that, Sebastian. Oisín needs you to respect that."

For the second time in my life, I'm speechless.

"It's not like that, Thomas," I try when I find my tongue. I shake my head, tensing and untensing my fists, feeling the sting of ripped, stretched skin. Another open scar to add to the collection. "It's not-"

"I didn't get to where I am by believing lies," Thomas deadpans. "I don't like seeing you hurt, kid, but you need to let this be. Let him go."

The numb shock wears off in a rush. All the anger I'd worked off on the punching bag comes back with enough force to send me rocking back on my heels.

"What the fuck do you care?" I snap, throwing my hands up. "Clearly, you've not cared all these fucking years. I'm not your Goddamn *kid*, Thomas!"

"You know as well as I do that blood isn't what makes family."

He's so fucking calm. So fucking calm because he's known this entire fucking time that I was in love with his son.

And that it didn't mean anything.

Not to Oisín. Not to him.

I can't stand being here any longer. I can't look him in the eye, even after everything he's done for me, and act like I can give up his son that easily.

I just fucking can't.

I'm pushing past him and storming out of the room before I can do something insanely stupid like hit him instead of the punching bag.

I'm not family. He might have taken me in, might have allowed me to live and saved me in the process, but I watched my actual damn family die in front of me. I know the cost of pissing off Thomas Cavanaugh.

The door to the gym slams behind me and I barely take in my surroundings as I make my way back to my room. Again and again and again, I see Oisín and Serafina kissing in my mind. I see her noticing me, I hear her ask who I am, and I feel the knife of his rejection twist in my back.

Distantly, I hear Nessa call my name but I don't stop. I can't fucking handle her telling me to get over myself again. She's my oldest friend, my best friend, and she's married. Married and happy and she doesn't fucking need me.

Nobody fucking needs me.

The self pity makes me feel sick to my stomach.

I can't even look at myself in the mirror as I strip the disgusting clothes from my body and turn the shower on. I let the water clean the cuts on my hands, and I focus on the white tile as if it'll erase every image of the day from my mind.

I expect Thomas to come barging in, demanding I pay for walking away from him, or Nessa, yelling at me for ignoring her.

Nobody comes.

17

Oisín

"You're a fucking cunt."

My sister may as well have slapped me across the face. It's not the first time she's insulted me, and it won't be the last, but the venom in her voice tears through me.

Nessa has never been one to hold back, and despite the fact my da only dropped the bomb that we're blood related a few weeks ago, we've been pissing each other off like brother and sister since she came to live with us at sixteen.

"Okay," is all I say back, glancing at her over my shoulder. She's standing in the doorway of the library, hands flexing repeatedly, blonde brows drawn together. I expect to find her wife at her side, but she's alone.

"Now that I know we're actually siblings, I'm not fucking holding back," Nessa continues, her train of thought clearly on the same track as mine.

"When have you ever?" I grunt, rolling my neck and hearing it crack. I'm so fucking tense I swear to God my entire body could snap in half and all I'd feel is relief.

"Why the fuck are you intent on ripping Sebastian's heart out and dancing on it 'til it stops beating?" Nessa snaps, crossing her arms over her chest as she steps further into the room. The door slams shut behind her, and the low light of the library casts shadows over her face.

Nessa takes after our mother, not that I remember much of her given she stole my sister away as an infant and didn't even bother coming back to check on me. But her blonde hair, green eyes and skin that takes a tan far better than my father's and mine does is certainly all Fiona.

Still, she's a Cavanaugh through and through. Her attitude wouldn't be as fucking dark otherwise.

"I'm not-"

"I fucking get it, alright? The arranged marriage shit is wild. You want to do what's best by your - our - Da, what's best for the whole bloody gang. I fucking *get it,* Oisín. I've done the same shit. For fuck's sake I even stole your first fiancée," Nessa rushes out, laughing a little at her last sentence.

I'd not even met Siobhán properly before our wedding, and I feel nothing for her. Whatever forces brought her and Nessa together are beyond my imagination, but they seem well matched, and knowing that their marriage has sealed the Cavanaugh-Branigan alliance is a weight off my shoulders.

"But you're being even more of a dick than normal. You're fucking avoiding the poor lad, Oisín. You've not even given him a second glance, or an explanation."

I sigh heavily. Her words are just another brick on my shoulders, and I'm sagging under the weight of it all.

I don't want to hurt Sebastian. But I don't know how to stop.

"I'm not trying to hurt him, Nessa," I tell her, pinching the bridge of my nose. I slide my glasses off my face and rub my eyes. I took my contacts out earlier, hoping I'd manage to relax and read, an attempt at a moment's peace while Serafina showered and unwound from her flight.

"Could've fucking fooled me," Nessa snaps. She drops down into the armchair in front of me and kicks her boots off. She leans back, lifting her legs to rest her feet on the low table between the chairs.

"Do you think this shit is easy for me?" I hiss, something inside me snapping. "Do you think a single second of this has been simple? Serafina deserves a committed husband. I can't fucking have him, Nessa. I. Can't. Have. Him."

"So you like her, then? It's not just for show?" my sister asks, brows furrowed.

"Yes I fucking like her."

I don't regret marrying Seffy. She's strong and capable and smart and above all that, she's brave and stubborn as fuck. I'm drawn to her, and despite the fact our marriage is one of convenience, I have no desire to try to get out of it.

But Sebastian.

Fuck me.

"So, what then? You just switched off your feelings for Seb? Just like that?" Nessa snaps her fingers and the sound echoes. "Don't try and tell me it was just sex. Not for that long, Ois."

I cringe, and my heart feels like it's been put in a vice.

"Of course not," I grind out. But I can't admit what I feel for Sebastian. I've never said it out loud and now is not the fucking time. Worse, my feelings for Serafina are only growing and I don't understand how I can have space for all that…all that warmth inside me. I'd expected my interest in Seffy to strangle whatever I felt for Sebastian, like ivy breaking down a house. Instead, the ivy is nestling against the stone and the house is still strong, just as steady as ever. Instead, the two have become inseparable.

And I can't fucking admit that.

It doesn't make sense.

"But I have to. I'll find a way to." My voice is losing its strength and I lean back in the chair, head hitting the soft, padded backrest. The idea of taking a sledgehammer to the stone makes me want to scream. I shove the thought away.

Serafina deserves a husband who is loyal to her. Who won't stray, or stumble because of some fucking fanciful dream.

But what about Sebastian? Doesn't he deserve that, too?

One thing's clear - I don't deserve either of them.

I twist my wedding band around my finger.

"Why?"

Nessa's question catches me off guard.

"What?" I whisper, frowning at her.

She tilts her head, regarding me with open curiosity like I'm some sort of zoo animal. My sister has a unique way of making anybody feel like dirt on her shoe with just one look. I admire her for it.

"Why do you have to find a way to turn off your feelings, *dearthár?*"

I blink at her like she's lost her mind. "Because I can't very well love them both, can I? I can't fucking have them both."

Nessa drops her feet from the table and leans forward, elbows on her knees. Her expression has softened and for a brief second, I can imagine how things would be if we'd been raised together, properly. Sure, we'd still be at each other's throats the way we were as friends, but there'd be this reassurance, too. A steadiness, a feeling that we weren't alone.

The longing in my chest grows even further.

I stamp on it until it shuts the fuck up.

"Sweet, stupid sibling of mine," Nessa tuts, shaking her head. "You think love is like your book? What, you just slam it shut and go *no thanks, done with it now*? Your feelings aren't just going to go away if you pretend they're not there, and they won't be told to stay where they're put either."

"Since when were you the expert on this shit?"

"Since I fell in love with the girl I swore I fucking hated, and threatened to kill," she says back, tone flat.

I scoff at that. "What's your point?"

"The point is that pretending you don't love Sebastian, that you haven't loved him for fuck knows how long, isn't going to make it go away. Pretending that you can only love one person isn't going to make that true." She pauses, inhaling deeply before meeting my eyes. "The point is that you're a fucking coward."

I'm stunned speechless. All I can do is gape at my sister as she stands, grabs her boots, and yawns.

She's halfway to the door before she glances over her shoulder at me.

"Pull your head out of your arse, Oisín. Before it's too late. You deserve to be happy. All three of you. But if you keep stomping on my best friend's heart, I'll have no choice but to stab you in yours."

I don't doubt that her threat is real. Nor do I blame her for it. I fucking hate that Sebastian is suffering and I hate myself for letting it happen.

But I don't know if I can fix it.

18

Serafina

Oisín is sitting on the edge of the bed when I finish my shower. His hands are open on his lap, his eyes blank as he stares at the wall. He hasn't even turned the light on.

I frown, holding my towel up with one hand and pad towards him, reaching to the right to flip the switch for the bedside lamp.

I'd needed to shower and recouperate after the flight and whatever the fuck happened downstairs. Between Nessa, Siobhán, Sebastian, Thomas and whoever else had gathered to watch my entrance, I felt like an animal in a zoo. Thankfully, Oisín had excused us shortly after, leading me away and up to his room. I didn't mind skipping the house tour as long as I got a shower, a bed and time with him.

Travel and stress had all my muscles tense, and even though it's only early afternoon and the time difference between home and here is negligible, I am so fucking tired.

But Oisín looks worse than I feel.

"Oisín?" I ask, stepping closer to him. My hair is escaping

the towel it's wrapped in, sticking to my forehead and cheeks.

He startles like my voice has woken him.

"Seffy," he says back to me, his voice distant. Slowly, he looks towards me, his eyes tracing up my bare, still damp legs, higher still to where I'm holding the towel around myself. Finally, his eyes are on mine, and though I search, I can't pinpoint what's different in them. "How was your shower?"

"Just what I needed," I answer, close enough to him now that he could reach for me. He doesn't. I frown. "Can I sit?"

"You don't have to ask," he says lowly. "Everything mine is yours, Serafina. *I'm* yours."

I blink at him, a smile on my lips, as I sit on the edge of the bed with him. "I've missed you, husband."

At that, his eyes darken, and finally, he reaches for me. His large hand cups my face, and I lean my cheek into his touch. He's colder than usual, though with my skin still flushed from the hot water, I can't tell whether I'm imagining things.

"Everyone seems…nice," I start. He only makes a noncommittal sound in response, and my concern grows. What am I missing? "Nessa reminds me a lot of your father. And Sebastian seems…well, if I'm honest, I think that man hates my guts, but I can't work out why."

Oisín's hold on me tightens. His other hand is on my thigh, the tips of his fingers under the hem of the towel, like he suddenly can't bear to be away from me.

"He doesn't hate you." My husband's voice is low and scratchy, and my heart stutters.

"But-"

"I'm yours, Serafina DeSantis," Oisín interrupts, leaning closer, tipping my face towards his. I let him, craving his touch after our weeks apart. I don't want the distance to ruin us before we even have a chance to really try.

I want to try.

Having this marriage be solely for appearances sounds exhausting, and though I don't need a husband to fulfil my duty to my father, having an ally close to me can't hurt. More than that, though, Oisín is just my fucking type.

Smart, brooding and fucking filthy.

"I know," I assure him, shuffling myself closer and loosening my grip on the towel. It falls from my chest, pooling at my hips, leaving me almost entirely exposed to him.

Oisín inhales sharply, and in the next second I'm on my back, with him towering over me and the towel nowhere to be seen. He braces his hands on either side of my shoulders, his face so close to mine our lips graze when he speaks.

"Yours, Seffy," he whispers, and I nod, reaching for him. I run my hand under the hem of his shirt, his stomach tensing under my touch.

"And I'm yours," I murmur back. "Now prove it."

I don't know what the fuck happened to make him act so distant, but I do know that we both need this connection. That if I can chase away that far off look in his eyes, I will. That if he can distract me from the fucking shit show I've left behind in Italy, then I need him to.

He crashes his mouth to mine, kissing me like he's starving. I swipe my tongue against his, his teeth nipping at my bottom lip until I gasp. I tug at his shirt, arching closer to him, desperate to feel his skin on mine.

He pulls away quickly, tugging his shirt over his head with one hand, throwing it off the side of the bed. His gaze is dark as he stares down at me, naked and panting beneath him.

Fucking hell, all he's done is kiss me and taken his top off and I can already feel how wet I am.

He sits back, holding my gaze as he grips my body, his thumb stroking the sensitive skin on the inside of my thigh. I shiver, his touch sending sparks through me.

Slowly, so fucking slowly, he pushes my legs apart, exposing every inch of me to his hungry gaze.

"Already wet for me," Oisín grinds out, stroking his thumb higher until his touch barely grazes my cunt. The tease makes my breath hitch, and I nod at him. He holds me open, leaving no room for shyness.

Not that I'd try to hide from him anyway.

I'm confident in my body, in the muscles I've earned from training, in the softness of my stomach and my thighs.

"I've been dreaming of eating this pretty little pussy ever since the first fucking taste."

I try to squeeze my legs together, desperate for any sort of friction, but he shakes his head, tightening his hold on my flesh.

"Hold still for me, Seffy," Oisín says darkly, forcing me to keep myself open for him as he lowers his body to mine. The sight of him, with his hair tousled and the muscles in his arms rippling as his eyes meet mine is too much to bear.

"Please, Oisín," I whisper, squirming.

"Be a good girl and hold still for me, angel. I'm fucking starving for you."

My eyes widen at his words, at the nickname that sends fire through my veins, but I don't have time to answer him. His mouth is on me before I can even try to formulate a response.

His tongue swipes through my centre and I clench the bedsheets in my fists in an effort not to buck against his mouth. He repeats the motion, collecting my need, burying his tongue inside me like he's desperate for every drop of my desire.

"Oisín," I moan, the relief of having him touch me like this heady. More, I want more, I want everything he has to give.

I feel him smile against me as he turns his head and nips at the sensitive flesh on my thigh. I jerk, the bite of pain feuling my lust, driving me wild. I'm so turned on I can't think of anything but his name.

"More," I beg, not giving a fuck that I'm pleading. I know he's teasing me, dragging this out for his amusement, but I need him.

I gasp, arching, unable to obey his command to stay still while the point of his tongue circles my clit. I curse, but my voice is breathy and strained as pleasure courses through my veins.

Oisín's hands leave my thighs only to grab my ass, lifting my hips from the mattress. My calves are resting over his shoulders, trapping him, and I'm all too aware that I'm crushing his head between my legs as he sucks my clit into his mouth. I can't stop myself, and Oisín groans against me, clearly content with having my thighs lock him in a death grip.

"Fuck, I've missed the sounds you make when my face is buried in your cunt," Oisín breathes, barely pausing in his ministrations to speak.

I feel every word against my centre, and *shit* I'm already so fucking close. Part of me wants to shy away from this, from the power he has over my body, over my *heart,* but I can't bring myself to.

I watch my husband fuck me with his mouth until I break apart. His tongue flicks over my clit, soft and warm and fucking *perfect*, and I shatter.

He doesn't pull away until I'm whimpering and oversensitive.

"Up, Seffy," he demands, voice low, and I barely have enough control of my limbs to listen.

I'm floating on the high of the orgasm he's just given me when I finally move, shaking as I push upwards. Oisín stands at the edge of the bed, watching me. I can feel my own release on the inside of my thighs, can see evidence of it on his lips.

I crawl onto my hands and knees, staring up at him. His trousers are tented making his arousal obvious, though he's made no move to remove them.

I want to shatter his self restraint the way he's destroyed mine. Slowly, with as much patience as I can muster when my fucking soul is desperate for him, I slide myself over the edge of the bed. The position presses my chest and face against the mattress, presenting my ass and cunt to my husband as I lean over the side of the bed.

"So fucking perfect," Oisín murmurs as he sweeps his fingers through my centre, parting me for him. Every touch feels like too much, but I don't care. I want more, I want everything.

"Fuck me," I breathe, arching back against him.

"So needy," he counters.

"For you. Only for you."

I swear the sound that leaves him is akin to a growl, and it sends goosebumps rippling along my skin.

"Mine," Oisín says as he unzips his trouser, the sound of the zip rasping against his words. "*Yours*, Seffy."

He presses his cock to my soaking cunt as he speaks, and I pant, pushing back against him. He swears as he shoves himself inside me. I don't care that I'm still recovering from my first orgasm, I don't care that he stretches me until it stings.

I don't care about anything except the way his cock makes me cry out, pleasure engulfing me.

I'm still shuddering at the sensation of my husband entering me, so lost in his touch that I don't even care about the squeak of the hinges as the bedroom door opens.

19

Sebastian

Fuck. My. Life.

Sure, Sebastian, try and talk to the man who ripped your heart to shreds. *Sure, Sebastian,* ignore literally everyone's fucking advice and keep prodding the wound. *Sure,* try one last time to repair shit with the man who's made it very fucking clear you're no one to him.

Sure, Sebastian don't fucking knock.

I'm a fucking eejit.

Serafina is naked. Naked and bent over the edge of the bed, her cheek pressed against the mattress, Oisín's hand on the middle of her back, keeping her still. She's crying out, calling his name, eyes fluttering closed as he fucks her. He's not even bothered undressing all the way, though his shirt is on the floor. His trousers are undone and barely shoved down enough to free his cock, which is currently balls deep inside his wife.

I'm frozen in the doorway, shocked still, staring at them with my mouth hanging open. I'm entirely convinced they've used all the air in the room, because there's no fucking oxygen left. My chest tightens and I tell myself it's because I can't breathe and not because this is like a fucking burning hot poker being shoved between my ribs.

My cock, however, isn't concerned with my broken heart.

The second they see me, they freeze.

"Sebastian?" Serafina pants, her brows furrowing as her gaze zones in on me.

Oisín's head snaps around, his eyes dark and pupils wide. He doesn't make any move to pull out of her, doesn't even bother removing his hand from her back. Serafina is still shocked, twisting to try to look over her shoulder at her husband with confusion clear on her face.

"I…" I don't know what the fuck to say. What the *fuck* do I say? *Sorry I caught you shagging but I was actually hoping to try and win Oisín back despite the fact he's married to you because I literally never fucking learn.*

Jesus Christ.

Serafina moans and my train of thought crashes and burns. Her brows are still furrowed, but her lips are parted in pleasure and Oisín's hand is between her legs. Despite the fact all I can see from this angle is her ass, I know fine fucking well what Oisín's doing.

Jesus. Fucking. Christ.

"Oisín," I whisper, and it comes out hoarse. I should leave. I really, really should leave.

But Serafina cries out again, pushing her ass back against Oisín. Her face is pressed into the bed now, and I wonder if pleasure has made her forget I'm here in the first place. Oisín's eyes are still on me, and when he withdraws from her cunt, his cock wet from her desire, I shudder.

He slams back into her, and she moans. The sound carries

past me and into the hall and I curse under my breath. Do I leave, and close the door? I don't know what the fuck to do.

Oisín's eyes have me under lock and key and I never have been able to disobey him. He's said nothing, but he hasn't told me to go, and neither has she and when Serafina opens her eyes again and smirks as I stare her down, I know I'm fucked.

I don't care.

I ease further into the room and close the door behind me, leaning against the wood. My cock pushes against the zip of my jeans but I relish the pain.

It's all I can do to focus on the discomfort as Oisín holds my eyes while he fucks his wife. Serafina whimpers, catching the bedsheets between her teeth and biting down as his fingers continue to work her clit. He fucks her hard, her whole body jerking with each thrust.

I close my eyes. I shouldn't be here and yet I can't leave. I can't fucking walk away. I'm so hard it hurts, but I refuse to give myself any sort of relief.

"Sebastian."

My name on Oisín's tongue, thick with lust, makes my eyes sting. I want him, and *shit*, I can't stop my eyes from opening again. Serafina is fucking glorious. I hate myself for thinking it. The woman is beautiful - strong and soft and sexy as fuck laid out beneath him.

I wish I could hate her. I wish I could look at her and grimace, look at her and blame her for stealing the love of my Goddamn life.

But I fucking *can't*.

She's gorgeous.

"Serafina..." I grind out through clenched teeth. Her

fucking name tastes as sweet as I imagine she does. I want to taste her on Oisín, I want to be between them, I want-

Fuck, I just *want.*

I'm shaking, but I can't stop. I can't do anything but stand there and watch them fuck, eyes flicking between them both, feeling Oisín's gaze on me.

I watch him drop his eyes to my crotch, and I don't doubt he can see the way this is affecting me. I don't doubt he can see the outline of my desire in my trousers any more than he can see the pain and need in my eyes.

I've loved him for years.

I've known her for a day.

But I want them.

More than anything, I want them.

I know the moment Serafina comes. She screams Oisín's name, burying her face into the mattress, her entire body shuddering. Oisín curses, slamming into her fast and hard, until his head tips back and he groans.

He meets my eyes, and I press the heel of my hand to my erection. I can't fucking stand it. I cup myself over my jeans, the pressure not nearly enough, but Oisín comes while holding my gaze and I want to sob in desperation.

He's not mine. But my body doesn't know that, or at least it doesn't care. I'm wound so tight I think I might snap.

Leaning against the door, I hold Oisín's eyes as he empties himself inside his wife while she moans and shudders beneath his touch.

I know how it feels to take his cum, I know how it feels to come with him inside me, I know how it feels to have him hold me down and use me.

I know how she feels.

I wonder if she knows.

For a minute, nothing but their combined panting fills the air and I commit the sound to memory.

If this is all Oisín will allow me to have, I'll take it. I'm no better than a dog begging for crumbs at his feet. He owns me.

And I don't want myself back.

"Oisín," I rasp, my voice alien to my ears.

Both their heads snap up, Serafina's eyes wide, Oisín's brows creased.

They don't want me here. I can't bear to hear them say it.

This feels like a slow death, but I'd rather a death at his hand than anyone else's. He hands me pain like it's pleasure, and I'm a fucking masochist.

Hurt me, I want to beg him. *Hurt me, then heal me again.*

God, I'm pathetic. He's made his choice, he's made it clear, but fuck I'm the fool that can't stay away.

Who else is there for me but him?

Serafina's wide eyes meet mine, the dark brown intoxicating. I could lose myself in those lust filled eyes, but I'm sure, so sure, that she'd hate me for it.

She might already hate me for this.

I want to fall to my knees in front of them and beg for forgiveness. I want to crawl to them and plead for relief.

But I don't.

I don't do fucking anything except stand there in the wake of what I've done, and try not to drown in it.

20

Serafina

Oisín eases out of me, and I feel the rush of his cum stick to my thighs. Vaguely, I hear him curse, but I can't tell whether it's because of the sight of me - still bent over with his cum spilling out of my cunt - or because of the man still standing at the door.

Sebastian is flushed, his blue eyes wide and his lips parted. His trousers are tented with his arousal, the hand he's cupping his dick with only emphasising the fact. His gaze is locked on my husband, and even when I strain to look over my shoulder at him, all I can catch is the sharp line of his jaw and the way his lips are pressed into a thin line.

What the fuck just happened?

And why the fuck did I like it?

Reality slams into me so fast I feel dizzy. Whatever lingering pleasure is still coursing through my body fades like I've been doused in icy water.

The silence consuming the room feels heavy, like some unspoken rule that everyone but me knows about has just been broken. I shudder. Neither man has moved, said anything, *done* anything.

Slowly, I stand, my legs shaking. There's no point in trying to cover my body, to hide the way my heavy breaths are moving my chest. I look between Sebastian and Oisín with new eyes, studying my husband like it's the first time we've met.

He's been lying to me.

And I've been made a Goddamn fool of.

There's a softness hiding in the fire of Oisín's eyes, a familiar tenderness untouched by any sort of regret.

Suspicion makes my gut churn. I hadn't even fucking paused to consider why Oisín never mentioned Sebastian despite the fact they've clearly known each other for years.

The stress has made me stupid.

"What just happened?" I breathe, trying to keep my voice steady. The last fucking thing I need to do is show any more vulnerability, given that Sebastian has just seen every inch of me.

Sebastian holds Oisín's eyes for a few more long seconds before he swallows thickly, turns and slams the door behind him. He leaves without a word, without an explanation or apology.

I can't even blame him.

I don't know what to say, either.

Finally, my husband turns to me. His eyes shine with more emotion than I've ever seen from him. The Oisín I know is reserved, any passion he shows saved explicitly for private moments.

Apparently I don't know him very well at all.

"Talk," I grind out.

"Serafina-"

"Fucking *talk*, husband." My voice is strained and tight, and it's taking every ounce of self control I've ever possessed not to storm out of this room after Sebastian and make the man tell me everything my husband's been hiding.

"Serafina, I don't..." Oisín's voice is quiet, his hands flexing at his sides. "I don't know."

I scoff, anger sparking. "No more fucking *lies!*"

There's a pause that feels like it lasts for a year before he speaks. "I wasn't trying to lie to you."

"No, you just left out the fact that you're in love with someone else while you said your vows to me."

Oisín tenses. I don't give him the chance to answer.

"You locked eyes with him while coming inside me," I spit out.

I ignore the fact that even mentioning what we just did sends a shiver of desire through me. I should be ashamed, I think, and maybe I am but I...I liked it. I grit my teeth against my own thoughts.

Oisín cocks his head at me, eyes narrowing. "Are you telling me you didn't like it?"

I want to scream at him. I want to shout and swear and make him regret everything he's ever done.

But I can't tell him he's wrong.

Oisín deflates as I pin him with a glare, shaking his head slightly. He sighs heavily, tugs his trousers back up, and sits on the edge of the bed. I stay standing, unable to stay still as I tap my foot restlessly against the carpet.

"I didn't want this to affect us," he begins, pushing his hands through his hair. "This wasn't supposed to happen, Seffy, you have to understand-"

"No, *you* have to explain!"

"Fine!" Oisín snaps, but his anger doesn't feel like it's directed my way. No, he's tugging at his hair like he can't bear to be still under the weight of all this either. "I...I thought I could leave it all behind, when I married you."

"Leave what? Sebastian?"

Oisín nods and my ears start ringing. Oh my God. Oh my fucking God.

"We were never...together," Oisín says slowly, like he's choosing each word carefully. "Not really. But we were close. Closer than close, I guess. Fuck, this is hard."

I let him pause to inhale deeply, though my chest is tight and my stomach is in knots and my stupid fucking cunt is still wet. The image of Sebastian watching me, watching Oisín fuck me, the way they looked at each other, replays over and over in my mind.

"We met when he was fourteen. Da took him in after his family..." Oisín trails off, shaking his head. "Da took him in. Him, Nessa and I were all close in age, and grouped together in training and well, life. He was annoying as fuck, but impossible to ignore. I could stay away from him no more than I could stay away from the library."

My heart clenches at the soft tone of his voice.

"So what, you thought fuck it, I'll fuck him?" I sneer, unable to keep my voice even. "And then *abandoned him for me?"*

"No!" Oisín is quick to shake his head, staring up at me pleadingly. "No. We knew we had no future. We couldn't. Fuck, I've known since I was a child that my fate is to help strengthen the Cavanaugh name. Sebastian knew it, too. He was fine when I was supposed to marry Siobhán because I'd at least still be here. But..."

"I've stolen you away to Italy," I snap.

"I chose to go," he eases. "I went willingly. I married you willingly."

"Is it more than sex Oisín?"

"Seffy..."

"I deserve to know."

He sighs, but concedes. "It shouldn't have been."

"But it is. That's why you never mentioned him to me, why he hated me from the moment he saw me, why you fucking stared at him while you *fucked me.*"

"Yes," Oisín breathes.

"You love each other," I whisper. I feel like I'm choking on the words. "You love each other, and I've...I've broken that."

"No," Oisín says, standing and stepping towards me. I step away, shaking my head. "No, Serafina, it's not...We knew we had no future. But he's...shit, he's hurt, still, and the man's stubborn as fuck."

"Can you blame him?" I ask, throwing my hands up. "He had years with you, all for you to fuck off and marry a woman you've never met. Of course he's pissed!"

"I'm not his."

"You're a liar."

"I'm yours, Seffy."

"Yes, so you've said," I murmur. "You should have told me, Oisín. You should have...*Cazzo*. I don't want to be second best, *husband*."

He flinches. "I didn't think it would be like this."

"What did you think? That you could abandon Sebastian, the man who's clearly obsessed with you, marry me and just forget he exists? How fucking cruel can you be? I knew you were a Cavanaugh, Oisín, but I didn't realise you were a cunt, too."

Oisín is so still his chest barely moves as he breathes. He's staring me down in a way that I'm sure would intimidate anyone else, but just makes me straighten my spine.

I'm so fucking angry, so *hurt*. For me, and for Sebastian. God, I can't even be mad at that man now that I know. I'd hate me too.

"I'm sorry," Oisín says finally.

"I'm not the one who deserves that apology," I grind out. I'm not nearly ready enough to hear him lie to me again.

"I didn't want to hurt you, Seffy."

"Oh, just Sebastian then?" I sneer at him, curling my hands into fists.

"I..."

"I have no interest in being married to a fucking coward."

"Serafina, please." Oisín steps closer again, reaching for me. I shake his hand off, glaring at him. "We both knew we had no future."

"You didn't even bother trying."

He flinches like I've struck him.

"There was nothing to try for," Oisín whispers.

My heart sinks. Hurt and betrayal make me feel nauseous. He should've told me.

I should've known better than to trust him.

"Fuck this, and fuck you," I say, swallowing the pain down. I don't have time for this distraction, not with my sister in trouble. I can't let him shift my focus.

Especially when I'm not his.

"I won't stand around fucking you and watching you fuck this up when my sister is in danger," I snap. "She is the priority here, Oisín, not you or your conscience. You can stand with me and pretend to be a loyal husband for the sake of the alliance, or you can stay in this room and rot. I don't care. But I'm going to find your father."

21

Serafina

I don't bother turning to check if Oisín is following. Fury burns through me, and there's fuck all that I can do about it.

This is my fault.

I was the one who married a man without even meeting his fucking family. I was the one who thought that maybe we had a future. I was the one who put my trust in a Cavanaugh.

I should have known better.

But the alliance has to stand.Trustworthy husband or not.

Thomas will help. I can fake this marriage long enough. I'm a fighter, and that doesn't stop just because I'm not currently carrying a weapon. Thomas *will* help.

He will, just as soon as I fucking find him.

I pause at the top of the staircase, breaths coming fast and heavy. Regret pools in my stomach. I should've made Oisín give me the stupid tour. It's such an amateur mistake that I curse myself. I don't know my way around. I don't know the hiding places or which direction the hallways will take me. I am at a distinct disadvantage, already off kilter from the sting of betrayal and confusion at my body's reaction.

"Need something?"

I still, every nerve in my body coming to life. I turn slowly, the sound of his voice sending heat and a fresh spark of anger through me.

Sebastian's leaning on the wall, lounging like this is just any other fucking day. Relaxed. He raises his brow in question.

"Not from you," I answer as smoothly as I can.

His eyes darken and he tilts his head to the side. "Ah, come on, Sef. Give me a chance. You have no idea what I could give you."

"I have an idea of what you've been giving my husband," I counter, trying to deflect the fact that his words make my core tighten.

For *fuck's sake*. I smooth my skirt down, regretting grabbing the first things I found in my suitcase before making my escape. My legs are bare, and the skirt only falls to mid thigh. At least the shirt I'm wearing covers my chest and arms, but it's useless.

I may as well be naked under Sebastian's eyes.

Again.

Sebastian pushes off the wall and steps closer to me. I don't miss the way his throat bobs with a thick swallow. Unfortunately, that means I'm also staring at the dark skull tattoo spanning his neck, following the lines lower to where a few spikes are visible at the edge of his t-shirt. What does he have etched into his chest? He's covered in art, too many designs to focus on, but I'm struck with the need to do just that. To find every picture, analyse it, trace the ink-

"Thomas," I blurt out, hoping to God that he didn't notice me staring at him. The sparkle in his eye tells me he knows exactly what I was just thinking.

This is ridiculous. There is no fucking way I can feel anything but contempt and pity for this man. The way my body reacts to his taunts, to the sight of him, is just residual heat. It has to be. He did *just* watch me get fucked, did just hear me scream as I came...

And I...

I turn away. The image of him, wide eyed and hard in the doorway, staring at Oisín and me, refuses to budge even when I close my eyes.

Shit.

"Sure thing," Sebastian says, grinning as he turns away, giving me his back easily. My hackles rise at that. Does he think that just because he saw me in a vulnerable position that I'm any less of a threat?

The insult has me reaching for a weapon that's not there. Apparently, I've left everything in Oisín's room - my knife, and my dignity.

I follow Sebastian, silent and seething. I don't have a choice, and that pisses me off. I'm surprised when he leads me downstairs and not up to where I assume more bedrooms and the offices would be.

The room we enter is certainly not an office.

"Aoife!" Sebastian calls out happily, striding further into the depths of the room.

I'm so struck by the walls of weapons that I barely take notice of the woman Sebastian is talking to. The entire space is essentially an armoury for every fucking weapon imaginable. Knives, guns, brass knuckles, daggers all line the walls locked in cases. There are more safes at the back wall, but they're closed and solid so I can only imagine what the fuck is stored inside.

The room itself is brightly lit, and fairy lights are strung up along the top of the walls. I blink at them like I'm hallucinating, the little sparkly lights far more confusing than the weapons.

"Sef?"

I jolt at the sound of Sebastian shortening my name again, gritting my teeth. Finally, I drop my eyes to the other figure in the room.

The woman is smiling at me, dark brown eyes creased at the sides, her curly hair falling in her face. She pushes it back, finding a hair tie on her wrist and quickly tying back the unruly strands.

"I'm Aoife," she says, extending her hand.

On instinct, I shake it, her palm warm against mine and introduce myself robotically.

"This place is…uh…*wow*," I try and fail to form even a sentence.

"The fairy lights are a nice touch, right?" Aoife says, dropping my hand to extend her arms out, gesturing at the room. "Figured since I was spending so much time in here, I should at least make it a little prettier."

I blink at her. "Right. Of course."

Aoife laughs at my reaction, turning back to Sebastian. "Thomas'll be back in a minute. You can wait up in his office, I'll send him up to you."

I get the feeling she wants me out of here, despite her welcome. Her eyes flick between me and the locked weapons, as though she's calculating if she can get between me and the guns if I were to lunge for them.

I respect her for it, and despite the fact that I would

love a tour of the weaponry she has, I can't blame her for withholding that trust.

"I hope to see more of you, Aoife," I tell her honestly, trying to soften my mood enough to give her a genuine smile.

Her grin is as bright as her lights. "Welcome to the family, Serafina."

Thomas' office is exactly what I expected, a stark contrast of Aoife's bright, sparkly weapons stash.

The space is lined with dark wood and smells like whiskey, coffee and leather. The large desk demands attention the way the man himself does, but it's filled with clutter - stationary, empty cups, a coffee pot with only dregs left.

"Your husband's coming," Sebastian whispers, and I glare at him over my shoulder.

The second he says it, I hear footsteps. Two sets, their pace nearly matched but one heavier.

Oisín and his father appear before I can answer Sebastian. My husband's shirt is wrinkled, and I focus on it to avoid the heavy look I can feel him giving me.

My father in law says nothing as he skirts around Sebastian to sit at his desk, the plush office chair creaking a little as he settles into it. Thomas clears a small patch of the desk to lean forward on, his eyes scanning all three of us. Oisín steps between Sebastian and I like he can block the other man from me completely. It takes everything in me not to step away from them both.

"Aoife said you were looking for me," Thomas says, gaze coming to rest on me. I meet his eyes, tilting my chin up.

"As much as I'd love my visit to be purely for pleasure,"

I begin, immediately regretting my choice of words when Sebastian clears his throat loudly. I want to punch him right in that fucking skull tattoo. "Unfortunately, my purpose here is business. We need the power this alliance allows us."

Thomas barely reacts, just a tick of the brow that reminds me of his son.

"My sister is missing." God, the words feel like acid in my throat. "And tomorrow, I'm going to return home to continue fighting to find her. I hope I won't be returning to San Jarno alone."

Thomas steeples his fingers together and inclines his chin towards me. "We're people of our word, Serafina. Our families are joined, which makes your family, my family."

I relax instantly. I can't fucking handle any more stressful men today.

"Oisín, go get Nessa, Anji and Aoife. Sebastian, you're dismissed."

22

Oisín

The last thing I want to do is leave my wife for even a second to go and round up my sister and the others. I've already wasted too much time sitting stunned on my bed, scrambling for any idea on how to fix things.

Sebastian scoffs loudly at my father's dismissal, shaking his head. He's on my left, Serafina's on my right, and I can't move.

"You're not serious," Sebastian says, disbelief sharpening his words. "I'm not staying here while you're off galavanting around Italy without me."

"It's a fucking rescue mission," Serafina hisses, though her voice is low.

My da bears her no mind, turning his glare Sebastian's way. "Given everything that's going on, you can't be trusted to keep your emotions in check," Thomas tells him, and I swear to God I can hear Sebastian's heart skip a beat.

"Excuse me?" Sebastian says, tone cold now.

"You're too close to this. To my son. Your emotions are a liability, Sebastian, and I cannot trust you to keep them under control. So, I will tell you once more, you are *dismissed*."

Sebastian inhales sharply, and I know that if I turned to him, I'd see fury brimming in his eyes. But I don't. I don't so much as glance his way. My eyes fly to Seffy, my heart twisting as I spot her narrowing her gaze in my father's direction. Her breaths are shallow. Too shallow, like she's purposefully controlling each inhale she takes. Fuck.

There's no way she hasn't realised that she's the last person to find out about me and Sebastian, when she damn well should have been the first. Guilt sours my stomach, and I can't bear to be in the room with them any longer. Tucking my head down, I do as I was told. I nod once to my father, turn on my heel and go to find my sister.

Siobhán refuses to be left out of the conversation. I sigh as the small crowd of us returns to the office, where Serafina has taken up residence in a chair across from my father. I've only been gone for five minutes, but my wife is lounging like she's never been more relaxed, and Sebastian is nowhere to be seen. My chest feels heavy.

I run my hand through my hair, the only action I allow myself before I shut down the cocktail of emotions swirling inside me.

It's so much fucking easier to feel nothing.

Siobhán shoves her way between me and Nessa with a grin. She isn't supposed to be here but I was all out of fucks to give.

It doesn't take long for Thomas to notice her, and once he does he rolls his eyes but says nothing. It's becoming apparent that he has a secret soft spot for her, the way he does for Sebastian. Though, given how he just snapped at him, perhaps Siobhán is higher in the food chain now.

I zone out of the conversation as my da explains what Serafina's told him. I watch my wife as he lists the details about the trafficking ring growing in the underbelly of San Jarno, about the family they suspect are behind it. I ignore the pain in my chest as he tells the others that the Russo's are denying any involvement in Francesca's disappearance or the trafficking.

Not once does Serafina look at me, and I swear if I let myself acknowledge the storm of emotions swirling inside of me, I'd be broken on the floor.

Instead, I straighten my back and return my focus to the conversation happening around me.

"Let me call Patrick," Siobhán says immediately.

It takes me a minute to place the name, and by the time I've realised she's talking about the new head of the Branigan gang, my da is already nodding.

"I don't want anybody brought in on this that isn't fucking bombproof," Serafina interupts, turning to look at Siobhán.

Siobhán offers her a small smile. "He's my cousin. Patrick Branigan? He's as good as anyone else in this room, I promise you that."

Serafina regards her for a few short moments before she nods sharply and turns back to my father.

"Call him," Thomas says simply.

I'm only half listening when Siobhán puts her cousin on speaker and Patrick answers on the second ring.

They spend far longer than I'd like chatting away as though they've not a care in the world. Based on the tight lipped expression crossing Seffy's face, it's evident she feels the same.

"Alright, enough's enough. Patrick, we need your help." My

father's voice cuts through their chatter, and I'm grateful for it when I see Seffy nodding at him.

I don't know how the fuck I'm going to handle any of the mess I've made, but the least I can do is help my wife find her sister.

"What can I do for you Thomas?"

Patrick's voice is clear and strong through the phone, and it drags me out of my stupor.

"We're heading on a little holiday to Italy, fancy a few of your crew joining us?" My father gently thrums his finger on the desk before him as he waits for Patrick to answer. I hold my breath, unsure of what to do.

"I've just the girl for you. Her name's Gráinne, best I've got and one hell of a partier. She'll liven shit up for sure."

I note the crinkle in Siobhán's brow and Nessa's gaze hardening, but I don't bother to question it.

If Patrick's telling us she's the best he has, then I fucking trust him to mean it. Enough blood's been spilled on both sides for neither one of us to want to fuck over the other anymore. And with Seamus dead, the streets of Killrover have never been more peaceful.

Nodding my head at my father, I take the phone from Siobhán's hand.

"Thanks Patrick, I owe you one," I say, ensuring that he hears me before I hang up.

He and my father may very well be the only thing keeping my marriage intact after the shit show earlier, and I'll repay them anyway I have to if it means keeping Seffy as my wife.

23

Sebastian

It's been hours since Thomas dismissed me from his office, and I can't stay away any longer. I'm going insane.

I've paced the halls of the house more times than I can count, and still, I want to punch him in the face.

To be completely honest, I'm not sure if he's the one I really want to see blood spill from.

I've been one of Thomas' best enforcers since I got here, and all it took for me to unravel was knowing that Oisín's getting his dick wet. All it took for Thomas to lose all trust in me was his son's rejection.

My hands flex at my side as I picture Oisín's face as Thomas kicked me out of the room.

He was so cold. So reserved.

Not once did he even bother to look at me as his father cast me aside like I mean nothing to this family, to this gang.

Closing my eyes, I force myself to take a deep breath for the hundredth time. I try to push my feelings deep down, locking them away, so that I can get through the rest of this day.

There's no fucking way they're going to Italy without me.

Yet, as soon as my eyelids shut, I'm flooded with images of Oisín and Serafina.

I can't unsee him fucking Serafina. Unhear the sound of the flesh slapping together or his grunts and her moans as they found pleasure in each other.

No matter what I do, all I can picture is his eyes locked on me, her face as she came, and his dick covered in their release.

I flinch as I remember Serafina's hurt gaze. The moment she realised that Oisín had betrayed her. Had betrayed me.

I've been threatened, beaten, and tortured to within an inch of my life.

And still, none of it hurt as badly as watching him come undone balls deep inside of her.

The scars hidden beneath my tattoos itch as I pace the hall one more time. I force myself not to scratch them. I've worked too hard to fall back into old habits.

I check my phone to find a text from Siobhán asking me if I'm alright.

I'm not alright. I'm not fucking alright at all, and a part of me wonders if I ever will be again.

Things between Oisín and I were frosty to begin with since his return, but now I doubt he'll ever speak to me again. At this rate, I'll be lucky if he so much as blinks in my direction.

I pocket my phone, not bothering to respond to Siobhán. I know she's worried, but I can't lie to her. I can't promise her that I'm fine, that things will be okay, or that I'll get over it.

Instead, I head back to the one place I know will hurt me more.

"Christ, there's fucking two of them," I huff as I reach the threshold to Thomas' office.

Nessa glares at me as my eyes swing between her and the newcomer, and I struggle to hold in my laughter. Both she and Nessa are leaning against opposite walls, their arms folded across their chests. Corded muscle bulges from both women's arms and there's a pistol strapped to both their hips. They're even wearing the same fucking cargo pants for Christ's sake.

The only thing differentiating them is their looks. The woman contrasts Nessa in looks completely with her short curly hair, dark skin, brown eyes and small stature. She seems softer too, less bitchy, but I've no doubt she's just as deadly as my best friend if she's mixed up with our lot.

I step toward the new girl, all too content with pissing Nessa off as I shove my hand out and formally introduce myself. Her eyes narrow into slits at my nearness, but she grasps my hand firmly, shaking it twice before clearing her throat.

"I'm Gráinne."

I smirk as Siobhán struggles to cover her chuckle behind a cough, before turning to close the door behind to Thomas' office. When I look back at the others I can't stop my smirk from transforming into a full blown grin as Nessa glares at me.

"Fuck off, Seb," Nessa hisses and I try to control myself.

Siobhán's laughter fills the air, and my chest tightens as Serafina huffs out her own dry laugh. I search the room, my smile slipping as I realise just how hard Oisín is working to ignore me.

Siobhán notices, and I give her a tight lipped smile before

I turn to face the man I've viewed as a father figure for half my life.

"What do you want, Sebastian?" Thomas groans, and anger rises within me once more.

I hate knowing he's disappointed in me.

Hate knowing that he views me differently now.

That he can't seem to trust me anymore.

But more than anything I'm fucking livid that he could feel all that so easily, for the small crime of loving his son when he was always going to be promised to another to strengthen alliances.

There hasn't been a break from the tension between Thomas and I since he found me in the gym, beating the bag with my bloodied knuckles.

I took his shit then, but I won't now.

I won't let him push me out. Not after everything I've given to him, to this family.

"I'm here to ask you to reconsider," I state and I force myself to not move under the weight of his glare.

"No."

The word cuts through the silence in the room, and I grit my teeth.

Thomas' word is final, and I know I shouldn't push him. I fucking know what happens when you cross that line, but shit, I can't seem to stop myself.

"You said I'm too close to this, too close to him," I start, clearing my throat as I nod my head in Oisín's direction.

My pulse throbs in my ears as I wait for Oisín to say anything, but instead he simply acts unbothered and pretends that I'm not here. That whatever he's looking at on his phone is more important than me publicly declaring I care for him.

That I love him enough to risk my life for him.

My chest spasms, but I ignore it and continue.

"But I don't see how that could be a bad thing. If anyone's most likely to keep your son safe it's me, and from what I've gathered, it seems like Frankie's gotten herself into a good spot of trouble."

Nessa hisses at me, practically begging me to shut the fuck up from between her clenched teeth.

I don't move as I hear something akin to a growl escaping Serafina, or Oisín's muttered curse.

I ignore Thomas too as he lifts his brow in warning, and push myself to keep going.

"Nobody else in this room knows Oisín as well as I do, and that's a fucking fact. I can tell you every move he'd make on a mission. Who he'd pick to come with him, what plan he'd think up for any situation, hell I can even tell you the exact fucking weapons he'll pick before he even knows he's going to pick them."

My breaths are shallow, but I keep going.

"I know him like the back of my hand. I know why he does things the way that he does, and it's because of this that I know you're making a mistake by not letting me come with ye," I state as I lock eyes with Thomas.

Silence thickens the room, and I swear the only sound I can hear is the seething rage simmering from Nessa as she grapples with Siobhán to reach me.

I spot movement from the corner of my eye, and slip my gaze towards Serafina.

Her hands rest neatly on her lap, her back is pressed into the arm of the chair and her legs are stretched out before her. Nothing in her posture tells me that she's annoyed, or even pissed at my refusal to be dismissed. If anything, I see respect glowing in her eyes.

Deciding to push my luck even further, I wink at her.

Her lips thin, and I grit my teeth to prevent myself from laughing.

She may be the reason that I can't have Oisín, but from the look on her face as she pieced everything together earlier, she's just as shocked to have learned of the two of us as I was to learn about her when Oisín first came home.

A small seed of guilt begins to gnaw at my stomach, but I rip it out at the root.

I won't let myself feel bad for loving someone.

I won't be ashamed of who I am.

Never again.

My eyes trail back to Thomas as I wait for him to finally say something. By now his knuckles are white as they grip the edge of his chair, and his eyes are narrowed into slits.

I've pushed too far, and I know it. But I won't sit back and let him treat me like I'm not an asset to this family.

Before Thomas can open his mouth to reprimand me for having the audacity to question his choices though, Serafina has lifted her hand.

His eyes narrow at her. The woman has balls of steel to raise a hand like that to Thomas Cavanaugh.

Giving her my full attention, I swipe my arms out, indicating that I'm ready for anything she throws my way.

I watch her as she tips her head slightly to the side. Her eyes narrow as she clasps her hands on her lap and asks me the one question I didn't expect, at least not in front of her father in law.

"Tell me Sebastian, just how do you think you're going to

protect my husband? By sucking his cock?"

I choke on my next breath as every single person in the room inhales sharply.

Fuck, I think I love her.

I give her my biggest smile while shrugging my shoulders. I won't deny my interest in Oisín any longer, and if this is the game she wants to play then I'm more than happy to go along with it.

"I've heard enough," Thomas growls and I sober as I realise that Serafina and I have been openly scoping each other out. "You're not coming with us, end of discussion."

Every hair on my body stands to attention as Oisín's gravelly voice travels across the office.

Not once before now has he dared to speak up, dared to look at me. Yet as I turn on my heels, he's glaring at me with a mix of rage, hurt, and disgust.

"You either let me come with you, or I'll make my own way there. But one thing's for sure Oisín, you're not risking your fucking life without me by your side." My voice is steadier than I'd hoped it would be.

My hands flex at my side, desperate to reach for him, but I won't do it. I won't give him any more of me than he deserves right now.

I owe him for saving me all those years ago. For giving me the escape I so desperately needed after everything that happened.

I owe Thomas too.

But I won't let either of them walk all over me anymore.

I'm done being good, obedient and nice.

I'm done playing by their rules.

24

Oisín

"What the actual *fuck?!*"

I slam the bathroom door behind me, sealing out the low hum of conversation from the main cabin of the plane. We're barely a third of the way through the flight and already it's gone to shit.

Because Sebastian fucking Byrnes has turned the plane's shower stall into his own personal den. The bottom of the shower has been padded out with blankets and a pillow and Sebastian is reclining with his legs stretched out and a game console in his hands.

"I was wondering how long it would take for someone to figure out I'm here," he says with a smirk, switching off his game and putting it down in the tangle of his blanket.

"You can't be here," I tell him, exasperation seeping into my words along with a horrible, heavy dose of worry. He was supposed to be back in Killrover - safe, far away and out of my eyeline. Far enough away to not be tempting me, damn it.

Except Sebastian is a stubborn fucker and I should've known he'd pull something like this. Hell, he even bloody warned us he'd do it too. It's a problem. A big fucking problem, least of all because he's disobeyed Da's orders and mostly because *how the fuck am I supposed to avoid him if he's here?*

The answer is obvious and utterly terrifying; I can't.

"Well that's odd, 'cause I *am* here," Sebastian snarks back, groaning as he stands and stretches his long limbs.

I can't breathe. I spent the entire time at home trying to avoid him, to distance myself, to make sure I was always far enough away from him to not give in to the bone deep need to grab him and drag his body against mine.

I *crave* him.

And I shouldn't. It's not right, pining after someone when I'm married to another I'm just as equally obsessed with. It's not fair, to fucking any of us, and I don't know how to make this better.

Sebastian cocks his head at me as he steps forward, looking for all the world like he belongs here on this flight, with me. And fuck how can I deny that?

He shouldn't fucking be here.

So why am I not hopping mad? Why am I not screaming at him and demanding he get on the next plane home the second we land? Why for the love of God am I not leaving this fucking bathroom?

"Sebastian…" I start, but his name is all I can get out. I have nothing else to say. Nothing that isn't utterly damning.

I can't fucking tell him that hurting him is cleaving me in half, or that I'm confused as fuck by my own feelings, or that I am so tired of lying about the years we spent together.

"Do you hate me, Oisín?"

"Sebastian…"

"Tell me you don't want me."

"Seb-"

"Say it, Oisín. Say *I don't want you, Sebastian."*

"Sebastian!"

"You can't," he says, stepping closer and closer until his lips graze mine with his words. "You can't fuckin' say it, because it's not true. You can pretend all you want, but I bet your cock still begs for my mouth."

Fuck, my dick swells at the promise in his words. I don't know what the fuck I'm supposed to say.

"My wife-"

"Is hot as hell and came hard as fuck with me watching," he says, his hands finding my hips, body caging me. "I'm a Goddamn masochist, because watching you fuck her was *heaven*. I want to hate you for what you've done, Oisín but I'm still starving for you. I'm begging for scraps, and I don't even have the decency to be ashamed of my own desire."

My eyes blur as my ears ring with the hurt and desperation turning his words raspy.

"I wasn't trying to hurt you, Sebby," I whisper, closing my eyes so I don't have to see his face. "It fucking *kills* me that I have."

"Look at me when you lie to me, Oisín," Sebastian murmurs and I can't bring myself to deny him. His face is blank, blue eyes boring into mine. "Fuck it, I'll take the crumbs. Tell me again how getting married and ignoring all my messages while I was fighting Branigans and worrying for your Goddamn life was all an accident."

He's not angry, there's no heat in his words, fuck he just sounds resigned. I'd rather he yelled, because I swear to God I'm shaking like each word out of his mouth is a punch to the gut.

"Sebby." His name again. Always his fucking name. My tongue struggles to form any other word. "Hurting you was never the goal. I just…I couldn't speak to you. I couldn't bear it."

Something flashes through his eyes, but he's lowering his head and dropping to the floor at my feet before I can pinpoint the emotion.

"Tell me you don't want me," Sebastian repeats, fingers hovering over the button of my trousers. "Tell me, Oisín, and I'll try and find the strength to stop…wanting you, too."

We both fucking know I can't say it. Shit, I can't do fuck all to deny him right now - the stowaway who follows me regardless of how much of a fucking asshole I am. His loyalty knows no bounds, and his persistence far outruns my ability to resist.

So with the mix of guilt, want and helplessness flooding my veins, I cover his hand with mine and yank my trousers down.

Sebastian wastes no time leaning forward and taking my cock in his mouth. I groan at the feel of him, hand in his hair, as he licks the underside of my dick with his tongue until I'm aching.

"I'm sorry," I mumble, voice thick with pleasure and pain. "I'm so fuckin' sorry."

I don't know who I'm apologising to - Sebastian, for discarding him like he doesn't matter in the slightest, like he never mattered to me at all, or Serafina for letting Sebastian suck my fucking dick in this Goddamn plane while she's sitting a room away. Or maybe myself, for thinking I could put duty over my heart, and being stupid enough to entangle the two so deeply that I'll never be able to pry them apart.

25

Serafina

"Nessa fucking Cav-"

"Tobin, actually, dear father," Nessa snarks back. Thomas' hands tighten on the armrests of his seat and a muscle in his jaw ticks.

They've been arguing ever since Thomas got back from the cockpit, Nessa clearly already bored enough to cause trouble. Thomas looks like he's contemplating opening the emergency door just to fling himself out. There's a deep line between his brows as he scowls in his daughter's direction, while she just shrugs back at him.

"For the love of God, can you stop your shit! At least until we're back on the fuckin' ground?" Thomas snaps, a tightness in his voice that wasn't there earlier.

I can't tell what's going on between them, but I'm too fucking tired for their shit. I've only known these people for a day but their dynamics are easy to learn. Nessa is as pushy as Sebastian, Thomas is a hard ass but a protective one, and Aoife stays out of it with a roll of her eyes and a soft smile.

Before Nessa can keep going, Thomas turns to the side and begins digging about in his bag.

It's then I realise that my husband's missing.

Well, not as missing as my fucking sister.

He disappeared when we levelled out, abandoning his seat next to me to move to the back of the plane, separated from the main cabin by a long red curtain.

It's been fifteen minutes and there's no sign of him coming back. Warily, I glance at the people around me. Thomas has a mask over his eyes and earplugs in his ears now, clearly trying to drown the rest of us out as best as possible.

Gráinne and Nessa are in some kind of stare off, both women's eyes narrowed at one another as they sit directly across from each other. Aiofe's in a solo seat to my left, reading a book with some sort of tentacled monster on the front called *The Kraken's Bride*. Anji sits directly in front of Aoife, his nose deep in his laptop, dark brows furrowed as he works on God knows what.

Nobody bats an eye when I stand, stretching my arms above my head. We've only been on this bloody plane for an hour but between yesterday's flight and the fucking turmoil of revelations, I'm stiff and stressed and sick of it all.

I stride towards the curtain separating the cabin from the back, where the door to the bathroom is. Further down here, at the back of the plane, is a bedroom, though the flight isn't nearly long enough to warrant use of it.

I squint around the space, going so far as to open the bedroom door just to check he isn't in there, before I hear it.

A strangled male moan, and then another low voice chuckling.

"Not as easy to forget about me when your dick's in my

mouth is it?"

I halt my inspection of the plane, that voice sending a frigid chill down my spine. I half expect my teeth to clack together as I fight the urge to shiver, tensing every muscle in my body.

In two strides I'm outside the bathroom door, pressing my ear to the wood, holding my breath.

My husband moans again and a sick sort of desire pools between my thighs.

I smack the palm of my hand hard against the door, and I hear Oisín curse. His voice is low and strained, thick with lust.

They haven't even locked the fucking door.

I slam the bathroom door open, step inside, and lock it behind me in one swift motion. I don't need any of his family to witness my utter humiliation. I don't even want to face it, for fuck's sake.

Both men are wide eyed and breathing heavily as they turn to me. The bathroom is large and luxurious, with a giant shower stall and grey marble effect acrylic panels make the space feel much brighter than it really is. The shower stall is, strangely, filled with a blanket, a pillow and a handheld game console abandoned in the pile.

Oisín is standing in the middle of the floor, trousers around his ankles, cock still wet with Sebastian's spit.

My husband stares at me, hair messy and tangled, skin flushed, mouth parted in what I can only assume is shock. He says nothing, and as much as I want to scream at him, I just stand there numbly.

Taking advantage of our silence, Sebastian flicks his eyes to mine and leans forward. He's on his knees, and I watch as his tongue darts out, drawing a long, slow line up the underside of Oisín's cock.

My husband's brow creases as his hand fists Sebastian's hair, forcing his head back sharply. Sebastian groans at the rough treatment, spreading his knees, making the tenting in the front of his black trackies even more obvious.

Yet as angry as I am, with shock still rocketing through me, I have never been this fucking turned on before. I can't breathe, my skin is on fire, and I swear I'm leaving a damp patch on the crotch of my jeans.

I can't think clearly.

The worst part, the damning part, is that I should be utterly and completely embarrassed. My husband, who married me a month ago, is already sticking his cock where it shouldn't be. But it's the shame of it, the shame of my own stupidity in not knowing, that makes me fucking squirm.

"Seffy," Oisín chokes out, his knuckles tight in Sebastian's hair. The other man is half lidded and grinning, leaning into the cruel touch.

My mind reels, memories of Sebastian watching us yesterday clamouring to the forefront of my thoughts. And I am furious, so fucking angry I want to put my fist through the damn plane windows but…

But they're so fucking *pretty* together. Shit, Sebastian is a work of Goddamn art, and not only because of the tattoos. The way Oisín is holding him, the way he kneels happily at his feet, the unspoken but clear dynamic between the two makes me swallow thickly.

Oisín has been my husband for five weeks, but he's been Sebastian's love for years.

Jealousy only makes me burn hotter.

I stare at them, leaning against the bathroom door as the plane thrums around us.

Oisín's eyes are pleading and bright as he stares at me, but he doesn't offer me any words. I don't know if I want him to.

When I speak, my voice is far steadier than I feel. I look Sebastian in the eye, cock my head at him and say, "Please, go ahead. Suck my husband's dick instead of helping us catch the fucking traffickers."

Sebastian's eyes widen and Oisín goes to release him.

"No, no," I snap, eyes narrowing. The mix of rage and lust and shock is all consuming now, and I'm lost to it completely. "Keep going. Don't mind me."

"Sef-"

"I *said,*" I hiss, pinning Oisín with a glare. "Keep. Fucking. Going."

26

Oisín

My wife's eyes are full of fire. She stares me down, a dare in her gaze.

I want to apologise to her. I want to say *this was a mistake, you're it for me, I'm sorry.* But I can't.

I don't want to fucking lie.

But I don't want to hurt her. I don't want to hurt Sebastian anymore either.

Nessa's words are stuck in my head, and I catch them just before they spill out on my tongue. *Pretending you can only love one person isn't going to make it true.*

You're a fucking coward.

I look between Serafina and Sebastian, my pulse so high I can hear it. Her, stern faced and demanding, standing in front of the door like she's blocking out the rest of the world. Him, on his knees, head tilted back with his hair in my grip, tongue licking the taste of me off his lips.

And I know I'm fucked.

"Sef-"

"I *said keep. Fucking. Going.*"

My grip falters in Sebastian's hair, and it's all the invitation he needs. His hand tightens its hold on my thigh, fingers digging into my muscle, as his lips wrap around my cock.

I can't stop the rough groan that rips its way from my throat at the feel of him. His tongue teases the tip before he hollows his cheeks and takes me deep.

This shouldn't feel so fucking good. I know that it's wrong. That I shouldn't want Sebastian to continue fucking me with his mouth while my wife stands there angry, embarrassed and God knows what else while I get off on the two of them.

I shouldn't fucking let this happen… and yet, as Sebastian takes me further into his throat, I can't stop the hiss of pleasure that escapes me.

Serafina inhales sharply as Sebastian takes me into his throat again, and I'm fucking lost between ripping him away from me and pulling her closer.

I don't need to reach for her, because she steps closer, heeled boots loud on the floor.

"Deeper," she demands of Sebastian, grabbing his hair roughly and shoving him further onto me. He gags, and she bites her bottom lip. I curse, trying to drag myself away before I condemn us all more than I have but her eyes snap to mine. "Don't waste his skills, Oisín. The least you can do is give him your cum, considering you refuse to give him anything else."

The remark stings like she's slapped me, and I grit my teeth to stop myself from telling her to get on the fucking floor for her disrespect.

But she hasn't agreed to that dynamic, to that side of me, and I've already subjected her to so much. Too much. She should walk away, and I can't, through the thick fog of need, figure out why she hasn't.

I'm not a good enough man to tell her to leave me.

Nor am I a good enough man to make Sebastian stop.

Sebastian makes a choked noise that I know would be a moan if he had any air. Serafina strokes his hair softly, petting him as his nose touches my skin. He swallows around me, and I swear louder still.

"Fuck, Sebby," I growl, wishing I could cup his throat, hold him to me, feel him take me.

"Sebby?" Serafina repeats, her tone disbelieving. "Sebby and Seffy." She snorts, shaking her head, and shoves Sebastian's before letting go. "Aren't you fucking lucky."

"Tell me, angel," I address her, the confusion over her actions boiling over, the pleasure of Sebastian's mouth pushing me closer to an edge we can't come back from. "Are you angry? Are you fucking furious at me? Or do you like the way my cock looks in his pretty mouth? Are you wet watching him gag on it? Will you whimper when he takes my cum? Will you kiss it off his lips?"

I know I shouldn't push my luck, that my marriage is hanging on by a thread at this stage, but I can't help myself. She's still here, watching us, and I'm wound so fucking tight that having both of them near me has me teetering on the edge of control.

Sebastian pulls away, gasping for air, his eyes shiny with tears from gagging. There's a wet spot on the tented fabric of his trousers, gleaming in the light. Serafina looks like she wants to slap me, but she does nothing but tense her fists at her sides.

"*Vaffanculo*," she hisses, and I grin.

Despite being in Italy for only a few weeks, I picked up on

enough. *Fuck you.*

"Gladly," I answer darkly.

"I have no idea what you just said but it was hot," Sebastian pipes up, his voice gruff and breathy still as he gulps for air.

My cock is painfully hard, aching for Sebastian's mouth again, but my eyes are locked with my wife's and her teeth are so deep in her lip I suspect it's bleeding.

"What do you want, angel?" I grind out. I try to keep my voice soft, but it comes out strained.

Serafina scoffs and shakes her head, finally freeing her lip.

"Do you want me to stop? Swear I'll never touch him again? That I'll never be with anyone but you?"

"You already fucking swore that in your vows," she points out, but her voice isn't as angry as it was.

"God and I have never seen eye to eye," I tell her. "I've broken every promise I've ever made in his house."

Serafina straightens at that, but says nothing. I can't fucking stop myself talking. I'm sure my words are too brash, but Sebastian has broken something in me, and Nessa's stupid words are still playing in my head, and I don't want to leave my wife.

I want too much. I want them both.

Is that a sin?

Gluttony, I think as I look between them. But if I'm going to hell, my fate was sealed long before this. Wanting to share my life with two people is perhaps the least sinful thing I have ever done.

Sebastian's eyes are on the ground, and I see his throat work as he swallows. I curse myself as I realise how much my words must have just hurt him.

Fuck, I need to fix this. I need them both to see that my

heart beats for both of them. That I never had a choice in loving either of them.

"I don't think that's what you want, angel," I murmur, reaching out to stroke Sebastian's hair soothingly. I've betrayed him, so badly that the knowledge hurts worse than a gunshot wound.

I was trying to do the right thing, and look where that's fucking got me. Three broken hearts, two potentially pissed off gangs, and Serafina's faith in our marriage completely fractured.

As I look between them both, the weight of everything I've done threatening to pull the whole plane out of the sky, the *wrong* thing feels as bright as the fucking sun.

"You don't fucking know what I want," Serafina accuses.

"We both know, Seffy," I tell her, extending my hand towards her. Beneath me, Sebastian rests his head on my thigh. "You can't walk away any more than I can."

"This is your mess, not mine," she says.

"I've always been a fan of getting messy," Sebastian interjects.

I can't fight the grin on my face. Fuck, I love his sassy mouth.

"Serafina," I try, her name sweet as sugar on my tongue. "If you don't want this, why are you still here? Why didn't you slap me in the face and file for divorce the second Sebastian watched us fuck?"

"Don't," she whispers. "I don't fucking know, Oisín."

"Let us help you figure it out," Sebastian offers, letting me go to crawl to her. The bathroom may be large for a plane, but there's only so far she can go without leaving.

"This is fucked," Serafina murmurs, but there's no bite to

the words.

"Do you want to be?" Sebastian counters, stopping at her feet and staring up at her.

He has a way of acting like he's in charge even on his knees, even underneath me, and it's clear that Seffy's experiencing that now.

"*Cazzo,*" Serafina swears, seconds before she grabs Sebastian's hair and crashes her mouth to his.

27

Serafina

Sebastian tastes like sin and Oisín. I can't stop myself from running my tongue along the seam of his lips, demanding he open, desperate and hot.

I know this is a mistake. It has to be.

I'm kissing my husband's lover.

The man I should want nothing to do with.

The person I should hate almost as much as I should hate my husband.

But instead of pulling away I push myself closer. Sebastian's hands find my waist and tug me down until I'm straddling him on the floor. Our chests press together and I can feel the hard length of him against the seam of my jeans as his fingers clutch my shirt, shoving it up.

I pull back just enough to hurriedly drag the whole thing off and throw it to the side, before his mouth is back on mine. His thumb grazes my nipple through the sheer lace of my bra, and I shudder, the touch sending a bolt of heat through me. I rock against him, my body seeking friction, whining when the thick denim of my jeans refuses to let me close enough.

Sebastian laughs against me, hands releasing me just long enough to pop the button and drag the zip down. I wriggle, frustrated as fuck when I realise that I can't get the damn things off unless I stand again.

Sebastian doesn't let me move. With the zip undone, he shoves his hand into the waistband of my jeans.

"You were right," he says to Oisín, holding my stare as he speaks, voice gruff and eyes bright. "She's fucking soaked."

I glance up as Oisín's shoes thud on the floor. He's tugged his trousers back up, but they're still undone. His expression is one I've never seen before - dark and intent and I can't look away. It's more than just the way he looks. It's the way he looms over us, a dark, all consuming force that Sebastian and I can do nothing but submit to.

I gasp as Sebastian's finger grazes my clit through my underwear.

"Should he make you come, angel?" Oisín asks, and Sebastian groans.

I nod, unable to speak.

"Tell him," Oisín encourages, and Sebastian drags his fingers over me again, slowly and so fucking gently that I want to sob in frustration. "He's really very good at following orders, given the right motivation."

"What…" my voice trails off before I can finish my question. I know what's happening. I've had a glimpse of their dynamic and now Oisín is inviting me in. "Sebastian?"

"I can stop…" he says teasingly, though his fingers are still pressed to the damp spot on my underwear. I rock restlessly, a groan stuck in my throat.

"Don't," I gasp, bracing my hands on his shoulders. "Don't you fucking dare stop."

Sebastian chuckles, pushing my underwear to the side and plunging two fingers inside me.

I shout out, pleasure sparking through me, the shock of it making me gasp. Oisín's eyes are fixed on us, wild even as he holds himself still a few feet away from us.

"God above, she's so. Fucking. Hot." Sebastian sounds pained as I shake on top of him while he holds his fingers still, as deep inside me as they can go.

"Sebastian," I pant, digging my nails into his shoulders as my hips jerk. *"Please."*

"Don't beg him," Oisín demands sharply and my eyes widen. "The only person you plead for is me, is that understood?"

Confused, I blink up at him. Does he not want Sebastian to touch me anymore? Despite the confusion, I'm still shifting my hips, trying to force Sebastian to fuck me properly.

He doesn't torture me the way Oisín does, his free hand holding my waist steady as he withdraws his fingers just to fuck me harder with them.

I fight to keep my eyes open under the onslaught of pleasure Sebastian's dealing me, staring up at my husband.

"You *tell him,*" Oisín says. "Isn't that right, Sebby?"

Sebastian grins, leaning forward to press an open mouthed kiss between my breasts.

"Tell me to do whatever the fuck you want as long as I don't have to stop touching you," he says against my skin, turning his head to take my nipple between his teeth.

His words and the sting of his teeth against my skin just makes me wetter. I press myself against him more and he groans in response.

I do as I'm told, finding my voice long enough to say, "Make me come, Sebastian."

He cups me entirely, pressing the heel of his palm against my clit as his fingers work inside me, curling to find my most sensitive spot. I can't think over how turned on I am, how the embarrassment of finding them together, of seeing my husband's cock in Sebastian's mouth, has turned into this.

I can't let myself think about how Oisín's words have twisted my heart and shattered my soul.

My eyes trace over Oisín as Sebastian drives me higher and higher. I must be hurting him with how hard I'm digging my nails into his shoulders but I can't stop. He's not complaining though and I can feel his enjoyment pressing against my thigh.

"Oisín," I whimper, cursing myself for how thready my voice sounds. Fuck me, I'm already so close. "Come here."

My husband's brow raises, a glimmer of shock lighting his eyes, but he indulges me, stepping closer. He glances at Sebastian, eyes filled with lust.

"Good boy," he murmurs, tone velvety and soft. "What do you need, angel?"

My mouth waters as I reach for him, releasing Sebastian just enough to grab at Oisín's waistband. He lets me tug his boxers down, freeing his cock. Despite how unaffected he keeps his expression, his cock is weeping as Sebastian fucks me with his fingers. He watches me intently as I pant and moan and squirm.

Silently, my words lost in a ragged moan as my cunt flutters around Sebastian's fingers, I let my mouth drop open and stick my tongue out.

"*Shit,* Serafina..." Sebastian groans, breath hot against my skin as he stares up at me.

Oisín's breath catches as I look up at him through my lashes, fingers still hooked in his waistband, mouth open and eager.

He curses, low and rough, and steps closer, his hand resting on Sebastian's head, fingers tangling in his hair like it's a habit, as he drags the head of his cock over my tongue.

I moan, the sound muffled by the concentration it's taking me to hold my mouth open in wait. I can't fucking help the way I'm bouncing on my knees, fucking myself onto Sebastian's hand. His mouth is still at my breasts, nipping and licking and sucking my skin, sending spirals of red hot need lower and lower.

"Fuck," Oisín curses before he shoves forward, his cock hitting the back of my throat.

I force myself to relax and breathe through my nose as my eyes water. I want to tell Sebastian to stop touching me because I can't think while I'm so close to coming, but the plane could fucking crash and I wouldn't want him to let me go.

I'm trembling between them. Oisín's hand leaves Sebastian to tangle in my hair instead, helping me as my orgasm washes over me. I choke on him, tightening around Sebastian's fingers, stars bursting behind my eyelids.

Sebastian doesn't let me go, fucking me through the pleasure, winding me higher and higher until I'm sure this is what heaven feels like.

Between Sebastian manipulating my orgasm, and Oisín using my mouth for his pleasure, I'm helpless to do anything but try and support myself on Sebastian as Oisín fucks my mouth.

The heady taste of Oisin's precum floods my senses. Spit drips down my chin, but I don't have enough control of my limbs to try and wipe it away.

Sebastian's fingers are still buried inside me, curling to

graze my G-spot lazily, like he's just happy to be touching me. Each stroke sends sparks through my veins, and I feel like I'm floating, suspended between them in the pleasure of it all.

Sebastian leans up, raising his head from my breasts, and through watery eyes I can see him watching us. He drags his teeth over his bottom lip, eyes fixated on my mouth, before craning his neck to get closer.

His tongue darts out, licking a long line up my neck before nipping at my earlobe.

"Come again for me, Sef," he whispers, and I feel his thumb drag my own wetness over my clit. I'm too sensitive, and I whimper around Oisín's cock. "I know he wants to feel you finish with him. And fuck, I want to watch you both lose it for me. I could come just from feeling your pretty little cunt squeezing around my fingers."

I grind down onto him, near sobbing with the overstimulation and the frantic pace Oisín has set. I gag on his length, losing control of my breathing, as he shoves deep.

"Fuck, angel, your mouth is a Goddamn *sin,*" he praises.

Oisín explodes as Sebastian bites down on my neck, the burst of pain sending me over the edge again. I choke as I scream my release, Oisín's cum flooding my throat. I try to swallow, but I'm gasping too hard for air, and I feel it coat my lips and drip out of my mouth.

Before Oisín can so much as pull away, Sebastian's tongue catches the cum from my lips, tracing the underside of Oisín's dick.

Oisín pulls back, and Sebastian's mouth is on mine before I can even catch my breath. His tongue sweeps against mine, catching every fucking taste of Oisín he can.

"Don't waste it," he chides with a smirk.

My lips tingle from his kiss, and my throat feels bruised. I cling to the sated, used feeling, relishing it. I stare down at Sebastian, the man I barely fucking know, who has my release on his hand and Oisín's on his tongue, and the biggest fucking grin I've seen.

My eyes widen, heat rushing to my cheeks as I see the wet spot on the front of his trousers.

"You were fucking serious," is all I can say, a heady bolt of satisfaction going straight to my head. Knowing he'd found his own pleasure just from touching me, watching us, feels powerful. "You are…"

"Delightful. Fabulous. Incredible," he offers up when I don't finish my sentence.

"Fucking filthy," I say instead.

He shrugs. "Same thing."

28

Sebastian

Nessa and Gráinne give us twin glares the entire descent into Italy. As much as I'd voted for the lot of us to hide in the bathroom until we'd landed, the air hostess had knocked on the door and politely asked us to return to our seats.

Despite the fact I had half a mind to ignore her and lock the door again, Serafina was already pushing past me back to the main cabin. With a shrug, I'd let her go, and Oisín had shot me a despairing look.

I'd only grinned and waited for him to bring me my bag from under my seat, changed out of the trousers I'd ruined, and stolen a free seat behind Nessa.

She leans backward, peering through the gap in the seats to pin me with a glare.

Thankfully, the pilot announcing we're five minutes out from landing saves me from whatever insult she looks ready to spew my way. I purposefully don't look for Oisín or Serafina as we descend.

Still, I can't pretend like I haven't just had the most mind blowing threesome of my life for long. That's fucking saying something, considering I've been in at least five. Six, if I count the time I offered to help show a man at *Sinners* how to eat his wife out properly and in thanks, he sucked my dick.

The plane hits the tarmac with a thud and I hear Gráinne hiss at the contact, the sound echoed by a low curse from Nessa. I snort at the blatant similarities between the two women, and I swear I can feel my best friend pin me with a glare for it through the back of her chair.

"Thank fuck for that," Anji says bitterly as the plane rolls to a stop.

I'm out of my seat in an instant, leaning over the top of Nessa's seat and grinning down at her.

"Get me off this fucking plane," she groans as she stares up at me, lip curling in a sneer. "I swear to God Sebastian, if I even so much as hear you say the word *wet* ever again in my life, I will send you skydiving without a parachute."

I don't bother trying to stop the laugh that spills out of me at her disgust. Nessa has absolutely heard far worse stories from me.

"Did you think I was celibate, Ness?" I tease back, ignoring the icy stare Anji throws my way.

"Don't even get me started on my fucking *brother*," she hisses, wincing. "I'd actually rather be shot again."

"You volunteering for target practice?"

"As long as you aim for the head, put me out my fuckin' misery," she mutters. Gráinne grunts her agreement, unable to so much as look me in the eye.

It shouldn't make me grin, but fuck it does.

Thomas doesn't even bother saying a word as he stands and practically throws himself out of the plane, taking the steps two at a time and abandoning his luggage to be ferried out by the hostess.

He hasn't even acknowledged the fact that I'd managed to sneak onto the plane, and defy him completely.

Arsehole.

Like the true gentlemen I am, I help Aoife with her bags, shouldering my own backpack before following the others out onto the tarmac.

The thick, warm air hits me hard as I step out. It's a far cry from the cold, damp air I'm used to at home, though it's not particularly hard to get warmer than Ireland in winter. But given that this is the first time I've left the country in my twenty-seven years, I try to hide my surprise.

The others are already walking to the three sleek black Ferraris waiting to the far left of the runway. Thomas strides ahead of everyone else. Oisín and Serafina are side by side, a united front.

I'd be angrier about that if I couldn't still taste both of them on my tongue.

By the time I've sauntered over to the group, four more people have emerged from the cars. Three are dressed in perfectly pressed expensive looking black suits. Chauffers, I presume.

The other, Serafina has her arms wrapped around.

"Welcome home, *figlia cara*," the man says quietly to her, patting her back before she pulls away.

Renato DeSantis is a few inches shorter than my six foot one, but with enough presence to make him feel seven feet tall. His dark eyes sweep over the small crowd we make up, and his black hair is neatly styled away from his face.

"*Bentornati*," he greets as Serafina stands beside him. Oisín and Renato exchange a nod that feels far more weighted than the one Thomas gives. "Thank you for coming on such short notice."

"Anything for family," Thomas answers smoothly.

"I'm pleased to see we share the same values," Renato answers, accent lilting his words. "I imagine you would do anything for your children, Cavanaugh."

"I have," Thomas says, eyes flicking to Oisín first, then to Nessa.

I notice the way Ness swallows at his acknowledgement, but I'm feeling nice enough not to tease her about it. I figure I should cut her some slack considering she heard me finger fucking her brother's wife through the flight.

"Then you understand," Renato continues, "that I will do anything to get Francesca back. *We* will do anything to get her back."

There's no preamble, no formalities or introductions and the tension in the air seems to be purely out of worry for the missing DeSantis child.

"There's a plan, right?" Nessa chimes in, her brow furrowed. "Because I just had to listen to some traumatising shit for the last three hours, the last thing I need is you throwing a half-baked plan at us and expecting us to go along with it unchecked."

Thomas looks like he might murder her, but she's unfazed. On the contrary, Renato seems almost impressed, and I fight to hide my laugh under a fake cough. Clearly, I'm unsuccessful because Oisín pins me with a warning look that I'm inclined to take as a dare.

"It was just payback for me guarding the doors of the Church while you confessed your sins between your wife's thighs," I tell her with a kind smile, making my expression as placid and innocent as possible.

Nessa looks ready to lunge for me, but before she can so much as move, Thomas is between us, fire in his eyes as he lands a heavy hand on both of our shoulders. I smile at him, fluttering my lashes and leaning into the innocent demeanour I'm sure I'm pulling off.

"Get in the fucking car," he hisses at us, and for a brief second I feel bad for adding more stress to his already overflowing plate.

The guilt fades almost as fast as it came, though. He didn't want me here to begin with. If I'm going to catch shit for simply existing in his presence at this point, then I may as well have some fun with it. Nessa huffs, but obeys, sliding into the last of the cars with Gráinne and Aoife. Thomas ignores the rest of us for Renato, following him and Serafina into the Ferrari at the front of the line.

The configuration leaves Anji, Oisín and me in the second car. Anji has already taken the front seat, and as I slide into the back, I see the earphones he has in, clearly set on drowning us out.

"So," I say, keeping my voice low for the driver's sake as the engine purrs to life. "Your wife is hot."

"Sebby, I swear to *God-"*

"Don't bother," I tell Oisín, waving my hand through the air dismissively. "He believes in me even less than I believe in him."

Oisín rolls his eyes at that, but I stare at him, committing the tilt of his lips to memory.

He hasn't kissed me in months.

I press my hand to my mouth, as though I can feel Serafina's lips lingering on mine.

"Oisín-"

"Don't, Sebby."

His voice is hoarse and thick, and he won't look at me. I reach across the empty centre seat, beyond caring if the driver or Anji sees. It's too late for pretending, and I never wanted to in the first place.

"Oisín," I say again, his name as close to prayer as I've come in five years. I suppose he and God are similar. They've both forsaken me. I crave their light as much as I shy away from it. I want them both to save me, as much as I want to be condemned.

"Please, Sebastian."

But his fingers don't jerk away from mine as I wind them together. I give him the peace of silence, but I keep his hand in mine the entire way to the DeSantis estate.

He doesn't pull away.

29

Serafina

It's odd to have half of the Cavanaugh clan in my family home. Thomas and my father are already discussing wine and whiskey while Anji, Aoife and Nessa are waiting around the large circular table taking up much of the meeting room. I know that it's only a matter of minutes before our underbosses and capos take their places around the table, too.

Gráinne waits to the side, eyes narrowed like she's scoping out every inch of the space while Sebastian lounges next to me, silent but difficult as fuck to ignore. My husband waits beside his father, face drawn and eyes dark.

Worst of all, my sister is nowhere to be fucking seen.

I feel her absence like an ache as the rest of my father's closest and most trusted members file in and take up space at the huge table.

Sebastian nudges me with his shoulder and I jolt, realising everyone is waiting for us to sit. I slide into the empty seat at Oisín's shoulder, Sebastian taking the one on my other side. Thomas waits a few more heartbeats before taking his, and my father stays standing.

The air is tense, but I doubt it's because of the families mixing.

"My daughter, Francesca Guilia DeSantis, is missing."

I forget how to breathe. The information isn't new, but it cuts me just as deep as the first time I heard it.

My sister. My best fucking friend. She should be here, sitting at this table, infecting the space with her smile and permanent bouncy energy.

I don't realise I have the edge of the table in a death grip until Sebastian pries my hand away and threads his fingers with mine instead. He squeezes once, and when I tear my eyes away from my father to frown at him, he squeezes again, harder.

Taking the hint, I tighten my hold on him, hiding my weakness from the others. Oisín's eyes flick to mine, and then his hand is on my leg, thumb stroking soothing lines up and down my jean clad thigh. I don't think about what this means, or how both of them seem content to lay their claim on me beneath this table. How things have changed so fucking much in the span of a single flight.

My father is still talking, explaining how Frankie's disappearance was discovered. And though I'm certain I'm crushing Sebastian's hand, he lets me, his face impassive as he focuses on my father and Thomas.

Between them, they ground me, and I have time to process the spiral that this meeting is sending me into.

I let myself take comfort in them as Papà continues, not allowing myself to question why I feel comfortable doing so.

"We've searched every fucking corner of this town, and found nothing," he says, and I know the admission weighs heavily on him when his shoulders tense. "Her phone was taken, and not a single hacker has been able to find it. Her room is undisturbed and there are no security breaches."

She's just…vanished.

"Francesca is a DeSantis," Papà says, voice gruff as it carries through the group. "She is as well trained as any of you. We spare no lives to get her back, *capisce?*"

"Have we considered that she just…ran away?"

It annoys me that I can't remember Gabriele's last name because I'm picturing his tombstone before he's finished his ridiculous fucking sentence.

"Shut your fucking mouth before I cut your traitorous little tongue out, *testa di cazzo*."

The only thing that stops me from leaping over the table at Gabriele for his mere suggestion is that Oisín's hand tightens on my thigh, holding me to my chair. On the contrary, Sebastian's grip on my hand loosens, as if he's preparing to help me fight the bastard.

I glare at Gabriele until he looks away, cowed. I let Oisín keep me seated, and Sebastian's thumb strokes over my pulse point. My heart jumps, betraying me.

"Are we to assume this is connected to the trafficking ring?" Oisín steers the conversation smoothly, though the question seems genuine.

My father's lips thin. "It would be…unwise to discount the chance. The Russos are steadfastly denying any and all involvement, even under…pressure."

My jaw ticks. If it's not them, then who the fuck is it? We don't have a single lead.

The questions keep coming, but I stop listening. My head is buzzing with *what ifs*. What if we never find her? What if we do, and we're too late? What if -

"Look, all I'm saying is, the princess might just have a sense of adventure," that bastard Gabriele whispers under his breath to Aldo. The second man raises a brow in what seems to be agreement and even Oisín can't hold me back.

I throw myself over the centre of the table, knocking a whiskey tumbler and sending glass shattering as it smashes against the floorboards. Gabriele wheels backwards on his chair, tipping back completely in an effort to evade me but the penknife in my hand is already at his throat.

I kneel over the man, his legs splayed and arms wide, sprawled on the floor, still half on his chair. A bead of dark red blood wells on the sharp edge of my knife.

Nobody moves to defend him.

"Say it again, Gabriele," I hiss. *"Io ti sfido."*

Gabriele's dark eyes are wide, the whites showing, his neck straining as he struggles to get away. I don't know why he bothers. If he hurts me, he'll die in a far worse way than with my blade in his throat.

"Apologise. To both of my daughters," Papà demands. Aside from Aldo's intake of breath, the air in the room is still, nobody daring to disrupt it.

Good.

Gabriele's swallow makes his Adam's apple bob, only serving to draw more blood. Satisfaction runs through me as I watch it drip down the side of his neck and stain the white collar of his shirt.

"Mi dispiace," the man beneath me croaks out. *"Ti chiedo tanto perdono."*

His apology is shit. He's shaking and I can practically smell his fear. He should know better.

"My sister would never *run away*," I spit down at him. "Her commitment is here, with her family, like yours should be. She is faithful, something you could do to learn."

Gabriele nods, the gesture sinking my knife in further.

"I take it back," he wheezes. The tightness of his voice sends calm through me.

"You're dismissed, Gabriele," Papà says, and I know well enough that's my sign to let him go.

I stand smoothly, wiping the blood off my knife on his white shirt before folding it back up and slipping it into my pocket. Nessa and Sebastian whistle their approval from behind me but I pay them no mind as I head back to my chair.

The wound in Gabriele's neck gapes a little as he stumbles to his feet, though it's nowhere near deep enough to injure him gravely. Blood spills through his fingers as he presses his hand to it, mumbling another apology before he leaves the meeting room.

I hope the fucker needs stitches.

30

Serafina

"Let me go and check her rooms." I turn from watching the door to look Papá in the eye. His eyes are hard but his stance is relaxed, even as he reaches for his wine and takes a long drink.

"We have searched every inch of this house," he reminds me.

"But I have not," I snap back. I force myself to take slow breaths, to calm the bloodlust still running through my veins. I want to punish someone for this, and Gabriele is the best punching bag I've found so far.

"I know Frankie better than anyone else in this world," I explain once I can speak without rage clouding my words. "If anything has been missed, I will find it."

I can see my father relenting even before he inclines his head.

"Go," he concedes, finally taking his own seat. "I'll finish updating everyone else on the cockroaches."

"*Grazie, Papà,*" I murmur, barely sparing a look back at the others before I'm out of the room.

The meeting room is on the bottom floor, along with the kitchen and living spaces. Only my father, my sister and I live here permanently, the other members put up in the group of houses we own on the main street of San Jarno. Growing up, I became accustomed to having visitors in our space, but our bedrooms were always off limits.

I take the stairs two at a time. The walls are white and the ceiling is tall. A large, ornate sky light fills the hallway with natural light. The wooden floors groan slightly under my footsteps, and I'm too caught up in my own determination to bother dodging the age-old creaks.

Frankie's room smells like vanilla.

The lingering scent of her favourite perfume makes my eyes water as I inhale deeply, as though I can keep what remains of her in my own lungs. The bed, with its pale pink duvet and stack of pillows, is still unmade and messy, as though just this morning she climbed out and wandered downstairs for her coffee.

My throat is tight. I'm still in the doorway, frozen and wide eyed. I force myself further in, kicking off my boots to feel the fuzzy cream carpet beneath my feet. Her desk is a mess as usual, stationary and books splayed open halfway, notes in the margins. I peer closer, squinting to make out her handwriting. But all I can decipher are the words *just fuck already* and *hot* scribbled under a scene where two characters are in the middle of a fight.

I huff a laugh, reading the annotations in my sister's voice, picturing her frowning at the characters, yelling when they made the wrong decision. How many times has she barged into my room just to rant about fictional people that I knew absolutely fuck all about? I'd listened every time, even when none of it made sense.

I'd give fucking anything for her to come back and do just that.

I shove my nostalgia away, ignoring the sick feeling in my stomach, and start picking apart her room.

The desk yields nothing except for the crumpled receipts Frankie hadn't bothered to dump - mainly for books and snacks. Her closet, her bathroom, her drawers are all as they've always been. It's messy, but that's not unusual. No matter how much I analyse every single item she owns, I can't find anything to suggest anyone but Frankie has been here.

I'm shaking with frustration by the time I collapse onto her desk chair.

"Come *on*, Frankie, help me find you," I beg the empty air. "You don't get to just fucking *leave me!*"

I stand too fast, sending the chair screeching to the left, and something rattles. I pause, breathing hard, and narrowing my eyes at the leg of the chair.

It's hit something under the desk, and when I kneel down, I find a small, simply decorated jewellery box. I recognise it immediately. We were given matching ones as gifts from Papà when we were children. I stare at the box, cradling it in my hands, stroking my thumb over the exterior.

He gave us these the year our mother died, with a piece of her jewellery inside each one. I got a sapphire necklace, Frankie got a diamond bracelet. The memory rises fast, and I cough to clear my throat and dislodge the uncomfortable urge to cry. The box's pale pink paint is chipped in the corners but the little dancing fairy on the lid is still perfect.

I open it before I can lose myself in the past. There's no point - I can't go back even if I wanted to.

Our mother's bracelet isn't there, but Frankie wears it religiously so that doesn't surprise me. There's a few other small, gold pieces - earrings, a couple of rings. They're all that delicate, feminine style that screams Francesca. I twist the ring on my left hand as I set the box down, the ruby digging into the pad of my finger.

I consider stealing one of her rings to add to the stack, and get so far as reaching in to grab one, only to knock the entire damn thing off the edge of the desk.

I swear, barely managing to grasp the edge of the box before it hits the ground. The jewellery spills out, skittering across the floor, but the box is mercifully in one piece.

I set it back on the desk and drop to my knees, grabbing at every piece I can find. My hand meets a silver anklet and I hold it up to the light.

I've never seen it before, and it matches none of the other jewellery my sister would normally wear. The silver chain is thick and simple, with a little butterfly charm hanging off it. I frown at the thing, holding it closer to my face.

Why the hell would she have this?

Shoving it into my pocket, I work quickly to collect the rest of the jewellery laying haphazardly on the floor. Once everything's been put back in its place, and the box is neatly stored beneath her desk once more, I settle on the edge of her bed.

I pull the silver chain from my pocket and stare at it. It's not even remotely like any of her other pieces of jewellery, and I can't see anybody that knows her buying this for her either. Sure, she likes traditionally feminine things, and as beautiful and dainty as the little butterfly charm is, anyone that knows Frankie would know that she hates butterflies.

She's terrified of them.

I close my eyes as I twirl it around loosely on my fingers. This has to mean something, but what?

My thumb grazes the underside of the charm and I pause my movement as my nail catches on an etching.

Lifting the charm so that it's at eye level, I rove my eyes across it with laser focus until I find what I'm looking for. There, on the bottom right of the butterfly wing, scratched and worn, sits the brand name.

I quickly pull out my phone and search the brand and *near me*.

Only one location that sells the brand pops up, and it's just twenty minutes away.

I slip the anklet and my phone back into my pocket.

There's no fucking way whoever owns that store isn't connected to Frankie some how, and I'll be damned if I just sit here and wait while the others twiddle their fucking thumbs.

I leave Frankie's room, not having the heart to look back as I do and race for the garage. Ripping keys off the hook, I press the lock button and wait to see which car lights flash. The second I know which one I have the key for, I dive into the driver's side and pull out of my family home.

One way or another, I'm getting my fucking sister back.

31

Oisín

For what feels like the hundredth time, I check my watch and wonder where the hell my wife is. When I first came to live with the DeSantis family, I made sure to scope out every inch of their home. I couldn't let myself settle into an unfamiliar place without knowing the strengths and weaknesses of my supposed safe haven.

I spent hours walking the grounds and inspecting the infrastructure. Because of that, I know the layout of the DeSantis' mansion like the back of my hand, and I know for damn sure that Francesca's room isn't big enough to require a fucking hour long search. The fact that it's even taken this long for Renato and Thomas to move through this debrief is enough to drive me crazy.

Gritting my teeth, I do my best not to let my frustration show.

I don't know why we're still here talking about Francesca instead of out looking for her.

It's obvious to me that the Russos have something to do with her disappearance, no matter how much they deny it. Even if they're not the ones who took her, they know *something* about her whereabouts. Someone has to.

My leg bounces beneath the table.

I have to find my wife. I have to talk to her.

We need to figure out how the hell we're going to get her sister back, and then, we need to talk about what the fuck happened on the plane.

Hell, I haven't even gotten a chance to properly apologise to her for any of it.

Guilt sours my stomach once more as I think about how she must have felt when she walked into the bathroom and found Sebastian and I like that. The guilt only worsens when I remember that Sebastian's hurt at the idea of me rejecting him in front of her.

Fuck, I've been such a coward.

I hate myself for not having the strength to give up Sebastian, and I hate myself even more for not having the strength to admit what I truly want before now.

I've played with both of their emotions. I'm not convinced that I deserve either of them. Not when I haven't even given them the chance to know each other, or consider what could be.

I'm selfish and I can't bring myself to stop. I can't let either of them go.

Though… given everything that happened on the plane, I'm beginning to question if either of them even want me to choose. And if Sebastian is more interested in Serafina than he first appeared to be.

My pulse quickens as I remember him sucking the taste of her from his fingers. Her soft moans mixing with our harsh grunts. Sebastian's desire to please both of us, like we were finally giving him the breath of air he'd been begging for. I subtly try to readjust myself in my seat.

Now isn't the Goddamn time to be thinking about how pretty they were together, or how perfect Sebby was with Seffy as he listened to her every command.

My leg bounces faster, my whole body shaking.

Normally, I'd never show this kind of weakness. To show your emotions to the people around you, especially those who could turn on you in a heartbeat, is to mark yourself as a target. I won't give any of the people that work for Renato the chance to turn on me, not when my marriage to Serafina is still so fresh.

My eyes track to Sebastian as he settles further into Serafina's chair.

As soon as she left the room, he repositioned himself so that he was seated beside me. I'd wanted to snap at him, to wrap my hand around his throat and tell him to behave, to punish him for acting like he could replace my wife so easily and so publicly.

I wanted to kiss him, and beg for his forgiveness when he rested his hand on my thigh, softly squeezing the muscle to settle my anger as Serafina stormed out of the room.

I'm in my own personal hell now as the minutes drag by, with Sebastian's hand inches from my dick, and Renato discussing all the ways Serafina and Francesca have been trained to prevent shit like this from happening.

I take a steadying breath through my nose, and shift to remove Sebastian's hand from my leg.

As much as I burn to have his hands all over me, and see them all over Serafina again, I can't afford to let myself feel that kind of hope.

I can't allow myself to want that, at least not before speaking with my wife.

Renato notices that my attention has shifted from the discussion at hand and he throws a quizzical look my way.

"I'd like to go check on Serafina," I state as I stand from my chair.

"Very well," both Renato and my father say in the same bored tone, and I can't stop the chuckle that leaves my lips.

I step away from the table immediately, and it isn't long before I hear the tell-tale sound of a chair being pushed backwards.

I know it's Sebastian before I even turn around. He reaches my side as I walk out the door.

Francesca's room is next to Serafina's, which I learned the hard way considering Francesca took it upon herself to walk in without knocking one too many times during the days after our marriage. Regardless, with what limited time I've spent with her, I like Francesca. She's bubbly and bright and easy to befriend, though obviously protective of her family. It was endearing when she threatened to castrate me if I broke her sister's heart, fake marriage or not.

Shit, I've given her reason to do just that.

Sebastian's steps are nearly silent behind me as we stalk up the stairs to the women's rooms. Francesca's door is still open, and I clear my throat before I call out for Seffy, not wanting to interrupt her if she's busy.

"Seffy?" I wait a few seconds, counting my heartbeats. She doesn't answer. "Angel? We just want to check if you're okay…I know you might not want to talk to me, but I…"

"Oisín," Sebastian interrupts, and I realise he's already gone ahead, stepping through the open door with no hesitation.

I sigh. Sebastian runs headlong into danger with no regard for his own safety, so waltzing into a stranger's room is hardly out of his usual style.

"It's empty."

"What?" I snap, moving to stand in the doorway with him. Our shoulders brush, and awareness sparks through me.

"She's not here," Sebastian says with a whispered breath, turning to me.

"What the fuck do you mean she's not here?" I shove past him, tearing into Francesca's room. It's empty. The attached bathroom is empty, too. "Fuck!"

Together, we step out, searching Serafina's room but finding it just as barren.

She's not fucking here.

Sebastian's ahead of me as we sprint back down the stairs, his long legs carrying him towards the meeting room. Panic pushes me on, fear curling around my throat, restricting each breath.

"She's gone!" I shout as we reach the meeting room, startling everyone still trapped in the debrief.

I watch both my father and Serafina's still.

"Excuse me?" Renato asks, his dark eyes narrowing on me.

"Serafina isn't fuckin' there," Sebastian repeats for me, gesturing out the door way. "The room's bloody empty."

Renato pushes back from his seat immediately, the screech of wood on wood making me wince.

"Search the house," he demands, and as one everyone rises, splitting off effortlessly. Even our people, unfamiliar in this territory, narrow their focus, following the DeSantis as they split off to search.

"You have footage?" Da asks, running his hand along his

stubble.

"*Certo*," Renato answers, already moving. "Come," he tells Sebastian and I as he and my da leave the table. "I am not losing another daughter."

Sebastian and I fall in line easily, following Renato through the house. I can barely focus on where I'm walking, my ears ringing. Sebby's hand brushes mine, and if I didn't know him better, I would assume it was an accident. But I know what he's trying to say.

He's here.

It will be okay.

And fuck if I don't believe him.

The security set up is in Renato's office - a wide, bright space with huge windows lining the outside wall. I know fine well that the glass is one way, Renato would never put the security of his family at risk for the sake of a little sunlight.

Despite the fact that Renato has declared me family, I hold back. Thomas takes a seat, but Sebastian and I stand at his back, waiting as Renato loads up the security feed.

Every fucking second feels like an hour as we wait, the click of the keyboard as loud as my own heartbeat.

"*Cazzo!*" Renato's voice jolts me, and the man is out of his seat in seconds, spinning the screen round so we can witness what he has.

Serafina, throwing herself into the driver's seat of a sleek blue car

and tearing out of the garage.

"Where the fuck has she gone?" Da mutters, face creasing as he

scowls at my wife on screen.

My heart is in my fucking stomach as I realise she could be

anywhere. Anywhere, because I didn't check on her sooner.

Fuck.

Fuck!

"Trackers?" Da asks, but I barely hear him through my own panic.

I'm already moving out the office door, standing in the hallway.

"ANJI!" I shout, loud enough I'm sure the entire house can hear

me. Good. Anji can track or hack fucking anything, and I need him.

"ANJI!"

Footsteps thunder up the stairs as I shout his name over and over.

Eyes wide and with a panicked Nessa in tow, Anji rushes towards me.

"What the fuck, Oisín?" he says, words coming out as fast as he

was running.

"Track the car," is all that I can get out. "Track her fucking car."

Nessa groans and runs her hands down her face, but Anji just

nods, already pushing past me to get to Renato's office.

"What the fuck is going on, *deartháir?"* she hisses, resting her hand against the door frame as she catches her breath.

"She's fucking gone, Nessa," I answer, feeling my worry bleed into my voice.

Her eyes soften, and the pity there is more than I can handle.

The car is parked on a street twenty minutes away. The second we have her location, Sebastian and I are out the door. The garage is the size of a fucking house, with rows of luxury cars lining the lot and in any other circumstance, I'm sure Sebby would be drooling over them. Instead, he snatches a key from the wall, where at least a dozen hang, and is revving the damn engine before I've even managed to sit.

The Lexus takes off so fast I'm flattened against the back of the passenger seat. One glance out the side of my eye confirms that Sebastian is in his fucking element, eyes narrowed and lips curved up in a devastating smirk.

"Twenty minutes, Anji said?" he asks, glancing away from the road to meet my eyes.

I nod once.

"I'll get us there in ten."

32

Sebastian

We get there in nine minutes. I'm sure I've broken at least six traffic laws, but given that Renato DeSantis runs this fucking town, I doubt I'll get a ticket.

Oisín is out of the car before I've even parked. I abandon the Lexus somewhere vaguely near the side of the street and join him, catching up just before he gets to the door of the small jewellers shop.

It's set on the side of a small side street, the light stone buildings boasting a collection of houses and shops. I give it a cursory glance, but the street's nearly empty, only an elderly couple walking away from us at the top, hands linked together.

My own hands itch to ruin the quiet calm of the street. I want to paint the pretty pale stone red with the blood of whoever the fuck was worth Serafina running out without any backup.

Tyres squeal along the road as Oisín and I slam through the front door of the little shop, but nothing could distract us from finding her.

Serafina fucking DeSantis is screaming at some poor man.

I've never been more turned on.

The man, who I can only assume is the owner of the shop, is wide eyed behind his desk. The mafia princess has her hands braced on the counter as she leans forward so every word out her mouth hits him like a slap.

The shop is small enough that her voice fills the whole space, though she's yelling in Italian and all I catch are the curse words: *cazzo, vaffanculo, testa di minchia, pezzo di merda.*

Her anger ramps my desire higher, and I have to adjust myself. Oisín rolls his eyes at me, but I swear I see his pulse hitch. He can't fucking hide how much he wants her, either.

"Sirs, please," the man says in pleading English as he meets our eyes over Serafina's shoulder. "I do not know what she wants of me. I do not have what she asks for."

I'm content to listen to her rip him a new one regardless of what he claims to not know, but the door opens behind us and Nessa, Renato and Thomas rush in.

If one pissed off gang member wasn't enough to make the man piss himself, six is. He's quivering, brown hair sticking to his forehead with sweat, suntanned skin paling.

I'm by Serafina's side before any of the others can interfere, grabbing the piece of jewellery from the counter and frowning at it.

"Did you make this?" I ask the man, rubbing the butterfly charm between my thumb and forefinger and finding the brand mark etched onto the back.

"Si." His voice shakes on the word.

"It's Frankie's," Serafina sighs, pushing away from the counter. "But she'd never have bought it. She wears gold, not clunky silver."

"Ah," I nod, chucking the piece back down so hard it *clanks* against the white marble style counter. "I see. So, here's the thing, lad. You tell her everything you fuckin' know about whoever purchased this, show us every record you keep, or that lovely lady -" I point to Nessa, whose smile does fuck all to make her seem less terrifying "- tortures it out of ya."

The man frowns, undoubtedly trying to pick apart my accent, and then shakes his head frantically.

"Ho già detto prima che non so niente!"

"Bugardio," Renato says lowly from behind us, and even my skin prickles at the obvious threat in his tone. "Nessa."

She straightens, raising her brow in expectation.

"Make him talk."

The man holds up as well as wet cardboard.

Nessa barely even needed to draw blood. She perched on the counter in front of him, twirling her blade between her fingers in one hand, and tapping her short fingernails on the countertop with the other as though to mark each second. He'd freely given her his name, Antonio, but refused to cough up the sales records until Nessa had proven her knife skills weren't a bluff.

With shaking hands and a thin trail of blood running down his cheek, good old Antonio produced his record book.

I'm almost embarrassed for him.

"Even more spineless than I predicted," Oisín mutters by my side, sneering at Antonio as he quivers. Serafina has only stepped to the side to let Nessa at him, watching her with a hint of respect shining in her eyes.

"It's here," Antonio insists, opening the heavy red folder. "All purchase transactions."

"Find the one for the anklet before I get bored," Nessa drones, pressing the sharp point of the knife into the pad of her index finger. A bead of blood wells, and Antonio blanches as she lifts it to her lip and licks it off.

I can only smirk.

"She uhh..." He trips over his words as he fumbles through the thick folder of transactions, receipts and files. "She was uh, tall and blonde. Had a rose tattoo. I only have a first name."

"Shocking how good your memory becomes under the threat of being flayed, isn't it?" I hum, tapping my foot on the floor. Oisín and Serafina are both stiff and stoic, but I'm just getting bored. I'm not even allowed to murder the guy.

"Here, here," Antonio says quickly, pointing to a particular page.

Nessa snatches it from his grip, eyes narrowing as she skims the document.

"Alyssa."

"Who the *fuck* is Alyssa?" Serafina snaps immediately, throwing her arms up.

"That's...that's all I have, I swear," Antonio pleads, glancing over his shoulder.

Beside me, Oisín shifts, and when I glance his way, his brows are furrowed.

"Do you recognise the description?" Nessa asks Serafina, showing her the book. "Blonde, tall, rose tattoo?"

Serafina shakes her head, jaw ticking and hands white on the edge of the counter.

"Any of ye?" Ness checks, answered with a resounding

round of *no*'s.

"It's a fucking dead end," Serafina nearly growls, shoving back off the counter and spinning, making to storm straight out the door.

Oisín catches her with a hand on her arm, and she glares at him.

"Wait," he murmurs. "He's hiding something."

33

Oisín

This fucker is lying to us. Again.

Three times in as many minutes, Antonio has glanced over his shoulder, wide, panicked eyes landing on the door marked *employees only*. Only for a second each time, quick enough that I'm sure he thinks he's being discreet.

Asshole.

Next to me, Sebastian goes unnaturally still. I spare him a glance to find his eyes bright and his mouth twisted in a feral grin. I've done enough work for Da with Sebastian to know he doesn't get angry, per se. He becomes fucking unhinged.

I welcome every second of it.

"'Fess up, Tony," Sebby says casually, taking a step forward. Serafina doesn't even flinch as he wraps his arms around her waist affectionately. "Or don't. Up to you. But seeing me all bloody turns him on, so you keep chatting or you can be my wingman."

I don't bother to check if Renato or my da reacts to his comment, instead I keep my focus trained on the man dripping blood all over the shop floor.

"Ti ho detto tutto quello che so," Antonio frantically insists.

"All I know in Italian is *vous le vous cochez avec moi?"* Sebastian muses, and Serafina fucking *laughs*.

"That's French, *idiota*," she scoffs at him, but her voice is brighter than it was a minute ago. Shit, I could kiss Sebby for taking some of her pain away with his nonsense, even just for a second.

"My point stands," Sebastian whispers to her. My wife's lips quirk up at one side. She's trying not to smile. And failing.

"Renato," I say, turning my head to meet my father in law's eyes and to avoid the reaction that seeing Sebastian and Serafina together is giving my body. "The door."

Renato frowns, eyes sweeping over the small shop before focusing on the closed door behind Antonio. He nods once, sharply, then mutters something to Thomas. Da tilts his chin in recognition, then slips outside.

I can only assume he's guarding the entrance, and anticipation quickens my pulse.

"Apri la porta," Renato instructs, thankfully appearing unbothered by the way Sebastian has wrapped himself around Serafina. We don't have time to answer the questions he's probably got brimming inside of his head right now. Fuck, I'm not even sure I *have* answers.

Nessa hops down from her perch only to shove past Antonio and push at the door.

"Locked," she says simply, turning back to the jeweller. "You heard the *big scary mob boss*," she teases, but her voice is dark. "Open. The. Door."

"No," he pleads, his voice shaky.

Sebastian sighs dramatically, releasing my wife only to tut

and take Nessa's place on top of the counter.

"Nessy, my dear," he says to her, eyeing Antonio. Sebastian's eyes are wide and I can practically see the excitement rippling off him. "How long can a man survive with no hands?"

"Took the last guy less than ten minutes to bleed out," she muses, twirling her knife again. Antonio is trapped between the two now, and Serafina is watching them with her head cocked to the side. "But I suppose we can't draw any conclusions without collecting more data."

"Antonio, care to help us out? Yano, for science," Sebastian asks, with a wide grin on his face as he flounces his hand in the air.

It's clear Antonio isn't following their fast paced, thick accented conversation, but the intention is there.

To prove his point, Sebastian holds up his hand and mimes cutting his fingers off with the other. Antonio gulps.

Shaking, Antonio reaches into a drawer under the counter, the rattling of metal filling the tense silence. There's something in the back, I fucking know it. No innocent man stares back at a locked door that much unless he's hiding something.

Sebastian snatches the ring of keys from Antonio's hand before he can even hold it up fully. He holds them out to Serafina like a gift, dramatically presenting them in the palm of his hand as he fucking *courtseys*. My wife rolls her eyes but takes them all the same, and I can't stop the grin that lifts my lips as I see Sebastian bat his eyelashes at her back.

"You can stay with me," Nessa glowers at Antonio, moving so fast he can't even try to run. She has him pinned to the wall, lined with glass jewellery cases, by the throat. He cries out weakly, and she tightens her hold.

Serafina shoves past them on the way to the door, the keys

jangling as she finds the right one. The second the door swings open, Sebastian pushes in front of her, earning him a death stare.

"If there's something in there," he says quietly to her as I join them behind the counter, "I'd rather they hit me than you."

We're quickly running out of space, with Nessa and Antonio in the corner and the three of us at the door.

Serafina softens slightly, but *tsks* at Sebastian as she reaches into the waistband at her hip and pulls out a gun.

"It's sweet that you think you could protect me better than I can protect myself," she coos at him. "But I wasn't raised to rely on men, and I won't start now."

She clicks the safety off the gun as though to punctuate her point and shoulders past a stunned and obviously turned on Sebastian. I glance back over my shoulder before we follow her, finding pride gleaming in Renato's eyes.

"Fuck me, I still don't get to stab anyone," Sebastian moans, and I try to hide my laugh as I turn to follow them both to the back room.

It's clearly a break room, furnished with a microwave, a small table with two chairs, and a mini fridge. All of that is shoved into the right corner, though, because most of the space is taken up by a fucking vault.

It's set against the back wall, easily as tall as Sebastian, with an electronic keypad in the centre of the door.

"I'm going to take a wild guess that it's not just pretty diamonds in this thing," Sebby says, rhythmically tapping the metal door.

Serafina clicks the safety back on before sheathing her gun again. Sebastian's gaze lingers on it at her hip, his tongue darting out to wet his lip.

"For fuck's sake," Serafina groans, kicking the door. "We need the code."

"Can I at least be the one to torture the fucker?" Sebastian asks, tone pleading.

"There'll be nothing left to torture if you lay a hand on him," I tell him, trying not to laugh as he pouts in response.

Sebastian doesn't do shit by halves, and as much as I'd like Antonio dead, I'd like answers more.

"What's the code, Ness?" Sebastian shouts instead as Serafina continues to aim his death stare at the vault.

"This has to be connected to Frankie," she murmurs, looking up at me. "It has to, right?"

"We'll find her, angel," I promise, Antonio's screech cutting off my words.

"I can tell you no more!" he screams, voice cracking. "I have given too much."

"You'll tell us *everything*," Renato demands.

Sebastian and Serafina abandon the vault to watch the scene playing out on the shop floor, and I brace myself against the doorway to see Nessa drag the man away from the wall by his neck to present him to Renato.

"You will, or we will cut the answers out of you," Nessa hisses.

"I will not speak," he chokes out as my sister's fingers flex. "No more. No more."

"You-"

"*Uccidimi,*" he cries, tears rolling down his cheeks. The four of us still as he begs. "They will do much worse to me."

"Who?" Nessa asks, her face close to his.

"I cannot," he repeats, shaking his head wildly.

"Who are you more afraid of than the fuckin' *DeSantis mafia?*" Sebastian asks, disbelief in his voice.

"Fuck whoever *they* are," Serafina snaps. "Just give us the Goddamn code!"

This whole thing is going to shit. We can't fucking afford to break apart right now, not when the answers are so close. I disappear into the back room long enough to grab one of the chairs, and drag it round the side of the counter. The legs squeal on the tile, and Serafina scrunches up her nose at the noise.

"Nessa," I say, keeping my voice even as I set the chair down in the centre of the floor. "Tie him down. *Deirfiúr*, make him squeal."

Nessa grins widely, though we both look to Renato for confirmation. After all, this is his territory, and if this fucker dies at our hand, he's the one who'll have to cover it up.

"Do whatever you must to find my daughter," he says simply, then steps back, apparently happy to let us do what we do best.

I do wonder, briefly, if this is a test. To see how valuable we are, what strengths we bring to the alliance. It doesn't matter if it is, because Nessa and Sebastian are no stranger to blood.

They both revel in it.

Sebastian eagerly begins to rummage about in the drawers, pulling out a spool of twine.

"Want my gun?" Serafina offers, sitting the weapon on the counter and Sebastian grins at her.

"There are *many* things I want to use your gun for," he tells her. "But torture is much more fun with a dull blade."

I swear her eyes light up, but I only frown at his insinuation. What the *fuck* does he want to use my wife's gun for?

I leave Nessa and Sebastian to it, ignoring Antonio's struggle as Sebastian binds him to the chair. Serafina stands by the counter, and I go to her only to lift her up onto its surface.

"Better view, angel," I murmur, kissing her cheek soft enough to feel her shudder.

Antonio starts to shriek as I pull out every drawer, determined to check every inch of this damn place. For all I know, this fucker is stupid enough to leave the key code written in his book.

"Hey, can I borrow your tie?" Sebastian's question is barely audible over Antonio sobbing. I snort, stopping my search to watch Renato raise a brow at a grinning Sebastian. "Uh...*per favore?*"

Unbelievably, Renato undoes his black tie and holds it out to Sebastian. Curiosity is clear in his dark gaze, and I think, for half a second, that he's intrigued by Sebastian's enjoyment. Sebby nods his thanks, then shoves the tie into Antonio's mouth, tying it around the back of his head in a gag.

The screams turn to muffled cries.

The record book and the rest of the junk in the drawers hold nothing of value. By the time I'm through with my useless search, Antonio has stained the floor red.

I lean against the counter in time to watch Nessa snatch the gag out his mouth and hiss,

"Ready to talk?"

Two long cuts mar his cheeks, his eyes are both blooming black and blue. He's missing both middle fingers, though strips of fabric have been tied around the remaining stumps to stop the blood loss.

"Non importa come lo fai, ma ti prego, uccidimi adesso,"

Antonio rushes, begging. I can't understand every word, but I catch enough.

Kill me.

When nobody answers, he begins to mumble something, low and fast under his breath.

Serafina slides off the counter, stalking towards him, hands flexing at her sides.

"This is useless," Nessa pants, shaking her head. "If he hasn't spoken by now, it's unlikely he will at all."

Renato nods in agreement. "Leave him to think about it," he drawls, adjusting the collar of his shirt.

"Want your tie back?" Sebastian asks, right as he reaches for the knife in Nessa's hand and buries it in Antonio's thigh.

Renato grimaces. "No. I think it's best if we search for the only other lead we have."

"Alyssa?" Nessa pipes up.

"Someone will know her," he says. "And someone will speak. I won't have our authority questioned."

"We'll finish here," Serafina tells her father, though she doesn't look away from the bloody, bruised Antonio. "Take Thomas and find her."

I can't tell whether she means Alyssa or her sister, but it doesn't matter.

"Be safe," Renato murmurs, ignoring the sobbing man to lean over and press a kiss to his daughter's hair.

He's no less terrifying for the act of love.

When the door closes behind him, all eyes return to Antonio. I lean in closer, trying to make out what the fuck he's chanting.

Serafina sneers down at him as it dawns on me.

He's *praying*.

"Dio non è qui," she says, and spits in his face.

34

Serafina

"Anji will get it open," Sebastian reassures me as Nessa slips out the front door. Oisín locks it behind her, then drags another chair out from the back to barricade it, trapping Antonio in the shop with us.

My father and Thomas have left to search for the woman Antonio mentioned, and Nessa's taken the bike she borrowed from the garage back to find Anji.

"He's literally the best in the fuckin' country," Oisín echoes Sebastian's faith in the man. I only nod, forcing myself to trust them.

Antonio has passed out, mid way through his prayer, my spit mingling with the blood on his face and streaming pink down the front of him. Fat, scarlet drops soak through the makeshift tourniquet bandages on his fingers, a small pool of the stuff collecting on the floor under each hand. Blood trickles down the leg of the chair from his thigh, and I can't help but appreciate the sight of it staining the tiles.

"He has to talk," I mutter as I stare at the unconscious mess of a man. "He fucking has to."

"Well he won't be talking 'till he wakes up," Sebastian pipes up, unhelpfully. His arms are bloody, but he doesn't seem to care. In contrast, he seems *giddy*.

Oisín must notice me frowning at him, because he huffs a laugh. "Sebastian's always taken great pleasure in getting his hands dirty," he says, trailing his eyes over the splatters of blood on the man's forearms.

"You would fucking know," I snark before I can stop myself. Now's not the damn time to be discussing any of this shit, but…what else are we supposed to do? We can't leave Antonio, and we've already searched the place for information.

I kick the unconscious man's chair, making his limp body shake, but he doesn't so much as stir. I try again, leaning down to slap his cheek, but the move only succeeds in spreading slick, warm blood over my palm.

I grimace, immediately wiping the stuff on my trousers. I'm no stranger to blood, but I don't want anything that belongs to this asshole anywhere near me.

Sebastian's eyes are bright as I look back up. My stomach flips as his gaze meets mine. His pupils are blown. He drags his teeth over his bottom lip, flicking his gaze down to where the blood has left a wet streak on my thigh.

"Do you want to talk about this right now?" Oisín asks. He's far too calm for my liking.

Sebastian talks immediately, before I can even think about the question.

"OR," he says loudly, holding up a finger like he's trying to tell Oisín off. "We can try having sex again and see if that helps the whole decision making process easier. Because I am team *don't abandon Sebastian again* and I'm more than willing to demonstrate my skills to persuade ye some more."

I blink at him. "You're suggesting you fuck me while we wait for the man you tortured to wake up from his pain induced nap?" I say slowly, my traitorous body waking up eagerly at the plan.

Not the time.

Not the fucking time.

"Absolutely," Sebastian says without hesitation.

"Sebby…" Oisín trails off, running a hand over his face.

"Oh get off your fake ass moral high horse," Sebastian groans, hands dropping to his side. "Don't spend any more time lyin' to your wife. You've fucked me, more than once, covered in the blood of whoever I'd killed. You've fucked me with the bodies just a room away. You've fucked my mouth while I'm panting with adrenaline from the fight and left me with blood and cum drying on my skin the whole drive home."

I'm not picturing it.

I'm not.

But my thighs squeeze together of their own accord and the tense combination of stress and anger has reached its boiling point, my body desperate to get rid of the sickening feelings.

"Sebastian, I swear to God I'll-"

"You'll do *what, Máistir*?" Sebastian taunts back, still staring at me. "Punish me? And admit you haven't turned off your fucking emotions? Admit that I can still get under your skin, that I'm always under your fucking skin. That I'm in your Goddamn heart and have been for years? Go on. Do it."

The silence that follows is permeated only by the steady, soft drip of blood and then my sharp inhale.

Oisín grabs Sebastian by the throat and shoves him back, walking him away from Antonio to the back room.

"Follow, angel," Oisín grinds out. "Come see what happens to disobedient little brats."

Sebastian is grinning, the hard outline of his cock pressing at his trousers, his eyes alight with excitement. He looks like he's won, like this is what he wanted, like my husband's hand around his throat is his personal heaven.

I follow without even questioning the demand, choosing not to analyse that. My own hand ghosts the skin of my neck, feeling my pulse skitter, wondering how Oisín's hand would fit.

I've had sex. Lots of it. Never like this, though.

Sebastian pants as Oisín pushes him down onto the table, legs spread so my husband can stand between them. His head is tilted back, and he's leaning into Oisín's grip, as though daring him to hold him harder.

"You just won't leave me alone," Oisín hisses, his face close to Sebastian's.

"You don't want me to," Sebastian counters.

"I can't fucking dig you out," Oisín groans. "Show Serafina how hard you get when I punish you, Sebby. Let her watch."

God, I'm so fucking hot my clothes feel like they're on fire. "What are you going to do to him?"

Oisín grins at me over his shoulder. "Use his disobedient little mouth until he can't remember how to speak."

I frown. "I think you're the one that needs to be punished, Oisín."

Sebastian laughs even as Oisín's hand tightens.

"Excuse me?" Oisín asks, shock rippling through him.

"Well, it seems to me that Sebastian should be...

worshipped," I whisper, though I may as well be shouting in the shocked silence. "You hurt him. Badly. Over and over again. Sebastian deserves an apology, husband, and you should be grovelling at our fucking feet."

Sebastian's eyes are wide now with something like panic.

"I'd really rather just be punished," he says with a wobbly laugh.

"Tough," I snap. I'm sick of this. Sick of seeing Sebastian hurt by my husband, by us. I want to hate him for having Oisín's heart, but how can I? He handed his own to my husband, only for Oisín to close his fist and burst it.

I don't want to fight Sebastian. I don't want to push him away, or deny him the love he so clearly craves. I want to give him a fucking chance.

Maybe I've lost my mind. I'm not sure that I care.

"Oisín…" Sebastian nearly whimpers as my husband drops his hand and takes a step back. Seb reaches for him, open palmed and desperate, fingers skimming Oisín's shirt.

My husband looks like I've slapped him.

"Oisín, please," Sebastian says again, face dropping. "You can punish me. I deserve it. Please, don't…don't stop touching me."

My entire body deflates at his words. This is my fault. I married Oisín without even considering the idea of someone left behind.

I'm tired of his hurt. I feel sick witnessing it.

Oisín's lips are parted, breaths shallow, and his skin is paler than usual. Instead of offering him comfort, I stride to him, grab his hand and drop to my knees in front of Sebastian, dragging my husband with me.

"Now isn't the time for talking," I murmur as I reach for

Sebastian, still perched on the edge of the table. His thighs are still spread, waiting for Oisín, and I run my hands up his legs, thumb sweeping across the bulge at his crotch. "But I've always found that actions speak louder than words."

Sebastian's dark brows draw together. His hair is messy and there's blood on his cheek from where he's wiped the back of his hand across his skin. That skull on his neck bobs as he swallows thickly.

It may be the first time since I've met him that he has nothing to say.

That's okay. What I want doesn't require words, anyway.

I snatch Oisín's hand and place our joined palms over Sebastian's cock. Sebastian inhales, his hands clutching the edge of the table.

"Can't you feel how needy he is, husband?" I murmur. "All for us."

"Fuck, it's always for you," Sebastian grinds out, staring down at us, long lashes framing his deep blue eyes.

"Seffy," Oisín whispers, hand shaking. "What..."

"Ssshh," I hush him. I can't answer. I don't know what this is, what I want, what we'll be. "Can I kiss the pain better, Seb?" I ask, glancing up at him and running my teeth over my bottom lip.

"Don't be gentle with him," Oisín says, and I tut.

How does he not fucking see it? The pain he's caused Sebastian, the pain that's still shattering his heart. He needs Oisín to fix this instead of barrel through and take control like he's so clearly done a million times before. He needs to be shown that he's cared for.

"Be gentler," I say back, keeping my voice soft.

I'm sure Sebastian would rather we just told him what to

do, if we just fucking used him, after all it's the only thing he's used to from my husband. But I can't fucking stop seeing the pain in his eyes, can't stop picturing his heart breaking in my hands.

He's not mine to care about. Yet.

But he is Oisín's, and I'll be damned if I play any part in shattering them more.

"Take his cock out for me," I instruct.

Oisín tenses, and for a moment I think he'll snap at me for talking back, but he doesn't. He unzips Sebastian's trousers and tugs. Sebastian scoots closer, lifting himself up just enough that Oisín can drag his clothes down to his ankles.

It dawns on me then that Sebastian has seen me naked, or at least nearly naked, twice and I've never seen his cock. It feels unfair, and suddenly I want to strip him completely and worship every inch of him.

I will, soon, I promise myself. Later, I'll memorise every single line of ink on his body.

Including...

"Holy fuck," I mutter, eyes widening as I realise what I'm seeing. His dick is *tattooed*. Not just tattooed, it's fucking pierced - a silver, curved barbell at the head of his cock. The length of him is tattooed in the same black ink as all his other art, an arrow shaft spanning well...his shaft.

My eyes widen as I imagine how much both of those things must have hurt, but *shit*, my underwear is soaked. Sebastian smirks at me, one brow raised as though taking in my every reaction.

"Like what you see, sweetheart?" he teases.

I answer him by leaning forward and tracing my tongue over the line of text tattooed between his hips, hovering just over his cock. I lap at each letter, ignoring the way his dick jumps at my touch.

"What does it mean?" I whisper as I pull away, hearing Oisín curse softly at my side before his hand darts out, thumb collecting the bead of fluid caught on the ball of Sebastian's piercing.

Sebastian shudders before answering, voice thick. "It says *tá, Máistir.*"

I don't miss the weighted look between him and my husband as he says the words. Oisín's tongue darts out to catch Sebastian's taste off his own skin.

"It means *yes, Master.*"

Oisín groans at the words on Sebastian's tongue.

"Fuck, *a rún mo chroí,*" Oisín whispers. Sebastian shudders, his usual sarcastic shell falling away under Oisín's watch.

I don't know what he just called him, but it's not the words that matter. His voice was reverent, far more godly than the dying man praying before he fell unconscious in the other room.

We need to talk. We will. But now…now I can at least give them this.

"He can still be your master," I say softly, despite my throat feeling like sandpaper. With the anger stripped away, I just feel raw. But it's not uncomfortable, and I've never been one to shy away from difficult things.

Sebastian's eyes snap to mine sharply. "Sef," he whispers. "Don't."

"Okay," I concede, allowing him the time he needs. He clearly doesn't trust me enough to believe me yet, but I'll make sure to fix that.

I turn to my husband to find a pained, desperate expression

on his face. Clearly, neither of them have the balls to do what needs to be done here.

But I do.

I lean forward, half pressed against Oisín, and take Sebastian's cock into my mouth.

The taste of him, salty and heady, floods my tongue and I groan. The piercing feels odd, and I flick my tongue over the ball at the head of his cock, earning myself a strangled moan which only serves to push my own desire higher.

I know if I run a hand over my jeans, I'll find the crotch and thighs damp and hot with my own need.

I press deeper, letting that piercing reach the back of my throat, drawing the flat of my tongue along the veins on the underside of his cock. Oisín says nothing.

I pull away, suddenly mad at my husband. The fucker is a damn coward, and it pisses me off. Because I know him, I do, despite this secret, despite how new our relationship still is.

"Tell me how he likes it," I say to him, voice thick with lust and frustration. I need Oisín to break. I need him to buck the fuck up and stop hiding. "Or, better yet, show me."

"Ah, fuck, please," Sebastian murmurs, hips thursting forward like he's still searching for the heat of my mouth. Or Oisín's.

My husband opens his mouth, not wide enough to suck a dick, but just to speak. I want to scream at him. Instead, I just cut him off.

"You're torturing us worse than that fucker in there," I snap, gesturing to the other room.

Logically, I can understand that what we're doing is fucked up. There's a half dead asshole just beyond that wall while I've got the taste of Sebastian on my tongue and yet not a single part of me feels bad for it.

I am not a good person.

I've never claimed to be, and I sure as fuck won't start now.

I reach for my husband, tangle my fingers in his dark brown hair and *tug*. His eyes flash with danger and I grin. *There he is.*

"You don't give the fucking orders here, angel," he snarls.

"I can't be your good girl unless you join in," I retort, unafraid of him. "And I certainly can't be good for Sebby unless you show me how he likes it. Look at him, husband. He's fucking *weeping* for us. He wants us. And you have the nerve to deny him. Again."

Sebastian gulps as he looks down at us. My spit and his precum wets the head of his cock, glistening in the flickering light. My mouth waters, needing another taste.

"Open your mouth," Oisín demands, and I drop my jaw happily. "Tongue out."

I'm sure my happiness is obvious on my face as I obey, vindication flooding me.

"Watch."

Fucking happily.

Oisín's fingers dig into Sebastian's thighs, warping the lines of the tattoos there, as he leans forward and blows a breath onto Sebastian's shaft. His cock jerks, and Sebby shakes a little.

"Máistir."

"Be good for once, Sebby, we've got a lot to teach our angel," he whispers, before taking Sebastian's entire length, until his nose brushes the very words Sebastian utters.

"Tá, Máistir."

I can't handle it any longer. I keep my mouth open and

tongue out obediently, even as I rise up on my knees just enough to undo the fastening on my jeans and shove my hand into my soaked underwear.

My eyes are glued to Oisín as I collect my own wetness with two fingers and drag it up to my clit. I'm so fucking sensitive that even that barest touch makes my eyelids flutter.

Oisín drags his teeth over Sebastian as he releases his dick, catching the piercing before he lets him go.

"Filthy fucking girl," Oisín groans as he looks at me. "Show him how wet you are."

I shiver as I hold up my fingers, shining with my desire. Sebastian groans, long and low. Fuck, I love the noises he makes.

How would that piercing feel inside me?

I suddenly need to know.

"No fucking. Not yet," Sebastian shakes his head. "I can't…I can't bear it, Sef."

My heart clenches. So does my cunt. "Let me taste you then," I beg. "Like Oisín showed me."

He nods once, sharply, like he can't deny himself this. I expect Oisín to move away, to give me space between Sebastian's legs, but instead, he hauls me onto his lap.

I feel his own arousal press against my ass and wiggle slightly, a sharp gasp bursting for me as his hand wraps around my throat.

Fuck. Yes.

"Take him deep, that's a good girl," he croons in my ear. "I want to feel him fill your throat."

I squirm again, desperate for him to let me take his cock, desperate to be touched. Moreover, I'm desperate to do exactly what Oisín just said.

Oisín's palm still cradles my throat as I lean forward and fight to take Sebastian as deep as I can. His piercing pressed against my throat and I gag, eyes watering, my teeth scraping against him. I panic, thinking I've hurt him, but Sebastian moans bucks into my mouth.

He likes the pain.

Oisín laughs as Sebastian's hand presses against my head, holding me in place. I struggle to find my breath.

"Breath through your nose, angel," Oisín hums, hand flexing on my neck. I haven't even taken him right down my throat yet and already I'm struggling. "Slowly, that's it. Sweet thing, look at her. So willing to let you choke her with it."

Sebastian groans at the same time I do, though mine comes out as a muffled whimper. I try to follow the instructions, focusing on inhaling through my nose, the impulse to gag lessening.

"Relax your throat now."

I go limp in his hold, and Oisín's arm bands around my waist, holding me upright.

"Make her take it like we know you want to," Oisín addresses Seb. "Use her pretty mouth. Let her choke, and drool and drink your cum."

I rock my hips uselessly, not able to get even the barest friction on my clit. I swear, all it would take is a soft touch and I'd fall apart.

Sebastian shoves my head down further without warning, filling my throat with his length. Again, I gag, spit pooling, and again I breathe deeply. My nose brushes the short hair at the base of him, and a sweep of pride rushes through me.

I sit there as Sebastian throbs in my mouth, until I can't help but swallow around him.

"Fuck, your mouth is heaven," he groans, sounding pained. I preen.

"Shit, I can feel him in your throat, angel," Oisín murmurs, fingers flexing on my skin.

Sebastian lifts my head back up, just enough to let me gasp, a trail of saliva hanging between us, from my tongue to his cock. Oisín leans over my shoulder, catching my mouth in a crushing kiss, spit and the taste of Sebastian sliding from my tongue to his.

"Please, please, *fuck*," Sebastian begs as Oisín pulls away.

"Whatever you want," I murmur back, meaning it and refusing to consider what that means. "Give me your cum, Seb. Let me taste you the way Oisín has. Let me have you the way he does."

I can't decide if the twist of his features is pleasure or despair, but the second my mouth is on him again, his lips part and his head tips back.

I gag less this time, anticipating the overfull feeling and the stinging in my eyes, breathing through my nose until my throat is full of him again. His hand pushes my head again and I relax, his hips bucking as he fucks into my throat.

Oisín's hand leaves my throat only to delve between my legs. His fingers press my clit over my underwear, the cotton barrier drenched and feeling all the dirtier for it. I can't moan with Sebastian so deep, but I squirm, eyes rolling back at the sensation of being caught between them like this.

Sebastian fucks my face in earnest, harsh, sharp thrusts that bruise my mouth and make tears stream down my cheeks. I love it. I need it. The crude, almost callous way he uses me for his pleasure is fucking *perfect*.

I feel used. I feel powerful. I feel like nothing but a toy. I feel like a goddess.

"I'm going to come," Sebastian groans.

I want to look up at him, to see his face when he does, but my lashes are thick with tears and my eyes are rolling back in my head.

Oisín pinches my clit, the sharp tug of pain and subsequent burning wave of pleasure wrecking me. I come so hard my vision spots as Sebastian empties himself down my throat. I choke on my own cries, struggling to swallow his cum past my whimpers, my body failing as all my muscles go lax with my orgasm.

I pull off Sebastian, gasping and moaning through my own pleasure. Most of his cum went down my throat, but some spills over my lip as I regain my own breath.

"Good girls share," my husband says and then his mouth is on mine, his tongue sweeping across my bottom lip, before I can even think about cleaning myself up. His tongue sweeps against mine, and though I'm fucking incapable of doing anything but cling to him, he moans.

"You taste so fucking good on her tongue," Oisín breathes as he pulls away, swallowing visibly.

"Holy-" Sebastian starts to speak, but the loud *bang* that shakes the fucking walls of the shop stops him.

A gunshot.

35

Sebastian

It's bloodier than before on the shop floor.

Serafina curses, snatching her gun off the tile, the handle slick with the now dead man's blood.

"He fuckin' offed himself," Oisín mutters beside me, eyes wide as we stare at the grim scene.

I've seen a lot of death, and this isn't any different. I sigh, zipping up my trousers and readjusting my clothes.

Antonio was never getting out of here alive, anyway. I'm pissed because we needed him to talk, and he can't very well talk now. Strangely, I respect him more for having the guts to keep himself quiet forever. He's loyal to whoever the hell he's hiding secrets for, I'll give him that.

We would never have made his death as quick as the bullet in his skull.

Still, it's a mess and I don't envy whoever has to clean this up. Serafina grimaces at her own weapon, her deep brown eyes angry.

"Careless," she curses at herself, clicking the safety back on her weapon before tucking it away. "Stupid fucking mistake."

I step closer to her, tucking her to my side.

"Not your fault," I whisper, trying to reassure her. "He'd have died anyway. You probably gave him mercy."

"He doesn't deserve *mercy,*" she hisses, but she leans into me. "He fucking knew something about my sister, I know he did. And now, because of my stupidity, he'll never tell us."

Oisín sighs heavily. "What's done is done," he says and I roll my eyes. "He may never have talked anyway. Besides, whatever we need, I'm willing to fuckin' bet we'll find in that vault."

Serafina is still glaring at the body like she can bring him back to life through spite alone.

The door to the shop rattles as someone knocks on it and we all jerk. Oisín curses low under his breath and gestures to me. I get the message instantly, dragging Serafina behind the counter and ducking down. I pull out my knife, and her hand goes to her gun again.

Silently, I press my finger to my lips. She nods, rolling her eyes and I can practically hear her telling me she doesn't need to be told what to do.

The click of the lock sliding open sounds as loud as the damn gunshot, and Oisín's rough voice follows.

"Shop's shut," he grits out.

A familiar laugh answers. "Not for us, fucker."

Nessa.

I jump to my feet immediately, and Serafina curses me before she does the same, her shoe slipping from the blood on the sole. We're going to have to burn these clothes.

"What the actual *fuck-"*

We surface just in time to see Anji's face as he and Nessa walk into the jewellers. Oisín locks the door immediately, leaning against it as he watches his sister's eyes widen.

"So..." I drawl out, shrugging. "We had an accident."

Anji frowns, avoiding the pools of blood on the floor as he steps around Antonio and the chair. He stares down at the fatal wound, eyes narrowed.

"That looks...self-inflicted," he observes, raising his gaze to flit between me and Serafina.

"Does it?" I muse. "That's convenient. What a sad story."

Nessa rolls her eyes. "You're not smart enough for that play," she teases, pointing a finger at me. "But I won't ask. Plausible deniability. Doesn't matter, I suppose. Bastard's dead either way."

I know the only reason she's not pressing the issue is because she knows I don't have a gun. Neither does Oisín. She's protecting Serafina from judgement, from our oversight, and I could kiss her for it.

"Nessa mentioned a vault?" Anji asks, moving the subject along.

I nod, motioning over my shoulder. "Big fuck off one in there."

Anji raises a brow, continuing his careful steps around the counter. Serafina and I make room for him, mainly because I plaster her to my front, enjoying the way it puts her ass directly in contact with my crotch. *Shit,* now I'm thinking about her ass. And whether she's ever been fucked there. Whether she wants to be fucked there-

"Sebastian," she hisses, elbowing me in the stomach. But she wiggles slightly and doesn't break my hold, though I know she easily could.

Let her feel how much I want her. Modesty has never been a particular value of mine.

"We need to call Da," Oisín says to Nessa, and I turn my head to watch him run his hand through his hair. "Need to get this shit cleaned up."

Nessa murmurs her agreement. "Renato's out interrogating half the town about that lead," she answers, fishing her phone out her pocket. "I'll get Da - Thomas, I mean - and Aoife to sort clean up."

Nobody mentions her calling Thomas her father. Mainly because I don't want a stab wound. The revelation is still fresh, though Oisín and Nessa have warmed up pretty fast to the knowledge that they're siblings.

The parent thing is harder for her though. For him, too. Given who their father is, and how Nessa's mother ran away with her and left Oisín and Thomas behind, I can hardly blame them for the awkwardness.

Hell, their situation's worse than mine, and both my parents are dead.

Nessa relays information to Thomas quickly and hangs up without a goodbye. "Give them thirty minutes."

"I can call in our clean up guy," Serafina says, finally pulling away from me. "They'll be here within the hour if it's me telling them."

Nessa grins widely. "Excellent."

Serafina grabs her phone, tapping out a text. I read it over her shoulder, not bothering to hide my curiosity.

It's in fucking Italian.

"I need to learn this stupid language," I groan under my breath.

Languages have never been my forte. Or reading in general. Stupid fucking letters are more of a tease than I've ever been, wiggling about and rearranging themselves on the page. It takes me twice as long to read a sentence as it does for Oisín to read an entire paragraph and that's in my own fuckin' language.

I swallow the lump in my throat and look away from her screen. Doesn't matter. Who needs fancy Italian words anyway?

Serafina.

That's who.

Frustrated, I drag my eyes around the room finding Oisín staring straight at me. It's like the bastard sees right through me.

I used to love that about him.

Now, it just makes my cheeks heat.

"What's your code, Seffy?" he asks.

She frowns, hesitating for the barest second before she hands her phone to him so he can read her text himself. It's a sign of trust that makes my stomach clench. They're fucking made for each other and I'm so jealous my teeth ache.

How am I supposed to walk away after everything we've done? How can I not?

Oisín's eyes scan her screen quickly before he hands it back. He meets my eyes as he translates it, "it's the equivalent of *spillage on aisle one*, and then coordinates. I'm guessing the aisle number is how many bodies."

I nod, looking away when Anji mutters something in the back. Serafina and I move at the same time, but she's faster, practically sprinting through the door.

Anji is peering at the screen on the front of the vault, murmuring something unintelligible.

"What's wrong?" I ask, voice sharper than I intend it to be.

He doesn't seem to notice, though, because he just taps his

fingers against the metal.

"Anji?" Serafina tries.

Again, he doesn't answer, just stares at the fucking vault like he's trying to read the damn thing's mind.

"ANJI!" I shout, finally getting his attention. He spins on his heel, glaring at me.

"I was thinking," he snaps.

"Well, we were asking," I retort quickly. "Can you get in?"

Anji sighs, scratching the back of his neck. "Don't insult me," he scoffs, but he looks wary. "I can do it…but it won't be quick. If I even fuckin' touch the thing wrong, it'll trigger the alarm. I don't think I need to explain why we very much *do not* want to trigger the alarm, Sebastian."

Serafina curses, her hands twitching at her sides like she's fighting the impulse to reach for a weapon. I smirk at that.

"I don't care what you have to do," I tell him, looking at the woman who destroyed my entire world, the woman I can't help panting over, begging her to rebuild it brick by fucking brick. "Just get it open."

36

Serafina

It doesn't take long for Thomas and Aoife to arrive at the shop. The minute I'm sure they have a handle on the situation, I ask Oisín to take me home. Of course, Sebastian follows us, all too eager to drive the Lexus again. I swear if I hadn't been questioning the guy's sanity while I'd watched him torture Antonio with Nessa, I sure as fuck am during the drive home. We race there in eight minutes, and Sebastian's grin is feral when he realises he's beaten his supposed personal record.

The fact that it's going to take Anji a while to crack the safe doesn't sit well with me. If I'm honest, it fucking infuriates me.

It's time that we don't have, time *Frankie* may not have.

Every part of me wants to go on a fucking rampage and force my way through the door. I'd go to hell and back for Frankie, and Oisín knows it... which is the only damn reason I didn't kill Anji on the spot when he said it would take time.

My hands ball into fists at my side as I make my way through the house, not stopping until I reach the threshold to Frankie's room. It looks exactly the same as it did before I ran off to the jewellers, clinging to the only hope I had at finding my sister. Now, with Antonio dead, and my father chasing down whoever the fuck Alyssa is, I'm beginning to think we're hitting a dead end.

Pain lances through my chest as I stare at her room, my eyes blurring with unshed tears.

I want to scream. I want to lash the fuck out and tear it all to shreds. I want to kill the motherfucker that thought they could take my Frankie without consequences. I want to scream at my sister for having the audacity to leave me. But mostly, I just want to see her, to hug her and know that she's okay. That she's alive.

Exhaustion seeps through my bones and I can't help but lean against the doorframe as I try to get a handle on the storm of emotions raging inside of me. My head hurts, my heart hurts, and my body is groaning with exhaustion. I know that I should crawl into bed. That I should give myself a second to process everything that's happened today. But I can't, not while she's out there, going through fuck knows what.

The house is too quiet, too empty without Francesca here.

I fold my arms across my chest as I rest my head against the wooden frame. I stay glued to my spot, my eyes raking over every inch of the space before me until a hand comes to rest against my lower back. I don't jump at the touch, certain that it belongs to one of my men.

Shit, when did I start thinking of Sebastian as mine?

It doesn't matter. There's no point in denying what we all already know.

Shaking my head, I stifle my sigh as I force myself to stand upright and step further into the bedroom. If I stay pressed against him for too long…God I don't even want to think about it. This man has a way of pulling at my heart like no other. Between him and Oisín, I know I'll fracture into a million pieces. I know I'll get sucked into feeling all the things I don't want to feel just yet.

He's gotten under my skin, and I can't afford to be distracted right now.

"Why are we here, Sef?" Sebastian asks, and I step away from his touch. It's the opposite of what I truly want to do. I want to sink into the feel of him. To wrap his arms around me completely as Oisín holds us both. But I can't let myself get comfortable.

Not until my husband finally admits what Seb and I already know:

He wants both of us.

He *needs* both of us.

And in truth, I need both of them too.

Everything's changed in the blink of an eye, and I'm not entirely sure what to do about it. The only thing I know for certain is that I'm not willing to let it go to shit.

"She wants to search the room again," my husband mutters to Sebastian, pulling me from my thoughts.

I can't stop my head from nodding. We may only have been married for about a month, but it's clear that the man pays attention. He's learned my tells, and how to read me like a damn book.

"You've been over every inch of this room already sweetheart, there's nothing left to find. Hell, it's a fucking miracle you found the anklet to begin with," Seb murmurs in my ear as he wraps his arms around my waist, refusing to let me go this time.

Realising that my fight is useless, I relax and lean into his touch. My body sags with the relief of no longer having to hold me up, and his thumb rubs soothing circles over my top on my stomach.

"There has to be another clue. There's no fucking way that the only thing in here to lead me to Frankie's location is that damn anklet," I hiss, the anger I feel at Antonio's death coating my words.

I step out of Sebastian's hold as I run my hands through my hair, pulling it back from my face. Gathering it in my hand, I lift it from my neck and gently massage the base of my skull. The weight of it feels like too much. I'm overwhelmed, tired, and fucking pissed.

I cross the room to Frankie's wardrobe and start tearing it apart. Every article of clothing she owns hits the floor.

By the time the wardrobe is completely bare, my breathing is strained, and sweat beads on my brow.

I glance at the men standing behind me. They're staring at me like I've lost the fucking plot. I raise a brow defiantly in response. Maybe I have lost it, but it doesn't give them the right to question me.

"Tell me what you need, angel," my husband demands, and I nod once at him, grateful that he knows not to push me right now.

"Tear this room to shreds. Anything that looks suspicious or out of the ordinary you bring to me."

"Sweetheart, there's nothing left to check," Sebastian says gently.

"There *has to be!*" I scream at him, stretching my arms out wide at the state I've made. God, what a mess. "This can't be it! There has to be something I'm missing, something I can do, something-"

"You've done everything you can," Oisin interrupts, holding his hand out like he's scared I'll bite it.

Sebastian has no such worries, walking straight up to me and scooping me into his arms. I thrash, but my shrieks are turning to sobs faster than I can even try to control.

"We will find her, Serafina," Oisín says, voice harsh. "*We.* Understand? You are not alone in this."

"I need her."

I'm horrified to find the words falling out of my mouth and completely unable to take them back. I need my sister. Sebastian's arms are steady, my head resting against his chest, his shirt already wet with my tears. I wipe furiously at my face, and Sebastian tuts.

"Don't hide your pain from me," he chastises, and I realise we're no longer in my sister's room.

"Put me down," I finally tell him. To his credit, he only hesitates a second before obeying, depositing me softly onto my own bed.

Oisín closes the door and walks over to us quickly, crouching in front of me. Sebastian is so close I can feel his body heat.

"Sebby's right. I think the time for hiding anything is over," my husband says, voice far steadier than my own.

My heart stutters. The air shifts.

"It shouldn't have been hidden at all," I say, scrubbing the salt tracks off my cheeks with my sleeve. I fucking hate crying. I'd much rather stew in the resentment festering inside me at the secrets my husband has kept. Anger is a much easier emotion to manage.

I'm pissed that he wasn't honest with me. Pissed that he wasn't honest with Sebastian. But more than anything I'm outright livid that he thinks he can continue to keep sweeping whatever this is beneath the rug, like it never fucking mattered to begin with. Like Sebastian never mattered, like my feelings on the whole situation never bloody mattered.

My husband has a hell of a lot to make up for, and I'll be fucking damned if he doesn't at least *try*.

"You're right," Oisín admits, ducking his head. "I'm sorry, Seffy. I broke your trust before I'd even earned it. I never wanted to hurt you, either of you. I was only ever doing what I thought was best. And I was wrong. Christ, I was so fucking wrong."

I still don't like the fact he neglected to tell me about Sebastian, but I'd be lying if I said I didn't understand why. And God help me but I believe him when he says he's sorry. Still, I can't help but wonder how the hell he's ever going to repair the damage between him and Sebastian.

"Does this mean I don't get to be your dirty little secret anymore?" Sebastian jokes, but his voice is hollow.

When I turn my head, I realise he's edged away from us, his lopsided smirk halfhearted. He won't meet my eyes.

Oisín's hand gently touches my knee, and our eyes lock. Something heavy passes between us, an understanding, bigger than just the two of us.

"No," Oisín says, both of us turning back to Seb. His hand remains on my knee, even as his other reaches for Sebastian's.

Sebastian jerks away, unable to hide the raw, unfettered pain in his eyes.

"No more secrets, I promise" Oisín continues, undeterred. I watch Sebastian's brow furrow. "*Tá mé i ngrá leat.*"

Sebastian jerks, eyes widening as his eyes snap to Oisín's. I don't need to understand the words to know their meaning. My heart squeezes, but surprisingly no jealousy spikes through me. Just relief.

"Oisín, don't," Sebastian whispers, squeezing his eyes shut. "I can't fuckin' stand it."

"Sebastian, *listen to me*," Oisín growls, grabbing Sebastian's hand in his tightly. *"Bhí mé i ngrá leat i gcónaí."*

"You…*love me?* Why are you telling me this now? Why is it that after shoving me aside for fucking years, you think you can just say that to me, in front of your wife no less, and expect me to believe you?" Sebastian breathes, staring down at their hands. There's anger and rope and raw pain in each syllable that leaves his tongue.

I can't handle the distance anymore, shuffling closer and leaning my head on his shoulder. I need the connection, and I think he does too.

"Because I tried to do what I thought I was supposed to," Oisín explains. "I married a beautiful, amazing woman and… but loving her doesn't mean I stopped loving you. No amount of stubbornness or denial could dig you out of my heart, Sebastian. I am a fool for thinking I could. For ever even wanting to. Forgive me, *a rún mo chroí.* I can't live without you. Either of you."

Sebastian's lips part but no sound comes out.

Oisín turns to me, giving Sebastian as much space as we can bear to process my husband's confession.

"*Ti amo,* angel," Oisín says to me, and I cover his hand with mine on my knee.

"*Ti amo anch'io,*" I murmur back to him, resisting the urge to lean down and kiss him despite the fact that I desperately want to. But we have to get through this, first.

I nudge Sebastian's shoulder with my head, trying to get his attention.

"I think I could love you, too, Seb," I tell him honestly, and he exhales sharply. "If you'd let me. If you'd...if you'd stay. I know I hurt you, by marrying him. I didn't know then, but now that I do, I don't want to ever forget. I don't want to pretend that you don't exist, or act like you mean nothing to him, or to me. I want you, Sebastian Byrnes."

"You have him," is all Sebastian says back, his hand weakly pointed in my husband's direction.

"No," I whisper, leaning closer and cupping his face with my free hand. He leans into the touch. "*We* have him."

"Don't lie to me," he begs.

"No more lies," Oisín promises. "Never again, my love."

"I want you too," he says, lifting his head, voice scratchy. "I want this so badly it fuckin' *hurts*. But not if I'm going to be left behind again. Not if I'm just going to be a second choice for you both."

I know then that we could sit here all night and make him promises that we want him, but that won't reassure him. So I do the only thing I can think of to convince him.

I straddle his lap and kiss him hard.

37

Sebastian

My heart ricochets in my chest.

The firm press of Serafina's lips against mine is the only thing keeping me grounded. My hands drop to her waist, pulling her closer as I swipe my tongue along the seam of her mouth, begging for entrance.

She grinds down on my crotch and I swear I see stars behind my eyelids.

This can't be real, it can't be happening.

I've wanted this for weeks, and yet all I can do right now is hold her with a bruising grip as the man I love watches us.

Tears roll down my face, and my breath stutters. The fear of being rejected by both of them is too much. I pull back from Serafina, needing to put space between us.

I know that both of them have said they want me… but how can I be sure that they won't leave me? That *Oisín* won't leave me again?

"It's okay Seb," Sef whispers against my cheek before trailing kisses down my throat.

I want to believe her, *God* I do. But after everything, how the fuck am I supposed to trust Oisín's sudden declaration of love?

A groan builds inside of my chest when Oisín's reaches for me, trailing his fingers softly down my spine.

"Please don't mess with me. Not like this," I beg. I hate the frown that contorts Sef's face. I hate knowing that I'm the reason it's there.

Fuck, how the hell did this happen?

How did I go from despising her for marrying the man I love, to wanting her just as badly as I do him?

How the fuck does she not hate me? More than that - how the fuck has she found it in herself to *want me?*

I'm getting emotional whiplash and I've barely had a chance to process any of the words they've said to me.

I lose myself in my thoughts, anxiety darkening my mood when I should be focused on the hot as sin woman sitting in my lap and the man I've been in love with for years at my back. Sef's tasting every inch of my exposed skin like I'm the treat she's been craving for the longest time, and all I can do is sit there and let the fucked up monster inside of my head ruin the moment.

When I stop responding eagerly to her touch, she looks directly to her husband, clearly wondering how the hell to handle me right now.

I can't blame her, Hell, I don't even know what to do with myself right now.

"Seb, I can stop-" Serafina tries to say, her gorgeous brown eyes narrowed with concern, but she's cut short by a hand resting on her shoulder.

"Sebastian, look at me," Oisín demands, and I twist my head in his direction.

His steady gaze helps to settle the anxiety wreaking havoc on my body, and I take a deep breath as he narrows his green-blue eyes at me. We sit like that for a minute, Serafina rubbing soothing circles on my shoulder, and Oisín taking deep breaths along with me.

"I'm only going to say this once more, *a rún mo chroí,* so you better fucking hear me when I say this. *You are mine, Sebby.* I'm never letting you go again," Oisín swears.

The lump in my throat threatens to choke me as he leans down to press his lips to mine. A tear escapes as I kiss him back. I have so much that I want to say to him, to both of them, but my stupid body won't let me. The lump in my throat is too thick, and my heart is pounding too hard inside of my chest.

I'm drowning in emotions, and I don't know how to save myself.

"Ours, husband. Ours," Sef corrects him with a pointed look, and I inhale sharply as she kisses the salty tracks staining my face.

"Tell me what you need, Sebastian," Oisín says, his tone dark, and I know exactly where his mind has gone.

He knows just what I need.

The one thing that works to save me from this headspace.

I need to fuck, and I need to submit.

I need them to take the pain away and make me feel whole again.

"You, I need both of you," I whisper, afraid that I'm asking for too much when their confessions are still fresh on their lips.

Neither one of them wastes any time proving just how wrong I am.

I'm stripped of my clothing immediately, left naked and hard on the bed as I watch them take the time to undress each other. Each inch of exposed flesh that greets my vision is confirmation that they're willing to accept me into their life. Into their relationship, flaws and all.

As soon as Serafina's free from her bloodied clothing, she plants herself back on my lap. The heat of her cunt presses against my dick and I tip my head down to kiss her. I capture her lips with my own and I kiss her with everything I have. Our teeth clank against each other as we battle for dominance, neither one of us ceding control to the other.

No matter how much I want to let go, want to let them take control, I won't let myself slide into that space so easily. They have to earn it. Prove to me that they deserve it after everything they've put me through.

I run my hands over Sef's silky thighs as Oisín settles on the bed behind me. The hard press of his cock tells me just how turned on he is by watching me kiss his wife. I decide to tease him a little, wiggling backward until my chest is resting against his, and Sef's perfect body is on display for us both.

I hiss as I feel Oisín's hands sneak between Serafina and I. One settles between Sef's slick coated thigh, and the other wraps harshly around my cock.

"Fuck," Sef moans, watching her husband press two fingers inside of her. I can't stop myself from lifting my hips and thrusting into his palm.

"That's the plan, angel," Oisín laughs, and I chuckle at the violent look she throws his way.

I watch as she removes one of her hands from my shoulder and leans forward to grab the nape of Oisín's neck. Her peaked nipples brush against my chest, and she hisses at the contact. She looks down, eyes widening when she finds the silver bars pierced through my nipples.

I lick and suck at every inch of her body that I can reach as Oisín's fingers pump inside of her. She lifts her hips, before roughly dragging him forward and melding their lips together. I'm wedged between them as they lick and suck at each other's mouth and fuck, there's nowhere else I'd rather be.

I jump at the feel of Serafina's hand wrapping around Oisín's, forcing his grip to move faster, up and down the length of my shaft. My eyes roll into the back of my head.

"Christ that feels too fucking good," I groan as Sef swipes the her thumb along my piercing.

She lifts her hand to her face and sucks the bead of my arousal into her mouth.

A soft moan leaves her at the taste of me and I swear I could fucking come from the sound of her alone.

"Don't push him too far, angel. We want him dripping and begging for that tight pussy before the night's over," Oisín says, and my eyes slip closed.

"Yes, Sir."

I snap my eyes open at the use of the honorific and feel my jaw drop as she gives me a knowing look.

I'm in for a world of hell, but I'll relish every fucking second of it.

38

Serafina

Sebastian's wide eyes are glued to mine as I bring my hand down and twine my fingers with Oisín's once more. His hips tip forward, desperate for the pleasure he knows we can give him, but neither Oisín or I are willing to let him fall apart. Yet.

"Be a good boy, Sebby, and I might just let my wife sit on your cock," Oisín taunts as he moves, pulling me from Seb's lap.

"I'll be good," Sebastian says in a rush. "I'll be *so fucking good.* The best. I promise."

A jealous groan falls from Seb's mouth as my husband lifts me in one smooth motion and plants me on his cock. My pussy stings at the sudden intrusion, but the burn subsides quickly as I settle myself, resting against Oisín's chest with my legs folded back, my feet resting on his thighs.

My cunt clenches around him, trying to adjust to the feel of him. It doesn't matter that we've fucked a hundred times in the last month, he's huge, and his cock will never feel like it's not stretching the shit out of me.

Once I can move without it hurting, I lift my hips and slam down on my husband's dick, hard and fast.

My chest heaves, and my breasts bounce in Seb's face as I ride my husband. I watch, completely enraptured, as Sebastian sucks on his bottom lip, his bright blue eyes tracking my every move. Pleasure rocks through my body, my limbs growing heavy as I take what I want, using Oisín to chase my own release.

"Christ," Seb groans and my eyes narrow when I notice his movements.

I stop what I'm doing, and lean forward to rest my hand on his when I catch him palming himself. He arches an eyebrow at me as he slowly drags our hands down the length of his shaft and back up, twisting slightly at the tip.

"None of that, sinner boy. This cock is mine to tease. It's mine to taste and fuck whenever I want. You don't get to take that from me before I've even had a chance to make you beg for us," I snap, loving the way his mouth twists into a wry grin in return.

"She's a little too good at this," Seb teases, his gaze swinging to the man behind me.

"Oh I know," Oisín hums, and my heart skips a beat at the approval coating his words.

"She's right though Sebby, only good boys get to come, and you're not behaving right now," Oisín taunts as he brings his hand down to my clit, circling his fingers in a swift motion.

I moan long and low as he teases my clit, fighting the need to close my eyes so I can watch Sebastian as he rests on his elbows, his eyes glued to our bodies.

"Look how good my little wife takes it, Seb. Come here, taste how sweet she is."

"Tá Máistir."

Wet kisses trail my skin within seconds as Oisín begins to thrust up into me.

My legs shake as Oisín ups the pace, his cock spearing me over and over again. Sebastian sucks my nipple into his mouth and teases the other with his free hand, sending sparks of pleasure through me.

His head slowly moves down my body, hands gripping me so tight I know I'll wake in the morning with fingerprint marks on my skin. Something stirs inside my chest at the thought of that, and I shudder with need.

Fuck, I want that. I want it so badly. I want every Goddamn person on this fucking earth to look at me and know that these men are mine. That I am theirs.

A cry rises in my throat as Sebastian settles between my thighs, his tongue replacing my husband's fingers.

"Jesus Christ, I can feel you eating her out, Sebby," Oisín moans as he fucks me harder.

"Fuck, I'm gonna come," I sob, my whole body vibrating with the need to let go, but I don't want this to end.

"Spread her open for me, *Máistir*," Seb pleads, not once lifting his lips from my aching clit.

Oisín does as he's been asked, shifting us until he's resting on the heels of his feet, holding my legs wide so that Sebastian can move closer.

I scream at the feel of his tongue entering me, him and Oisín taking turns to fuck me.

Pleasure consumes me as I fall apart, my eyes slipping closed, every muscle in my body pulling taut. I can't breathe, I can't see, and I can't fucking stop myself from trying to wriggle my hips, begging for the earth shattering orgasm to never end.

"Fuck she tastes like heaven, *Máistir,*" Sebastian praises, as he continues to chase every single fucking drop of my release.

Oisín simply grunts in response, not bothering to form words as he buries himself deep inside of me. I feel the warm gush of his cum coating me as he finds his release.

Sweat drips down our bodies, neither of us able to speak as Sebastian keeps swallowing our combined taste.

Eventually, my husband's cock slips free from my body and I watch in awe as Seb dips lower to lick him clean. He's still hard, despite just coming inside of me, and I want nothing more than to watch him fuck our lover.

It shouldn't be so hot. I shouldn't want to keep watching, but as I hear Oisín whimper from behind me, and watch Sebastian trail gentle kisses along my husband's dick, my body starts craving more.

I shuffle up the bed, my overheated skin pressing against the cool headrest behind me and lift my hair from my neck. I'm fucking sweating, and dripping, and I want, no - *need* - more.

Oisín twists his fingers into Sebastian's hair, lifting him from his cock before flipping him over to face me. Seb settles on his hands and knees, his dark messy hair tumbling into his eyes as he lifts his chin to look at me. Oisín nods when I swing my eyes back and forth between them, and I know that I'm finally going to get the show I've been secretly hoping for.

"Crawl to me, sinner boy," I hum.

His eyes darken, and the mattress dips as he moves his body in my direction.

Using his hair like a leash, I drag him forward and press

my lips to his. He opens for me immediately, grunting as I tug hard on his hair. I can taste myself and my husband on his tongue.

"I want to watch my husband fuck you, sinner boy. I want to watch you fall apart on his cock, and I want to feel you come inside me. Do you think you could do that for me? Or do I need to beg?" I ask, my eyes searching his.

He swallows once, looking over his shoulder to Oisín before quickly turning back to me.

"Sweetheart, you could ask me to rip out my own fucking heart and I'd do it for you without question. For both of you. If anyone should be begging for anything, it's me. I don't deserve you, but for some reason you're determined to keep me. I'll do whatever it takes for you to never change your mind about us, because I'm too fucking selfish to let either of you go."

My heart shatters inside my chest at his words.

I wasn't kidding when I told him that I could love him if he'd let me.

I want him as selfish as I am - digging his claws into us, keeping us close. I want so much it's consuming me, and knowing that he's being taken by the same desperate desire is a relief.

His arms band around me as my husband steps towards the bathroom. I meet his eyes, biting my bottom lip in silent question. Oisín gives me a sly grin, inclining his head in a nod. I turn back to Sebastian, pussy pulsing with need in anticipation.

"Come fuck me then, sinner boy," I say, my throat tight with emotion as I sink into his arms.

39

Oisín

I take a second for myself as I slip into the bathroom, leaving Serafina and Sebby to fall into each other. Hushed moans bleed through the door, and my dick is already begging for release again.

Christ, it's impossible to ever be fully satisfied when I have both of them around me. I feel like I'm constantly on the brink of coming in my pants, dying to touch them every second that I can.

I never let myself think that I could have them both.

My whole life I've known that I had a duty to do. An expectation to make a strong, good alliance for our family.

Each time I'd been with Sebastian prior to the marriage, I'd had to painfully remind myself of that. No matter how much I'd wanted to say fuck it all, and keep him for myself.

God I've been such a fucking fool, and for far too fucking long.

Looking in the mirror now, I barely recognise myself. It's like the weight of the world has been lifted from my shoulders. I know that we still have a long way to go, and that the trust

Sebastian lost in me will take time to rebuild, but I'll do fucking anything to show him just how sorry I am. How much I mean it when I say that I'm never letting him go again.

More cries seep through the door and I smile, delighting in the fact that they find pleasure in one another. However, I know that if I leave the brats alone for long enough, they'll find a way to ruin each other completely before I've had a chance to stop them.

Determined to get back to the bed, and fuck my man until he begs me to stop, I turn for the door.

I halt immediately when I find Sebastian fucking Serafina against the wall beside the door. The little shit knew I'd be able to hear them better, and the smirk on his face confirms it as his eyes meet mine.

"You want to play games?" I ask, a thrill shooting through my chest at the excitement that lights up his face.

"Always, *Máistir,*" he answers, not once slowing the pace at which he's fucking Serafina.

"Has he been a good boy, angel?" I ask Sef as I step behind Sebastian.

I reach behind me, blindly searching for the cabinet, not wanting to take my eyes off either of them. When my fingers finally grasp the handle on the drawer, I quickly turn around to search for the bottle of lube I know Serafina keeps there.

The second I have it, I give them my full attention again.

"He's been very good, Sir," Sef breathes on a strangle moan as Sebastian uses one hand to hold her up, and the other to pinch her clit.

Her head tips back, knocking against the wall with a thud, and I swallow my own groan. Her long neck is exposed and all I can think about when I look at it is how pretty she would be with Sebastian's tattooed hand wrapped around her like a necklace.

"Spread your legs wider, Sebby," I tell him, as I squirt the cool lube onto my hand. I fist my hard dick, pleasure zipping down my spine as I pump myself quickly, coating my cock.

I drop the bottle onto the bed before stepping up to shove my cock between Sebby's cheeks. At this angle, it's going to be a tight fit, but it's not the first time we've done it like this.

I don't bother to stretch him out, knowing that Seb loves the bite of pain that comes with having his ass fucked. Instead, I reach down between us, placing the head of my dick at his entrance, and thrust into him in one brutal, quick stroke.

His hips falter, and Serafina screams in pleasure as Sebastian grips her tighter.

"Keep fucking her, Sebby," I order him, not giving him a chance to get used to the feel of me.

Barely audible curses fall from his lips as I sink my teeth into his shoulder, tongue meeting the raised skin of a scar. The bite mark will barely be visible amongst the ink coating his skin, but I'll know it's there nonetheless, as will he. Something inside of me snaps as Sebastian dips his head lower, and copies my bite on Serafina's shoulder.

She screams, her hands gripping tightly onto the nape of his neck as he drags his mouth lower and bites down harshly on her peaked nipple.

My hips snap forward at a punishing pace and I work myself hard to fuck the man I've been in love with for years. His legs buckle beneath him, unable to support him any longer as Serafina and I ring every ounce of pleasure we can from his body.

"Oh fuck, oh fuck, please-" Sef begs, and I loop my arm beneath Sebastian's to grip her chin.

"Look at what's ours when you come," I demand, and immediately Serafina's eyes lock with Sebastian's.

Using the wall behind her for leverage, she does her best to match him thrust for thrust until she falls apart on his cock. My balls draw tight as I listen to her come, Sebastian grunting at the feel of her clenching around his dick.

"She looks so beautiful when she falls apart, doesn't she?" I praise, knowing how much she loves it.

"Fuck yes, I need to see it again," Sebastian moans, and his wish is my command.

I up the pace, forcing him to fuck her harder while moving my tangled arm lower. From here I can just barely reach her clit, but it's enough that between the two of us we can make her come once more.

"I can't," Serafina cries, but I know my wife's body better than anyone else, at least for now.

"Yes you can, angel," I hiss back, gritting my teeth with the effort it takes not to explode inside of Sebby's tight ass.

"Come for me sweetheart," Sebastian begs. He shifts the hand holding her up, sliding his finger backwards to toy with her tight hole.

"Oh fuck!"

"That's it gorgeous, drench my cock," Sebastian murmurs as his arm moves swiftly, fucking her ass with his finger.

I move the hand that holds Sebastian's hip lower until I'm cupping his balls, squeezing gently. His knees nearly buckle once more, but he locks them just in time.

"Jesus Christ, you're going to fucking kill me," he whines, and a smile spreads across my face.

I keep fucking him, not bothering to dignify him with a response. My knees lock and I lean heavily on his back until I hear Sebastian grunt his release. Serafina moans, happy to be filled with his cum. In a few short thrusts I'm coming too, unable to stop the tidal wave of pleasure that bursts from me.

My eyes slip closed, my head tipping back as I continue to fuck into Sebastian. I lose all sense of reality and time as I empty myself inside of him. Short pants escape me as I struggle to catch my breath, slick sweat coating the three of us.

"I can't feel my body," Serafina whispers and I smirk at her.

"I'm not sure I even have a body anymore," Sebastian replies, a dry chuckle on his lips. I don't bother to hide the laugh that escapes me.

"Bath, now," I say, still gasping for breath as I pull out of Sebastian.

Watching my cum trail down his legs shouldn't be such a turn on, especially after what we've just done, but it never stops being so fucking hot.

"Mmm, yes please," Serafina mumbles, reminding me of what I've just said. Her head rests against Sebastian's shoulder, her eyes slipping closed as Sebastian rubs gentle circles into her back.

"Come on, sweetheart," Sebby coos, pulling her away from the wall.

I step back into the bathroom, and twist the taps until I hear the roar of water filling the clawfoot tub. I thank the heavens that it's big enough for the three of us to fit as I pour the body wash into the water. Bubbles fill the tub just as Sebastian steps into the room with Serafina. He presses a gentle kiss to my lips, and I relish the feel of it. I choke on my laughter as Serafina mutters about *dumb boys fucking her senseless,* and Sebastian nips at her earlobe in response.

He settles into the bubbles, Serafina curled against him, as I climb into the tub resting behind her. My legs tangle with Sebby's beneath the water, and I shuffle closer. The heat of the water seeps into my bones and I release a contented sigh as I soak for a few minutes.

"Are you ready to give me back my dick yet, sweetheart?" Sebastian asks and my eyes widen with shock.

He's still inside her?!

"No. I licked it. It's mine now," Serafina snaps, and I sink my teeth into my bottom lip, trying not to howl with laughter at her attitude.

Sebastian looks at me, unsure of how to handle the situation, before murmuring, "fuck it," and settling deeper against the side of the tub.

We lounge like that, tangled and connected, until the water cools. Only then does Serafina allow Sebastian to slip out of her so we can clean the cum from their skin. Relaxed, well fucked and sated, I carry her back to the bed, Sebastian close at my side.

Immediately, she throws herself under the duvet in the middle of the bed, wet hair splayed on the pillow around her. Sebastian stands at my side, eyes fixed to her, one hand keeping his towel on his hips.

I grab the fabric and pull, baring him again. I laugh lowly as I realise he's already at half mast, though I refuse to indulge him again. We all need to rest. Including our cocks.

"She's...perfect," he says, voice soft.

My throat tightens as I nod in agreement. I tug at his hand, encouraging him forward, and we arrange ourselves on either side of Serafina, whose breathing is already slow and heavy with sleep.

Sebastian curls around her front, and I wrap around her back, our legs tangled with hers. My arm stretches over her waist until my hand rests on Sebastian's hip.

His eyes are already closed, and I don't know if he'll hear me, but it doesn't matter. Sleep is already softening me and my eyes are heavy.

"You're perfect, too," I murmur, squeezing his hip, before sleep claims me, too.

40

Serafina

"Get the fuck up!"

I jolt awake, panic flaring through me, immediately reaching for the nearest weapon. Where the fuck is my gun? My hand smacks against my bedside table, finding the first thing I can grab - a heavy paperback book Frankie left in my room the last time she tried to convince me to read her recommendations.

I throw the book hard in the direction of the voice, my eyes still blurry with sleep.

"Ah, *fuck!*"

Sebastian rolls over, long limbs spread out like a starfish, and I blink rapidly. Seb raises his arm into the air, middle finger extended in the direction of the door.

Ah shit.

I've just hit my father in law with a book.

And, *oh my God,* he's just seen me naked in bed with his son and his enforcer.

Fuck. FUCK.

"Get the fuck out, Da!" Oisín shouts, voice thick as he bolts upright, shoving half of Sebastian's body off him.

We're a tangle of limbs and sheets and discarded clothes. Thomas looks despairingly at us all, and I have no explanation that will make this situation better.

"Sort your shit out," Thomas demands, but his voice is more exhaustion than anger. "Anji got into the vault. Aoife's ready to kit you out, you have five fuckin' minutes."

Mercifully, he's already walking away when he shouts the last words, because I'm out of the bed in seconds with zero regard for my nudity. The bedroom door is still open and I'm scrambling over the men's laundry to get to my wardrobe.

"It's too early for a heist," Seb groans, and I'm saved from having to throw a book in his direction too because my husband smacks him in the chest.

"Get up and get dressed, asshole," I hiss at him.

"Shit," Sebastian mumbles as he falls out of bed, tripping over the blanket tangled around his legs.

We're silent as we dress as quickly as possible. All I can hear is the pounding of my own heart. What if the vault gives us answers? What if there's something in there that leads us to Frankie?

What if there's not?

I refuse to let myself contemplate that idea. There will be answers. Or there'll be fucking hell to pay.

Sebastian and Oisín flank me as we hurry down the stairs to join the huddle of people in the meeting room.

Thomas wasn't fucking kidding.

Aoife looks like the goddess of war or some shit. She's surrounded by weapons, ensuring all of the Cavanaughs are kitted correctly, chastising Thomas because *you always need another knife, idiot.*

I'm already carrying my gun, but I let her wrap a harness around me and give me a second one. She winks at me as she adjusts it, the black leather supple and comfortable to move in.

She's been here a day and she's already made herself at home. I recognise the holster and the guns are ours, and I wonder what it took to get my father to trust her enough to let her help us.

Come to think of it...

"Where's Renato?" I ask loudly as Aoife moves onto my husband. Thomas raises a brow at me.

"Debriefing your lot," he tells me. "He's in his study, if you need him."

I appreciate the way his voice softens ever so slightly when he speaks to me, like he recognises why I'm searching for my father. I don't doubt my own strength or my ability to face whatever we're about to find. But I've lost my sister and my mother and...I need my father.

I turn to go find him, just to reassure myself that he's ready, too, only to smack straight into his chest. He laughs, wrapping an arm around my shoulder in a hug before I pull away.

"Siete pronti?" he asks lowly, and I nod once.

At our back, I feel the Cavanaughs still, and I know our men are waiting outside the room already.

We're ready.

I just don't know what for.

The two women my father has assigned to guard the store let us through with a stiff nod. I recognise them vaguely as

Polina - a blonde with high cheekbones and icy eyes, and Kitty - a redhead who wears a smile even when she's firing the gun on her hip. My chest aches a little. If things were different, could they have been my friends?

As we step over the threshold, I realise how much Frankie's absence is revealing things to me. How fucking…lonely I've been. For so long, my sister has been my only friend. Why would I need anyone else when I had her, and the legacy I knew one day I'd take over? I'm polite to everyone who works under our name, I have a reputation for being a good party guest, I make a point of never being rude until it's time to strike.

And it's left me isolated. By my own design.

Kitty meets my eyes as I glance back, a smile on her lips. She inclines her head at me, as though she's encouraging me, and I vow then and there to make more of an effort. I need to have loyalty within the gang if I ever hope to replace my father as Boss. More than that, I need friends.

Sebastian and Oisín don't leave my side, and I hold my breath. I have them. I am not alone.

I stand straighter as the doors close and lock again behind our group. The jewellers smells of bleach. There's not even the hint of a stain on the floor. It's so fucking clean we could eat off of it.

You'd never know a man died here. That more might, today.

Papà has men roaming the entire city, tracking down anybody who matches the description we got from Antonio. Given that our forces have been spread out, I'm grateful we have the Cavanaughs. Nessa, Gráinne and Thomas wait behind us, alongside Mattia, one of my father's most trusted men, while Papà moves to the front. He spares me a glance over his shoulder and I nod.

We're prepared to act as soon as we find out what's in that fucking vault. Every desperate inch of me hopes it's coordinates, or at least something that will give us a location. We can be out of here and heading straight to my sister in seconds. I don't give a shit how many men I have to kill to get to her.

Fuck, even if the vault is protecting information on who *they* are, I'll take it. Anything will help because as it stands, we're out of leads.

These bastards won't fucking best us.

I refuse to let them.

"Open it," Papà instructs, moving into the backroom.

Anji is waiting by the vault, the locking mechanism hanging open. There are wires and a small computer set up on the table he's dragged over from the corner to use as a desk. He looks none the worse for having been up the entire night working on this, and I admire him for it.

"The alarm has been deactivated," Anji tells us. "But I have no fuckin' clue what's in there."

"It's *something*," Sebastian says with a shrug. "Something worth dying to protect. That's all the information we fuckin' need. Now open it, Anj."

Anji nods, brushes his hair off his forehead with his forearm and turns to the vault. I can't see what he's doing given that my father is standing in front of me, but I hear it when something *clicks*.

The door creaks as it opens, and Anji steps to the side.

All hell breaks loose.

The first gunshot ricochets off the metal interior of the vault, and instinctively, we all dive for cover. I can't even fucking see what's inside the damn thing because Sebastian flattens me to the floor.

"YOU SAID YOU DISARMED IT!" Thomas shouts as another bullet flies.

"I DID!" Anji snaps back, and I manage to get out from under Sebastian in time to see him aim his gun into the vault and fire twice. "It's a fucking *tunnel.*"

Oh Dio.

"Move out!" I yell before my father can beat me to the command, surging forward the second I get my feet under me. Movement blurs all around me, but all I can focus on is that fucking vault.

And the person climbing out of it.

They're dead before I can even question who it is, Oisín's bullet in their skull.

Someone's shouting something, and I hear my name, but my ears are ringing. Fuck this. Fuck everyone. More people spill out of the vault, out of the hole in the wall that it hid. All of them armed, all of them angry.

Gunfire and shouts fill the air with shock and smoke, but none of us hesitate to fight back when the strangers pull their triggers again and again. There's more of them than us, but they're far less well trained, and despite the fact we're outnumbered, their men fall and ours don't. Something grazes the skin of my leg and I hiss, looking down briefly to realise a bullet has just missed me.

I don't have the chance to figure out who shot the damn thing because Sebastian jumps in front of me, pinning a man to the wall, knife in his hand. I don't know where his gun is. I don't know what the fuck is happening.

I shoot, again and again, blood spraying, a body dropping

in front of me. The world stills as I move to push past it.

Because the corpse at my feet is a tall woman, with blonde hair and a rose tattoo on her exposed arm.

My sister is in that fucking tunnel.

I know it the second I make eye contact with the glassy, lifeless blue eyes of Alyssa.

I'm not fucking waiting for the order to find her.

There's a lull in the rush of people spilling from whatever infested nest we've uncovered and I charge forward, shooting the remaining person who appears at the mouth of the vault without even thinking. I kick their body back, and they fall in a heap at the mouth of the tunnel.

The thing is *huge*. How the fuck did this happen, under our feet, without us knowing? How long has this been here?

I don't have time for answers. I throw myself into the vault, passed the body, and into the tunnel.

41

Oisín

"SERAFINA!"

Red flashes across my vision as my wife disappears from my sight, running down the fucking *tunnel*. Alone. With no Goddamn backup.

"SEF!" Sebastian screams her name seconds after I do, and I turn to find him pinned to the wall by some bastard with a knife in his hand.

Shit. *Shit.*

I scan the room quickly, finding all of our members fighting, Thomas being circled by two of the fuckers who ambushed us. There's not a single ally free to follow my wife.

A bullet hits the wall by my head, and no matter how many routes I run through in my mind, there's no clear path from my place by the counter to the vault. There's no one to cover me even if I could get through the frenzy of the fight. The intruders may be less trained than our men but they're making up for it in sheer enthusiasm now. Bullets are firing so fast I can barely hear anything past the ringing in my head.

I shoot, a cool, calm anger sweeping over me like I've

plunged into icy water.

Serafina.

Again, another bullet, the fucker I aimed for moving just seconds before it would've hit him in the stomach.

Serafina.

Again, again, again.

I can't fucking get to her.

A low, rough shout comes from my right and I curse. Sebastian. My eyes find his. There's a thick cut on his cheek, a divot that looks like it might be from a ring, and his shirt is torn, blood blooming thick and fast through the fabric.

I will him to move, to duck, to turn enough that I can hit the man

holding him against the wall without hitting Sebastian. He bares his teeth at the man who's stabbed him, his lips stretching into a grin before he lunges. His sudden movement throws his attacker off balance and the knife drops between them as he stumbles to the side. Sebastian doesn't waste a second of the opportunity.

He doesn't even reach for a fucking weapon.

No, he *bites*.

The man screams, the sound sharp, as Sebby rips his fucking ear off his head with his goddamn teeth.

Blood sprays in a wide arc as the man clutches his head, swinging his other hand in a clumsy, off centred punch. Sebastian laughs as he grabs the man's fist and yanks him closer, kicking his knee up straight into his balls. He doubles over, and Sebastian's eyes gleam, his bloody face lit up as his hands grip the man's head.

And twists.

I can't hear the sound of his neck breaking over the gunfire.

Sebastian is wild now, any control he had left is gone. The dead man is limp and heavy, but Sebastian holds him up as someone fires again. The bullet embeds itself in the dead man's chest, giving Sebastian enough time to snatch the knife off the floor and throw it.

All the air leaves my body as my head smacks hard off the floor.

Fuck.

Someone's on top of me, their weight holding me down. My vision swims as I try to recover my consciousness. My head is pounding from the hit I took. I can't tell which way is up.

I blink hard, trying to get my body to respond, recovering my vision just in time to stare down the barrel of a gun.

Oh fuck no.

I raise my hand to grab the gun, to point it anywhere but at me, to dislodge this asshole, to do anything -

Too late. Too fucking late.

They pull the trigger.

Click.

I don't believe in luck, or karma, or God. But the second the sound of the empty chamber clicks right in my face, I become a man of faith.

I surge upwards before the person above me has the chance to so much as react to their failure. Where the fuck is *my* gun? Doesn't matter. I can kill well enough without it.

I have them pinned beneath me in seconds, nausea rising fast as my body protests to the movement, vision spotting again. Doesn't matter. My hand is around their throat, dragging them upwards just to smash their head down hard and fast. The sound of their skull hitting the floor is almost as satisfying as Sebastian laughing loudly behind me.

I know I won't get him back into his own body for at least a few hours. I don't care. We need him wild, we need him unhooked from reality, we need him murderous and manic.

My attacker's eyes roll back as the second smash renders them unconscious. There's less satisfaction in killing someone who isn't even aware of it, but needs must. I slit their throat quickly, leaving them to bleed out alone.

I'm breathing hard and fast, head spinning, limbs aching as I get to my feet and turn again.

Just in time to see Gráinne, bloody and with a gun in hand, charge down the tunnel after my wife.

42

Serafina

The tunnel is dark and grimy as fuck. I can't fucking imagine what it was ever used for originally, but now the cockroaches who have infested this route have let it rot around them. There's rusted candle holders mounted to the walls in intervals, a few of them holding dying flames. The smell of shit, piss and sickness is thick in the air, and no matter how well accustomed I thought I was to the scent of bodies and blood, I choke on it as I run.

What the fuck is going on down here?

The floor is sticky and slippery in places, and more than once I have to catch myself on the damp wall to stop myself falling. My hand comes away slick with what feels like blood, but smells like decay.

I can't afford to stop. Not when, breaking through the cloying air, is the soft, intermittent sound of shuffling feet and metal scraping on stone.

I round a corner, utterly fucking lost and cursing myself for it. There's a fork where the tunnel separates into two paths, both equally as dark and dank as the one I've just come down.

I shouldn't have come alone. My lungs burn as I catch my breath, seeing nothing that would distinguish either tunnel from the other. There's nothing. I have nothing.

I can't even pinpoint which side the sound is coming from. I even hold my own breath, letting the quiet settle in, but the clanking doesn't come again. Did I imagine it? No. There has to be something down here. There is. The fuckers that ambushed us have something down here and every heavy, hard thump of my heart is convincing me that the *something* is my sister.

I resist the even stupider urge to call out for her.

I edge closer to the wall on the right, flattening myself against it. The cold seeps through my clothes and I shudder, trying to force my heart rate to calm so the sound of my pulse doesn't echo in my ears.

Nothing.

Fuck-

I still completely as the sound of soles slapping on stone echoes from somewhere in the tunnel.

Running. Someone's running.

Fuck.

It's nearly impossible to pinpoint where the person is coming from, the pounding of their feet bouncing off the walls. I grip my gun steadily, finger hovering just over the trigger and exhale slowly.

I realise nearly too late that the steps are approaching from behind me.

I spin just as the person comes close enough for me to see them in the dingy gloom. My gun is raised, every muscle in my body tightening as I instinctively ready myself for a fight.

"Ally!" a familiar voice shouts seconds before I pull the trigger.

My finger hovers over it as I frown, narrowing my eyes as the person steps forward, arms raised in surrender.

"It's me, Serafina." I recognise the Irish accent now, and as I lower my weapon, Gráinne's face comes into view.

"Fuck, I nearly killed you," I hiss at her, my voice sounding too loud in the silence.

"Good thing you didn't," she says back, keeping her voice low. "I'm the only fuckin' backup you've got right now."

"More than I had minutes ago," I mumble, happy for her presence. "Split?" I ask simply, gesturing to the two paths ahead. I can only pray our interaction hasn't drawn attention from whoever the fuck is down there.

"Best go together," Gráinne whispers as she steps closer. She's armed to the teeth, a dagger in her hand and a gun at her hip from first glance. "If there's more of them..."

She trails off, but I nod. "We stand a better chance together," I finish her thought for her, flicking my eyes between the two routes before us.

"Preference for which?" Gráinne asks, her words short and snappy as she whispers.

I shake my head, pointing randomly to the one on the right. Gráinne agrees with the incline of her head and together, we step further into the dark.

We keep our footsteps as light as possible as we ease on, the tunnel turning sharply to the right. Gráinne and I press our backs to the wall as we round the corner, and finally the flicker of light comes into view. Two lanterns, the orange glow breaking up the thick shadow. Logically, I know that there is no electricity in what must be centuries old tunnels, but the fucking *candlelight* makes this so much more eerie. I half expect a bloody zombie or ghost to leap out at me, something out of a horror novel, monstrous and hungry.

The dull scrape of metal on stone makes my skin crawl. We pause in sync, raising our weapons. Our eyes connect, and I nod slightly.

Nothing I imagined prepares me for the sight that greets us.

Heavy metal rings are bolted to the walls, thick chains hanging off them. They swing like they've been disturbed, scraping against the wall. There's *shackles* secured to the floor. Handcuffs, too, the silver metal either rusted or...bloody.

The brown-red stains are everywhere. The flicker of the candlelight moves over the nightmarish scene and I have to blink rapidly to be sure I'm not fucking imagining this shit.

It's *barbaric.*

Mercifully, there's nobody hanging from the wall, though there's spatters and drips of what has to be dried blood seeping into the stone and floor. Somebody's been held here. Multiple somebodies, judging by the sheer darkness of the stains.

I have tortured and killed and hurt more times than I can even remember. I know every way to hurt a man without killing him, every way to prolong his pain until he's desperate for death.

But this...

Whatever has happened here, beneath my fucking city, is far worse. Whatever happened here happened beneath my feet, under our noses, right in front of our Goddamn eyes. How have we not known? How-

A bullet hits stone beside my head. I dive away from it

before I can even register what's happened, throwing myself headlong into the open cavern before us.

Gráinne and I react instantly, our weapons firing as a group of bodies rushes towards us. They must have been waiting, hiding around the next fucking bend, and *shit* they've got us right where they want us.

Alone, and outnumbered in an unfamiliar maze.

Two of them go down as our bullets connect with flesh, but there's three more to contend with. Gráinne curses and grunts as she surges forward, body slamming the man at the front of the group before he can aim again. Time slows as I duck and move, the other two running towards us with determined grimaces. I trip the one on the left as I spin low, dodging the other's blade. He goes down, reaching for me as he does. I barely manage to avoid his grasp, sidestepping him to sink my knife into his friend's stomach.

I'm not fast enough to avoid him the second time. His hand closes around my ankle as the man I stabbed raises the butt of his gun, metal flashing in the candlelight. The one on the floor tugs, and my balance wavers.

A dull, hard *thud* resonates through my very fucking bones.

And everything goes black.

43

Sebastian

These fucking tunnels smell like death and illness.

It took far too Goddamn long for us to clear out the fuckers who ambushed us and rush their vile little lair. Minutes, too many minutes, where Serafina was down here alone, only Gráinne chasing after her.

Distantly, a quick succession of gunshots echoes off the walls. Our entire group moves faster. Oisín curses. I push ahead, sprinting, the taste of blood still coating my mouth and the tiny, sharp sparks of pain from the stab wound pushing me faster, faster, faster. I have felt much worse, and ran much farther, towards things that mattered far less.

My fucking future is alone down here in this filthy, rotten little maze, and I refuse to lose it.

I refuse to lose her.

The tunnel forks up ahead.

"Half each!" Thomas barks out, not bothering with full sentences. The order is clear. Split, cover all ground.

Without even looking, I know Oisín and Nessa are at my back as I sprint ahead down the tunnel to the right. I can't stop moving. The need to spill more blood, to paint myself in it, to make the streets of this town run red with the stuff is burning through me. I sink deeper into the feeling, until the entire world around me goes nice and still and calm.

It doesn't matter that there's fucking chains and bolts attached to the walls, that the blood stains are so big there's no way a person could survive that loss. It doesn't matter that there's six bodies on the floor, because nothing matters except Serafina.

Serafina

Serafi-

The body on the floor. Dark hair, sticky and wet. Arms splayed to the side. She's warm. And in my arms. How did she get in my arms? She's so bloody. Her nose is burst, the blood covering her mouth and neck. We must look similar then. She's warm. The blood is still spilling, thick and deep red, dripping onto my skin and clothes as I cradle her. Unconscious. Breathing. Stiffly, slowly. But breathing. She's warm-

A hand on my shoulder snaps me back into my own body. Fuck.

"Serafina," I breathe, eyes meeting Oisín's. Immediately, I thrust her limp body into his open arms. "Get her out of here."

"Sebastian-"

"GET HER OUT OF HERE!" I demand, because whoever hurt her could still be out there. I can't afford to assume that they're among the dead, but even if they were, I need to rip something limb for limb right the fuck now.

"Get to Gráinne," Oisín tells me as he clutches his wife close to his chest. "And then come back to me, Sebastian."

I don't make him any promises. He's right. Gráinne isn't among the bodies and we can't just leave her.

I take off again, barely even noticing the multiple other shackles and cuffs I pass as I run. This is a fucking torture operation.

"What the fuck is going on down here?" Nessa's voice makes me jolt. I assumed she'd gone back with Oisín to get Serafina to safety. In the orange light, she grins at me. "We kill them all, Seb."

I know my answering grin is bloody, but she's unfazed.

The first fucker we find is alone and dead before he even gets his mouth open enough to scream. It's too fast, too easy. It does nothing to ease the blood lust that's turning my vision red.

The next two we find are already down - one from a headshot and one with a nasty looking gash across his face. That one's still alive.

I kick him in the gut, and a low, ragged groan spills from his mouth. Nessa sneers down at him. He's not even really conscious, and the blood loss will catch up to him soon, but I kill him anyway.

The tunnel seems endless. A trail of bodies and barely any left for us to dispose of. Gráinne has been thorough, and I'm both impressed and pissed off.

There's no way to know exactly who hurt my girl, so they all have to die.

It feels like we've been running for hours though it can't really have been more than ten minutes by the time we discover the tunnel is, in fact, not endless.

There's a soft, broken sort of mewl in the damp air as we come face to face with the end of the tunnel.

Two women are already there. The wall is solid and as grimy as the rest of them, though the bloody marks are far fresher. Still wet and gleaming. There's two bodies on either side of what looks like some fucked up, huge St. Andrews cross. It hasn't been used for pleasure. No, the cuffs hanging from each point are bloody and swaying.

Gráinne's back is to us, her hair clumped with sprayed blood, the thick muscles in her back tense.

There's someone in her arms.

"Francesca?" Nessa speaks softly, like she's trying to coax a feral cat closer to her.

Gráinne turns, and the girl in her arms groans.

Jesus, Mary and Joseph.

She's naked. Shivering, her body wracked with shudders. Her dark hair is matted and filthy, hanging limply over her face. Gráinne sets her down carefully, and I step forward on instinct. The girl jerks, whimpering at my movement and I stop instantly.

She's terrified. Nessa tries to get closer, but the woman's reaction is the same, turning her face away and making that horrible, pained noise.

"Stay there," Gráinne tells us in a low voice, and Nessa and I nod.

I feel fucking useless, trying to avert my gaze from the poor woman, not wanting to strip her of her dignity even more. Gráinne strips off her jacket, grimacing at the garment.

"It's bloody, I'm sorry," she whispers to the woman, but Francesca doesn't seem to care.

With shaking hands she reaches for it, sliding her arms through the leather sleeves. It's big, given that Gráinne is nearly as tall as me and has about twenty more muscles than

I do, big enough that even sitting, it offers her at least a little privacy.

"Here," Nessa says, crouching down but not getting closer.

I watch my best friend place her knife on the dirty, stained floor and slide it towards the other women. Gráinne frowns at her.

"Always helps me feel better," Nessa offers by way of explanation, and Gráinne doesn't get the chance to answer that before the woman in her jacket lurches for the weapon. She clutches it tightly to her chest like it's a lifeline, finally looking up at us.

"Tunnel's clear," I grunt out.

I want to shout at Gráinne to hurry the fuck up, because I don't trust for a second that some fuckers won't come after us again, but the state of the girl stops me.

"I'm going to pick you up, okay?" Gráinne, murmurs gently. She scoops her up in a bridal carry as softly as possible, but the woman still groans at the movement.

My eyes are glued to her. She's limp in Gráinne's grip, but still conscious, her eyes puffy and heavy though they're open. Her tanned skin is pitted and discoloured with bruises and cuts, and her wrist, hanging over the side of Gráinne's arm where she's being cradled, is raw. She's been hurt, but carefully. None of what I can see is even near a fatal wound.

"As fast as possible," Nessa is saying quickly as Gráinne begins to move. "We'll cover you."

Francesca DeSantis is alive.

But at what cost?

44

Serafina

Someone's kicking me in the head. Repeatedly. Wearing fucking steel toe boots.

"Che cazzo?" I mumble, my tongue heavy and dry. The words scrape against my teeth. My whole face feels fuzzy.

Something cold and wet presses against my forehead and I jerk, my body stiff and distant. What the *fuck?* There's a voice, speaking low and slow next to my head, but I can't make out what they're saying. Their words all blend together into one indecipherable string of letters.

My eyelids are glued shut. It takes me reaching up with a stiff arm and peeling my lashes apart to get my eyes open. Even then, everything blurs and nausea rises.

I close them again, defeated.

"Breathe, angel," the voice coaxes, and it takes all my limited concentration to process the words. I know that voice.

"Oisín?" I mutter, swallowing roughly.

"Here, sweetheart." This voice is new, but achingly familiar.

Something cold presses against my lips. My teeth clink off the edge when I part my mouth, and icy water flows in.

As soon as I get drops on my tongue, it's gone again, and I manage to push myself up to chase the water.

"Sit up properly so you don't choke," Oisín says, strong hands cupping me and helping me push my body upright. God, I feel like I've been run over. My fucking head won't stop pounding.

"Water," I demand, though even through the blurry, ringing feeling, I know my voice is scratchy and quiet. Still, the second voice laughs. The sound sends chills over my skin. Sebastian.

They're both here.

The glass returns again, and I chug down the remaining contents. My stomach turns almost instantly as the water hits it, protesting. I grit my teeth, refusing to vomit.

"Take it easy," Oisín cautions, and there's fuck all I can do but listen to him. My body won't let me do anything else, no matter how much I want to leap out of-

Bed?

"Where am I?" I demand, my voice far stronger now the water has soothed my throat.

"Home," Sebastian supplies.

I blink rapidly, forcing my eyes to clear. It works, but not fully. Things are still hazy, but now I can make out my room, and two human shapes in front of me.

"No," I protest, shaking my head. Mistake. Big mistake. Fuck. The pounding is all consuming, like there's a Goddamn hammer being taken to the inside of my skull. "What happened?"

The way I frown makes my scalp sting. Immediately, I raise my hand, prodding my hairline and finding thread. Stitches. My hair feels clean, though, and it's pulled away from my

face. Someone's washed me, and braided my hair.

"Thought you might castrate us if we put you into bed bloody and covered in gross tunnel dirt," Sebastian jokes. "Plus, we had to get that head wound cleaned up. Did as much as we could without fucking up the stitches."

The care in his voice makes my panic rise higher.

"What happened?"

"You got knocked out," Oisín takes over from Sebastian. The bed dips as the taller of the two human shapes sits down. "Hard. Fucker split your head open and broke your nose."

Now that he's mentioned my nose, I begin to analyse the pain radiating through my skull. A tender touch of my finger confirms my nose is swollen and sore as all hell, and my skin feels too tight. Though it's the internal construction works happening in my brain that concerns me most.

"Concussed," I say out loud.

"Doc says you're to rest and have as little excitement as possible," Sebastian says. "And we have to watch you at all times. Make sure you don't choke on your own puke in your sleep and all that."

I make the mistake of pulling a face at the mere mention of that, and every injury screams at me for it.

"I'm so sorry, Seffy," my husband murmurs, his hand gently stroking at my hair.

"I'm fine," I lie, trying and failing to untangle myself from my duvet. "Frankie. I need to get to Frankie."

"Sef-"

"I said I am *fine*, Oisín!" I snap, finally finding my feet only to feel the water I've just drunk rise rapidly in my throat. My hand flies out blindly, catching the bedpost as the dizziness overwhelms me.

"Sweetheart, listen-"

Sebastian's hand lands on my arm and I shake it off immediately, the sound that rips from my throat nothing short of a growl.

"I need to get to my fucking sister!" I grit out through the tidal wave of nausea.

I'm so fucking angry my whole body is shaking. Then again, that could be the concussion. Or the gut wrenching, skin chilling *terror*.

I got knocked out. Down in those filthy fucking tunnels.

I didn't find my sister.

I need to go back, injuries be damned, men be damned because fucking Sebastian is touching me again, holding me still. I struggle, my back to his chest, every shake of my head sending a new earthquake of pain through me.

"FRANCESCA!" I scream, flopping uselessly in Sebastian's arms. "Let me go, you fucking *asshole! I need to find my sister!"*

Nothing exists except the waves and waves of sickness, and the resolute determination to get out of this house and back to where I'm so sure my sister is. I left her.

I fucking left her.

I'm aware that I'm shrieking like a banshee, but I can't stop. I think I might be sick. Or pass out. Fuck it, I'll fight to get to her until at least one of those things happens.

Nothing, not even my stupid fucking injuries, will stop me from finding her now. Not when we finally know where she is, not when I was so close, I was SO GODDAMN CLOSE-

"Sef!"

I still like I've been electrocuted.

"Sono qui! Va tutto bene."

Soft hands cup my face, and my eyes are still blurry but

now it's because I'm fucking crying.

My sister.

"Francesca," I whisper, and Sebastian finally lets me go only for me to crush my sister to me in a hug that must hurt both of us. Neither of us complains, though.

"*Va tutto bene. Sono qui, Serafina. Va tutto bene,*" Francesca whispers, voice muffled in my shoulder, repeating the words over and over. I can't decide whether she's saying them to me or to herself but I don't care because she's *here.*

I can't get my stupid tongue to say anything back except her name.

"Frankie," I choke out, barely able to believe she's here.

"Heard you screaming from my room," she laughs as she pulls away.

"You look like shit," I tell her, the sound of her laughter like a balm.

"You look worse," she shoots back.

My heart is so fucking full it might burst out of my chest.

"You beat me back here," Frankie continues, tone teasing. She's skirting around the bad stuff, the dark stuff, but I let her. "Thanks to these two." She gestures behind me to my husband and my…Sebastian.

Can I marry him, too?

I clear my throat and let my body stumble backwards into Sebastian's chest. He directs me to the edge of the bed and my sister follows, sitting close to me. We get comfy, fluffing up the pillows and tucking ourselves under the blankets the way we did when we were kids and she'd sneak into my room when she couldn't sleep.

"Who *is he?*" Frankie mouths at me, the bruises on her face and swelling of her bottom lip doing nothing to distract from the curiosity on her face.

I snort. We've both been beaten to shit and yet *Sebastian* is where she wants to start this conversation.

"My husband's lover," I tell her, earning myself a choked noise from Oisín. "My lover, now, too. Don't be weird about it."

Frankie rolls her eyes dramatically, and rests her head against my shoulder.

"Sef, I've just been betrayed, kidnapped and kept under the actual ground for days. The news of your threesome isn't even close to the freakiest thing I've heard this week."

"Frankie..." My voice is soft, but I can't bear to dodge the bullet anymore. She sighs beside me.

"I know, I know," she says quietly. There's a brief pause, then her heavy sigh. "I guess I should start with the fact that it was my own fault, really. I let a pretty face fool me."

I say nothing. I want to hear every detail of what happened, and I want to commit it all to memory. If only so that I can ensure every fucker involved, anyone who even laid a pinkie finger on my sister, dies.

"Her name was Alyssa Caddel."

45

Serafina

"She's dead," I say, my voice thick with anger.

The bruises dotted along my sister's body fuel the rage coursing through me. As badly as my head is pounding, I want nothing more than to find the bitch's corpse and fucking kill her all over again.

"I know, I saw her body as Gráinne was carrying me out of the tunnel," Frankie murmurs, her eyes squinting shut. She hisses at the movement but doesn't make any complaint.

"What happened, Francesca?" Oisín asks, concern darkening his tone.

"I... I thought she loved me. I thought that we were meeting up to go on our first real date. She was supposed to take me to the jewellery store to add another charm to an anklet she'd bought for me six months ago-"

I cut her off with a raised hand. "The chunky silver one with the damn butterfly charm on it?" I ask rhetorically, my mouth tilting downward with disappointment for my sister as she nods.

Shit. Frankie's one of the purest, sweetest souls I know. No matter how much violence or bloodshed she's been exposed to, and fuck there's been plenty of it given the family business, she never allowed it to harden her. She refused to build the kind of walls I worked so hard to place around my heart. She wanted nothing more than to love. To be loved. I hate that her feelings, and her willingness to be vulnerable were used against her.

"Yes," she whispers, a tear trickling down her face. She wipes it away quickly, the white bandage on her wrist catching my eye

My vision swims as I remember the fucking chains and cuffs bolted to the walls of the tunnel. Nausea rocks me and I press my hand to my stomach, desperate to push past it.

"Why didn't you tell me that you'd met somebody, Frankie?" I ask, my heart shattering as I look at my sister.

I thought we told each other everything. I thought I knew her like the back of my hand. I never would have believed her capable of hiding an entire six month long relationship from me.

"It was the first time I'd felt any... attraction for a woman. I wanted to explore my sexuality before I said anything to anyone. I didn't want to come out until I was sure of who I am," she says, a sob rising in her chest, and I nod my head in understanding.

Our family has never been one that cares about such things. Who a person loves or is attracted to is none of our business, and I know that Frankie knows we would never have judged her for being with a woman.

However, I also know how deeply unsettling it can be when you find someone who makes you question everything you thought you knew about yourself. When the attraction is so strong you can't help but let it change a piece of you. Shape you into somebody new, someone who's willing to redefine how they label themselves.

Hell, I never thought I'd have two men at my side, sharing the weight of the world with me. Yet here I am, with my husband and his lover. My husband and *my* lover.

"I can understand that," Sebastian says, and I nod in agreement with him.

"I'm sorry. I'm so fucking sorry, Frankie," I mumble while reaching to clutch my sister's hand.

"You have nothing to be sorry for. I should have told you. Maybe then none of this would have happened," she cries, shuffling closer to me on the bed.

We hold each other tightly for a few minutes, the guys settling on the end of the bed near us.

"Francesca, we need to know what happened when you got to the jewellers," Oisín states, an uncomfortable grimace twisting his handsome face.

I watch, horrified, as my sister shrinks into herself. Her eyes glaze over, and sweat breaks out across her body. I can practically see the memories flit through her mind. The litany of bruises and cuts coating her skin tell me one side of the story, but I know that a beating alone wouldn't be enough to break my sister. Not when we've been trained to withstand almost every kind of torture a person could think of.

"They wanted to use me. To...sell my body. They thought that if they could take one of my father's heirs and break them, it would force the other mobs to see how *weak* Papà is. They wanted him away from our territory. To use me as a distraction. The tunnels were being used as a human trafficking system..."

Frankie trails off, her throat bobbing as she tries to push past her trauma to tell us what's happened. Sebastian scoots closer, wanting to comfort her, or me, probably both, but he doesn't lay so much as a finger on my sister. Fuck, I think I love him for that small act alone.

"Do you know who was at the head of it all?" Oisín asks, and my sister visibly *winces*.

"No."

That single word has rage boiling my blood once more. How could none of us know that this was happening? How could none of us know that those fucking tunnels were right beneath our feet, and being used for such horrendous purposes? Hell, there had been rumours of the Russos pushing into the skin markets, and we were so fucking sure they were true. But with how hard Papà's men pushed the fucker we questioned, I'm certain now that the poor boy was telling the truth.

I don't feel guilty for his death. If anything, it gave us the answers we needed. It cut the Russos from our hit list, but we're sure to face shit for killing one of their men.

Oisín's hand rests softly on my shoulder, squeezing gently as he offers me silent comfort. Stress gathers tight between my shoulder blades.

Sebastian's hand lands softly on my thigh. He doesn't interject, but I can tell from the gleam shining in his eyes that he's watching Oisín's face. My husband must have his *plotting someone's demise* look going on, and I'm almost sad to not be seeing it. There's nothing sexier than a man who's willing to fight for the people he loves. But I can tell that my sister is hiding something. Something dark and twisted.

I lift my hands, cupping my sister's face while trying my

hardest to not hurt her. The swelling along her eye is significant, along with the glaring purple bruise across her cheekbone. Her lip is split, bleeding slightly as she chews on it with anxiety.

"I need you to tell me what they did to you, Frankie. I need to know how I can help you," I plead with her, desperate for her to tell me everything.

With one look at my sister's crumpled face as she shakes her head, I have my answer.

They fucking raped her.

Frankie's shoulders rattle as her head drops, her body curling into the foetal position beside me. She buries herself in the blanket as she clutches onto my arms for dear life. I hold her tightly as she cries, tears streaming down my own face.

"Una volta che saprò chi c'è dietro, Francesca, ti prometto che non ci sarà un solo pezzo del bastardo lasciato intatto dal mio coltello. li distruggerò. Te lo giuro sorella."

I swear to you sister, once I find them, there won't be a single inch of the bastard left untouched by my knife. I mean every word.

I stroke her hair gently as I vow to figure it all out. Vow to end the fuckers that dared to violate my sister. Vow to tear the world apart to seek out revenge.

Eventually, the mattress creaks as Sebastian and Oisín leave the room, giving Frankie and I the chance to grieve the innocence she lost. The life she lived, and the future she would no longer have.

We sit like that, holding each other through the pain until our eyes finally slip closed, and we fall asleep.

46

Serafina

Papà has sent everyone else in our employ home.

I know because the house is quiet and still as I slip out of bed, leaving my sister sleeping. Frankie is curled up tight in a ball, her arms wrapped around herself tightly. Like she's trying to hold herself together.

I rip my eyes away from her, guilt and anger burning in my gut. I can't stand it. I can't fucking *stand it.* I want to burn the whole Godforsaken city down so that I can be certain there's not a single person left alive who dared to hurt her.

Instead, I go in search of coffee.

My head is still murky as fuck but I can move without feeling violently sick now, so that's a bonus. It's early, given the bright streaks of sunlight beginning to push through the windows. The house is cold, and I wish I'd thought to grab something warmer to tug over my nightdress.

The stairs creak as I ease down them, holding tight to the bannister. The last thing any of us needs is me injuring myself more.

The kitchen is warm. I pause in the doorway, brow

furrowing, as the hot air reaches me.

"Serafina?" Papà's voice is tight, but welcoming. I step into the room properly, nudging the door shut behind me to keep all the warm air in.

My father is sitting at the large table, a cup cradled in his hands. There's no steam coming off the coffee, though. I wonder how long he's been here. He's wearing all black, and his gun is on the table.

I realise with a jolt that he hasn't slept at all.

"I came in to check on you, but I didn't want to wake you," he says, nodding his head to the chair next to him. I sit silently, abandoning my search for coffee, suddenly very awake. "You both needed your sleep."

"So do you, Papà," I tell him.

He shakes his head, the movement minute. "How am I to rest, knowing what happened to your sister, Serafina? What could have happened to you?"

I wince. "We're okay."

My father, for all the brutal, murderous, literal mafia boss he is, cares about his children more than anything. Frankie and I have been doted on. He taught us how to fight, how to defend ourselves, encouraged us to be loud and angry and violent.

He has done all he could to keep us safe.

And I know, sitting beside him at stupid o'clock in the morning, that he thinks he's failed.

"We found the others, too," he says, changing the subject. "When we went down the left tunnel."

"Others?" I whisper.

Papà nods. "Three of them. Two women and a man. Boy, really. Only nineteen. Left in similar…states as your sister."

I swallow the bile rising in my throat.

"Are they..." I can barely get the fucking words out. "Alive?"

Papà nods and I exhale sharply.

"*Sí*. Doc's got them somewhere safe. But we need to get them out of the city. Out of the damn *country*."

Despite the warmth, I freeze. "You think they're in danger."

Papà meets my eyes then, and I swear I see myself in the dark brown depths. He looks exhausted, but no less determined and ruthless for it. Never, not even after Mamma died, has he lost that resolve.

"We don't know who the fucker in charge of the operation is," he says darkly. "Until they are resting in pieces at the bottom of the fucking ocean, those they've ruined can't find peace. They can't be found at all."

I nod.

"What about Frankie?"

Papà looks away. "She won't leave the house."

"You want to keep her here?"

"You disagree?"

"No."

I don't. And I don't know if Frankie will hate me for it, but she's not safe anywhere but in this house. I'm not even sure if she's safe here, if I'm honest with myself, but I know we can keep her safer here than anywhere else.

Unless...

"Thomas sent Oisín to us to keep him out of their enemy's hands," I say slowly. I hate myself for what I'm suggesting, but I can't bring myself to shut the fuck up. Because this might be the only way to keep her well and truly safe.

"Serafina," my father starts, but his voice ends in a sigh. I know he agrees with my unspoken question.

"The Cavanaughs are family now, right?"

Papà's hands clench tighter on his mug.

"If you're sending the other victims to a safe house elsewhere to keep them out of the cockroach's grip..."

"Lo so," Papà mutters. *"Hai ragione."*

"Strarà bene, Papà," I whisper, pushing my chair away from the table, the legs scraping against the tile. *"Vuoi un caffè?"*

He nods yes, and I boot up the espresso machine, staring as the shots pull. Steaming espresso pools in the glasses, thick crema settling on top. My mouth waters. I'm half convinced this will revive me and chase away the lingering effects of my injuries.

Papà is analysing me from the table when I return with our drinks. I'm even nice enough to steam his milk for him, though I prefer my espresso as it comes. I grimace when he adds milk to his long black, the long standing teasing rivalry over the correct way to drink coffee between us not at all diminished even in the wake of the last few days.

I sip my coffee, try to ignore the pounding in my skull, and lean my head against my father's shoulder - still clothed with his suit jacket. We sit there as the weight of everything that has happened, and everything that's about to, settles over us like dust.

47

Sebastian

"WAKE THE FUCK UP!"

Oisín shoots upright in an instant, a dagger somehow already in his hand. Normally, I'd be all for having him pin that to my throat the way he is now, but we have far bigger issues than my dick.

"Jesus fucking Christ, Sebastian," Oisín pants, releasing his weapon at last and dropping it on the side table. His curly hair is messy from sleep, and his voice is thick. "What the hell is going on?"

"Serafina."

"What about Sef?"

"She's fucking *gone.*"

He's out of bed and running the second the last word is out of my mouth. I follow without hesitation. Guilt and panic and anger swell inside me as we race to Serafina's bedroom. Sure enough, the bed is occupied but only by her sister.

Francesca is curled tight on herself right on the edge of the mattress, the blankets all tucked up around her. The duvet on the other side is rumpled and folded over.

There's no sign that anyone else has been in here, but that does little to squash the sickening fear wrapping itself around my throat.

"Shit," Oisín curses under his breath.

"I'm so fucking sorry," I rush to say back, already moving down the corridor and throwing open doors.

"Where were you?" Oisín asks as he follows, opening a door on the other side of the hallway.

"I just went to fucking pee," I tell him honestly.

It was my shift to watch the girls, because neither Oisín or I could bear to leave Serafina alone. It didn't matter how *safe* the house was, or how capable she is. She and Frankie were injured and exhausted and neither Oisín or I would be able to sleep anyway without knowing they were under close watch.

I'd failed.

"We'll find her," Oisín assures me, but his voice is strained.

Sweat breaks out on my skin, cold and clammy. Panic is choking me in earnest.

I slam open another door further down the corridor, only to immediately slam it shut.

"What the fuck, Sebby?" Oisín asks as the door rattles, my knuckles white on the handle.

"Nothing!" I rush to say, but he doesn't believe me for a second.

Oisín shoves me to the side with his shoulder and I don't bother fighting him. If he's determined to see what's in that room, that's on him.

"What the FUCK!" Oisín shouts, shock and horror making his voice higher than usual. The door slams shut once again, and this time I hear Thomas' muffled curse from the other side.

"So, no Serafina," I surmise, resisting the urge to burst into hysterics, but only barely.

"No, just my fucking *da* shagging Aoife!" Oisín hisses, face pale as he turns away rapidly shaking his head.

"Well, they weren't shagging," I argue, muffling my laugh. "Yet. Hell, his pants were barely off-"

"Sebastian, I swear to everything good on God's green earth, if you finish that fucking sentence I'll kill ya myself," Oisín snaps, visibly shuddering. "I'm going to erase that image from my mind right the fuck now."

"Yeah, good luck with that, babe. Pretty sure even I'll never be able to unsee that," I tease him, ignoring the middle finger he shoots my way.

Quickly, we check the rest of the rooms before sprinting down the stairs.

In the space between my own fast breaths, I catch the faint clinking of...dishes?

I feel Oisín glance at me, but I'm already moving towards the kitchen. Nobody has turned the lights on anywhere in the damn house, but when I inhale deeply, I can smell coffee in the air.

"Seffy-"

Oisín and I shove into the kitchen. Serafina's wide brown eyes meet ours inquisitively, her full lips parting in surprise. She's still in her nightdress, a black silky thing. Despite its modest length, it's the single sexiest piece of clothing I've ever seen. Then again, anything that woman wears is. Her face is still bruised, her hair still sticking up oddly from sleep and the stitches pulling at her skin, but *fuck* she's gorgeous.

Oisín drags her into his arms before she can even greet us.

"What's wrong?" she mumbles against his chest.

He hasn't bothered getting dressed, and his blue pyjama bottoms are slung low on his hips. He's shirtless, and now that the relief of knowing Serafina is okay has chased away my panic, my cock jumps to attention at the sight. Oisín is slim but strong, and I trace the muscles on his back with my eyes as his arms flex tighter around our girl.

"You weren't in bed," I answer her, crossing to force myself into their cuddle. They part immediately for me, dragging me into their warmth. My heartbeat calms. "We were worried."

Serafina *tuts*. "I'm fine, *idioti*."

Still, she doesn't pull away from us. It's only when I hear a low chuckle that I realise Renato is in the room, too. I don't care enough to pull away from his daughter and her husband. They've let me in and nobody will pry me away from them again.

Renato doesn't make any comment on it. No, he just shakes his head a little and smiles. The man looks exhausted.

"I am glad my daughter has you two at her back," Renato says gruffly. We pull away from each other to find Serafina blushing, but unapologetically so.

"Papà..." Serafina starts, stepping away from us.

Fuck that. I grab her hand and tug her back between us, where Oisín wraps his arm around her shoulder.

Renato holds his hand up, interrupting his daughter. "I don't need an explanation, Serafina. I just want you to be happy, *capisci?*"

Seffy nods at that, squeezing my hand. Renato's lips quirk up in an almost smile before he points his finger at me. I raise a brow in question.

"I have a job for you."

"Sebastian, for the love of God, be *careful!*"

Oisín chokes on a laugh at Serafina's plea. "Angel, Sebby doesn't know the meaning of that word."

I pretend to look offended. "I *do.* I just reject the notion entirely. It's a waste of bloody time, effort and life."

I hear Serafina mutter something in Italian that I can only imagine means *I love Sebastian more than anything and he can do no wrong.*

"We should've just hired a fucking demo team," Sef continues to complain and now I'm actually offended.

"And deny him all this fun?" Oisín counters.

"Stop doubting me, you arseholes," I grumble, brows furrowing.

The explosives are in place, and despite the fact I really want to experience every second of this place falling apart, I grab the ear defenders from the counter.

I shoo Serafina and Oisín away, shoving the ear defenders on so I can't hear them anymore. They do the same, though Sef is still frowning like she doubts me. The urge to prove her wrong consumes me.

The mere idea of her hiring anyone else to get to play with explosives is ridiculous. I'm well versed in blowing shit up. In fact, as a child, I made a whole game of it - rigging shit up in the alley I called a garden when Mam was taking meetings in the house.

When we're across the street from the jewellers, my thumb hits the button.

At first, there's just the low rumble of rocks. Then, gloriously, the pillow of smoke blooming from the windows before, finally, the whole street shakes like a bomb's gone off.

Because it has.

Annoyingly, I wasn't allowed to decimate the entire fucking row of buildings like I'd wanted to. The shop is still standing, though the windows are black with smoke and debris now. The front one has shattered, though the glass still clings to the frame, large spiderweb cracks spreading across the front.

We wait, silent, as a few heads poke out of windows and doors around the street. One glare from Serafina has their eyes widening and scurrying back inside. Christ, I'm hard. It's so fucking hot when she's all intimidating and shit.

Once I get bored of waiting, I storm back over to the shop. I'm not stupid enough to inhale the smoke, and cover my mouth and nose with the neck of my t-shirt. I only dive into the wreckage of the innards of the shop long enough to ensure I've done my job. The entrance to the tunnel has collapsed completely. The vault is melted and crumpled, and the stone and plaster has folded inwards. It's unrecognisable.

Perfect.

Nobody's getting in here.

I return to find Serafina and Oisìn closer than before. Serafina's shoulders visibly drop in relief when I give them a nod, and Oisìn inclines his head.

"Good boy, Sebby," he murmurs as I inhale fresh air greedily.

"Don't call me that unless you're going to fuck me in the smoke, *Máistir,*" I warn him. Serafina's glance burns holes in my back, a shiver of awareness running through me.

"I'll thank you thoroughly later, Seb," she whispers as she brushes past me.

I curse, adjusting myself in my jeans not so subtly.

"You're still supposed to be on bed rest, angel," Oisìn chastises.

"I've already disobeyed those orders," she says with a shrug. "May as well keep misbehaving."

"Bad girls don't get rewards, sweetheart," I tell her. "Trust me," I add on with an exaggerated wince.

Serafina looks like she's thinking, catching her bottom lip between her teeth. "Will you punish me, *amore?*"

Jesus, she's going to be the death of me. From the look on Oisín's face, he will be too.

"Neither of you are getting fucked six ways to Sunday if we don't get home soon. Besides, we need to check on Francesca, and let the others know the tunnels have been shut down," Oisín grumbles as he walks back to the car.

We follow behind like the good little pets we are.

I drive us back to the DeSantis mansion, testing the speed limits once more, living for how Sef squirms in the passenger seat the whole ride there.

As we pull into the garage, I take stock of how she's looking. She's not bothered to hide the bruising across her face with make up, choosing instead to display it with pride. Her hair is pulled up into a slicked back bun, and she's wearing one of her killer *I'm a boss ass bitch* suits. She seems more herself today, more alive. But knowing what happened to Francesca seems to have destroyed a piece of her, and I can't blame her for it.

The things that were done to her sister… they'll haunt both of them for the rest of their lives. I'd blow this whole fucking town to the ground if it means keeping her safe and lifting the weight of the world from her shoulders.

I zone back in to realise that both Oisín and Serafina have been staring at me, waiting for me to move.

"You good, Sebby?" Oisín asks, and I can see his brow raised at me through the rearview mirror.

I nod once, not feeling like now is the best time to explain the dark, vengeful turn of my thoughts.

We climb out of the car and make our way into the house, none of us bothering to speak. The excitement that coursed through me earlier while blowing up the shop has dampened. All I want is five minutes where somebody's life isn't in danger and to fix the damn hard on that's been driving me nuts since we left that Godforsaken city. I just want to make them come and cry with pleasure until we pass out. No more worries, no more pain, and no more fucking assholes interrupting our fun. Is that too damn much to ask for?

I hear murmurs behind me as I climb the stairs leading to Serafina's and Francesca's rooms, but I'm too focused on making my desires a reality to pay attention to them.

I storm the steps, not bothering to wait for them to follow. When I reach the top, I pause outside Francesca's room, wondering if I should pop my head inside and check on her, but decide that Sef will most likely want to do it herself.

Sure enough, just as she reaches the empty space beside me in the hall, she tips her head in Francesca's direction before cracking the door open and slipping inside.

Oisín's hand finds mine, leading me away. I want to stay, to ensure they're both okay, to say *fuck their privacy, they need to be protected,* but I stamp down on the caveman instincts raging inside of me.

Francesca needs peace and her sister, not some overprotective asshole thinking they know what's best for them.

Still, I'm grumpy as fuck when Oisín drags me into Serafina's room and closes the door behind us.

"On the bed, Sebby," Oisín says the second we're alone.

I still, his low, demanding voice sending shivers through me.

"But-"

"Are you *questioning me?"* Oisín asks, voice darker still. He takes a step towards me, gaze fixed on me, and my lips part.

"Sef..." is all that comes out my mouth in answer.

Oisín's hand is around my throat before I can say more. I lean into the contact, letting him control me. It's familiar, as comforting as it is exhilarating. Oisín thrives on control and I thrive on doing whatever the fuck he wants.

He might call me a brat, but we both know it's all for show. My loyalty to him knows no bounds.

That extends to Serafina now, too.

"Our girl was bad today," Oisín tells me, walking us backwards towards the bed with his grip on my neck. "She needs to be punished, Sebby. Be a good boy and help me, won't ya?"

My eyelids flutter. *"Tá, Maistir."*

48

Serafina

Frankie is tired. She'd barely woken up enough for me to check she was still breathing before she tucked herself back under her blankets. Worry lines my heart but I don't want to force her out of bed. She needs the rest.

The hallway is empty when I ease back out of my sister's room. My head swims and I steady myself on the wall, taking slow, deep breaths. This goddamn head injury is a massive inconvenience. The pain, I can deal with, but I hate being unsteady on my feet.

I drag my hand along the wall to balance myself as I trudge towards my room. It feels wrong to sit here and do nothing, but with the massive clean up job happening to dispose of all the bodies, the collapsing of the tunnels and decisions to be made about the future, there's little more I can do.

I stumble the second I enter my room.

"*Dio mio,*" I breathe, shoving the door shut behind me and leaning against it. Heat flashes through me, not helping the dizziness, and my thighs clench.

"Not sure there's room for God in here," Sebastian pants,

looking up at me. His dark hair hangs over his forehead, his pupils wide, his lips parted.

Oisín has him spread out on the bed, chest flat to the mattress. His knees are bent and spread wide and his back is arched, giving my husband the perfect angle to fuck his ass with.

I can't breathe. Oisín is still fully clothed, and his fingers are between Sebastian's legs. I watch as he pulls away, three fingers slick with lube, and stands. Sebby moans a little at the loss, sagging against the sheets

"Come sit, angel," Oisín croons, beckoning me.

My legs shake as need rockets through me. That nickname, in his dark tone, makes me quake. I manage to make my legs work enough to get to the bed, scrambling up to sit at the pillows. Sebastian takes up most of the mattress, and I'm happy to let him. He looks fucking *beautiful* - smirking, needy and every inch of tattooed skin on display. I spot the stitches our doc used to hold his stab wound together but pay them no mind. He hasn't complained of pain since the tunnel, and I certainly don't think they're going to hinder him now. I quickly check him over, looking for any other signs of injury.

In places, the tattoos adorning his skin are raised and bumpy, though the ink covers most visible scars. I haven't asked him about them, and he hasn't offered the story. I'm patient, I can wait.

"Tell our little angel what's going to happen, Sebby," Oisín murmurs as he kneels at the end of the bed behind Sebastian.

His fingers find Sebastian's hole again, and I watch the muscles flex in his arm as he slides three in.

Sebastian tenses, a low moan rumbling in his throat. "You disobeyed, sweetheart."

I frown, getting comfortable despite the headache, and undo the buttons of my jeans. Oisín meets my eyes over Sebastian's body, brows furrowed in disapproval.

"I wasn't aware I had rules to follow," I snipe back, raising my ass enough to wiggle my jeans off.

"Doctor's orders were sleep and rest, Serafina," Oisín grumbles. I raise my brows in shock. Is he *telling me off?* "You asked if I'd punish you."

"And fucking you two is supposed to be punishment?" I ask, trailing my hand down my stomach, gripping the fabric off my t-shirt and pulling it up. I throw it in the same direction as my jeans, keeping my eyes on my husband.

"Oh, angel," Oisín tuts, shaking his head. He thrusts his fingers hard into Sebastian, and the other man cries out, hands tightening on the sheets. "You're not getting fucked."

I blink. "Excuse me?"

"You can sit there, wet and needy, but we're not touching that pretty cunt."

"What the-"

"You need to learn to take care of yourself, sweetheart," Sebastian grins, raising his head.

"That's not fair!" I complain, glaring at them.

"Be good for us, Seffy," Oisín says, voice suspiciously gentle. "And maybe I'll let you come. But no fucking, not until you're head's healed. I won't have you hurt again."

The sentiment might be sweet, and I can hear the edge of his voice that makes me think he is genuinely worried, but I'm too pissed off to care. Watching the two men I adore fuck is *too damn hot* and I can't sit here and not be allowed to join in on the fun.

I pout.

Sebastian laughs at me. "She's a brat," he taunts, twisting to look at Oisín over his shoulder.

My husband rolls his eyes. "Of course I get stuck with two fuckin' brats."

"Hey!" I argue, on Sebastian's side now. "It would be way less fun if we were good all the time."

Oisín smooths a hand down Sebastian's spine, pushing the man down hard into the mattress again.

"But way less stressful," Oisín mumbles, but his lips quirk up in a smirk.

"What if I promise that I'm fine?" I try, running a finger over the edge of my underwear.

"You're not getting our cocks, angel."

I huff, frowning in earnest. "I'm going to make you fuckers pay for this shit."

Sebastian groans. "I can't wait."

"Show our girl how good you take my cock, Sebby," Oisín hums.

Suddenly I'm not sure I care that I can't have Sebastian's dick because the idea of watching my husband ruin him sets me on fire.

"I want to taste her," Sebastian whispers as my husband unzips his trousers, shoving them down just enough to free his cock. My mouth waters. *Dio,* I married one of the hottest men alive.

And our lover is the other.

"Seb-"

"I need her pretty cunt to muffle my moans," Sebastian says before Oisín can tell him no. "Don't want to wake the house. They're all resting after the fight. I'm just trying to be *good, Máistir.*"

Oisín curses, reaching around to grab a small bottle beside him. The cap clicks, and I watch as he coats his length in it. The sight of his fist wrapped around his shaft makes my clit pulse.

"Do not make her come," Oisín finally grinds out. With his other hand, he grabs Sebastian's hair and tugs his head up. The man grins at me, and I waste no time spreading my legs wide.

Oisín pushes Sebastian's face between my thighs. My underwear is still on, but it's soaked, and somehow the pressure of Sebastian's tongue through the cotton is *devastating.* It shouldn't be this hot, being used to muffle screams while my husband shoves his cock into Sebastian's ass in one harsh thrust, but fuck I have to close my eyes against the burning wave of pleasure.

"I think our girl likes being used," Sebastian mumbles against my cunt. "She's fucking soaking, *Máistir.*"

Oisín, deep inside Sebastian, pauses to meet my eyes. His hand is still in Sebastian's hair, the other tight on the man's hip.

"Is that true, little wife? Do you like us using that perfect little body?"

I can't hide the shudder that rips through me. Sebastian presses even closer, and my thighs tighten, trapping him there.

"He's going to bury his tongue in that hot cunt just so nobody hears us, do you understand?" Oisín pushes, beginning to thrust as he talks to me. "You will not come. You will not be fucked. You are there for our pleasure only, Serafina."

I must be on fire. I don't understand why that is so unbearably hot, why the idea of being used and degraded, nothing but a toy for them to play with, is turning me on so fucking much. My underwear is soaked, so much so that I wouldn't be surprised if the white fabric is see through, and sweat drips down my spine.

I want that.

Oisín knows it, too. I trust him with this, trust Sebastian with this. I know they care about me, value me, and I know they'll look after me in every aspect of our lives.

Especially in bed.

"Take every fuckin' inch, Sebby," Oisín snarls, dropping my gaze. The muscles in his jaw ticks as he fucks Sebastian in earnest, the other man's legs shaking with each harsh thrust.

Sebastian moans against me and I curse.

"Quiet," Oisín snaps.

I bite my lip to try to obey, but Sebastian's teeth scrape over my clit, gentle enough not to hurt, and I whimper. Oisín's hand leaves Sebastian's hip, reaching under him to grip his cock. Sebastian shakes, and then his hand is between my legs, shoving my underwear to the side, tugging hard until something rips.

I gasp against the sharp sting of the material pulling against my skin. When I look down I see a red mark marring my tanned flesh, but it only heightens my arousal.

Fuck, I'd give anything for both of them to mark me over and over again.

"Fuck, that was hot," Sebastian groans, as his hips shove back to meet my husband's brutal thrusts.

"Give our needy girl your mouth, Sebby," Oisín commands and my eyes roll into the back of my head, my back arching as Seb sucks on my clit.

My arousal coats his chin and my thighs, and he times

his tongue entering my me to match the pace my husband is fucking him at. I can feel myself clenching around him, desperate for the release I know neither of them will give me. Somehow, it only makes me want it more, instead of pissing me off like it might have in the past.

"That's enough Sebby," Oisín pants as he continues to fuck Sebastian with punishing strokes.

"No," I mewl, hating the idea of Seb moving away from me. But Oisín's having none of it.

He grabs Sebastian by the shoulder, lifting him until Seb has no choice but to wrap his arm around Oisín's neck to keep himself upright. The hand that rested on Seb's hip moves to wrap around his torso, holding him closer to Oisín.

Separately, they're walking works of art. Together, they'd set the world on fire.

My heartbeat ricochets inside my ears, my thighs tighten, and my pussy throb as I desperately seek any bit of friction I can get. I've never been this fucking torn between wanting to watch them, and wanting to be in the middle of them.

"Please, Sir," I beg, hoping that the mix of me begging and using the honorific will be enough to get me in his good graces.

"Only good girls get to come, angel," he growls, as his hips slow.

"Ah fuck," Sebastian groans, his hips tilting forward as my husband wraps his hand around his lover's dick.

My nipples are so fucking hard I can feel them scraping against my bra as I take heaving breaths. I drag my hand up my body, making a show of removing my breasts from the cups before pinching and tweaking my nipples. If neither of them is going to touch me, then I'll fucking do it myself.

I watch my husband, a smirk twisting his lips as he watches me in return. When my free hand begins to trail down my body toward my dripping cunt, the smirk falls from his face.

"I said *no*," he growls, his dark tone spiking my pulse.

"You said I can't have your cocks, but you also said that I need to learn to take care of myself, Sir," I tease, using the words he threw at me earlier back in his face.

Sebastian barks a laugh. Oisín's jaw clenches as he continues to fuck our lover with shallow thrusts, his cold eyes focused on me as I insert a finger, then another, and another, into my aching pussy.

Fuck, that feels good.

My breaths stutter as I pump my fingers inside of myself, coating them with my arousal before drawing them out to circle my clit. When my hips lift from the bed with pleasure, my husband snaps.

"Restrain her hands, Sebby," Oisín commands.

My eyes widen. My body freezes. My breath hitches at the thought of being held still, the tiniest thread of hesitation weaving through me. My cunt, however, only gets wetter at the idea of them using my body while I lay there, incapable of moving away.

The thread of hesitation burns away as heat spirals through me.

"If you can't behave, then we have no choice but to force you to."

Sebastian whimpers as Oisín removes his cock from his ass, Seb collapses onto the bed right between my fucking thighs. A knowing smirk darkens his face as his breath hits my damp skin, and I know for sure that I'm in for hell.

I answer him with what I can only imagine is a perfectly

innocent smile as my husband crosses the room and begins rooting around in my closet. I don't know what the fuck he thinks he's going to find in there, but I don't stop him, or tell him that the box of sex toys beneath the bed probably has everything he needs already in it.

Trailing my eyes back to the man between my legs, I watch curiously as he makes his way up my body. Not a single inch of his skin touches mine, yet I can feel the heat radiating from him as he hovers above me. Sweat is beaded on his brow from the rough fucking he's taken, and something inside me is begging to lick every inch of him and taste it myself.

"Hands, Sebby," Oisín snaps when he sees what we've been up to in his absence.

"Sea, Máistir."

Sebastian's hands find my wrists. He stretches my arms up, leaning over me fully to hold my arms above my head. I wriggle, protesting weakly. His grip on my wrists is hard but not painful.

There's a gleam in his eye that should concern me, but instead I'm just flooded with curiosity. Sebastian's as shit at following rules as I am, because this position presses the hard, hot length of him against my aching cunt.

If I could just figure out how the fuck to move...

If I wasn't injured, I could spin us, flip him onto his back and ride him before Oisín had the chance to stop me. But, as much as I've whined otherwise, I really don't want to worsen my head wound. The concussion is far better, though still making me dizzy, but there's a shit tonne of bruising from my nose and the stitches in my head are still too fresh to fuck with.

I'm needy, not stupid.

And I can get what I want without having to wrestle a six-foot-something man for it.

I arch, widening my legs, hips screaming at the stretch. Sebastian's eyes meet mine knowingly, but he doesn't pull away. No, he cants his hips forwards, rubbing his cock through the wet folds of my pussy. I force myself to swallow my moan, not wanting Oisín to see and stop us. It feels wrong, dirty, disobeying like this and I can't get enough of it.

Sebastian narrows his eyes at me, then leans closer, catching my lips with his. He kisses me hard, teeth and tongue and the taste of myself on his mouth. I arch as he rubs against me, the piercing at the head of his cock nudging against my clit. I whimper, and he bites my lip hard to silence me.

"Naughty fuckin' brats," my husband taunts.

I startle, adrenaline flooding me, as I realise we've been caught. Sebastian doesn't even move. A low chuckle leaves his lips, still pressed against mine, and he stays hovering over me, his cock teasing me where I need him most.

"You being a bad influence on my good boy, wife?"

I shove Sebastian off as the insult registers. "He's the bad influence!"

Sebastian laughs whole heartedly at that, winking at me without a care in the world for whatever punishment we're about to get. "You've got that right, sweetheart."

Oisín just glares at him.

"Hey, you've had years to get used to it," Sebastian argues, batting his lashes dramatically at Oisín. My husband just shakes his head, ignoring Sebby's taunts as he steps closer to the bed, something in his hands.

"Keep your arms right there, angel," he demands.

"Or what?" I ask, though I keep them stretched above my

head.

"Or the second you're cleared by the doc, I'll have your ass so red you can't move again," he threatens.

My eyes must widen at that, because I catch Sebastian's smirk.

"Maybe Sebby should demonstrate what you mean," I say slyly, letting Oisín wrap something around my wrists, securing them to the headboard. It's soft and stretchy, and I know I could get out of it if I wanted to. But I don't. I really fucking don't.

"Traitor," Sebastian hisses my way, rolling over to nip at the flesh of my thigh in retaliation. I yelp, trying to move away, which only accomplishes a small tide of dizziness and my wrists rubbing against each other.

"Keep your teeth to yourself until she's healed," Oisín chastises, double checking my wrists are okay.

"I'll fucking tattoo my bite on her when she's healed," Sebastian grumbles, narrowing his eyes at my husband in challenge.

"You're fuckin' lucky I love you, you brat," Oisín growls.

I swear Sebastian's pupils turn to hearts. The grin he gives my husband is bright enough to light up the whole room. There's no jealousy, hearing them and watching them love each other, only a sense of *rightness*.

"But our girl wants to see that perfect ass turn red under my hand," Oisín continues, and Sebastian only rolls his eyes. "Keep your eyes on her while you show her how well you can take it, Sebby. Let her know what she's in for."

Sebastian grumbles something about *this isn't fair* but obeys anyway. He likes to act like a brat, but really he's a golden retriever who's eager to please. Eager to love. If golden retrievers were vicious and bloody half the time, that is.

I love each side of him equally.

"Count each strike for him, wife," Oisín tells me before gripping Sebastian's hip, leaning down to say to him, "I'm going to fuck you while I spank you."

"Fuck, yes," Sebastian agrees eagerly, pressing back against Oisín.

Oisín doesn't bother teasing anymore. No, he's as feral as both Sebastian and I, slamming into Sebastian hard enough to shake the bed. I whimper at the sight of Sebastian's face scrunching in pleasure as my husband's hand comes down hard on his ass.

I squirm uselessly, out of reach of them and unable to so much as touch myself now.

"Poor little angel," Oisín taunts, voice strained as he fucks Sebastian hard. "Such a pretty, needy little cunt. Stay nice and still for me, Seffy, and maybe I'll let Sebastian taste it again."

The other man is silent, face buried in the blankets, fists curled around them. His tattooed chest is rising and falling with fast, heavy breaths, a low groan emanating from him. At Oisín's mention of eating me, he raises his head long enough to nod.

I grin widely, trying to force myself to stay still even as I shake with desire. Oisín spanks Seb again, I count out loud, and he curses.

"Please, fuck, Oisín *please*," Sebastian begs now, voice cracking.

"What do you need, *a rún mo chroí?*"

"I need your cum," he moans, and fuck the sound is so hot I'm burning. "I need *hers*."

"Filthy, needy boy," Oisín whispers. His eyes meet mine again. "Keep your hands to yourself, Sebby. She only gets to come if you're gentle."

Sebastian agrees, moaning again when Oisín slips his hand around his cock.

"Hold still for him, angel. Let him make you feel better," my husband says to me, and I nod gently.

Even if they won't give me their cocks, the least they can do is make me come.

I cry out when Sebastian buries his face between my legs again, fighting to hold my thighs open for him. His tongue licks a long line from my ass to my clit and I jolt, whining.

"That's it, Sebby," Oisín groans. "I want you coming with my cock in your ass and the taste of my wife's cunt on your tongue."

"Oh *fuck*," I swear, tugging hard at the tights holding my hands to the headboard. The fabric holds strong, and I curse myself for not buying the cheap, thin tights that rip if you even look at them wrong.

Sebastian's mouth finds my clit once he's done lapping at me, and he sucks on it. My cry of his name is broken, pleasure spiralling so high and fast that I can't keep up. Watching them together has me so soaked my thighs are slick with it, and every touch of Sebastian's tongue is sending me straight off the edge.

"Fuck, yes," Sebastian moans against me, before sucking *hard* on my aching clit.

I see stars. I swear I black out from the pleasure, my eyes falling closed even as I try to keep them open, to keep watching.

"Fuck, take it," my husband demands, and Sebastian moans

against my sensitive flesh, his own orgasm crashing into him.

I manage to force my eyes open in time to see Oisín slump forward, caging Sebastian in with his arms, Sebastian's cum coating his hand. He reaches forward, pushing a limp, panting Sebby into the mattress, and swipes two fingers across my mouth.

Immediately, my tongue darts out, tasting Sebastian with a small groan. For a minute there's nothing but our harsh breathing and then Sebby groans from where he's pinned, still between my legs.

"Sleep," he huffs, and Oisín eases out of him.

"You're covered in cum," Oisín reminds him.

"You know I like it," Seb argues, raising his head just to lick at the wet arousal on my thigh.

"Well, I like clean sheets, so move," I tell him, trying to clamp my thighs closed again.

Sebastian groans, but my husband drags him up and shoves him in the direction of my bathroom. I see a streak of Oisín's cum trail down the back of his thigh and force myself to look away before I try to convince one of them to fuck me again.

"Think you can stand long enough to shower, angel?" Oisín asks, leaning down to kiss me as he unties the tights and frees my hands.

"I've told you a million times that I'm fine," I reply with an eye roll. "Besides, orgasms are powerful healing tools."

Oisín raises a dark brow at me in question. "Is that so, wife?"

"It is indeed, husband," I chirp as I slide off the bed and move towards the bathroom, where the sound of the shower filters out through the door Sebastian's left open. "Just ask our boyfriend."

Oisín's grin is so wide his eyes crinkle at the sides. I love him. I love them both.

49

Sebastian

Serafina rolls over for the third time in the space of two minutes. The room is dark, the curtains drawn and the lights off, but if I squint, I can make out the strong line of her nose and the way her eyelids flutter and her mouth parts as she exhales.

"Can't sleep, sweetheart?" I murmur, smirking as her eyes open wide.

Clearly, she thought I was asleep. Oisín is, soundly, on the other side of me. His arms are wrapped around my waist tightly, his legs tangled in mine.

"You'd think I'd be dead to the world after the last few days," she mutters back, frustration clear in his voice. We're both whispering, trying not to wake up the only one of us who's managing to rest. "But I…I can't stop thinking…"

I reach for her, drawing her closer so I'm sandwiched between her and Oisín. She's wearing his t-shirt, so he's shirtless, but I'm naked and *fuck* it's heaven. Seffy lets me drag her against me, and rearranges herself a little so her head is resting on my arm like a pillow. Her hand settles above my latest war wound, but it doesn't hurt. I'm sure she can feel the hundreds of scars marking my torso like this, but she says nothing. She simply shuffles closer, and places a tender kiss on my chest.

"Do you want to tell me about it?" I offer, not really knowing how to comfort her. Normally, my solution to everything is to murder whoever hurt the people I care about. Violence is always the answer.

Serafina shakes her head, her silky hair shifting against my arm.

"There's no point," she sighs. "It's nothing new. Just…my sister."

She doesn't elaborate, and I don't push.

"Do you want me to talk instead?" I ask.

I don't want her to think I'm making this about me, but I want her to know that I'm no stranger to the mess a family in the mafia can make.

She nods, leaning closer, her breath warm on my chest. Fuck, she smells so good. My cock jumps at even the feel of her in my arms, and I have to concentrate to force the blood back to my head.

"I realised, that aside from loving the hell out of your husband, you don't know all that much about me," I tell her teasingly, and she huffs.

"Aside from the fact you look hot as fuck covered in the blood of my enemies?" she teases right back, laughing softly. "I know that you're sarcastic, and stubborn and never fucking learn when to back down. I know that you're as loyal as a Goddamn hound, that your smirk is dangerous as fuck, and that no matter how hard you try to hide it, your heart is huge. I know what matters, Sebastian. Enough to lo-" she pauses, inhaling deeply. My heart stutters in my chest. I wish I could see her face. "Enough to love you, Sebastian Byrnes."

I go completely still.

"Serafina…" I whisper, my own heartbeat pounding in my ears. "Fuck, sweetheart, I love you too."

I crush her mouth to mine before she can even think about taking the words back. She kisses me hungrily, hands pressed against my chest, fingers finding the raised peaks under my tattoos before she tugs at one of my nipple piercings, making my fingers flex on her waist.

"Okay, now you can introduce yourself to me," she mutters against my lips, pulling away when I go to kiss her again. "No, go on, *sinner boy*. Give me a tour of every shadow in that pretty head of yours. I want to know my husbands equally."

"Call me your husband again and I'll fuck you until we wake yours up," I warn her. My words are dark and filled with lust, but there's a sinking feeling inside me that I hate. I'm not her husband, or his husband, and I never will be.

It's okay. It is. I have them, and that has to be enough. It's more than I ever thought I'd get.

"Go on," she urges again. "Tell me about you, Seb."

Because her hand is still resting on my chest, her thumb tracing circles over my heart, I start there. "It's okay to ask about them, you know."

Her movements pause for a second. "The tattoos…or what they cover?"

I smile. "Both. It's the same story, really," I begin, getting comfortable. "I grew up with my mother, in the middle of Killrover, for the first fourteen years of my life. I lived with her until Thomas Cavanaugh killed her."

Serafina makes a strangled noise, her nails digging into my

chest.

I laugh, but it's bitter. "Not his fault," I clarify. "Ma did betray the fuck out of him. And, honestly, he's a better parent than she was. Ma could have loved me, I think. But she was scared too."

"Scared? Of her own son?"

I sigh, unsure of how to explain. Nessa and Oisín both knew everything already when Thomas took me in, and I've never had to tell the whole story before.

"I reminded her of my da, I think. Not that I ever met the man. He worked with Thomas. Was an enforcer back in the day, before Thomas even took over the Cavanaughs. He was right by Thomas' side when he *did* take over, close to him. My mother loved my father, that I know. And then he died."

"I'm-"

"Don't say you're sorry, Serafina," I tell her. "There's nothing to be *sorry* for. This is just the way it is. Anyway, Ma got pregnant, and Da got killed. Mission gone wrong, bullet to the skull. Quick, at least.

"Ma never got over it. Some part of her died with him, or, at least, rotted. She *hated* Thomas. Blamed him for not protecting my father, for getting him killed. Never mind that this job is dangerous, and Da knew fine well what risks he took. But Ma wanted someone to blame, and Thomas was easy. For fourteen years, she stayed close to him. He helped her pay rent, helped buy my clothes, though I never really met him as a child. He looked out for me, the son of his friend and enforcer, and tried to help make things right. And in return, my ma tried to get revenge."

"What did she do?" Serafina whispers when I pause to catch my bearings.

I don't remember this shit often. I've never wanted to live in the past, mainly because it's painful as fuck. But I can't escape it.

"Contacted a Branigan member," I say finally. "Said she'd help topple the Cavanaughs if they took out Thomas. Obviously, she never succeeded. Thomas caught her, he suspected she was up to something. They raided our flat, while she was meeting with the Branigan member in our living room."

"Dio..."

"Ma was dead before anyone even realised I was in," I continue, voice void of emotion. "I think I should feel sad. But Ma never let herself get close to me, or me to her. She was there, she kept me alive, but that was all. Far from maternal, always cold, kept herself at arm's reach from the kid that looked too much like her dead love."

"How..."

"I should've been at school," I explain. "But I hated it, so I never went. They weren't planning on offing her, the plan was to kill the Branigan and bring Ma in for questioning. But she freaked out, tried to stab Thomas, and sealed her own fate.

"I was fuckin' nuts, even at fourteen. Always in fights at school, when I went, I pissed off all the teachers cause I couldn't read a sentence out loud. Got my *d*s, *b*s, *p*s and *q*s all mixed up. I felt stupid, and only got more angry when they tried to help me. I was a *problem.* I got my first stick and poke from the drug dealer next door when he found me scouring the alley outside for shit to blow up. Nice guy, Nick was. Sold good weed, too. Anyway, I watched my Ma die, then grabbed the knife she'd dropped and brandished it at Thomas."

Serafina chuckles at that. "You and your fucking weapons."

"Longest love affair of my life," I agree, kissing her hair. "I expected him to kill me, too. Instead, he put his gun away and stepped closer to me. I remember thinking *what the fuck is this man doing in my house and how am I still alive?* I was shaking, for all my bravado. Never been in a real fight at that stage, just scuffles with boys my own age. You know what he said to me? He said *just like your Da. More bravery than sense.*"

"We're coming back to the stick and poke thing later," Serafina mutters, stroking her palm over my inked skin.

"It was shit. A lopsided, lumpy *cross* of all things-"

"Never would've guessed you were a man of God," Sef snarks.

"Old sky bastard doesn't even know my name," I snort. "I've still got it though, I'll show you in the morning. Anyway, Thomas motherfucking Cavanaugh got close enough that I could've stabbed him. I doubt he would've let it get that far, but in the moment, he was in reach. I was angry, and scared, and very fuckin' lonely. And instead of killing me, or casting me out, or leaving me to fend for myself, Thomas took me in. Said he couldn't leave Liam's son, and muttered something about *what's another kid anyway*? I was around the same age as Ness and Oisín, and Thomas figured three couldn't be much worse than two.

"He was wrong, of course. I gave him a run for his fuckin' money. But he taught me how to harness the anger that had run my life for so long, explained all the shit my mother never did, and gave me an outlet for all the pain. I'm very good with pain, Serafina."

My girl grins. "My sinner boy," she murmurs, kissing me softly. "Always so stabby."

I snort. "Shit at school, great with knives."

"We all have our talents."

"God, I love you," I mutter back. My cock's getting hard again. She pulls away, feeling it stiffen against her stomach.

"Keep talking, Sebastian," she says lowly.

"I'd been with Thomas for four years before I was tortured."

"Tortured?" she repeats, that shock in her voice again.

I don't know why she's surprised. I work for the biggest fucking gang in Killrover.

"Yeah," I answer simply. "Fucked up a mission. Got myself stuck in some shitty basement, out of bullets and backup. Like I said, sweetheart, *I'm very good with pain.*"

"What did they do to you?"

"Lots of cuts, on every inch of my body they could get at. Deep enough to hurt like a motherfucker, and to scar, but not enough to bleed me out. They wanted information on some shipment or another. Fuck, I don't even remember now. Fuckers knew to avoid all the good spots - big veins, arteries - to keep me conscious but delirious. Peeled some skin off, put cigarettes out in the wounds, took a blow torch to my back, blah blah blah. Thank fuck they didn't go for my dick, though."

"Priorities," she breathes, amusement lacing the word.

"They were stupid as shit, too," I tell her, smiling. "Got high halfway through their torture session, passed out, and left a lovely dagger a few metres away from the chair I was tied up in. Shuffled over, cut through their rope, and slit their throats before they even realised I wasn't another one of their hallucinations."

This memory is easier than the ones of my mother. Sure, it haunted me for fucking years. Sure, I'd wake up sweating and screaming and wielding a knife I didn't remember grabbing. Once, Oisín found me with a blade pinned against his throat, wild and in the grips of a flashback.

"I got myself out, back to the manor, and collapsed at the front door. Thomas saw me on the security feed, and he and Oisín dragged me inside, cleaned me up and called our doc. Not much she could do about a lot of it, aside from bandaging the worst wounds. But they nearly all scarred. Hundreds of slashes and burns."

I pause, shuddering, holding Seffy tighter as I remember the state of my own skin. It wasn't the pain that broke me, it was the feeling of complete failure. I'd failed – by not being prepared enough, by underestimating the job, by not defending myself well enough. I'd let them hurt me, because I hadn't done enough to stop them.

I failed at being a son, and then it felt like I had failed at being a Cavanaugh.

"I couldn't stand to look at myself," I say, fighting to keep my voice steady.

I haven't had a bad episode in at least a year now, thanks to years of processing and determination to rid myself of the flashbacks and anger for fear of hurting someone I love by accident. But I can feel myself shaking now. I hate it.

"Every time I saw myself, I saw what had happened to me. Until then, I could hide it. Or, at least, pretend it hadn't happened. But suddenly, it was like everything that had ever happened to me, everything that I'd ever done, was on my skin for everyone to see. I hated it."

"Sebastian," Serafina says, and I brace for the pity. It doesn't come. "You're beautiful."

I kiss her hair again, inhaling the scent of soap still on her skin. "I covered nearly every scar with tattoos. The first was the deer on my chest, covering the largest burn mark. It felt like...a reclamation of sorts, I guess. It was addictive. I'd taken that scar and covered it in something I chose, in *art*. It sounds cliché but..."

"It's not," my girl interrupts, shaking her head. "Why a deer?"

I smirk at that, sinking back a little into Oisín's sleepy embrace. "*Oisín,*" I say by way of explanation. "It means *little deer.*"

"That's disgustingly adorable," Seffy murmurs, but I can hear the smile in her voice. "You've got two tattoos for him, then? The deer and the..."

"The one above my dick?" I finish for her, grinning. "What can I say? I love the bastard. And I knew when we first got together that I couldn't keep him. I wanted a reminder of him on me, so I could have him...close, even when I couldn't have him at all."

Serafina is silent for a moment. "I never wanted to take him from you," she whispers.

I shake my head immediately. "It's not your fault, sweetheart," I clarify. "I've come to realise, everyone is just trying to do what they think is right. Even if they're wrong, you know? Even if it hurts. Thomas, Oisín, fuck even my Ma, they weren't trying to hurt me."

"But they hurt you all the same."

"Yeah," I concede, swallowing hard. "That they did. But I wouldn't have it any other way."

Serafina snuggles closer, kissing along the antler of the deer tattoo over my heart. "Neither would I."

I hold her, content, letting the weight of my past settle over us. It doesn't feel oppressive, just familiar. A weight I'm used to carrying.

"I had my *mamma* for nine years," Serafina says, and I have to concentrate to process what she's just said.

"Sweetheart," is all I say, pressing my lips to her forehead. I don't tell her I'm sorry. I don't try to make it better. There is no salve for this kind of ache, so I just hold her and let her talk.

"She was beautiful, and kind, and brutal as fuck," she remembers, voice light. "Ran the family with Papà. Then she got sick. Really sick. Didn't matter how much money Papà threw at doctors, or treatments, or specialists. She was more sickness than human, and nobody could fix it. Frankie and I were only children, and they kept us from the worst of it. Mamma died, at home, in her sleep. She fought, she really did, for months. I used to think she was a superhero…I still do."

"Of course she is," I agree immediately. "She raised you."

Serafina sighs softly. "I think she'd have liked you," she murmurs, relaxing in the wake of our mutual confessions. "Oisín, too. Though she'd have had his balls for the mess he's made."

I laugh at that, and Oisín stirs a little behind me, groaning in complaint that I've woken him. Serafina and I giggle.

"Smart woman," I whisper to her, the three of us getting comfortable.

"I love that asshole, though," she murmurs, tucking herself up against my chest. Her words are muffled with a yawn that I echo.

"Yeah," I agree as her eyes closed. "I do, too."

50

Serafina

"You've healed well," Dr Hunt surmises as he packs up. "The bruising will fade soon, as will the headaches, and the stitches will dissolve within the next ten days."

"Grazie dottore," I say as I stand, Dr Hunt patting me on the back. He's practically family, considering he's been treating Frankie and I since we were born. Doctor Alfred Hunt is a long term friend of my father's, but paid handsomely to look the other way with things like gunshot and knife wounds.

He's also damn good at his job.

My father leads Dr Hunt out of the house and I turn to my men with a smile.

"See, told you I was fine."

Sebastian's smile is nearly feral. "Oh, I'll be testing that theory tonight, sweetheart."

Oisín doesn't argue with that. "*We* will," he adds.

I shiver. Sure, Sebastian's mouth is fucking *sin* but watching them last night gave me ideas. Ideas I desperately want to play out.

My father comes back into the meeting room before I can even think about suggesting them.

"Francesca won't be joining us," he says softly as he takes his place at the round table.

My throat goes dry. "Oh."

I knew Dr Hunt was checking her out, too, but I thought she'd been okay...

"Her injuries are still healing," Papà continues, leaning over the smooth wood to lay his hand on mine. "And she's requested to be given...space."

I nod, though my heart feels all wrong in my chest. Family meetings without my sister aren't family meetings at all. My father wants to speak to me, but I don't want to discuss business without her. I don't want to do anything without her.

But she needs space. I can, and will, respect that. Even if it feels like swallowing rocks.

"Oisín, Sebastian," I murmur, and both are at my side in an instant. A bit of the wound in my heart closes over at that. "Would you get us some coffee please? Now that the concussion is gone, this headache just needs caffeine."

I try to keep my tone even but I know it comes out all wrong. Still, they don't question me, Sebastian squeezing my shoulder and Oisín nodding at my father before they ease out of the room.

"They're good men," Papà comments.

I smile at that. "That they are."

There's a brief pause, and the air grows heavy. Worry collects in my gut. My father's brows are creased in a way that screams *you're not going to like what I have to say.*

"Watching my daughters be hurt is the worst pain of my

life," Papà says, leaning back in his chair. "You and your sister are my weakness, *cara mia*. And too many people know that."

"Papà..."

"Let me speak, Serafina," he says sternly, and I nod, swallowing. "You are strong, capable and powerful. And now, you have two men who would die for you by your side. I will not be head of this family forever, Serafina. And the time for my heir to step up is drawing closer."

A chill runs through me at the implications of his words. "You can't mean..."

"*Sono fiero di te, Serafina*," he says, voice rough now. "And your Mamma would be, too."

"*Grazie*," I manage to whisper, throat tight at his praise and the mention of Mamma.

"You're ready, *mia cara*," he continues, patting my hand. "Two or three years, to establish your place in the family, to make and cement the connections you need, to allow your marriage and...relationship to stabilise."

"And then..." I can barely get the words out now. He can't be saying what I think he is, and yet there he is, brown eyes shining with pride and words sure. "You're stepping down?"

"It will be time," he surmises with a nod. "You have proven yourself, and I do not doubt you will continue to do so. With your marriage as a powerful alliance, you have the makings of a leader."

I've known this was my destiny, of course, but suddenly it seems all too real. In just a few years, Papà intends to retire and have me head the family. Head the city.

I can't think of anything to say that will summarise my shock and excitement, so instead I throw myself into my father's arms. He catches me, squeezing me tightly to him.

"Help your sister, yes?" he questions when I pull away. "We are nothing without family, Serafina."

I nod. "We'll return to Killrover with her," I tell him with surety. She needs to leave the country, and Oisín's family will need to return too. We can go with them, and ensure the alliance stays strong and that my sister is safe. "And I'll bring her back home when the fucker who hurt her is dead."

By the time Oisín and Sebastian return with the coffee, my father and I have put plans in place for my sister. I wish she was here to discuss them with us, but she's asked to be left in her room and we have to respect that. Papà assured me that Gráinne had been stationed at her door, and that she was safe, but it still leaves a sour taste in my mouth.

With my men filled in on the plan, we leave my father to tell the others and make the necessary arrangements.

True to my father's promise, Gráinne is standing like a guard outside my sister's room when we head back up the stairs.

"Can I speak to her?" I ask, not wanting to barge in or upset Frankie.

"She's asleep," Gráinne supplies, giving me a sympathetic smile. "I'll let you know when she wakes, if you want?"

I nod, shoving down my worry and guilt. She'll be okay. She needs to rest. She's been hurt and she's tired and I can't even imagine the wheel of emotions she must be feeling.

I want to fix it all for her, and I can't.

Sebastian squeezes my hand as we file back to my room. I sigh as the door snicks closed behind us, running my hand through my hair. My face is still bruised like a bitch, but the pain is negligible now.

"We should pack," I say as Oisín and Sebastian sandwich me between them.

They're so fucking warm, and their touch grounds me. I don't know how I got so lucky, when I don't even believe in luck. If luck was real, Mamma would still be here and Frankie would never have been taken and I wouldn't have stitches in my head right now. No, it wasn't luck. It was Sebastian's stubbornness, Oisín's possessiveness and my willingness to do what needed to be done and marry a Goddamn stranger.

"We have time," Sebastian whispers, tugging my back against his chest.

"We leave tomorrow," I counter, but I don't try to pull away. His arms feel nice around me, and my husband steps closer, wrapping his arms around us both.

"Exactly," Oisín murmurs, resting his chin on my head.

I'm not short, but between the two of them, I feel like I am. I tilt my head back in time to see my husband press a kiss to Sebastian's mouth.

I'm not fast enough to hide the shudder it sends through me. Sebastian chuckles, pushing his crotch hard against my ass. I can feel the hardening length of him through his trousers.

"I think the little angel likes the idea of being pinned between us," Oisín murmurs to Sebastian, speaking like I'm not there. It should piss me off. In any other situation, I'd take a man's finger for doing that. But now…

Now I'm learning not to question what I like when it comes to these two. If I want them to fuck me like I'm nothing but a toy for them, then why can't I have that?

Sebastian's chest rumbles with his agreement, then his

breath hits my neck as he dips his head. "She's missed our cocks, haven't you sweetheart?"

It's only been a matter of days. But, fuck, he's right.

"Yes," I breathe, letting my worries melt away as I lean back into Sebastian. Oisín's hand drifts to my hip, his thumb dipping under the waistband of my cargo pants.

"Do you want it slow and sweet, Sef?" Oisín asks, but his voice is teasing. He knows fine fucking well what I want. But he's going to make me say it.

Fine. I have no fucking problem speaking my mind.

"I want you to use me," I tell them, keeping my voice strong. "I want to be between you, to be your toy. To be fucked until I can't take it anymore."

"Fuck, she's perfect," Sebastian groans, grinding his hips against me. I push my ass back, eager to feel him.

"I love you both," I say, quieter as a flash of heat goes through me. Oisín's lips are at my neck, and the way his tongue teases my pulse makes my cunt flutter.

"We love you too, sweetheart," Sebby answers, and my husband whispers his agreement against my skin.

"Good," I gasp out, needing them and needing them *now.* "Now fuck me like you don't."

51

Oisín

Sebastian and I crush Serafina between us as he kisses me. My wife's chest is pressed to mine, her back to his chest, and her little gasp when Sebastian's tongue meets mine has my cock weeping.

She wants to be used, like the perfect little toy she is, and we won't deny her.

"Whatever my angel wants, she gets," I whisper to Sebastian, ensuring I'm loud enough that Seffy can hear me. "Whatever my good boy wants, he gets too. And I think you want my wife's tight little ass."

Serafina squirms between us as Sebastian moans. He's always so fucking vocal, and it drives me insane.

"Maybe I want your ass," Sebastian brats instead, despite the fact I can see evidence that he's sinking into the headspace of being my good boy. He thrives on this, but the man can't ever keep his smart mouth shut.

I love him for it. And I intend to make sure he never has to question that again.

I reach around Serafina, mindful of her comfort even as I

prepare to carry out her wish to be used, and place my palm over the skull on Sebastian's throat. His tattoos are intricate and detailed and his artist is incredible. I have plans to visit them when we're back home, to prove my loyalty will never waver again.

I squeeze Sebby's throat as I slip my thigh between my wife's legs. Even through the layers of our clothing, she grinds down, seeking pressure.

I refuse to give her it.

"I want to feel you inside her," I snarl at Sebastian, losing myself in our game. Fuck, I want this, want them, so much it hurts. Literally - my cock is so fucking hard, pressing against my zipper, that it's uncomfortable. "I want to feel that pretty piercing of yours in our toy's ass as I fuck her desperate cunt. I want to fill her so full of cum that she's dripping. I want to taste all three of us on her skin."

Serafina whimpers at my words, and I swear I can feel the heat of her pussy against my thigh. Sebastian swallows hard against my palm, eyes half lidded and pouty lips part. God, he's pretty.

"Perfect little toy for us to use, Sebby," I taunt, pushing them both in the direction of Serafina's bed.

The second we get home, I'm finding somewhere all three of us can sleep together. Fuck, I'll build a whole new property on our land so I can have a bedroom so big the bed will fill a whole wall.

"Be a good boy and get her hole ready."

With a push, Sebastian falls back onto the bed, dragging Serafina with him. I waste no time, aware that we teased the fuck out of her last night and wanting to cement our future with our flesh. We're returning home, and we're returning *together.*

I'm careful not to rip Seffy's favourite cargos as I drag them off her tanned legs, taking her underwear with them. I don't go slow, I don't kiss her, I don't touch her more than to get her naked. It takes effort not to pinch her pretty, peaked nipples or tease the tight bud of her clit, but I refrain.

That's the game, after all.

"On the floor, face between her legs," I order Sebastian, stripping him with the same fast efficiency as he stands before sinking to his knees. "Don't touch her cunt, Sebby. Only her ass, understand?"

I want to use her, not hurt her. I refuse to do this without prepping her properly, especially while this is so new. Neither Sebastian or I are small, though he's longer, and without stretching her out, there's every chance it wouldn't be pleasurable for her. Still, that doesn't mean I'll be kind about it.

I watch for a moment as Sebastian throws Serafina's legs over his shoulders and ducks his head. His dark hair tickles her thighs, and I catch the glisten of spit as he lets it drop off his tongue and run down her centre. He traces its path with his tongue, avoiding her cunt, until the tip of his tongue presses against her ass. Serafina jerks, eyes widening at the sensation.

I undress as I watch them, my wife squirming as my love relaxes her until she's moaning, her hips bucking in search of more. She won't get it, not yet. His tongue works her over as I shed my own clothes and find the lube.

Instead of passing the bottle to Sebastian, I drip the cold gel onto my palm and settle behind him, reaching for his cock. He's so hard his head is slick with precum, and when I coat his length in the cold lube, dragging my hand over him, he groans against Seffy.

"Give me your hand," I demand of my wife as I drag Sebastian away from her to his feet.

Serafina shakes as she dutifully extends her hand to me, palm up. I coat her index and middle finger in the lube, watching her brows furrow.

"What-"

"Toys don't talk," I snap, watching the way my words make her breathing hitch. "Fuck your ass with your fingers. Get yourself ready for Sebastian."

I watch only long enough to make sure she obeys. With her thighs spread wide, her cunt glistening with her need, she whines as she slides one finger into herself.

I don't want to look away from the sight of her, but I have another needy brat to attend to. Sebastian is practically drooling, eyes darting between Serafina and me, pulse thrumming at his throat.

"This doesn't feel real," he mutters, so quietly that I'm not sure he meant to say it out loud. I grab him by both the throat and the dick, squeezing, my fist sliding over his length easily with the slick of lube left on my palm.

"It's real, *a rún mo chroí,*" I assure him. "Come on, sweet brat, let me show you how real it is."

Sebastian leans into my touch as I kiss him, tongues fighting for dominance, my hand still working him over. I pull away when Serafina moans, two fingers in her ass now, wet enough that her cunt is dripping onto the sheets.

More than ready.

"Our toy is ready to be used," I muse as we return to the mattress.

Roughly, I grab Seffy, dragging her to me. She squeals, grabbing my shoulders to balance herself, fingers still damp with her own need and the lube.

"Fuck, please," she murmurs, wrapping her legs around my waist in an effort to get me inside her faster. "Both of you, fuck, *I can't wait*."

My hand meets her mouth, shutting her up. I'm gentle, covering her lips and pressing just enough that she can't talk. A fresh wave of arousal rocks her, and she shifts her hips desperately. Fuck.

"Keep your filthy little mouth shut, or we'll leave those holes empty and weeping," I warn her, though it's a lie. I won't leave her needy, not after I denied her last night, but the warning is enough.

Serafina relaxes against me, going limp in submission. My lips skim her ear as I whisper, "We won't be gentle. If you need to stop, pinch me."

She nods frantically, and I remove my hand to let her answer. "Wreck me," she pants.

"Fucking gladly," Sebastian supplies, grabbing her hips.

Her soft flesh dimples under his tattooed fingers as he lifts her, once again squishing her between our bodies. His cock glistens with lube, and his hands are tight on her ass as he lowers her onto him.

"How does our toy feel, Sebby?" I ask, holding Serafina steady with a tight grip on her waist.

"Like heaven," he grinds out, fingers flexing as he struggles to go slow. Finally, he exhales in a rush, Serafina shaking between us, as he sinks into her up to the hilt.

I wait, letting her adjust, and checking to see if she'll pinch me. When she only wriggles, I laugh darkly.

"You're wrong," I say as I drop my grip to her thighs, spreading her wider for me. Pinned against Sebastian, her soaked cunt slides against my shaft, coating me in her desire. I notch the head of my cock at her entrance, even that barest bit of contact making my pulse rise. In a few sharp, hard thrusts, I'm buried in her cunt - hot and impossibly tight with Sebastian already in her ass. "Our fucktoy feels like sin."

52

Serafina

I'm sweaty and shaking and stretched wide open between them, and I couldn't fucking be happier. I'm stuffed full, my thighs shuddering with the way my husband keeps me spread for him. His hand has left my mouth for my thigh, but I keep myself quiet anyway, playing my role.

But fuck, I don't know how long I can stay silent for.

Not when they start moving.

"Ah, fuck, yes," Sebastian groans as Oisín rocks me between them, the men working in tandem to keep both my holes full as they thrust. "*Shit*, I can feel you inside her. God, that's so fucking hot."

I want to agree, but I can't speak. I can't even *think*. The sensation of their skin on mine, my breasts pressed against Oisín's chest, Sebastian's vice like grip on my ass, their cocks so fucking deep inside me, is too much. I'll never get enough.

I'm jostled between them, their hands harsh, their thrusts harder. Oisín's hitched breathing and Sebastian's low groans fuel the fire spreading through me, and my clit throbs with the need to come. Just one touch, that's all it would take. I resist the urge. I asked for this, and I want it to last.

I tilt my head to the side, teeth sinking into my bottom lip to keep my moans in, the pain anchoring me. Oisín releases one of my thighs to grab the back of Sebastian's neck, tugging him close to him and forcing me to take their cocks deeper. I whine, unable to stop it, the small pang of pain at the new stretch only driving my need higher. My men kiss, hungrily, messily, thrusting faster now, wild with desire.

"I want to feel you come," Sebastian begs, lips wet with their spit and brows drawing inward. His thrusts are desperate, falling out of rhythm with Oisín. "I want to feel you come with me, *Máistir.*"

"Ask. Nicely," my husband grinds out.

"Please, please," Sebastian pleads, swearing and gasping. God, *I'm* going to come.

"Fill our pretty little toy like a good boy for me," Oisín demands, releasing Sebastian's neck only to stick the tip of his thumb between the man's lips. Sebastian sucks immediately, tongue winding around Oisín's finger, his blue eyes bright.

Why is that so hot?

I'm beyond questioning it, or us. Everything about these men turns me on, individually and together. Fuck, one heated glance from them and I'm dripping, and being used by them for their pleasure is intoxicating.

I feel both degraded and powerful, and I never want to let go of that feeling. These men are the sweetest poison I've ever tasted.

Oisín withdraws his thumb, and Sebastian sticks his tongue out, mourning the loss. My husband curses at the sight, releasing me completely. Sebastian's grip on me keeps me steady through their fucking, though, and even if it didn't, the way I'm digging my nails into Oisín's shoulders would. When did I start clawing at him? I'm not sure, but I can't stop. He doesn't tell me to, and I'm out of control now, wild and whimpering as the need to come becomes almost painful. But I want their cum dripping out of me, I want them to feel each other use me.

Oisín's now free hand raises, and he shoves two fingers into Seb's open mouth. Sebastian chokes a little at the intrusion, moaning, sucking and licking at Oisín's digits like he would his cock. I want to make a comment about how I'm not the only one who wants to be filled, but then Oisín's thumb, wet with Sebastian's spit, finds my clit. He circles it, once, twice-

I *die.*

I know I'm screaming. I know I should shut the fuck up. I know, I know, I know, but I can't. I can do nothing except shatter, endlessly, between the bodies of my two men. They're still moving, fucking into me, drawing my orgasm out until my voice is hoarse.

I can't tell where the first orgasm ends and the second begins, because Sebastian shouts his own release and I'm seeing stars again.

"Fuck, that's it, Sebby, come for me, oh *God,*" Oisín groans before he's coming too, set off by either me or Sebastian, thrusting himself deep.

I shudder, trying to find air, completely trapped by both their bodies. I can feel their cum seeping out of me, hot and wet and sticky. I relish the filthy feeling of it cooling on my skin as we all try to catch our breaths.

My head rests against my husband's chest, and Sebastian's weight squishes me against him. I can barely breathe for the scent of sex and my own lingering pleasure and I don't care.

If I never breathe again, at least I'll die happy.

"Can I spend the rest of my life like this?" Sebastian asks, echoing my own thoughts.

"In my wife's ass?" Oisín chuckles in response and I can't help the laugh that leaves me.

"I may be your wife," I whisper. "But I'm his girl, too."

"Of course you are," Oisín corrects quickly, "but both of you belong to me. You're mine, and I'm never letting you go."

Sebastian snorts. "Clearly, you can't ever rid yourself of me. Don't bother trying again."

I find his hand with my own, twining our fingers together. "They can pry you out of our cold, dead hands," I promise, squeezing.

"Keep talking dirty to him and you'll make him fuck you again," Oisín says, voice light.

I glance up at him, seeing a softness in his eyes as he looks at Sebastian and I. I know, without a doubt, that this is where I'm meant to be. Just a few years off being the head of our family, with the loves of my life, and the future at our fingertips. Speaking of...

"What happens when we get back to Killrover?" I ask, glancing between Oisín and Sebastian. "Because I'm not hiding shit from anyone."

Oisín winces. "We should never have hidden at all," he says. "I had my head up my arse. I wanted to do right by my da, and the duty I had to the family, but in truth, I think he just wanted us to be happy. I tried to prove that the people I fucked were just flings, the men and women I brought home always left the next morning."

"You fucked other people?" I ask, shocked. Oisín and Sebastian both seem far too possessive for that.

But Seb nods at my back. They're both still inside me and none of us make any move to change that.

"We never asked each other for exclusivity," he explains. "Both because we were trying to avoid the pain of eventually losing each other, and because I think we always knew we had enough space in our hearts for other people."

I swallow thickly, bracing myself for what I'm about to say. "I don't think I can share you both with anyone else."

Even the thought of it makes me want to rip the hypothetical person's hands off. These men are mine, and each others', and nobody else's.

"My heart is full," Oisín murmurs, and mine beats hard against my ribcage. "You two are all I'll ever need."

"You're what we needed, Serafina," Sebastian echoes. "I'm officially only a slut for the two of you now."

He says it dramatically, like it's a hardship, the sarcasm in it making us all laugh.

"Back to your original question," Oisín redirects, smoothing his hand up and down my spine. I'm so relaxed I feel boneless, sated and limp and doing nothing to hold myself up. "I'm going to build us a home. I know we'll be going back and forth between San Jarno and home, but I want us to have somewhere that's just...for us."

"Where?"

"On our land," my husband continues. "Close enough to the manor to still be near the family, for security and business, far enough so that my family won't have to hear me making you two scream."

"I am tired of trying to keep my mouth shut," Sebastian says, voice bright with excitement.

"Never again, sinner boy," I mumble, smiling against Oisín's chest. “We like you loud.”

53

Sebastian

We've been back in Ireland for three days and already I'm back in Avery's shop. This time though, for the first time in all the years that they've been tattooing me, I'm not alone. Over the buzz of the tattoo gun, I can hear Serafina already planning her next piece, and Oisín reminding her she only got her first tattoo five minutes ago. I've gone last, hoping to sneak a peek at the others' designs, to no avail.

I've barely any free space left on my body, but I'm lying face down on the freshly cleaned table, arms flat at my sides. The familiar, stinging sensation of ink pressing into my skin soothes me, and I'm as relaxed as ever as Avery works. Oisín and I coordinated our design somewhat, but Serafina's could be anything.

It didn't sit right with me that I had ink for Oisín but not for Sef, and when I told them I was going to get that fixed, Serafina persuaded Oisín to come with me. Fuck, the idea of seeing them with ink, ink that represents *us*, is enough to have me trying not to get hard on Avery's table.

"You're running outta space, Seb," Avery laughs behind me, bracing one knee on the edge of the plush table I'm lying on. They're shorter than me by about a foot, something I've teased them about every time I've come for the past decade.

"You'll find more. Sure I've still got some clean skin on my balls," I tease, voice muffled by the bench.

Avery snorts, wiping a dry paper towel over the fresh ink. I hiss, the scrape of it worse than the actual needle.

"Bastard," I accuse them.

"Pfft," Avery replies, adjusting their position to reach my left shoulder blade now. "I've tattooed your fuckin' dick, Sebastian. You can deal with this pain for fuck's sake."

They're not wrong, but I still shoot them the middle finger.

"Your...*friends* are nice," they continue carefully.

"Lovers," I correct. Though, I have plans to make our relationship concrete. Not that they know that. It'll be my surprise, after we leave here.

"You've told me all about your little deer," Avery muses, pressing the needle to my skin again. "But less about the angel."

"She was...unexpected," I say with a laugh, trying not to move.

For the rest of the session, I tell Avery the story of Serafina and Oisín. The artist stops tattooing me to provide commentary, shock and intrigue in their voice. By the time my newest tattoo is finished, Avery is determined to introduce themself properly, despite having just tattooed the two.

We reappear in the reception area of the small tattoo parlour. It's owned and run by Avery, though there are two other artists who work with them - Sof and Trig. Avery has done every single piece I have, aside the stupid stick and poke still on my ankle, and I'm loyal as fuck to them. It occurs to me as Avery eyes up my lovers, that I consider them a friend.

The small, heavily tattooed artist at my side narrows their eyes on an unsuspecting Oisín. Serafina's dark brow furrows in confusion, her wrist shiny with the second skin covering her fresh ink, but a smile tilts her full lips. Avery is shorter than all of us, with messy dirty blond hair that permanently looks like they've just rolled out of bed. Their tattoos are a patchwork of their own skill - early work with bobbly lines, to newer, incredibly detailed work. The fine line scythe tattoo above their brow quirks as Avery rearranges their expression into a neutral one.

"So, *little deer*," Avery says, their smile a little feral. I grin, staring down at their short form with amusement. "You take good care of your angel and your devil, okay?"

Avery's voice is steady but laced with poison. They're hot as fuck - what with their mosaic of art, messy hair, bright green eyes and lip piercings - but I've never seen them act like the badass they look like. They've always been nice to me, sarcastic but caring, and over the years, we've grown comfortable in each other's presence. Avery has seen me at my worst, and helped me get to my best. Clearly, they hold a grudge against Oisín.

"Or what?" Oisín asks, though there's a glint to his eyes that tells me he's only pushing them to see what will happen. Sef and I know fine well that Oisín would never hurt us again.

"Your name doesn't scare me, little deer," Avery says with a shrug, turning their back to us to slip behind the desk.

I hand them over a wad of cash in payment and watch them roll their eyes as they count out my overpayment.

"Maybe it should," Oisín replies carefully, though amusement is bright in his eyes even as he crosses his arms over his chest.

Serafina dismisses the whole pissing contest to continue flicking through the flash book Sof has out on the coffee table, full of available designs.

Avery tries to hand me back my change and I glare at them. They never charge me enough. Fuck, I owe them so much more than money for all they've done for me. They know it, too, though they refuse my gratitude every time. I don't know where the fuck I'd be without Avery helping me claim my body back, and it's not worth thinking about. One of these days, when I eventually do run out of fresh skin, I'll find a way to repay them.

Avery just eyes Oisín over the counter, resting their elbows on the glass. Their tank top slips down one shoulder, exposing the trippy swirl design inked there. It's one of my favourite tattoos out of all the ones painting their skin.

Oisín sighs, and I hear his footsteps as he gets closer. His arms wrap around my waist from behind and the contact jolts me. It's still odd, having him care for me publicly. I love it. I think he does, too, because he hasn't stopped touching me or Sef since we cemented our desire for a future together. It's like whatever tense, tangled ball of string that was holding his heart together has unravelled and he can finally breathe.

"Thank you for taking care of Sebastian when I failed to," Oisín murmurs, so quietly I think I've misheard him. Avery's eyes widen, their lips parting.

"For the record, I tried to talk him outta both tats he got in your name," Avery counters, still pushing Oisín. I smile widely, showing them how much I appreciate them.

"For the record, you're a good person," Oisín answers

smoothly, chin resting against my shoulder as he folds himself around me. "I am not a good man, but I have never felt guilt over that until I realised what I had done to Sebastian. You may hate me, but if you ever need anything, the Cavanaughs are in your debt, Avery. We look after our own, and that's you now."

Avery looks like they'd be less shocked if Oisín had just pulled a gun on them. I can feel Sef's eyes on us, and in seconds she's at my side, too, her smaller, calloused hand resting on my hip as she tucks herself against my side.

Relief makes Avery's face calm.

"I just did my job," they lie.

We all know they've done more than that. Avery gave me a safe space in their studio, and their life. They helped me reclaim my skin, to turn pain into something beautiful. This is where I came when I was hurting, when I wanted to crawl out of my own body. They have grounded me, always knowing what design I needed. They've covered every mark I hated in intricate black ink, and they've never asked questions. I offered my story to them eventually, when it became clear that they were a friend.

Avery has never judged me. Never asked for anything in return for being my tattoo-artist-slash-therapist-slash-safe-haven. Fuck, even getting them to take my tips is hard enough.

"You protected my boy, made him confident again," Oisín continues, his voice rough. Fuck, I might cry. What the hell? Avery's eyes are glassy too, their hands splayed on the counter. "I hope you'll accept us into your studio again, Avery. It would be an honour for Serafina and I to carry more of your art, the way Sebastian does."

Who knew I'd get so emotional over some fucking tattoos?

Avery smiles, a genuine one that shows off the smiley piercing that clinks against their teeth.

"You're welcome here, as long as you don't hurt Seb again. He's special to me, ya know. Sits better than anyone I know for a dick tat, too."

The humour is much needed, chasing away the sentimental tinge in the air. I escape Oisín's arms to jump the counter before Avery can escape, dragging them into a one sided hug. They like to say they're not a hugger, and I'd respect the fuck out of that boundary if it wasn't an absolute lie. They go soft in my arms, and I kiss the top of their messy hair.

"See ya soon, Aves," I say as they push me away with a mock glare.

"I want the cherub in that book," Serafina calls out, pointing to the flash sheet.

"Sof will be happy to do it for ya," Avery says, nodding at her. "Bring the boys with you when you come in, angel. See if you can convince the little deer to get his junk tattooed next."

Oisín makes a pained face at that, and I burst into laughter.

"Love ya," I call out to Avery, who just rolls their eyes and shoos us out the door.

"Home?" Oisín asks as the grey sleet of Killrover greets us.

Serafina wrinkles her nose as the slushy rain hits her and I laugh at her expression.

"What, our little sun goddess can't handle a bit of rain?" I tease, but I'm already shoving my hoodie over her head and pulling up the hood.

"You'll get cold," she argues, but she makes no move to take it off again.

"Nah, I'm way too hot for some Irish weather to tame," I

say with a smile, and Oisín's hand slips into mine.

I turn my head, meeting his lips hungrily, suddenly fucking desperate for them. Serafina kisses me when Oisín pulls away, nipping my bottom lip with her teeth.

"But no, we're not going home," I answer Oisín's original question. "I have plans."

"That's dangerous," Serafina mutters.

"Do you trust me?" I tease.

Both of them answer yes without hesitation.

54

Sebastian

The Church of Blessed Hearts is an intimidating place. Beautiful building, really, except for the fact that it's in the middle of Killrover. This city isn't a godly place, and we are far from godly people, and yet I can't think of anywhere better to do what we're about to do.

The church's old stone, weathered and grey, climbs towards its imagined heaven. Shockingly, the stained glass windows are intact - given that Siobhán shot out her wedding in this church, the building carries no sign of it. Higher still, as though it's trying to reach the thick grey clouds of winter, the bronze bell is set proudly in the steeple.

This is where Oisín's first wedding was held, where Shivy ran the fuck away in her wedding dress and straight into Nessa's arms. It's the perfect place for the next step.

And the priest is crooked as fuck.

The doors are locked, but that doesn't matter. I pick the ancient lock in seconds, while Serafina grins at me.

"Why the fuck are we back here?" Oisín groans as the heavy doors swing open. Immediately, Sef and I duck inside, escaping the shite weather.

Oisín remains, face stony, lips pressed together in disapproval.

I fill Serafina in quickly on what happened before Oisín was sent to Italy, and she just shrugs. Of course, she knows already, but she seems unbothered by the whole thing.

"Where else could possibly be better for your third marriage?" I ask Oisín, who finally steps inside. His curly dark hair is wet and sticks to his forehead, and his eyes are dark with suspicion.

"What the fuck are you on about?"

Serafina echoes his statement, their confusion clear. No matter, it'll be very obvious what I mean soon.

"Father Donnelly!" I call out, turning away from the closed door and practically skipping down the aisle between the rows of pews.

The worn red carpet beneath my feet holds so much pain, so much discarded hope, and I am determined to renew it. Fuck, this church hasn't seen God in a long time. It's well known that Seamus Branigan, former head of the Branigan gang AKA our sworn enemies until the bastard died and Patrick took over, used to conduct dirty business in the confessional booths here.

The priest doesn't answer me, and the church appears empty. I know the bastard is here, though. He's always fucking here.

"FATHER!" I call out again in a sing-song voice, ripping open the curtain to the confessional booth to seek him out. Damn. Empty.

Serafina and Oisín are muttering their confusion at my back but I ignore them. I sidle through the door to the right, where I know the large recreational room and bathrooms are.

The large space is empty, but the slider on the bathroom door is red, indicating it's occupied. Gotcha, fucker.

I slam my palm against the wooden door hard, making the whole thing shake on its hinges. The yelp from inside makes me grin.

"Found ya, Father," I taunt, wiggling the handle just to mess with him. "Out ya come now, I've got a job for you."

"I stopped doing *jobs* when Seamus died," he squeals from inside, his voice shaking. "I'm clean!"

I laugh at that, kicking the door some more. "This one's easy, Father Donnelly, promise. I swear it in the Lord's good name. Come on out, priest, before I break the door down."

"I work only for God-"

"Alright, fine, we'll do this the hard way."

Father Donnelly is a liar, and worse than that, he's a coward. The lock on the door breaks with a good few, hard kicks, and uncovers the priest with his pants still down.

He fumbles, eyes wide, tugging his clothes frantically until his feeble dick is covered.

"What does a Cavanaugh want with a man of God?" Father Donnelly asks, sweat beading at his brow.

"What we always wanted," I say, like it's obvious. The Father is wearing his fancy ass priest outfit - complete with the white collar. I grab him by it and he stumbles after me. "A marriage."

I yank him back into the church proper, the old fucker shaking like a sinner in - oh wait. Like exactly what he is. Not that I'm going to judge his morals, my own are fucked and his lack of loyalty to the rules he preaches are exactly why we're here.

Oisín is standing near the altar, muscles tight and brows drawn close. Serafina, in contrast, is stretched out on a pew, tapping her boot against the floor. Both of them go still as I drag the priest out and deposit him at the front of the church.

"Sebastian..." Oisín starts, at the same time Serafina says, "What's going on?"

"Get up here, sweetheart," I tell her, extending my hand.

Serafina cocks her head, but stands and walks to us. The priest is sweating properly now, his eyes nearly bulging out of his head. I turn to him, with Oisín and Seffy on either side of me.

"We're getting married."

Serafina chokes on her breath but Oisín just tenses. The priest, however, shakes his head emphatically.

"I can't," he insists. "I can't marry three people."

I roll my eyes. Jesus, this isn't rocket science.

"Do I look like I give a single fuck about if you can or can't?" I ask, using my free hand to stroke the butt of my gun tucked into my waistband. "You *will.*"

"Even if I wanted to," Father Donnelly stumbles to explain. "Neither God nor the law will recognise the-"

"I don't answer to your god or the laws," I drawl back, sighing. "But right now, Father, you answer to me. I will ask *once more* out of courtesy, because I'm sure you don't want more bloodshed or bullets in your church; marry us, priest."

"This is perhaps the most romantic thing anyone's ever done for me," Serafina muses at my side, grinning widely. Oisín scoffs at that, but he doesn't argue with my plans.

"I even got rings for us," I say, producing the box from my pocket.

Two gold rings, engraved with the delicate but strong pattern of the trinity knot that encompasses the whole circle. A third, thinner and shinier with a row of emeralds, the trinity knot design covering the second half.

"Sneaky fuckin' bastard," Oisín breaths at my side, but he's smiling.

Serafina's eyes are bright as she stares at the matching rings in my hand. The priest looks like he's about to piss himself, but fuck if I care. I just need him to say whatever the magic words are and tell us to put on the rings and kiss. Ta-da. Married.

"Better make haste, Father," Oisín grumbles at my side. "Don't want a repeat of the last wedding I had here, do we?"

Serafina taps her nails against the metal of her own weapon impatiently, sending an obvious if unspoken signal to the priest. He's outnumbered, unarmed, and out of options.

"Father forgive me," he murmurs, and I scoff loudly.

I wonder if he asks forgiveness every time he commits the same sins, if his knees are bloody beneath that robe from kneeling so long. I wonder how many prayers it takes to wash away a life of corruption.

"I need your names," he grinds out as the three of us stare him down.

I fucking adore my lovers even more for going along with my plan. The law may not recognise this marriage, given that there's three of us, but we will and that's what matters. I supply our full names, and the priest inhales shakily.

"Oisín Cavanaugh, Sebastian Byrnes and Serafina DeSantis, have you come here to enter into marriage without coercion, freely and wholeheartedly?"

"I have," the three of us echo in unison.

"Are you prepared, as you follow the path of marriage, to love and honour each other for as long as you all shall live?"

Again, the three of us echo our consent.

I roll my eyes at half of the religious bullshit Father Donnelly spews for the rest of the mock ceremony, though I answer happily when prompted. After what feels like a lifetime, Father finally cuts to the chase.

"Oisín Cavanaugh, do you take Sebastian Byrnes and Serafina DeSantis to be your…spouses? Do you promise to be faithful to them in good times and in bad, in sickness and in health, to love them and to honour them all the days of your life?"

My heartbeat is so loud I almost miss Oisín's answer. The three of us have our hands joined, and I swear they must feel my pulse jump through the connection.

"I do," Oisín says calmly, surely, like it's the easiest answer he's ever had to give.

Father Donnelly nods, and though he looks like it physically pains him, he repeats the vows to Serafina. Her *I do* is soft and full of her strength.

Finally, he turns to me. "Sebastian Byrnes, do you take Oisín Cavanaugh and Serafina DeSantis-"

"I do," I interrupt, giddy and blood buzzing with the rush of adrenaline. This is better than racing, better than fighting, better than bloodshed.

I feel *alive.*

Father Donnelly swallows thickly, casting his gaze downwards as he mutters, "What God joins together, let no one pull asunder."

I take pleasure in knowing he's going to hell for this, but really it's the least of his sins.

I have no gods except for the two people beside me. My angel. My *Máistir*.

"You may exchange rings," he tells us, and Serafina's hand finds mine.

Together, we slip Oisín's ring on his finger, the triple knot band settling comfortably against his original wedding ring. They look perfect together. Fuck.

Oisín's eyes gleam as he pulls Serafina to him, and he and I repeat the gesture, guiding her emerald and gold ring to sit atop her ruby one. The colours are perfect together - us, and her, forever joined.

Finally, the loves of my life slide my ring over my inked knuckles. It sits, warm and shining, over a space that has seemed so empty until now.

I think I might be crying. I'm also hard as fuck. And the stupid fuckin' priest is still talking.

"You may now seal the marriage with a kiss."

Gladly.

It's messy and uncoordinated but it's fucking perfect. Oisín crushes my mouth to his as Serafina presses her lips to the corner of mine. I'm passed between the two of them, mouths and tongue and teeth meeting until the three of us are laughing and smiling and panting.

I forget the priest is still there until he shuffles backwards.

"I suggest you make yourself scarce, Father Donnelly," I tell him with a wink as he scampers back. "Neither you nor your god will approve of what we're about to do."

55

Oisín

I don't wait for the pathetic excuse for a holy man to disappear. Sebastian's shirt is tugged over his head and Serafina's already unbuttoning his jeans before we hear the slamming of the door that signals the priest has scampered off to one of the back rooms.

Sebby pulls away from us for a second, turning his head in the direction of the confessional booth. The curtain covering it is still wide open from where he yanked it back earlier, and his eyes gleam. The way he moves exposes the new tattoo across his shoulder blades, shiny with salve and the second skin covering Avery applied to all of us.

"Sinner boy," Serafina breathes as he turns back to us. Her eyes are wide.

His brow furrows before realising why she's wide eyed.

She steps toward him, hand outstretched to trace the edges of the ink. The wings are intricate, each feather so detailed it looks *real*. Sebastian really could be our fallen angel with wings of darkness, come to damn us all. I'd let him. Fuck, I'd let him drag me to hell if it meant I got to keep him.

It dawns on me then, I *do* get to keep him. I cast my gaze down to the set of rings adorning my left hand. I get to keep them *both*.

"For our angel," Sebastian says with a grin, the tattoo rippling as he moves.

"It's beautiful," Serafina says honestly, letting her hand drop as he turns to face her.

My sight sticks to the large stag across his chest, older but just as beautiful as his newest addition.

"Let me see yours," he says, momentarily distracted from the idea of fucking.

Serafina grins wickedly, dragging her skin tight black top over her head. Her tattoo's on her wrist, and there's no way she needed to get undressed to show us, but neither of us are complaining.

She holds out her arm as I come to stand beside Sebastian, chuckling as I realise what she's got tattooed.

A clover.

"You're missing a leaf," I say, staring down at the delicate ink on her wrist, right above her pulse point. The clover's three leaves stare back at me.

"No," Serafina counters, looking pointedly between the both of us before back down at herself. "I'm not missing anything. Besides, I don't believe in luck."

Sebastian's smiling so wide his eyes are crinkled. The outline of his cock is visible against his jeans, and I refuse to delay our consummation longer. I shuck my own shirt off, throwing the fabric onto the first pew with the other's.

My own tattoo is on my bicep. Sebby and I had coordinated a little, both of us getting angel wings, though mine are smaller due to the placement. Above them hovers a set of devil horns. Avery has managed to make it dark and moody without being too cartoony and it's perfect.

"Sinner boy and angel," I say with a smirk as their eyes fall to it. "Start of a sleeve, according to Avery."

I've always left the tattoos up to Sebastian, but there's something *right* about having a representation of them permanently on my skin. I doubt I'll ever be as covered as Sebby, but I can envisage a sleeve of Avery's work. A tribute to us. To our life.

"I'm going to fuckin' come in my pants at the sight of those on your skin," Sebastian groans, jaw tensing.

"We're permanent, sinner boy," Serafina says softly, leaning up to wind her arms around his neck and kiss him. It's slow and languid and so fucking hot that I'm burning alive.

The church is echoey and dark, the sound of rain pattering off the large stained windows and high roof.

"Fuck yes we are," Sebastian answers as he pulls away and peel my eyes away from them long enough to stride to that damn confessional booth.

The memories I have of this church are nothing but anger and fear and this is the perfect way to replace them.

"Come here," I tell them, and for once neither of them baulk at my order.

They stride towards me and I grab Sebastian by the waist, pulling him into the side of the booth I imagine Father Donnelly sits in when he's pretending to know God. Sebastian yelps as he lands on my lap, his ass grinding down onto my hard length.

"Take a seat, angel. Let's confess all those filthy sins, huh?"

Serafina's eyes go wide, and Sebastian moans on top of me. Still, she steps into the other side and pulls the curtains closed. Enclosed in the small space, the world ceases to exist. There's nothing but the three of us, the rings and ink and words binding us together.

"Stay quiet while she confesses," I whisper to Sebastian, sliding my hand across his toned chest. "She's a dirty little sinner. She needs advice, doesn't she, Sebby? She needs to be shown the light again, huh? So keep that loud mouth of yours shut or she'll never be saved."

My fingers find the barbell piercing Sebastian's nipple, tugging on it as he squirms.

"So much pretty jewellery for me to play with," I whisper, my other hand twisting his wedding ring.

My hand leaves his chest, trailing down his toned stomach to slip my hand under the waistband my wife so kindly unbuttoned for me. I resist the urge to wrap my hand around his hard shaft, instead gliding the pad of my thumb over the head of his cock, playing with the piercing there.

Sebastian shudders, and I hear the moan he tries to hold back. Through the mesh grate of the confessional booth, my wife's breathing is heavy, her anticipation sweet in the air.

"Have you been a good little lamb?" I ask her, continuing my slow circles and teasing Sebastian's pierced cock.

"I have strayed from the flock," Serafina purrs back, her voice low and sultry.

Good God, I've got the world's hottest fucking sinners on my hands and she may not believe in luck but I sure as fuck do. There's no way in heaven or hell that I deserve these two. But I'm sure as fuck going to try to earn them every damn day of my life.

I figure orgasms will help.

"What sins have tempted you away, angel?" I ask her, unable

to stop her pet name slipping out my mouth.

Sebastian's cock weeps in my hand and I soothe him with a kiss to the shoulder.

"Wrath. Greed. Pride," she whispers through the mesh. There's little light, but I can see the barest outline of her face. "And lust. Over and over again. I can't help myself."

Her voice is breathy, and I don't doubt she's playing the game for me the way I am for her. Sebastian wiggles onto my lap again and I grind my teeth.

"What causes you to lust?" I ask our wife as my husband desperately tries to get my hand on him properly.

I know how much he wants to be edged, though. Delayed gratification makes Sebastian feral. He hates being denied as much as he craves it. And I only want to give him what he wants, what he needs, what he craves for the rest of our days.

"Tell me your sinful thoughts, angel," I prompt again. "Confess them so we may purge you of them. So we may make you heavenly again."

"I think..." she starts, and I hear the tell tale sound of her unzipping her trousers. "I think about being used. Being pinned between two men-"

"Any men?" I ask, unable to stop the possessive bite in my voice.

"No. Only these two men. A sinner boy and my...Sir."

"What do they do, in your dirty little dreams?"

I'm torturing us all with this, I know I am, but I won't stop. I'm so hard I could come with just a touch. But this church has wrecked Sebastian, and I will give back to him what this place has taken. Organised religion has never been where we found worship. The church may not want to recognise our marriage, or our relationship, but we'll make sure the very stone of Blessed Hearts remembers us.

"They touch me," Serafina whimpers. She's pressed close to the mesh now, and I swear I can fuckin' sense her sweet need. "They pin me between them. They kiss me, on my mouth, my neck, my tits. My cunt. They take me. *God,* they take me."

"Oisín," Sebastian whines, pleading. His skin is clammy with sweat already, the close air of the confessional booth heating.

"Ssh," I whisper to him, scraping my teeth along his neck. "The confessor can't know you're here, Sebastian. If you can't keep your mouth quiet, I will have to fill it. Do you need it filled, Sebby? Do you need your *Máistir* to give you what you crave?"

Sebastian nods rapidly. As much as he likes being touched, he thrives on giving pleasure. Always has. I'll let him lick our wife's need up the second this ruse breaks us. Hell, if he's good, I'll get her to lick him too. I'll watch them at my feet, wet and filthy and pleading for release.

"Yes, yes," Sebastian pants. "Please. I need to taste you. Badly. So badly. Fill my throat and keep me quiet, *husband.*"

That fucking breaks me.

It's an awkward manoeuvre but we manage it. On the limited floor space, Sebastian arranges himself between my legs. I shove my trousers down just far enough to free my aching cock, then cup Sebby's face with one hand.

"Do not touch yourself. Do not make me come. You are there to warm my cock and keep that mouth of yours quiet, understand?" I tell him, keeping my voice quiet to build the illusion we've created.

What better way to consummate an *illegal* marriage but to fuck your husband's mouth in a confessional booth while your wife confesses her many sins in the space to the left?

"Ta Máistir," Sebastian whispers, leaning his head on my thigh for a second. "This is the only prayer I'll ever want to do," he murmurs before leaning forward and taking me into his mouth.

Fuck. He obeys, not sucking or teasing, just slowly tracing me with his tongue and warming my shaft in his hot mouth. But, God, I'm dying for more. I've fucked up because now I'm not only edging him, but myself.

To my right, Serafina whimpers. My attention snaps back to her, even as Sebastian takes me deep in his throat.

"Is your pussy wet, angel?" I ask her. "Is it craving those little fantasies of yours?"

"Yes," she confides.

"Does she need to be taken care of? I'm sure I can find it in my heart to cleanse you if you confess while you take care of the ache, sweet girl."

"I...I can't be good," she whispers, and fuck if I didn't know she was the literal heir to her family's gang, I'd believe this innocent lamb act. Sebastian moans around me, lost as I am in this game.

I tut, tapping on the mesh between us. "You need to learn some self control," I tell her, making my voice harder. "So that you can...fight these urges. Even now, I bet your hand is between your thighs. I bet that greedy little cunt is making a mess of your fingers. I bet when you stand, there'll be a wet spot on the velvet. Tell me, angel, am I wrong?"

"No, no," Serafina moans. "God, your *voice*."

"Listen to me and obey," I urge her, my hand winding through Sebastian's hair. I can't keep my hands to myself for a second longer. His hair tangles in my fingers and I tug in the way I know he loves. Sebastian rewards me by groaning around my dick and I no longer care about keeping him quiet.

"Don't make me stop," Serafina asks, and somehow not being able to see her, touching herself right next to me, makes me burn hotter.

This feels forbidden, like we're breaking every rule, but I fucking love it.

"No, angel, I won't make you stop. But I will ask for forgiveness for you, if you do it exactly as I say, okay?"

"Okay."

"Spread your thighs wide." I hear the rustle of fabric, knowing that she's obeying. "One finger at first, Seffy. Slowly, slowly, let your cunt beg for more."

"It's not enough," she mewls.

I click my tongue off my teeth. "How wet are you, angel? Is it coating your thighs yet? Is your underwear sodden? Make your needy little clit wet with your desire, Serafina."

She's gasping, and fuck, so am I. At my feet, Sebastian pulls off my cock to plead with me with his eyes. He's so pretty like that, in the shadows of the booth, shirtless and jeans unbuttoned, begging me to fuck his face.

"What do you need, pretty boy?" I ask him, and his face lights up at the name. Fuck, this man. I'm so gone for them both it feels unreal.

"Your cum," he pants, shifting uncomfortably. "And hers."

"The little lamb next door is confessing," I tell him, loud enough to make sure she hears. "Do you want to ask her if she needs help making her desperate cunt feel better? Do you want to show her how *good* sinning should feel?"

"My hand isn't enough," Serafina says again. "It's not

enough. I need...I need..."

"Do you want our sinner boy's pretty mouth on your clit, angel?" I ask her. It takes strength to sit myself on the bench while Sebastian slips from my side to hers. "You're not allowed his cock. You're not allowed to touch. I want you to show him your pussy, angel. Spread yourself wide for him. He's so eager to please. Let him pray between your legs, Serafina."

"Yes, yes, please let him," she agrees.

"Tell me exactly what he's doing, angel. I need every detail."

"He's on his knees," she answers immediately, happy to paint the image for me. "God, he's beautiful."

"Sebastian, is the angel obeying? Can you teach her some control?"

I know he knows exactly what I'm asking him to do. He answers immediately.

"Yes."

"Talk, Serafina," I remind her as her gasp echoes through the booth. I'm so hard I might fucking explode. But, God, this is so worth it.

"He's...licking me," she tells me, and there's a thump from her side as she smacks her hand into the wall between us, her palm splayed over the mesh. "His tongue, *fuck*."

"Every. Detail."

"His mouth is on my clit," she moans, voice choppy. "It feels so good, *so good*. God, yes, like that, fuck!"

"Is this how you pictured it in that naughty head of yours?"

"More," she says. "I want his cock. Please."

"Sweet little angels don't beg for cock in a confessional booth," I tell her. "I thought you wanted to confess?"

"I don't want heaven if this is how good hell feels," she

admits. "I just want this. Forever."

That's my breaking point.

I stand and yank back the curtains, taking in the fucking glorious view. Serafina's hips are tilted, her feet braced on the wooden walls on either side of Sebastian's head. His dark hair blocks my view of her, but she's obeyed, one hand between her legs to hold herself open for him.

And *fuck* she is soaked.

"I-" Our wife's eyes practically roll back in her head. "Don't stop!"

"Stop, Sebby," I command, and like a good little pet, he stops immediately. His mouth and chin are wet when he tilts his head to look up at me, eyes glazed with desire.

Serafina whines and the sound goes straight to my cock. "No," she begs. "It *aches*. I need him. I need him."

Frantically, she reaches between her legs, spearing two fingers into her slick cunt. Fuck, I can *hear* how wet she is. The furrow between her brows tells me all I need to know - her own hand isn't enough.

"I see now that you were right, angel," I tell her, urging Sebastian to his feet. He slips past me to wait outside the small space as I scoop my desperate wife into my arms. "You're in need. Nothing will fix this except us, isn't that right?"

"Yes," she says, clinging to me, mouth at my neck. She sucks on my pulse and I tighten my grip on her.

"Welcome to hell then, angel."

56

Serafina

The wooden pew is hard and unforgiving beneath me, a stark contrast to the velvet of the confessional booth bench. I'm beyond giving a fuck, though, because my entire body is fucking *vibrating* with the need to come.

Oisín's instructions were intoxicating. And now, denied release, I'm convinced I might actually die if one of them doesn't fuck me right now.

"Return the favour, angel," Oisín tells me, gesturing to Sebastian.

He's kneeling on the floor in front of us, annoyingly with his jeans still on. The fabric is offensive, blocking my view of him.

I stand on shaky legs, reaching for Sebastian. He rises enough for me to tug on his jeans, wrestling them off him. His cock is so hard it looks painful, leaking and desperate.

The pair of us are.

"What a fucking sight," Oisín hums, sitting on the spot I just vacated on the pew. "Make a mess of each other. I want to watch."

As if I could burn any hotter. God, the mouth on this man. Hell, the mouth on both of them given that I'm craving Sebastian's on me again. I drag Sebastian back to the floor with me, the carpet here feeling surprisingly new and clean.

"Spared no expense replacing it after the blood ruined the last one," Oisín chuckles as Sebastian lies down on the floor like he's ready to be sacrificed.

Oisín smiles, pride and desire warring on his handsome features. He crosses one leg over the other and stretches his arms out along the back of the pew.

"I came for service, but this is far more interesting," he mocks as I crawl on top of Sebastian.

I don't even have time to arrange myself. Sebastian grabs my ass and drags me onto his face. I'm half scared I'll suffocate him with the way he shoves his face between my legs, apparently not caring a damn about breathing.

In the next second, I don't care either.

I nearly buckle as Sebastian's tongue glides over my sensitive flesh. He flattens it against my clit and shifts my hips, encouraging me to use him. *God.* I do, leaning forward to brace myself on the floor, hands on either side of his torso, and grind myself on his tongue. The wet heat of him feels so fucking good against the ache of unfulfilled need.

So good that I nearly forget to obey Oisín's demand. *Return the favour.* Happily. I lean forward, dropping to my elbows, pressing my body against his, and take his cock in my mouth. The salty taste of his precum hits my tongue and I shudder. His hips kick up at the first feel of me and I relax my throat in anticipation.

The metal of his piercing is warm and slick with spit as I

pull away, gasping when two of his fingers plunge inside me.

"Enough," Oisín says, and I want to cry.

It's not enough. It's not nearly enough.

Sebastian protests as Oisín crooks a finger at me, demanding I come closer.

He uncrosses his legs, and strokes his cock roughly. My gaze is fixed to the sight, mouth watering. I want the taste of him and Sebastian on my tongue. So badly.

"Ride Sebby for me, angel," he instructs, and both Sebastian and I jump into motion. We don't need to be told twice.

Sebastian grabs me, pulling me back against his chest so we're both facing our husband. My legs are spread wide over his lap, and my eyes are on Oisín's as Sebastian pulls me down roughly. The full length of him sinks into me in one thrust and sparks fly through my body. Yes *this* is what I need.

"Thank you," I mumble, somehow knowing it's what Oisín needs to hear.

"Thank *God*," Sebastian pants at my back, ever the brat.

His hands slide up my waist to cup my breasts, pinching my peaked nipples and sending another bolt of heat straight to my clit.

I'm going to come, and I'm not sure I can stop again.

"Mouth," I manage to get out, bouncing myself on Sebastian's cock. His piercing hits every sensitive spot inside me, and I'm barely fucking lucid now. But I crave… "Fuck my mouth, Oisín."

Oisín shoves his cock into me hard. I choke around it, fighting to remember how to breathe as my orgasm threatens to take me under. I want their cum, and I don't want to wait for it.

I fight to relax my throat, gripping Oisín's thighs desperately. I scratch him, trying to tell him not to hold back. I don't know if he understands me, or if his control just snaps, but his hand flies to my hair. He bundles the long locks in his fists and *fucks me* with hard, fast thrusts that leave no room for air. But I don't need air, I don't need anything except these two men.

My husbands.

I can't hold back my orgasm any longer. Not with Oisín gripping my hair and the taste of him and Sebastian on my tongue. Not with Sebastian meeting my every thrust from beneath me. Fuck, even the press of the carpet against my knees sends sparks through me.

I try to scream as my orgasm rips through me, but all I can do is choke. I don't care. The world ceases to exist, there's nothing except us, and the stars dancing in my vision. Through the ringing in my ears, I hear them curse. Sebastian moans loudly, and heat courses through me again as Sebastian fills my cunt with his release, and Oisín floods my throat.

Oisín pulls out before I can actually choke, and I swallow what I can, which is most of it. I catch what's escaped from my mouth with my finger and suck the taste of him off my skin.

"Christ," Sebastian says, squeezing my tits once more like he doesn't want to let them go. "You're right, Sef. Heaven can go suck a dick, I want hell."

I laugh, and Oisín grins, reaching for me. I'm pulled off Sebastian and lifted to the pew again, squirming on the uncomfortable wood.

Oisín pushes my thighs open and I gasp at the cold air that greets my pussy. I'm a mess of my own cum and Sebastian's, and as I glance down at myself, I smirk.

"My wife," Oisín says, kissing my damp thigh.

Sebastian pushes him to the side, trying to get between my legs too. Oisín chuckles.

"My husband," he adds, kissing Sebastian deeply.

I'm not sure it's possible to come again after that but as Oisín leans forward and drags his tongue through the combined release dripping out of me my cunt clenches, desperate to be filled again.

"You taste perfect together," he praises us, lapping at me a few more times before he pulls away. "The loves of my fucking life. My angel and my sinner."

"My sweetheart," Sebastian says, grinning widely. I swear he has hearts in his eyes as he looks between us. "And my *Máistir*."

I grin at them both, the three of us sweaty and delirious with happiness and adrenaline in the wake of our orgasms. I lean forward, and they both catch me easily, wrapping me in their arms.

"My husbands," I murmur, pressing a kiss over Sebastian's heart, and then Oisín's.

Oisín's heart beats steadily against my ear as I rest my head on his chest. My legs are on Sebastian's lap, and his head is on Oisín's shoulder. We're a tangle on the church floor, the sound of rain and echoing of our breathing filling the cavernous space.

I've never been so content.

Oisín's breath skims my hair as he cuddles both of us closer. "My forever."

57

Sebastian

"Libby!" I shout out as the three of us tumble through the diner doors, dripping wet and laughing. The diner's nearly empty, thanks to the shit weather, but Libby trods out of the kitchen seconds after I've finished calling her name.

"You bringing trouble?" she asks immediately, brandishing a pot like a weapon. I snicker, grinning wide.

"I'm after a slice of wedding cake for my spouses if ya don't mind," I say, claiming the same booth we sat at for the peace talks with Patrick. God, that feels like months ago and yet it's only been a few weeks.

Libby's weathered face splits into the widest grin I've ever seen from her. I've known this woman since I was fourteen and I can count on one hand the amount of times I've seen her smile.

"You're telling me I wasn't invited to the wedding?" she scoffs, her signature scowl back in place.

I pout at her, trying to worm my way into her good graces again.

"It was an...*intimate* affair," I tell her honestly, grinning.

Oisín and Serafina slide into the same side of the booth as me, all of us smushed together like eager kids on a first date. It's disgustingly adorable, and I'm disgustingly happy.

"I've got just the thing for you," Libby promises, slipping her order pad into the front of her apron as she shuffles off, pot still in hand.

Oisín just smirks a little at her, while Serafina furrows her brows.

"How are we gonna explain this?" Sef pipes up as she settles into the worn leather of the booth.

I stretch my arm over Oisín's shoulder so my hand grazes Sef's too. She leans in, pressing into my touch and his. Oisín's hand rests on my thigh, his other twined with Serafina's. We fit together easily, like the three of us were built for each other.

"To who?" I ask, because I'm not in the habit of explaining myself to many people.

"Thomas-" Serafina starts, but Oisín cuts her off before she can continue her list.

"Simple," our husband says gruffly. "I tell him I was sick of choosing between two pieces of my Goddamn heart. He's a gang leader, sure, but he's still my Da. He'll be happy it worked out without Sebastian murdering either of us."

I feign insult. "I'll have you know, I'm a lover not a fighter."

Both Serafina and Oisín laugh at that, and I jostle them, elbowing my husband in the ribs. I couldn't give less of a fuck whether our threeway marriage is *legal,* I'll be calling them my spouses as loudly and proudly as I can for the rest of my damn life.

"He is a *hell* of a lover," Serafina points out as she shoves us back over to make room for herself at the edge of the leather booth.

"Hell of a fighter, too," Oisín agrees with a smirk, yanking me closer to press a kiss to my cheek.

The gentle, easy contact sends a rush of warmth through me and I fucking *melt.* This is all I fuckin' wanted - a love that's as bright as the goddamn sun, one that I didn't have to try and dim under the cover of darkness and secrecy.

"Here ye go!" Libby interrupts, plopping a heavy tray down on the table.

It's laden with three glasses, filled with a hefty measure of amber liquid, and three giant slices of what looks like vanilla cake with thick buttercream icing.

My mouth is watering. "Thank you," I tell Libby with a nod, but she waves off my thanks.

"Eat. Drink. Be merry and all that shite," she smirks as we each grab a glass and plate off her tray. "But don't fuck on my table, that's where I draw the line."

She points directly at me as she says it, but I can only take it as a complement.

"Wouldn't dream of it, Libby," I assure her. Though the idea of laying my spouses on this sticky table top and eating cake from their bodies is exactly what I'll be dreaming of tonight.

Libby waits until I pick up my glass as I raise it in silent cheers, and take a sip. I splutter, the burn of the liquor making my eyes water as I choke it down. The bastard woman only laughs, winks then strolls off.

"What the fuck is this?" Serafina mutters, eyes wide as she handles her own sip better than I did.

"It's like moonshine," Oisín says hoarsely, shaking his head even as he drinks again.

Libby's definitely does not have a liquor licence, nor the facilities for brewing alcohol, so I can only imagine the old woman spends her free time at home making this shit. It's as strong as paint stripper, and I'm half afraid to try it again.

God, I love her. Is she taking applications for grandchildren?

"I wanna be Libby when I grow up," Serafina says with a chuckle as she sets her glass back down.

"But less grumpy please," I request, pulling my plate of cake closer.

"No guarantees," my wife snarks back.

Oisín's fork sinks into my slice before I can even take a bite. I'm halfway through chastising him for it - because *seriously* you've got your own - when he shoves his forkful in my mouth.

"It'd be remiss of me to miss the tradition of feeding my wedded spouse the cake," he says by way of explanation, licking the fork clean of icing.

There's that damn warmth again.

The cake is good, and I repay the gesture by feeding Oisín and Sef bites, too.

"So..." Serafina murmurs after a long silence during which the three of us stuff our faces with our wedding cake, looking at our husband. "How fast can you get that house built? Because I'm not adverse to making us all sleep on the floor in a pillow fort, but like fuck are we staying in separate beds in separate rooms in your family manor."

I snort, grinning widely.

"I'm flexible," I pipe up, wiggling my eyebrows. "I can squish myself between the two of you on a double mattress."

"Sebby, we could have the largest bed on earth and you'd

still sleep half on top of me," Oisín grumbles. Sef starts to talk but Oisín silences her with cake. "You're not any fuckin' better," he mutters at her, but his eyes are sparkling and his lips are curved in amusement.

He loves it as much as we do, the asshole.

"Answer our wife," I press, mostly to piss him off but also because I haven't stopped thinking about the house idea since he brought it up. I've gone from my ma's flat to Thomas' mansion and never once had a place of my own, not really. The idea of owning a house, filled with the two loves of my life where we have the privilege and privacy to fuck on every surface without worrying about one of their damn father's walking in sounds like a dream come true.

"Suppose now's as good a time as any to give you a wedding present," Oisín sighs, sipping the homebrewed liquor again with a wince.

The stuff is truly poison and yet we're all sipping at it anyway. Libby's persuasive like that.

"Construction starts next week," Oisín finishes and I nearly smash my glass as I drop it in shock. Thankfully, only some of the liquid sloshes over the side, the glass remaining intact. "Four bedrooms - so we can have our own space if we need it - and a custom sized bed for the main room."

"Holy shit," I whisper, shock rippling through me. "You're serious?"

"What, the tattoo and the ring wasn't serious enough for ya?" Oisín laughs, but he's nodding, dragging Serafina onto his lap as she leans into him. "I'm not giving either of you up for anything. I've wasted too much time resisting happiness, and I won't spend a single second more on that bullshit. So, Serafina DeSantis and Sebastian Byrnes, spouses and pains in my ass, any extra requests for our new house?"

Serafina pinches his arm for the tease, then wraps her arms tight around his neck, kissing him hard.

"A red room," I smirk in answer to his question, and he doesn't even bother rolling his eyes at me.

"Whatever you want, Sebastian," he says with full sincerity, Serafina pressing kisses to his neck. Her hand darts out, grabbing my shirt and tugging me so hard I tip forward into them. "Anything you want. I'll give you it. Name it, Sebby. It's yours."

"You," is all I can say. "Her."

Serafina pulls away from Oisín to slam her mouth to mine, kissing me deeply, the last of alcohol and sweet vanilla icing on her lips.

"Forever," she whispers against my mouth as I chase her taste.

We're both leaning our full weight on our husband, but judging by the way his hand is digging into my thigh and a groan is building in his throat, he's more than happy with his position.

"I said *no fucking on my table!*" Libby shouts, the sound of banging following her reprimand. The warning makes us pull away, laughing, eyes bright and hearts brighter.

"Come on, let's go," Oisín murmurs, grabbing Seffy and shuffling out the booth as I follow. "I'll show you where our home's going to be. We can christen the ground."

"Fuck yes," I answer, dropping a handful of cash on the table as payment before running out the diner doors with my laughing, squealing new spouses following suit.

For the first time in my life, I run through the streets of Killrover without a single worry about what the future holds, without trying to pretend it doesn't exist at all. The future doesn't feel like a rock in my throat, or a pit in my stomach. No, the future feels *sure*. Safe. Warm and so bright my eyes sting.

Because they'll be by my side.

Forever.

Epilogue

Francesca

"I'm not staying here."

My sister's blank face stares back at me. Her dark eyes are a mirror of mine, but her hair is longer and currently messy, as though someone's wound their hand through it. I wince at that image. The idea of anyone even fucking touching my hair like that makes me want to shave it off.

Matter of fact, I'm half inclined to do that anyway.

"Frankie, I'm sorry, I know this isn't ideal, but we're trying to keep you safe," Serafina says softly, twisting the rings on her left hand. There's a new addition to the stack but I don't comment on it. I don't have the energy to.

"I'm not," I say again. My tongue feels heavy as the words leave my mouth. I reach for the water that should be on the side table, but the glass is empty. When was the last time I ate or drank? The hours seem to slip by like sand through my fingers, and I'm not even sure what date it is.

I do know that I've been in this unfamiliar house, in this unfamiliar bed, for days and now the only familiar thing I have left is leaving me.

I won't stay without her.

I won't do it.

She left to return to her actual home for a few hours - I think

- and without her here the manor feels even more foreign, more unbearable. My sister has been off with her guys, or off trying to fix the mess I've made, and the strangers footsteps along the hallway sound like a death toll.

I haven't left this guest room since we landed in Ireland. The bed is cold and all wrong, and the door doesn't have a lock on it.

I. Can't. Stay. Here.

"I'll go with Gráinne."

Serafina looks stunned. "You'll…what?"

"I'm *not* staying here, Fi." I mean it. I'm in no state to fight her over it, and I hope I won't have to. But I can't stay here.

I want my home, my bed, my room. But I know that no matter how much I ask, I can't go back there. I need Gráinne.

"But…I'm here," Serafina says gently, reaching out to lay her hand on mine. I pull away, escaping the touch. Hurt flashes across her face before she smoothes her expression.

Guilt slips through me like an oil spill. I can't find the words to tell her I'm sorry.

How do I explain to her that I don't want to be here? How do I explain to her that I haven't slept because I can't stop listening for movement outside the door? That this house isn't any safer than ours back home? That nowhere is safe.

My eyes are blurry, and I struggle to focus on my sister's face. The full body ache that lives in my bones makes me feel heavy, and I struggle to sit up.

Serafina's expression is soft, and I can't stand the pity. I look away.

"I can't just let you go," she says.

"Please," I whisper, my voice cracking. "I can't…I need *space*." I gesture limply to the shadow of feet standing guard outside the door to my room. Serafina blinks.

"Gráinne isn't a Cavanaugh," Serafina explains.

I know this. But I don't care. I don't give a shit.

"Fi," I say, unable to get out more than her name. "Please."

My sister looks torn, but there's a resignation in her face now. An understanding.

"I...I'll get Siobhán, okay?"

Siobhán Branigan, cousin to the current head of the Branigan gang, daughter of the now deceased former head - Seamus Branigan. I know a lot about them. Gráinne told me stories, when I was half alive in Italy, her voice a soothing constant from outside my door.

The mattress shifts as my sister stands to leave.

She returns a while later with Siobhán and Nessa, but I can't focus on what they're saying. I can't focus on anything because my skin feels wrong. Something's fucking touching me. I rip off the duvet, ignoring someone's startled shout, and tear my night dress up past my waist. I swat, uselessly at my own skin, trying to rid myself of the phantom sensation.

A strangled noise winds its way past my teeth as I scratch at my thighs, sure I can feel the pads of rough fingers there. I need the feeling *gone*. Now. It's unbearable.

Someone's hands grab me, pulling my arms away from myself. I screech, my throat burning. Let me go. Let me go. Let me-

A new voice breaks through the chaos of my brain, the chaos of my room. A familiar one, a safety line that my soul instantly recognises. Soft, low and even, the voice guiding me out of the fog.

"Hey, dandelion."

Gráinne's here.

Acknowledgements

To Sam, for making the perfect cover and putting up with our chaos. We appreciate you so much!

To our beta and ARC readers, you guys are the bestest. Thank you for supporting us and helping bring our world to life.

SCARLET

To my partner, I love you endlessly. You take my chaotic, stressful nonsense in your stride and never ever fail to support me through it all. You're my real life book boyfriend, and I can't wait to call you my husband.

To my child, mummy says put this book down (but I love you more than all the stars in the sky).

To my friends - online, in person, wherever you are - for sticking with me, I love you all.

Nadine...The universe threw so many bloody challenges at us while writing this, but it's done. We did it. Sebby's sad, smutty story is out there in the world. Breathe. I'm so proud of you, and honoured to call you my wifey (I will be taking your fiance's place at the altar).

To our readers, who have made posts, edits, videos, who've messaged or commented to tell us how much they loved

Broken Vows. I hope Fractured Faith made you fall for the Blessed Hearts world even more. We have so much more chaos to come and we literally cannot express how fucking grateful we are that you're on this journey with us. Our stabby, queer, stubborn as fuck characters mean so much to us and it's truly an honour to see them matter to you, too.

To you. Yes, you, reading this right now. Thanks for being here.

Scarlet xo

NADINE

To my fiance. Thank you for being my rock while I struggled to get this book done. For listening to me rant endlessly about the workload, the pressure I felt, and the stress that rested on my shoulders. I'd be lost without you. You're a light in my life, one I never want to let go of.

To my mam, for supporting me through it all despite the chaos we were living through. You've taught me to reach for a source of strength I never knew existed within me. You've shown me how to be a better, stronger, and more resilient person. I couldn't have learned all that from anyone better. Thank you for being you.

To my sister. Thank you for encouraging me to keep writing each moment you could. Thank you for making me laugh each and every day even when you had so little to laugh or smile about. I love you loads my little monkey.

To Scarlet. I genuinely cannot put into words how grateful I am to have you not only as a co-author, but as a friend. Writing this book had us both on the brink of numerous mental breakdowns. The universe quite literally put us through fucking hell while we wrote this. I can't thank you enough for the kindness, patience, understanding and love you have graced me with during this process. You are an amazing friend, partner in crime and wifey.

To our readers. I never thought in a million years that anyone would care for Broken Vows as deeply as you all have shown you do. I can't thank you enough for your support, your love, and the kind words each and every one of you have sent our way. The edits, the reels, the messages, each one fuels me and reminds me of why I started writing to begin with. I hope that Sebastian, Oisín and Serafina were able to add to the joy you feel when you think about the Blessed Hearts world.

Nadine x

About the Authors

Scarlet King is lives in Scotland with her partner and child. She loves coffee, book stores, and ignoring her responsibilities in favour of writing. She has a bad habit of falling in love with fictional characters and hopes that someone out there will fall for the ones she writes, too.

Nadine O'Keeffe is a queer dark romance author from Ireland, where she lives with her partner. She loves book, music, coffee, and her cat (even though she swears she's a demon in disguise). She can often be found ignoring the real world in favour of fictional ones, because, let's be honest, they're far better.

If you want to keep up with what the authors are writing and what chaos they plan on causing next, you can find them at the links below:

Instagram: @scarletkingauthor @authornadineokeeffe

TikTok: @scarletkingauthor @NadineOKeeffeauthor

Facebook Reader Groups: Scarlet King-Dom and Nadine's Hunters

Websites (for signed copies and swag!): www.scarletkingauthor.com

If you liked this book, please consider leaving a review! A star rating and a few lines helps authors out massively. If you post about this book on social media, please feel free to tag Scarlet and Nadine so they can thank you!

Also by Scarlet King and Nadine O'Keeffe

Also by Scarlet King:

The Revenge Duet - a paranormal why choose dark romance duet (MMFM)

Thieves and Thorns
Revenge and Roses
Ribbon and Rope

The Surrender Duet - a paranormal why choose dark romance duet (MMMFF)

Honey and Hellfire
Sugar and Surrender

Blessed Hearts - a connected series of queer, dark romance mafia standalones:

Broken Vows (FF)
Fractured Faith (MMF)
Shattered Souls (FF)- coming 2024

Lord of Wild Things - a monster romance standalone COMING SOON

Run Rabbit Run - a sapphic stalker standalone romance COMING SOON

Also by Nadine O'Keeffe:

Blessed Hearts - a connected series of queer, dark romance mafia standalones:

Broken Vows (FF)
Fractured Faith (MMF)
Shattered Souls (FF) - coming 2024

Run Rabbit Run - a sapphic stalker standalone romance COMING SOON

Printed in Great Britain
by Amazon

38360677R00223